The Dog's Tale

A Life in the Buda Hills

†

Other works by the same author:

Around the World in Twelve Stories. (fiction)
Celestial Seductions. (poetry)
Cleopatra & Asia Calls. (plays)
Stories of All Ages. (fiction)
Asian Galaxy. (play)
Medea & Other Poems. (poetry)
Glimpses of the World: Stories, poems & letters from China
Chinese Women's Long March to Tiananmen. (play)

In praise of The Dog's Tale

The 'person' who tells this story is a dog. A dog who (as he himself puts it) does not intend to give up his animal nature. Yet of course he understands human speech and is able – if not in speech, then certainly in writing, and entertaining writing it is! – to express his thoughts about the world. His world is an interesting one: it is the city of Budapest in Hungary, in central Europe, in the years right after the fall of the Iron Curtain. Rani Drew, in her animal guise, writes with attention, caring, and an easy-flowing style which will make this book a favourite with readers.

— Nádasdy Ádám, Poet & Translator (Hungary)

How does one summarize a narrative that conflates myth and history, fable and animal psychology, Magyar and Gypsy lore, to produce a multifaceted mosaic across which shimmer Confucian sages, ancient heroes from the Mahabharata, livid wounds of the more recent Balkan wars, carnivals, picnics and canine mating rituals? Rani Drew directs her ensemble cast with the gentle wit and lightness of touch of a consummate puppeteer: her 'not so shaggy' dog's tale provokes without preaching.

— Jaysinh Birjepatil, Novelist (U.S.A.)

Few writers have risen to the challenge of asking the impossible question: What place do humans occupy in the canine imagination? It is this profound epistemological reversal that Rani Drew explores in a work that plaits Indian legend from the Mahabharata and the Buddhist Jatakas with Sufi myth and the modernist discourse of the RSPCA. The result is a rich hybrid that resists easy classification but achieves a difficult end – evoking empathy for a voice, a bark, that is radically 'other'.

— Rukmini Bhaya Nair, Poet & Critic (India)

This is our world through the eyes of a very special dog. The canine observer/ narrator, unschooled as he seems to be, is a savvy purveyor of the human scene and an articulate critic of its pretensions and pettiness, codes and cruelties, though gracious enough to celebrate its acts of generosity, courage, and creativity. The wide-ranging novel, with its psychological and cultural insights, its reflections on the diversity and flux of modern Europe, and its interplay of Eastern and Western literary genres, emerges as an impressive tour de force.

— Riad Nourallah, Poet & Translator (UK)

⋮

To the desire for freedom in all living beings.

☙

Bronze statue in a Budapest square

THE DOG'S TALE

~ A LIFE IN THE BUDA HILLS ~

RANI DREW

‡

Paperback ISBN 978-8792632-04-3
First edition.

Published by

Whyte Tracks
Tuborg Havnevej 19
Hellerup
2900 Copenhagen
Denmark

Introduction

In this ingenious novel, The Dog's Tale, Rani Drew, poet, playwright, university instructor, once again shows her commitment to values that should make this world a much better place than it is: friendship, respect, love, and, above all, a chance for everyone to have freedom of thought and movement.

We read the autobiography of a foundling – one of the most salient narrative structures in the history of the novel – but this time the foundling is a dog who, in order to realize that he belongs to the wild, has to define himself against human characters, the young woman who finds him and her mother, who both lavish loving care on him. In his reluctant search for identity he acquires some understanding of most of our basic human affections, like love, hatred, anxiety, sense of loss, confinement and freedom.

Like the main hero, the novel is also a kind of a mongrel, a mixture of genres: tales, songs, plays, and puppet shows are inserted in the main body of the text as well as lively dialogues which come fully alive thanks to the neatly appropriate style and descriptions of places thoughtfully observed and sensitively rendered.

The story is set in Budapest. The author, who spent nine years in Hungary, has the flair to lovingly reconstruct the culture of a country that she learned to appreciate. Although the events are described through the eyes of a dog, the narrative has a leisurely tempo that allows room for a survey of the whole history of the country, at the same time convincingly re-creating the feel of life in Hungary in the 1990s.

Ágnes Péter,
Professor of English,
Eötvös Loránd University, Budapest.

Acknowledgements

Two of the chapters, 'The Boy At the Gate', and 'The Nights', were published in *Text's Bones, Spring and Summer 2003,* by Skrev Press. I wish to thank Daithidh MacEochaidh, Skrev's editor, who saw the potential of a novel in the dog stories and suggested I weave them together into one tale.

My thanks to Annemarie Skjold Jensen, my present publisher, whose suggestion of extending the tales brought new dimensions to the story.

Further thanks are also due to Eszter Wardrop-Szilágyi for checking accents on Hungarian names and to Kálmán Faragó for his readiness to bat my out-of-the-blue questions about Hungary.

My special thanks to John for many proof-readings of the text, and to my children, Sandhya, Anita and Iqbal, for continuing to take a critical interest in my writings.

- Rani Drew

PREFACE

The Dog's Tale gestated in Hungary in 1989, after the collapse of the Soviet Union. The narrative unfolds during the volatile changes taking place in Eastern Europe in the following decade. I arrived in Budapest in 1990 to teach drama at the University of Budapest and stayed until the Millennium, writing and staging my plays in the culturally rich theatres of the city, a legacy of the Soviet Era. It wasn't long before the arts faced the onslaught of Western capitalism and the suspension of state subsidies.

For me, the political changes looked a rich picking. A canine seemed the ideal vehicle to tell the Magyar story. Hungarians are great dog lovers. Behind the gates of every well-to-do house are huge dogs, the likes of which one rarely sees in the UK. The gentility of owning dogs or being masters of well-behaved pets always brings up questions of the behaviour of humans themselves. Once I started on this theme, there seemed no end to what could be brought into view. Some stories came out from plain observations, some from witnessing street happenings, others from tales brought by travellers.

Then there was the perception of the dog himself. What does the world look like to a house-bound pet? What must it be like to be domesticated? Does the loss of the original natural state remain somewhere in the pet's psyche? How does this surface from time to time? How does the consciousness of slavery lead to a desire for freedom? Do stray dogs retain their animal nature more than the house-bound? Do they have a concept of freedom?

The Dog's Tale traces the course of a dog's growing up as a domestic animal. And how despite being indoctrinated with human values from childhood to mid-life, he finally comes to abandon them in favour of a life in the wilds.

⋮

CONTENTS

⋮

A Word First

‡

How did I, a dog, come to claim a place for myself in this comfortable home up in the Buda hills? A question that can be answered only by starting at the beginning. There is no life without birth, and although this house was not the place of my real birth, it became the place of my second. Since the story of my birth is a blank in my memory, I have to start with the story of my adoption as if it was the first, the beginning of all my stories. Call it a story within stories, but one which is necessary to tell. Yet even this one is not my story. It is a story about me told by my mistress - not only to me but to others as well. That's how all stories of childhood go. No one knows what it was like 'then'. We can only be revealed to ourselves by others. It's their memory that creates our childhood for us, which lies outside our perception. Yet we insist that our recollections are from our own memories. I am no exception to the general tendency and will tell the moment of my second birth, my adoption, as if nothing could be clearer in my mind than that event.

One fine morning, I found myself abandoned on a slope by the busy highway between Szentendre and Budapest. Not only do I not know who my parents were but I cannot even recall my previous owner, who left me to perish in a thicket by the roadside. I suppose I must have been a mere puppy. All I remember is that I woke up to a constant sound of whizzing and swishing of vehicles. Instinctively I felt I was in a forsaken state. Fear crept into my bones, and I shrivelled up to an even smaller size than the puppy months had accorded me. I have no idea how long I remained there without food or water. Nor how long after was it when I heard someone saying something to me, someone kneeling on the pavement above and making sweet sounds of encouragement to me to climb up the slope. Truly, I would not have lost a minute to obey the call, so compassionate was the face of the young woman, but I could hardly move my limbs from weakness. Then I looked down the slope and knew that only danger and death awaited me at the bottom.

My survival instinct triumphed and I started to crawl up, bit by bit, what seemed like the summit of a mountain. The constant flow of sweet words were like a rope thrown at me to grab tight and heave my weak spirit up up up and more up and finally to the top. At my emergence from the abyss where fate had left me to perish, I was met with two outstretched arms and gathered up in a warm loving hug. I was out of the bush, out of the jaws of extinction.

After five years as I look back to that afternoon, I am certain that was the real moment of my birth. It was the preamble to a new life. A good home, two caring mistresses, and a house that looked up to the hills. In short, a life enviable by all standards, human and canine.

†

2

THE FACT OF GENEALOGY

‡

In this country, people say 'what does a dog have to tell about its life?' Then they go into an ecstasy, 'O istenem, it's a wonderful life. This country is a haven for dogs,' they chorus, 'let all the dogs of the world come here to live: big and small, fierce and timid, wild and domesticated.' Others declare with even greater passion, 'We love every sort of dog. We are even called a dog culture. Every bit of our life is steeped in dog nuances: our language, our emotions, our neuroses and our fixations - all are rooted and fixed in dog responses.'

As a dog I listen to this passionate claim so often that I have almost come to believe in it myself. I am not exaggerating when I say that one single phrase of the Hungarian language can epitomise the national character of the Magyars. So, for example, when describing someone's predicament as 'kutya a baj', they mean to say (i) that the trouble is not real, but in the mind, and (ii) that having a family and home alone rules out the existence of any problems. Like its Magyar owner, the dog too has nothing to complain of. Now according to this view, I, a dog, should stop here and go no further as I have an excellent home presided over by the most charming mistress, live in the best part of Budapest, eat the best food and go for leisurely walks in the lovely woods just above our road. What need is there for an autobiography? This then could be the beginning and end of a dog's tale, making it the shortest story ever told.

The same people will go even further and say that animals cannot tell stories because they lack thinking and speaking faculties. The aesthetics of speech, they declare, are the prerogative of humans alone. Now I object to this claim and will expose its fallacy. But I will limit my defence to the dog community, since I consider other pets to be outside my discourse. Before I go into epistemological proofs of my assertion as a story teller, I must, true to all autobiographical modes, establish my genealogical credentials first, since it is an important factor in one's social standing in this country. And though I am without the knowledge of my canine genealogy because I was found abandoned by the road side, even then I would say I am a Magyar breed - not a pedigree but a mongrel. I know I have no right to claim such racial roots, especially as I cannot back my statement with a clear hereditary descent. Moreover I cannot even prove my parental connection, let alone descent from dogs in King Mátyás' time, the beginnings of the Magyar nation.

I know I am on slippery ground here, and can easily be challenged by the vigilant pure breeds in this country, yet I won't retract a single syllable from my statement. I feel so strongly of this soil that I am prepared to take all risks. I may get branded by the experts with having only the blood of some minor breeds that were brought across the borders by immigrant communities who arrived in waves in the Carpathian basin; I may even be declared to descend from the wild canines of the Gypsies who forced their way into the homeland of the Magyars from the east. Well, let them say what they like about my descent. After all, I stand to lose nothing.

†

3

A DECLARATION OF RIGHTS

‡

It is common knowledge that the origins of modern western philosophy stem from the time of the Renaissance. 'I think, therefore I am' became the foundation of European humanism. If you reverse this paradigm to 'I am, therefore I think', it becomes perfectly valid for all beings. Now don't get me wrong when I use the word 'humanism' for non-humans. I do not intend to give up my animal nature, but having lived in proximity with human beings, I'm afraid I have developed - for better or worse - a desire to articulate my perception of this world, in a non-animal way. This then establishes my claim to the two most important faculties that humans are privileged with: one, the ability to think, and two, to use speech to translate thoughts. In fact, I cannot be accused of hubris since there have been plenty of writings where animals think, speak and evaluate human actions. I am talking not only about the great tradition of fables, but also of stories where insects, birds and animals give an impartial view of difficult events in human life. What I am about to relate is certainly claiming something more far-reaching than humans assert about animals.

I have given much thought to the question of how closely dogs are related to humans. And I would say that compared with other animals, dogs are much humanised and hence could be considered their poor relations. Now the proof of that is a chance discovery I happened to make the other day. I was carrying my mistress's letter to her one morning, when my eye fell on the stamp. Believe it or not, it had the picture of a dog speaking, actually speaking, and not too happily either. Words were flying out of the dog's mouth, 'Do this, do that', it was grumbling, 'why don't you ask the cat?' That's it, I thought, that's what makes dogs a part of human society. Work! the work ethic. 'Thou shalt live by the sweat of your brow' was handed down to the first man, according to the Christian religion. Now tell me why does a cat not do things? If you look around, you'll find that among all the house pets, the dog is the most domesticated, and happily so, I will add. And the funny little things called birds, they chirp and flutter around the house, dipping into water and grain provided for them in idyllic surroundings and in containers, but do they do anything for their patrons? No. Nothing whatsoever. Cat, it's the cat I begrudge most her luxurious living since she goes on her fours as I do, yet she goes scot-free from having any obligation whatsoever to her owners. Oh, yes, I know, I know I have called Cat a she, and you would accuse me of sexism, but is it my fault or society's which has passed on these macho attitudes to me? Cats are always regarded as she's whereas dogs always as he's. Hence, I can't be blamed for using the language so prevalent these days which I have to admit is sexist through and through. Now, she (I'm sorry I find it difficult to shake off my gender bias towards the feline species) - the cat - never involves herself in the household. She comes and goes wherever she likes, and whenever she likes. If you ask me she has no sense of obedience and loyalty, which is the first principle of the human family.

While I am at it I might as well air another grudge I have against this cat who seems to think she can share this terrace with me even though she does not belong to this household. Now, I wouldn't mind if she showed some gratitude and humility. On the contrary, she abuses the peace and quiet of my space. One thing I cherish outdoors is listening to birds, but does she respect that? No, she lies in wait for them, fixing her eyes on every hop and flutter of their downward movement as they come to pick bird-seed put out for them. But ill-fated is the one who is too slow to elude the vicious pounce of the stealthy killer. And it's always too late when I run to make her let go of the poor victim. By that time the creature is squeezed out of most life and left there to breathe its last. Oh, it's savage to kill birds! How tragic that these noble ariel dwellers, sky-goers or twice-born, as some cultures call them, fall prey to such a pernicious animal. Forgive me, cat-lovers, for my rant against cats, but unfortunately I have my reasons. If you witness the gruesome grisly hunting habits of this cat, as I do, you would understand my stand against the whole feline community.

Now to return to the people who boast of their dog culture and stand by the domestication of even wolfish canines, and think there would be nothing for me - a dog - to say about my life up here in the hills, they have a surprise coming to them. I have a lot to say, and that too not always about myself, but about what I see and hear around me.

The next thing for me to do is to establish my right to tell my story. Again, I can hear the same people say if I have all the worldly comforts of a Magyar home and have no problems, what stories could there be to tell? But I will prove that good stories are not made of personal well-being, they come from the life of others. Moreover, a comfortable life, such as a dog's, does not exclude observations of the forces that mould our perceptions. If we look closely, we will discover that the most assiduous human thinkers led rather comfortable lives, looked after by their devoted wives and patronised by the rich. Of course, there were also thinkers in whose cases this was not true, but by and large I would say my statement does hold about what makes one tell stories. I will show that this privilege applies not only to humans, but to animals also.

As I said above, the most important philosophical paradigm which proved the humanity of the homo sapiens was 'I think, therefore I am.' Now, nowhere does the statement specify the type, content and the range of the faculty that performs this function. And the assertion of being an organism in itself would develop and stretch the faculty of perception and hence of thought. This is how it happened with humans, and might with other beings too. You will witness in my autobiography that not only can I think but also analyse and oppose my own thoughts, and all this because 'I am, therefore I think'.

This may seem simplistic, even nonsensical to you, but to my mind the statement plumbs great wisdom. It widens the sphere of awareness to all beings. And with the increase of environmental concerns and animal rights, no living being's claim to knowledge can be invalidated, least of all mine which rests firmly on empirical observations.

The notion of labour too is considered special to humans only. Animals, it is claimed, exert themselves only when they need to. For the rest of the time, they enjoy the feel of living, luxuriating in their surroundings. Humans, on the other hand, claim they have a spiritualised notion of the body. To prove whether they are right or wrong in setting themselves apart from other organisms is not the point of my discourse here. I don't want to involve myself in the ethics of work, nor am I keen to come up on the side of the humans against animals. I am merely stating that the faculties of thinking and speaking are not the prerogative of humans alone.

I apologise for this digression from the dog-cat rivalry I was dwelling on earlier, given rise to by the stamp on the letter I carried. I am afraid some of the human limitations have rubbed off on me - the result of my long association with them. I cannot help making some typical differentiation between domestic pets, a Magyar tendency to make pedigree distinction among animals and people. Yes, back to my obsession about cats and dogs! Now, if you analyse the statement of the stamp which I spoke about above, it concludes that the dog is in the same category as the human, whereas a cat is not. Why not? you will ask. Because, I say, a cat does not involve herself in others' affairs. She remains aloof and detached from all things. She performs no function in the house. She does not guard the house against thieves and burglars, nor does she do any chores like carrying letters or wood logs for the fire, or fetch a ball, or clap, or ask for food and so on. She does not involve herself emotionally with happy or solemn occasions in the family. I think a cat is a sad case when it comes to thinking and speaking. Yes, yes, cat lovers may resent my claim, but they cannot disprove it. They may also assert that a cat has her own speech, i.e., she miaows, she arches her back, rubs her body against you and many other things, but here I am not talking about private speech. A speech is not speech if it is not understood by another. Now, in support of dogs, I can produce a human witness who claims that dogs speak a language that is clearly understood as a syntactical formulated string of words.

A little girl called Zsófi, who lives up on the next road above us, stops by my fence every morning on the way to her school. I make sure that I am there at the fixed hour, even if I have to disobey my mistress as I do not want to miss my usual chat with her. Don't ask me what we talk about. One can never reproduce what one talks to people. But we do and it can be anything under the sun. Once I heard her tell her mother,

'You know, Mummy, that dog tells the most interesting stories'- which I do as you will soon find out - but would her mother believe her?

No. 'Come on, Zsófi,' she said in an irritated tone, 'don't be silly, darling, dogs don't talk.' And pulled her daughter away from the gate.

'But this one does, Mummy. I can tell you some of the stories it has told me, shall I?'

'We'll miss the bus if you don't hurry,' the mother said, stepping up the pace.

Here was the truth then, straight 'out of the mouths of babes'. But if you also don't believe Zsófi, then there is no point in going on with listening to me talking about my life in my new home, with my new owners. You can stop here.

†

⋮

4

MY NEW HOME

‡

It was about five years ago that on a cold December morning I was brought to my new home. I was received by an old lady with noises of surprise and delight. She took me in her arms from the young lady and made sweet comforting sounds to what must been a poor little rag-bag of fur and bones. She rubbed down my back and smoothed my ears, snuggled me into her coat.

'It's your gift from Szent Miklós, Zsuzsi,' she said.

'Yes, mother, but he forgot to leave it in my stocking. I had to fetch my gift myself, didn't I?'

'True, true, but worth all the trouble,' she said lovingly to me, 'aren't you? Where did you find it?'

'Long story. First some coffee.'

And while making the coffee the young lady started to tell her mother how she retrieved me from a ditch. I was snuggled up in the bosom of the old lady while all the details were unfolded about my terrible plight that morning.

'Never mind, it will be all right now, yes, it will,' she informed me lovingly.

'Where are we going to put him?'

'Tomorrow I'll get a kennel, but tonight he had better sleep in the warm here.'

'I want him to sleep in my room. Would you like that, eh?' I was asked to give my consent, which I'm sure I did by giving a weak yelp. Thereupon, the old lady started to sing a Christmas carol to me.

'He's a wee little thing, but crafty enough to milk so much sympathy out of you. But first he could do with some real milk, mother. You do that, and I'll bring some blankets down.'

'Oh, yes, let's go and have some warm milk, little one, before you kip down.' And with a flourish she took me to the kitchen. The way I lapped up the warm white liquid it must have been my first meal in days.

Such was the love and adoration with which I began a new life in the Buda hills, in the home of a beautiful young mistress and her equally young-hearted mother. An hour after arriving, welcomed with love and warmed up by hot milk I snuggled down into a well-blanketed bed and was asleep instantly.

Next morning I opened my eyes to bright sunlight. Immediately, I was taken out to the terrace by the old lady for training and orientation. It was a cold day but the sun was shining brilliantly. The old lady followed me around, talking and chatting to me as if I was a child. 'Now, listen, drágám, I'm your grandmother, Nagyanya, and you are my grandson, unoka. So, remember, always, always.' I was over the moon to have her attention, and to please her I performed my ablutions promptly. Having done my bit, I headed for indoors again, was fed and returned to my cosy place for more rest. I looked for the young lady but she didn't seem to be around.

After a little while the old lady took me on a tour of the house upstairs and downstairs; I stopped at every object, sniffing and smelling things, which brought warnings of one sort or another from her against doing this or that. I couldn't believe my good fortune. All this amidst chatting and singing a line here and there. Then I was asked to go down to my bed and have another lie-down. This was to see if I remembered where my corner was. Of course I knew. Who would forget the place of rest and sleep? Here I am, I whispered to myself, my small body burrowing into the blankets, from rags to riches by some stroke of luck - or 'szerencse', as the Magyars would say.

I don't know for how long I had slept before I woke up to the sound of people talking. A man was standing with my mistress and her mother and they were all looking at me.

'He must be about a year old, looks a mixed breed, hard to tell, really.'

'We are not bothered about the breed, are we, Zsuzsi? Anyone can tell he's not pedigree,' she said putting the man in his place.

'Quite, mother, but I am interested in his background,' my mistress said, trying to tone down her mother's sharpness.

I got up and started to sniff and lick everyone's feet. Immediately the old lady picked me up and took me out for my toilet training. The young lady and the man followed us. I was aware that I was being watched closely by the man. So, as the old lady was guiding me to make sure I did the right thing at the right place, I pricked up my ears to hear what the man was saying about me. Would I find myself back in the thicket again? The smell of misfortune hung over me.

'About a year, yes, I think no older than that.'

'And abandoned on a highway. He could have died of cold.'

'It happens often. People get puppies as a gift for their children and when the children's interest wears out, the poor animals are left anywhere.'

'So young and vulnerable? Oh, people.' The young lady was incredulous.

'You'll be surprised what's done to animals. Now, that one has a very interesting side to it.'

'That's the sort of thing I want to know.'

'From what I can see he may be a hedgehog breed,' the man deliberated.

'Hedgehog? What can that mean?'

'Well, once I had a visitor from Greece and on looking at the dog I was taking care of for some friends, he said, "That's a hedgehog dog." Now, like you, I asked him what did that mean in real terms. And he told me the following story about his own dog. I'll tell it in his own words.

'"My dog," he said, "had a mania for catching hedgehogs. She used to bring them to me first, never minding the prickles, but when she found I either released them over the wall, if still alive, or disposed of them if dead, she took to burying them herself, to mature for her future delectation. I usually managed to find the tell-tale mound and remove the body while she was shut up indoors, but sometimes she would stand guard over it all night, growling if I approached, only two green eyes to be seen in the dark." When I saw your puppy, I was reminded of this man's story.'

'Goodness. Did the dog eat them ever?' The question betrayed a nervousness in the young lady.

'No, no. That was the interesting thing. The dog was going through the motions of old, from when it used to hunt for its masters.'

'Like dogs fetch balls these days?' the mistress prompted.

'Exactly,' the man confirmed. 'A mere ritual now of what was once a necessity for survival.'

'Might he have been a hunting dog?'

'Very much so, but a different sort. Now this hedgehog dog, the one I told you about just now, probably had something of the breed that came to Europe with the Gypsies. As they were always on the move, the Gypsies trained their dogs to hunt hedgehogs for their food. According to anthropologists some nomadic tribes keep only dogs as pets. And I think the Gypsies followed the same practice as they moved westwards.'

'And this dog, you think has something of that breed in him?'

'From his movements, yes, I would say that. Just now when he came out, he ran straight for that tree, sniffing the undergrowth.'

'And hedgehogs dwell under trees?'

'Well, hedges and thickets. A tree would only be a substitute memory of the original growth.'

'How interesting!' A pause in the conversation. I stopped in mid-motion. What's she going to do with me? I felt paralysed. Would I be taken back to the highway thicket and left to the four winds?

'Ah, so I have an authentic dog, if not a pedigree?' she said, at last.

'That has to be seen yet, but certainly your puppy meets that description on first impression.'

'Very interesting.'

'Have I disappointed you?'

'Not at all. As I said, I have an authentic Gypsy dog here. And as long as the Gypsy community doesn't come claiming him as part of their ancestry, I shall be proud to have him. It is a him, isn't it?'

'Oh, yes, an authentic Gypsy "him",' he laughed. 'No, jokes apart, it may all be too far-fetched, and too early to predict, but he's a nice puppy. Your mother seems delighted with him,' he said looking at us. 'Do you think you should tell your mother? She might not like the idea.'

'What, about him having Roma ancestry? I wouldn't be her daughter if she didn't.'

'That sounds good. I'll be off then.'

'So, I'll bring him over for vaccination. Oh, yes, any idea of a good authentic Gypsy name?'

'Béla. I've always felt Béla to be a Gypsy name.'

'Like Bartók Béla or King Béla?' A shock wave stirred the air.

'There may be a connection?'

'In the 11th century? The Gypsies hadn't even set out for Europe by then.'

'A mystery, indeed. Still the name is found in India, a very common one too, and generally among low-caste people.'

'Excellent,' she burst out laughing and then turning to me, called out. 'Béla, Béla, gyere, gyere, come here, come here.' The call was enough to unhinge me from my paralytic state and I ran to her. The old lady was surprised by this sudden naming. She picked up the call, rolling the name off her tongue in a sing-song – Bé..la...Bé..la Bé..é..l..a. The sound filled the air with my name, making my existence unique, one among billions.

'See, it has brought an obedient response. Well, if there's nothing more you want to know, I'll push on now.'

'I'll bring Béla around, probably tomorrow or the day after. Oh, yes, how long is the life span?'

'Between 12-14.'

'Long enough,' said my mistress, seeing the man off at the gate.

I was relieved to see him go. You never know what he might have said next. I was still in the grip of the trauma triggered by his words. All that speculation about my breed and ancestry could have brought to an end the short spell of a comfortable life for me. Words are dangerous things. So, when I saw the young lady turn to me and call me, I didn't care what the name was, I ran to tell her I would be the best dog in the world. She picked me up and I heard her tell her mother about my breed, my origins, and my life-span.

Even so, my nerves remained on edge and that night I slept badly and had nightmares. I saw myself crawling about in the middle of a road where cars were coming and going at break-neck speed. But somehow I escaped being crushed under the wheels of any of them. I was whimpering and squealing as I tried to cross the road to a safer place and was failing to do that. I could hear myself whining. Then I was awake and the young lady was holding me in her arms, and the old lady was saying 'Mi a baj? Mi a baj, drágám?'

'I'd better take him to my room. He's scared and nervous, poor thing.'

But all through the night I kept on having dreams of being left alone in different places to perish one way or another. I found the old lady by my side whenever I woke up whimpering. Eventually she took me to bed with her and I slept snuggled up to her.

I must have alarmed them so much that next day the young mistress took me to a vet psychologist. I sat in my mistress's lap while she was asked all sorts of questions about me. I heard her explain that I was new to the house but seemed quite happy and full of beans earlier in the day, then something seemed to have upset me which left me traumatised. The psychologist asked what else happened in the evening, whether someone had visited them. A quiver passed through me as the mistress told about the dog expert who was called by her to examine me. I began to tremble and gave out some squeals. The lady noticed my condition. Immediately she administered a pill to calm me down. 'Are you planning to neuter him?' she asked, while holding my mouth clamped against my expelling the pill. 'We haven't thought about it yet, he's just arrived,' my mistress informed her and then added, 'I suppose we will eventually. Is it a good idea?' The psychologist was rubbing my neck now to make sure the pill did go down. 'Oh, yes, it's absolutely necessary,' I heard her say. 'The reason I asked is to let you know that he will have traumas on that account, from time to time.' The pill was beginning to have its effect, their voices were fading out.

Next thing I knew I was in the old lady's lap, and my mistress telling her about the psychologist's analysis of me: that I had taken a scare from the expert's words about my breed and was suffering from insecurity. The way to get me better, the psychologist told her, was to reassure me in every way that I was very much wanted here.

'That's easy', the old lady said, planting a kiss on my head, 'I can do that all right. Oh, yes, I will do that most happily. I will tell you stories every night and sing a lullaby to make you sleep soundly.' Then looking at me intently, she reminded me, 'Now listen, drágám, from today I'm your granny and you are my grandchild. So, you call me Nagyanya and I will call you unoka. Yes, agreed?' She then turned to her daughter and said, 'What about you, Zsuzsa, do you want him to call you Anya? We might as well sort out the relationships now. What do you say?'

'No, I don't want to be called Anya,' her daughter sounded quite definite about it.

'Whatever you like then.' The old lady said to me, 'Now, listen, Béla, while er...er...the mistress is away at work, you and I will have a lot of fun together,' and lowering her voice, pretending we were going to share a secret she added, 'while the cat's away, the mice will play, oops!'

The young mistress laughed. 'You don't have to be mice, Anya, since I won't be a cat. I don't mind what you do, as long as he – your unoka - doesn't chase or kill my beloved squirrels. I won't stand for it. So, watch out, little doggie, let me warn you, yes, you little puppy, don't you dare, okay?' She bent down and gave me a pat on my nose.

'Why would you do that, Béla, eh?' I was too small to enjoy the banter between mother and daughter. But I could sense that it was a good beginning and that I had come to the right place.

'Remember, I am your Nagyanya, always and always,' and she gave me a tight squeeze. I licked her hand to say how secure I felt in her care.

'Now then, Nagyanya promises she will tell you stories,' she put on a strict tone, 'on one condition that you will always do as she says. Agreed?'

I gathered that she believed in negotiating her every move. I had no objections of course, since I had no option other than doing as I was told. I gave a sniff, as a sign of my agreement to all the conditions laid down.

Well, that was five years ago. Since then, I have gone through five seasons, but still I have not caught a single hedgehog for my mistress. Nor have I shown any sign of ritual performances or compulsive mania for killing and burying my kills. Only once did I pounce on a squirrel and unwittingly injured it. That was when the old lady died, two years after I had settled into the comfort and love of the wonderful mother-daughter home my good fortune had brought me to.

†

⋮

5

BEDTIME STORIES

‡

Next morning, the Old Lady announced that she was going to bathe me and groom me if we were to have a daily routine of story telling. I was curious to know what a bath was and what grooming meant? I was just getting used to thinking of myself as a dog, and now what? I was taken to the bathroom where a tub half-filled with water lay in wait for me. I didn't like the look of it, but before I knew it the Old Lady lifted me and put me in. To my surprise, I started to splash in it, and liked the feel of the water. 'Just a minute, just a minute, stay still, I must scrub you down with soap, we don't want the filth and dirt of the roads in this house.' She kept up a running commentary while she gave a close inspection to every part of my body, soaping it, scrubbing it and then pouring lots of water over it. I was enjoying it so much that when she came to take me out, I found myself resisting. 'Now, now, don't you do that to Nagyanya,' I was warned in no uncertain terms. Next, she wrapped me in a big towel and gave me a good rub everywhere. 'A good dog must look clean, that's what I say. Besides, drágám, I want you to know yourself. Now, do you see that mirror over there in the corner? It will show you what you look like.'

'This is a mirror, Béla,' she said, pushing me in front of something big and shiny. 'There! See what a handsome lad you are?' I couldn't see anything. The thing was flashing in my face. I started to squeal. The Old Lady got quite startled by my reaction, she took me in her arms and soothed me. 'Now, now, there's nothing to fret about, drágám, you don't like it, I'll put it away, all right?' And she did. 'Instead, I'll tell what you look like.'

'Now, where should I start? Let's see.' She stood me away from her while informing me about my body. 'First your size: you are neither very big nor very small, I would say you have a medium build. Now your features: your face is longish, which matches your beautiful long ears that come all the way down to your shoulders. Your eyes: they are gentle and long - humans call them "almond shaped"- and your nose is beautiful, like a red berry, I love it. Next your colour: you are black and white both. The black starts from your forehead,' she said tracking it, 'then covers your ears, which are fully black and go all the way down to your shoulders. Your snout too is black, it blends well with the black over your eyes. The rest of you is white but speckled with black lines or dots. Your body is gentle and your limbs trustworthy.' I wasn't the least interested in what I looked like. She looked at me steadily and said, 'But you don't know what you look like, do you? Only the mirror can tell you that. What your face is like, your eyes, your hair, your mouth, and that there's no one else like you in the world, that you are unique and different from millions of others. See, without the mirror we won't know that.' I began to show my nervousness at the re-appearance of the mirror.

While she combed my coat slowly, she promised to tell me stories every night. I licked her hand to let her know how much I appreciated her attention. 'Like Shaharazade in the Arabian Nights, my stories will also add up to 1001, maybe even more.' She flicked a finger on my snout and said, 'Don't be like that horrid king. You are my nice unoka and you love your Nagyanya. After every story, I will also sing you a lullaby to send you to sleep, like I used to tell Zsuzsa when she was little. That's a promise.'

...

The Old Lady – somehow at that time I couldn't think of her as my Nagyanya, maybe my species don't have a sense of family - proved as good as her word. Not a single day passed when she did not sit me down and tell me a story before my bedtime, ending with a song to soothe my spirit. The first night remains memorable in my mind, to this day. She started with an announcement that instead of calling her stories Arabian Nights, she will call them the Shaggy Dog Stories. 'Isn't that a good idea?' she said. After all a dog wants to hear what is closest to his heart, something about his own species. And what are shaggy dog stories? - a question I could hardly answer. 'They are stories about stories that go on forever, and never finish! Ha!' She stopped and looked at me. 'Eureka!' she exclaimed. 'You know what? It just occurred to me that Shaharazade's stories were nothing but shaggy dog stories.' I was still confused by her quick-moving discourse, when she launched into another preamble.

'Now then, Béla drágám,' she said, with the opening flourish of a story teller, 'I'll start with animal stories first, then move on to the stories of tribes, kings and invaders. So, as I said, your first bedtime story is a dog story. Now then, are you ready?' I gave some sort of indication that I was, but can't recall whether it was a bark or a sniff or a lick. 'It's about a shaggy dog - no, you are not shaggy, drágám. You are beautiful and lovely and I just adore you. You don't believe me?' she feigned surprise, and then gave me a long steady look. 'You know, I think we should try the mirror again.' She waited to see my reaction. I gave a whine at the thought of being subjected to that thing flashing in my face. She drew me to her and said, 'It's all right, szívem, you don't have to but I want you to understand the value of a mirror.' She waited until I stopped whining, 'A mirror makes us recognise ourselves, just as we recognise others.' After a long pause to work out how to explain the importance of a mirror, she said, 'If it wasn't for looking into the mirror, we would not know who we are, what we are, and how we are not others. I am Ilona and not Margit Néni or Erzsi Néni or Zsuzsa or even Béla - that's you. Do you understand what I am saying?' How could I understand what she meant by all those words?

'I know the mirror is supposed to be only an outward reflection of who we are,' she continued, 'but what we really are inside nothing can tell us, except our inner self which is also like a mirror.' She paused as if working out a very complex thought. 'It's true. When we think, we talk to ourselves and try to look into the consequences of our actions. It tells us when we are bad, when we have done something wrong and why we shouldn't have done it. It's a sort of god that keeps us on the right path, and each one of us,' she emphasised, 'has our own god, very, very different from other gods. That's the true mirror, without which we would not know what is good and what is bad.'

It took me some growing up to understand what she was saying that evening. Stories too are like mirrors, I have come to know now. But at that time, her wisdom was no more than so many words, and much beyond my limited comprehension. At that time, I was waiting to hear the story of the shaggy dog. My patience was running out. I gave a bark, moving my body to show I wanted to leave the bathroom. I pulled her to the door, she pulled me back, 'Shall we try the mirror once more, Béla?' and even before I knew it, she had turned the mirror over quickly to catch me unawares. I backed away with a terrible whine. 'All right, all right. Too bad you don't want to see how lovely you are,' she picked me up, showering kisses on me. I was sorry to see her so disappointed. Years later, I did come to understand the importance of the two mirrors, but can't remember whether it was only after the death of the Old Lady.

SHAGGY DOG STORY

:

'So, listen.' She tilted my face and made me look at her. 'It's a real story, it took place in London. A gentlemen there lost his dog – yes, that's true, dogs do go missing, especially dogs with a shaggy coat, because they can't see where they are going. So, this gentleman advertised repeatedly about his dog in The Times – a very posh English newspaper. To his grief, no response from anyone. Then an American in New York saw the advertisement, and was touched by the man's devotion to his dog, and took great trouble to find another dog that matched the description. On his next business trip to London, he brought the dog over and visited the gentleman's house. He was met by the butler and explained that he had brought a replacement which was shaggy, like the missing dog. The butler looked at the dog and exclaimed in a horror-stricken voice: "But not as shaggy as that, sir!"'

Nagyanya clapped her hands and roared with laughter. I'm afraid I couldn't join her. I tried but found I couldn't laugh, although I felt my tail moving. 'Now, never mind this man's lost dog, don't you ever go missing, szívem. I tell you what, we will put our address on your collar. If you ever lose your way, you just point to the collar and someone will bring you back. Okay, my lovely unoka, Nagyanya loves you. Now, I'll sing you a lullaby to send you to sleep.' I can still hear her voice as it floated in the air, sending me into the sweetest sleep I could remember.

Tente, baby, tente,
Sleep little cavalier,
Evening is here.

Tente, baby, tente,
The stars up in the sky
Greet you from on high.
Tente, baby, tente

After that I was carried to my bed where I slept peacefully, without any trauma or bad dreams.

GODS AND DOGS
:

And so bedtime stories formed a daily pattern. Not a single day went by when the Old Lady didn't sit me down for a tale and a lullaby. If I know anything about my country – I assume it is mine – it is on account of those sessions. Much as the Old Lady had changed her mind about the Arabian Nights, nonetheless, the count of stories must have almost come to 1001 before I was bereft of her existence.

Next day, from the time I woke up I waited for the bedtime-story session. After supper Nagyanya settled me down next to her on the sofa and started, 'After yesterday's shaggy dog story, I shall tell you other dog stories – dogs with humans. Okay, are you ready?' I was quick to indicate I was. 'Now then,' she started in her customary style, 'the question is when did human beings start to have pets? When did human life begin?' She paused as if she expected me to answer the questions. But how would I know?

'Now then, I will tell you stories about humans and dogs from three religions.' I hadn't the slightest clue what a religion was, but decided not to interrupt. She continued. 'It's a general thought that most religions do not have dogs in their scriptures. To find out if it's true, we'll do a check on each of them. First we'll start with the Bible. You know, the other day, I was thinking about the Great Flood in the Bible, when God in his anger decided to drown the world he had once created. It tells us that Noah, who was a good man, decided to save some living beings, in memory of God's creation. So he put pairs of birds and animals in his Ark. The question is was the dog among those he chose? People say, oh, no, there's no dog in the Bible, because the dog belongs to a lower species and hence is not important enough. I refused to accept this. So, I read many different Bibles to find out. And believe it or not, I discovered one story which mentions a dog in Paradise!' By this time, I knew I was from the dog species, so I was dying to know the story.

ADAM AND DOG

:

'In the beginning there was nothing, then God said let there be a world, and he created a man whom he named Adam; then he made Paradise for Adam to live in happily. After a while, Adam went to God and said, "Lord, the Paradise you made for me is big, and I am the only one living in it. Can you not give me a companion?" God felt compassion for Adam and after some deliberation created Dog to keep him company. It proved to be a good relationship. Dog wagged his tail at all times in obedience to Adam. This made Adam a happy man, in fact too happy to care for anything, even God. After some time passed, an angel came to God and reported, "Lord, Adam, your first creature, has ceased to be humble. He is too happy to be considerate of anyone, even Dog who obeys him at all times." God was puzzled. "What could make my perfect creation, Adam, so thoughtless of his loyal companion?" God asked. The angel replied, "It's Dog; Dog is so obedient to Adam that he has lost all regard for him." God was pained that Adam turned out to be less than perfect. He had understood Adam's loneliness, because in a way God too had felt lonely despite being surrounded by many angels. So, He gave the matter a great deal of thought, and decided to make another companion for Adam who would remind him that he was not the only being in the Garden of Eden, that he was only mortal and limited in many ways.'

I could hardly work out who would it be.

'So, God created Cat as the new companion for Adam. And guess what? Cat would not obey Adam in anything. When Adam gazed into Cat's eyes he was reminded that he was not the supreme being in Paradise. This is how Adam learned to be humble.'

'What do you say, drágám?' At that time I had no idea what cats were like, so I made a low rumbling sound. 'All right', the Old Lady said. 'Tomorrow, I will tell you a Chinese story about Cat and Rat. But a lullaby now to send you to sleep.' She put my head in her lap, and stroking it gently she sang yesterday's lullaby. For a while I floated on the softness of the sound, until it started to fade away.

Next morning, the day had hardly begun when the Old Lady announced we were going for a walk. 'Let everyone see what a lovely dog you are.' I was waiting for her to tell me a story. Then I remembered stories were for bed time. That meant a long wait. I calculated: first the morning walk, then lunch, followed by a siesta, followed by the evening meal, followed by the last walk of the day. The evening I reckoned was way down the line, and the story some distance away. But it would arrive, I was sure.

THE CHINESE ZODIAC
:

'Now, yesterday's story was about Dog and Adam,' the Old Lady started with a flourish, 'today's is about Cat and Rat.' That should be interesting, I mused. 'Now then, the Chinese Zodiac is round like the earth itself, and is divided into twelve sections, managed by 12 animals. Each section is then allotted to one animal. How did this come to be?' I waited. 'This is known as a story within a story,' she declared.

'A long time ago, the First Chinese Emperor – he was called the Jade Emperor – announced to the entire animal kingdom that he would be holding a race for animals to compete for a place in the Zodiac. The first twelve to cross the finishing line would each be awarded one year in the lunar calendar – you see, the Chinese still go by the Moon, not by the Sun like in our part of the world. The news spread quickly and excitement grew in forests, lakes and mountains. At that time, Cat and Rat were the best of friends. They did everything together: eat, play, sleep. There wasn't a day that would go by where they didn't say 'hi' to each other. But later they became enemies. How did it happen? This is what the story is about.'

'When Cat heard the news of the Jade Emperor's race, he immediately told Rat who jumped to his feet and said they should both enter it. After many sleepless nights, all Rat could think of was winning the competition. But he said nothing to Cat who was happily dreaming about chasing butterflies. Finally the day of the race arrived. All the animals gathered at the starting line and with a big bang the race began.'

'Now drágám, just watch how clever Rat is. With fantastic speed, Rat and Cat rushed to get there first. They scurried through prickly bushes, ran over grassy meadows until they came upon a vast river. The current was so strong that they could not swim across. Just as they were thinking of what to do, the sturdy Ox came upon them. Being full of ideas, Rat suggested, "Ox, since your eyesight is very poor, let's help each other. Cat and I will get on your back and direct you across the river.' That sounded like a great plan to the other two. Ox was very strong and had no trouble swimming across the river.'

'As the party neared the other side, Rat let out an excited shriek. "Look, look! The Jade Emperor's palace!" Sure enough, bright red festive lanterns were shining all around the magical kingdom. Now, even though Rat and Cat were the best of friends, Rat wanted to be first more than anything in the whole world. So without even a whisper, Rat pushed Cat off Ox into the fast moving river. "Meoow-oow", yelped Cat. "What was that?" Ox asked. "Oh…oh…nothing…it must be the wind. Quick! Quick! We're almost there," shrieked Rat. As they reached the shore, Rat leapt off Ox's back and ran to the finishing line, dancing and cheering.'

'The Jade Emperor awarded Rat the first spot followed by a very tired Ox. Shortly after, the strong and powerful Tiger roared to the finish with the lucky Rabbit hopping right behind. From the sky, the noble Dragon descended to the ground. Through the bushes the Snake slithered to take its place. Next came the Horse and Goat in a tight race. From the trees, Monkey swung in from vine to vine. Rooster scrambled in with a few feathers ruffled, trailed by Dog – your ancestor, szívem – who was in a very good mood. Finally, last but not least, Pig trotted up wanting to know when dinner would be served. As the Jade Emperor congratulated all 12 animals on completing the race, Cat, who was soaked head to paws, scampered in to the palace. Jade Emperor thanked Cat for joining the race but said he was just too late to win a place in the Zodiac. From that day onward, Cat swore he and Rat would be enemies forever.'

'That is one version of the Chinese Zodiac, the other is a Buddhist one. Gautam Buddha, a Prince of a small kingdom at the foot of the Himalayas in India, was bothered by the suffering of mankind. What could be the source of human suffering? How can humans liberate themselves from this state? He left his comfortable life to find the answer. During his wanderings he saw much cruelty against animals. He was appalled by the Hindu practice of sacrificing animals as an offering to their gods. He opposed the cruel practice of animal sacrifice. Thus compassion for all beings became one of the eight principles of Buddhism. How did the animals come to be in the Zodiac? The legend has it that before his departure from this world, Lord Buddha summoned all animals of the Earth to come before him, but only twelve actually came to bid him farewell. To reward the animals who answered his call, Lord Buddha named a year after each of them in the order they had arrived. Hmm,' she suddenly stopped and asked, 'Is Cat missing in Buddha's Zodiac too?' How could I know? I gave her a blank look. 'I'll have to find out,' she said, tying a knot in her hankerchief to remind her.

'Anyway, Cat or not, the Zodiac is divided into 12 sections, hence, a 12 year cycle for each animal, and each year is guided by the qualities of the animal. So, for example, people born in Year of the Dog are thought to be loyal, honest and make good leaders.' I was beginning to understand what being a dog meant. Nagyanya was saying, 'You see, how different it is from the Bible story? In the Buddhist view of the universe, animals are not only accommodated in the universal scheme but even given a prime space. Aren't you proud that a whole year is named after you?' She rubbed my back, and added, 'I wish, I too had a year to myself – the Year of Ilona!' That was the only time I heard envy in her voice.

'Tomorrow, I'll tell you the story of Man's sincerity for a Dog. But now, to bed with a song and a lullaby.' While she was singing me to sleep, I was wondering if this was how Shaharazade sent her king to bed every night, all the 1001 nights! My heart went out to her.

YUDHISHTRA AND DOG

:

At last the evening arrived. I snuggled up to Nagyanya on the sofa and waited for her to begin the story. 'Now, Béla drágám, this story is the opposite of Adam and Dog, because here Man preferred to forego life in Paradise rather than abandon his dog. This is how it goes.

'After the death of Krishna - who was the reincarnation of God - Indians are always having reincarnations – the Pandava family were left grief-stricken. Krishna had led them against their evil cousins, the Kuravas, and helped them to recapture their lost kingdom. Yudhishtra, the truth-seeking eldest of the five Pandava brothers, could no longer face life without Krishna. Renouncing the world of power, wealth and fame, he abdicated the throne of Hastinapur in favour of a great-nephew. The five brothers and the queen Draupadi embarked on a pilgrimage, on what they knew was their final journey. As they wandered from one sacred city to another in search of salvation, they stopped in Varanasi for a short rest. It was here by the sacred river Ganges, that a dog attached itself to them. When they resumed their journey and began to ascend towards the Himalayas, the dog continued to follow them. The small band pressed on, but the journey was proving difficult. It wasn't just fatigue and obstacles that were the cause but the heavy load of their karma – the Hindu word for sin – that started to take a toll on each of them. One by one they began to perish. Queen Draupadi, the twins Sahadev and Nakul, Arjun the archer, and mighty Bhim, in turn gave up the ghost.'

'Yudhishtra, who had lived a life of almost unblemished righteousness, was the only one left. He continued, the dog still following him. Numb with grief and loneliness, yet impelled by destiny, Yudhishtra pressed on. Suddenly, a glow of light appeared revealing Indra – the sky god – in his golden chariot. Indra descended from the chariot, and invited Yudhishtra to board it, saying that it would make his journey easier, since it would carry him straight to heaven. Yudhishtra was reluctant at first, and wanted to make sure that his brothers and wife were already there. However, on Indra's insistence that he would meet them in heaven, he acquiesced. Yet, as he prepared to board with the dog, Indra laughed and told him that there was no place in heaven for a dog. Yudhishtra reacted strongly. He shook his head, and expressed his refusal to comply with Indra's command.'

'The dog, Yudhishtra explained, had shared all his troubles. It had demonstrated its devotion by continuing to remain with him. Surely, he argued with Indra, his deeds must earn him a place in heaven, and that his own merit would be negated if he failed in his duty towards the dog. Indra looked at the dog who was listening to their conversation and replied, "The dog, O Yudhishtra, though faithful to humans, is considered a lowly creature by the Hindus; for that reason he is not allowed even in the temple precincts, let alone in the Swarga." But Yudhishtra did not waver. "If this is the price your heaven demands of me," Yudhishtra declared to Indra, "then I will not pay it." And then, sadly but firmly, he turned away from Indra's chariot. As he started to walk further, the dog began to change form. Dharma, the God of Justice, Yudhishtra's celestial father, stood before him. All along, it was Dharma in the form of the dog who had kept pace with his son, until the final test was played out with Indra. Having proved his mettle, Yudhishtra ascended Indra's great chariot and left for heaven.'

'Did Yudhishtra miss the dog?' Nagyanya asked wiping her tears and pulling me to herself. 'What do you think?' she asked me. I wasn't too sure of what Dharma was. 'He must have,' she answered, 'after all, the dog had become Yudhishtra's companion, a real fellow traveller. Don't you think?' I wished she would stop asking me these difficult questions, because I hadn't a clue. 'Lonely, bereft and at the end of his life, yet Yudhishtra was still ready to give up heavenly comfort for the sake of his dog. Isn't that wonderful?' It was, and like her I felt moved by human loyalty to an animal. I snuggled up to her. She seemed no less loyal to me. Could she be a reincarnation of Yudhishtra?

We sat in silence. After a while Nagyanya started to sing, softly and slowly.

> *Sleep, baby, sleep, little rabbit sleeps too.*
> *Evening's on the village, little girls are dozing.*
> *Sleep, baby, sleep, little rabbit sleeps too.*
> *Evening's on the village, bells are ringing.*
> *Tomorrow, God's big lamp will make the sky bright,*
> *Baby and the rabbit will wake to the light.*

Before the music began to recede, I heard her say, 'Remind me to tell you the Jataka story of the Fox, Dog & Horse.' Even in the increasing fuzziness of sleep I wondered how was I to remind her?

SIRIUS – THE DOG STAR
⋮

Sure enough, I was getting addicted to story time. To work out how far away was the bedtime, I would calculate all the hours in the day by looking at the sun and its journey downwards. After a quick stroll for my post-dinner performance, I would rush in and hop onto the sofa, and wait for Nagyanya to join me.

'Now, Béla szivem, you will like tonight's story,' she announced. 'It's an ancient tale. Long ago, when the astronomers first spotted this great star, they thought it looked like a dog and named it "Dog Star". Isn't that nice?' she said giving me a peck on my mouth. I squealed with joy and moved closer to her, indicating that I did and wanted to hear more.

'Now then, the fantastic feat of the Dog Star was that it was not afraid of getting closer to the sun – others who did the same before him suffered tragic consequences. Do you know the story of Icarus?' Did I? I gave her a blank look. 'The story goes like this. He and his father were imprisoned in the Labyrinth of Crete – I won't go into that story, too many shaggy dog stories otherwise, – and wanted to be free men. The only way to get out of the Labyrinth was to fly out through the top into the open sky. Daedelus, Icarus' father, who was a descendent of Hephaestus, a Greek god, made wings with wax and feathers for himself and his son and wearing them they flew upwards and out to the open sky. But Icarus didn't stop there, the lust of flight was upon him, and he continued to fly until he got too close to the sun. Immediately the immense heat melted the wax of his wings. His wings scorched to cinders and he plummeted down into the sea and was instantly drowned.'

'But not so Sirius, our Dog', she gave me a tight squeeze. 'He was wise enough to stay in the vicinity of the great god, not challenge it head on, like Icarus. The sun was flattered by his wisdom and smiled at him. This is how the great Dog Star was able to shine alongside the sun, giving us hot weather, doubly hot, all through the month of July. That's why people call it High Summer; some even call the days Dog Days. They say, if it wasn't for Sirius' humble bravery in courting the proximity of the sun, we would continue to shiver in shilly-shallying spring and never get hot summer. It's right too, isn't it? Aren't you proud of your fellow dog, drágám?' she asked me with another kiss, this time on my snout. How could I not be proud of my link with a star in the celestial regions! I made my feelings clear by responding to her and licking her face in return. I loved hearing her tell all these stories, which otherwise I would not know. Here, I admit, humans have the better of animals. After her death, in all the years I remained in the house, not once did I forget this superb story, which during the High Summer never failed to remind me to look up to the sky, despite the glare of two suns. After all, but for the feat of my compatriot, we would not have the Dog Days.

Nagyanya remained true to her word. Not a single day went by when she did not sit me down and tell me stories. Starting with stories about dogs, she went on to other animals. If I came to know anything about the animal world it was because of her. It was as if I had a trip to the wilds with her and experienced the world of animals, how they lived with each other and how they survived the occasional contact with humans. Wolves, foxes, lions, tigers, cheetahs, jungle cats, deer, antelopes, elephants and scores of other animals continued to make their appearance one by one, what seemed to be forever, with no end in view. 'I have to confess these are not stories I made up – I wish they were,' she said showing regret, 'but stories that came from India, and just like your forbears they slowly travelled,' she dramatised with her hands, 'out of the land of their origin over the mountains, then across to Europe, with stopovers on the way. People found such wisdom in them that they turned them into moral stories, i.e. lessons for humans how to be good, and vice versa, for animals. They came to be called 'Aesop's Fables', after a Greek named Aesop who compiled them.' So started my long journey into the animal world, a world which in the end I came to choose over the human world.

†

6

HISTORY LESSONS

‡

One day the Old Lady announced that she had thought of something new for me. 'If you were a human child, you would be going to school, where they teach children many things, including the history of their country. And I totally agree with this sort of teaching, knowing the past of your land is essential – who were the first people, and who came later. Did these tribes live together happily or did they fight with each other? Was it because they believed in different things, or was it because they feared each other? Why did they choose kings to rule them?'

This was getting too complicated for me. Nagyanya noticed that my interest was wilting and my eyes closing. 'Don't you dare go to sleep, Béla. Knowing history is more important than music. I don't care what Bartók Béla says about the importance of music in children and that music predates the birth of language in our brains. I don't agree with him. My question to him is: where does music come from? I say it is from our perception of the world. We need words to describe what we perceive, only then,' she emphasised with force, 'and only then can we sing about it.' She stopped with great aplomb as if she had defeated the argument of a worthy adversary. I extended my paw to her in an appeal to cut to the chase, I wasn't sure how long I could keep my attention going. I think she took the hint. 'All right, all right, I get your message,' she snapped.

Next morning, when we went out, Nagyanya walked quietly. She usually talked to me about whatever passed on the street or anything that looked interesting, so her silence worried me. I thought if I made a bit of a song and dance about something, it would make her speak. But before I could decide what, she gave a tug at my lead and said, 'Listen, Béla, I know last night you got bored by my talk about history; so I've been thinking how to make your lessons interesting.' I gave a bark to deny the accusation. 'Oh, no, don't tell me you didn't. I know you were, so no point in apologising. Never mind, listen to my plan.' We were passing a bench, so I jumped on to it as if to say, tell me now. She laughed and sat down. I waited to hear what she'd say.

'I think I should combine my idea of history together with Bartók Béla's about music. All this, szívem, to make the lesson interesting for you. Yes?' Yes, I gave a few sing-song barks, yes, music please. 'Good,' she said. 'I will make a puppet show of kings, and of invaders and of people!'

I had no idea what a puppet show was, and certainly not what all these kings and invaders were. I must have looked so nonplussed that she drew me to her side and said, 'Don't worry, you'll understand when you see it. But you have to wait. I can't do it right away, because I have to prepare puppets first, which will take a few days.' No bedtime stories? I looked up. 'Bedtime stories will continue. That's the nightly affair, yes, every night. The puppet show will be the day affair.' It was hard to grasp this 'day and night affair'.

'The question is when should we have it?' she asked, and then answered herself, 'I know, after you finish your breakfast. How's that, eh?' she said, tickling me. I was happy to see her pleased with her plan.

A week passed but no puppet show materialised. I was getting curious about it, but was happy that the bedtime stories continued as usual. Every evening Nagyanya told a new story, centring on a different animal who chanced on some traveller journeying through the forest.

†

PUPPET THEATRE

:

Another week was passing by and yet no sign of the promised puppet theatre. One morning, as I started getting ready to go on the regular walk, the Old Lady said, 'No walk today, school this morning, the time the children leave for school.' I didn't know what a school was, so I continued to tap around her, insisting on going for the walk. 'No, no, no, drágám, no walk this morning, school instead.' I had never seen her so determined. 'To my room, that's where your school will be,' and she marched up the stairs. I had no option but to follow her, still puzzled about this school business.

'That's the Puppet Theatre,' she said pointing to a very big cardboard square under the window. A room within a room, it had curtains and lots of colourful pictures on all sides. 'You sit here, in front of the stage, from where you can see what's happening. I'll be behind the curtain, this one,' she said going behind the box, 'so you won't be seeing me.' True, I couldn't. She came out again to say more. 'You will hear the music of Bartók Béla, as background to my history stories; on stage will appear lots of little figures who will act out historical events. I'll show you.' She went behind the stage and came out with a cluster of doll-like figures, strings coming out of their arms and heads. I must have shown a blank expression that she said, 'How the puppets work is like this: I pull the strings to make them turn, run, sit, stand and many other things, but they won't be speaking; I will be, though it will seem to you they are. And yes, the curtain in the front – not the one at the back from where the puppeteer moves the puppets – will have the topic of the day's lesson. For example, today's lesson is "Tribes & Chieftains",' she pointed to the stage curtain. 'Is that clear?'

I'm not sure if I took in everything she said, but I gave a snort to say yes, and not knowing how long this thing would go on, stretched out to give myself a relaxed posture for the ordeal.

I was still in the process of arranging myself when the music started with a blare and the curtain went up.

Tribes and Chieftains

A play in two Acts

:

The players:
Avars (3)
Kavars (4)
Árpád
István (Chief of the Magyars)
Elders (5) (The council of Elders)
Audience

...

Voice over.

Four centuries brought Roman rule to an end. The Romans left everything in the hands of the Vandals who flourished for a while before they were invaded by the Huns, who in turn were swept aside by other wandering tribes, until in the 9th century, the Avars came on the scene. A horde of seven tribes, they were linked with each other by the same language, the one we speak now. (Nagyanya stuck her head over the curtain: take note, drágám, language comes before music). Not long after, the tribe of Kavars arrived. A clash seemed inevitable, but instead it turned into a unification of the two.

The curtain goes up, music fades in. ***Ahoy!***

A call is heard; in response comes the call, ***Ahoy!*** Avars enter from stage left and Kavars from the right. They have spears in their hands.

Tribes and Chieftains

Avars:	We are the seven tribes of Avars, and this is our land.
Kavars:	We are the Kavars — only three tribes. Together we can make ten, stronger against invaders. What do you say?
Avars:	(*Putting their heads together*) Yes, good idea.
Kavars	(*the two groups embrace each other and shake hands*) We are all one tribe now, loyal to each other against any outsider. Agreed? (*The Avars nod their heads*) What do we do next?
Avars:	The Romans were here for four centuries. Do you know why?
Kavars:	That was a long time ago. Since then other tribes must have come.
Avars:	They did, but they hardly left a mark behind. Yet the sites of the Romans are still here. You know why?
Kavars:	(*Think*) Because they had good leaders?
Avars:	Correct. So, to be like the Romans, we must choose a chief who will lead us against other tribes.
Kavars:	Good idea. You never know, the Romans may come back. And they will wipe us out in no time.

Avars: So, let's choose a leader. (*Announcing*) Who wants to
            be the leader? (*One hand shoots up*).

            Anyone else? (*No other hand. To the man*)

            What's your name?

Man: Árpád.

All: Árpád! Cheers for Árpád. The first leader of the Avars
            & Kavars.

            (*Cheers*)

**Béla: This is fun. I like history. And hear Nagyanya!
            Amazing she can change her voice to suit so many
            puppets.**

Avar I: What will you do for us? What will be your agenda?

Árpád: My agenda will have ten points:

            One! I will give ourselves one name. The Avars and
            Kavars together will be called Magyars.

            (*clapping*)

            Two! We shall have a standing army. All the young will
            be trained to be soldiers.

            Three! Draw a territory and call it Magyarország.

            (*Hurray*)

            Four! Build forts to keep the invaders out. (*Clapping:
            Good idea*)

            Five! Create a look-out system to spot the enemy.
            (*Bravo*)

Six! Divide the people into workers and soldiers. (*Here! here!*)

Seven! Set up a Council of Elders.

(*Yes, indeed*)

Eight! Make a Magyar Flag and raise it.

(*Yes. Three colours!*)

Avar 1:	What about food? Do we have Magyar food?
Árpád:	We can. We can even give names to the dishes, if you like.
Avar 2:	We can call our soup as gulyás…
Kavar 1:	What about the thin bread, you know what I mean?
Avar 3:	(*Excited*) We can call it palacsinta.
Árpád:	(*Impatiently*) All right, all right, we can work out names later.
Kavar 2:	Nine can be the national cuisine. (*Cheers go up*)
Árpád:	(*Puts up his hands to silence them*) Right now (*determined tone*) we must decide on one other important issue.
Avar 4:	What's that?
Árpád:	Elect me as your Chief.
Kavar 2:	(*Surprised*) But we have. We have chosen you as our leader.
Árpád:	Not the same. I want the title Chieftain of the Magyars.
All:	(*To each other*) Shall we? (*Lots of noise*) Yes. We elect Árpád as our Chieftain.

(*Loud cheers*)

Béla gets up and dances around.

Árpád: Hang on, why not make me your king?

Kavar I: We don't know what king means. Maybe in time we will. (*To others*) Isn't that right?

All: Yes, right, we can do that later, later. (*Pause*) By the way, did the Romans have kings?

Avar: Can't think of one.

Kavar: Right, then we wait. (*To Árpád*) Let's move on to other things. Shall we build some Baths, like the Romans? We want to look clean.

Árpád: (*Not too happy*) Yes, by all means, go ahead.

Kavar: Well, aren't you going to lead us? Make us do things to improve our lot?

Árpád: Yes, I will, I will. Let's start with a flag. Do you have any preference for colours?

All: (*variously*) Red....white...green.

Árpád: There! I knew you would choose the same colours. (*He unfurls a flag in red, white and green.*) Magyars! My people, from now on we call this land of ours **Magyarország**. Let us work together to make it prosperous. We will make it rich with food, build canals, houses and forts for protection against invaders.

They start building, digging irrigation, making weaponry.

Béla: **Oh, what fun. I begin to understand how the system works.**

Voice over: *And so the nation of Magyars was born. Árpád proved to be a good chieftain. He consolidated the tribe of Magyars and kept other tribes at bay. In time Árpád had sons who like him led the Magyar people into prosperity. It is the 12th century A.D. Watch István, Árpád's great-great-grandson, Chieftain of the Magyars, addressing the Council of Elders.*

István:	Council Elders, I have called this meeting to say that our frontiers can no longer hold aggressive tribes back. There are too many of them, and they keep coming in waves. We need to rethink our warfare strategies.
Elder 1:	Are we in danger? Is the enemy at the gates?
István:	Not yet, but if the word spreads we are not strong, they will be.
Elder 2:	And how can we become strong?
István:	I should have more powers and be made a king.
Elder 3:	Well, if you want, you can be one. We don't mind.
István:	Not like this. I want the Church to sanctify my Kingship.
Elder 4:	What does that mean? What is the Church?
István:	The Roman Church (*Ah! The Romans!*) – The Church will enthrone me as the first Christian King of the Magyars.
Elder 5:	That sounds good, we have no objection. (*Pause*) Are there special gains in being Christianized?
István:	(*Earnestly*) Since I will be backed by the Church, if there's an attack on us other Christian countries will come to our help. (*Pause*) But there is a condition.
All:	What's that?
István:	In return I must convert all pagan tribes to Christianity. We already have Christian missionaries living here, who were invited by Prince Géza, my father.
All:	(*looking at each other*) Are we pagans?
István:	You were, but now all Magyars have become Christians, and better human beings.

Elders:	Was there something wrong with us?
István:	Do you know about reading and writing? As Christians we must read the Bible and for that we must learn the alphabet.
Elders:	Alphabet?
István:	Yes, alphabet. So that we can write what we say, and read what we want to say. Latin will show us the way. It was the language of the Romans.
Elders:	Ah, the Romans again!
István:	(*raising his voice*) So, my good people, with your support, I will apply to Pope Sylvester to crown me as the Christian King of the Magyars. I will ask for the Coronation to take place on Christmas day, the year 1000 A.D.
	(*Sky-reaching cheers*).

Burst of hymns. A Catholic procession headed by a Papal Bishop carrying the Crown, which he places on István's head and drapes a rich cape on him. He performs the ceremony with panache. The curtain falls amidst singing and ceremonies.

Béla gives happy barks by way of clapping.

†

Nagyanya came out from behind the puppet box and sat down with me. 'Okay, today's lesson is over, which means we can go for a walk.' I jumped up. 'Did you enjoy it, your first history lesson?' I licked her foot to indicate I did. 'All history starts with people, ordinary people like me or Margit Néni or Kati Néni or Aladár Bácsi or Ádám Bácsi, you know all the people you meet up and down this road. Only then come kings and invaders, battles and wars. That's why I started with the Avars and Kavars. To make sure you have understood everything, I will explain more. That's what they do in schools,' and she added, 'I will also tell you about the Romans. I couldn't make a puppet show with them, because I couldn't make their cut-outs, rather complicated as they are. Let's go now. We'll walk and talk.'

Surprisingly enough I was quite interested to find out who the Romans were and why they came here and what they did for us. This was a complete turn around for me. Earlier I was bored by even the mention of history, but now the stories made sense. The Puppet Theatre was certainly working for me, although it was scary to see little people being pulled up with strings by an unseen hand, in a most wilful vicious way. I dreaded being in their place. So in some way it was a relief to get out of the dark room.

As we set out on our usual trail up the hill, Nagyanya continued with the history. 'Now then, drágám, about the Romans, they went everywhere. They had a good army, so they kept marching up north to different settlements in Europe, always looking for natural resources, you know the way the US looks for gas these days. They would settle down for a few centuries and then off they would go again. That's what the Romans did in our country too. And you'll be surprised, after two thousand years, we still have evidence of their being here. I tell you what, one day we'll take a trip to Óbuda to see the Roman sites. Ruins they may be, but they tell many stories, stories of gods and goddesses. The nobles' mansions, the baths, the military settlement, and of course, the amphitheatre - Rome par excellence. But some people are very disparaging of the Romans, labelling their culture as "bread and circuses", "more muscle than brain". But I think it's unfair to say that.' I must have shown some lack of interest for she gave me a quick look, as if to say 'Pay attention, will you?', and then carried on.

'In a way the Avars were pagans like the Romans, and migrants like them too, but unlike the Romans, the Avars put down their roots here, and created the nation of Magyars.' I was getting hungry, so I began to whine a bit to convey to Nagyanya the urgency of getting home, but she paid no attention to me. On the contrary, she sat down on our usual stopover bench, and patted the space next to her for me to hop on to. I was back in the labyrinth of roots and origins.

'That proves the Avars were our first ancestors. I could really be an Avar, just as you could be an Indian who came with the Gypsies. After all, we all have to come from somewhere. And how many of us really know our ancestors? Some people deny that they may have any genes of the Avars in them, but I don't. I'd be proud if someone said to me, "You, Ilona, are an Avar!"' She clapped her hands in glee and gave me a kiss on my head! 'Others say, the Magyars came from Asia. Why not? I don't mind. That would make me and you with the same roots, won't it?' I gave a loud snort, indicating that I was ready to go home. To my surprise Nagyanya took the hint and got up. I set out at great speed hoping she wouldn't stop again, but her train of thought went rushing on.

'Many of the Magyars are uppish, they don't like to think of themselves as Avars, they prefer to trace their genes back a thousand years earlier to the Romans, who took off from a tiny place like Rome, and established a mighty Roman Empire all over Europe. So, to be traced back to them is a matter of pride for some Magyars. But I say that the Romans too were migrants - maybe mightier than some - because they came and they went, leaving a lot of debris behind. But the Avars stayed, that's what makes them our first ancestors.'

We were almost home. I ran ahead and waited at the gate wagging my tail rapidly to tell her that my tummy was rumbling hard. She looked at her watch and understood my haste. It wasn't long before I got my lunch. Within five minutes of lapping it up, I was flat out. Listening to history had finished me, and that too human history, nowhere as interesting as animal stories.

...

Next morning, again I was marched up to the bedroom, made to sit down in front of the Puppet Box and told what I was about to see was the hardest but the most heroic period in Magyar history: Christian Kings & Islamic Invaders. Again I hadn't a clue what that meant, but since I had enjoyed the puppets the day before, I looked forward to the show. Nagyanya said it would interest me because it was all about the Béla Kings – not one but four! Béla I, Béla II, Béla III and Béla IV! She said that she had chosen my name because King Béla IV was the best of all Magyar kings. So, I was quite curious to see them today, even though they would only be puppets. I had understood one thing about history - it's always in the past.

†

Bélas & Mongols

A play in one Act

:

The players:
Béla IV
Margit
Priest
Messenger
Nobles
Audience

The curtain goes up.

Voice over: *For two centuries, following the death of the first Christian king, reasonable peace prevailed in the land. New immigrants came from the west, and the royal power increased under Béla III, who brought smaller kingdoms into the Magyar fold. The dynasty of the Béla Kings were the best of the Magyar Kings. Nagyanya's head came over the curtain. 'That's why I named you Béla… Béla…. Béla …' she said singing,*

(I wagged my tail rapidly and snorted loudly to stop her from sending me crazy with repeating my name. Thankfully, it worked.)

BÉLAS & MONGOLS

The time is 1241 A.D. King Béla IV sits on the throne, surrounded by his nobles.

Béla IV: *(to the courtiers)* My grandfather, King Béla III, made this country strong. Many kings bowed to his will. They accepted the authority of the Magyar King. *(Angry)* Look at us now? Why are we in this state? Within half a century Magyarország is in tatters, and the Mongols are about to descend on us. Before we know it, they will be our rulers and we their slaves.

Noble I: We understand the situation, but we are not to blame for it.

Béla IV   *(outraged)* Are you not? Twenty years ago, out of sheer greed, you forced King Andrew II to sign the Golden Bull, reducing him and the kings to come after him to mere puppets in your hands. *(Pause)* How are you going to stop the Mongols now? *(Waits)*.

        A messenger runs in.

Messenger   Your majesty, the Mongols have broken through into our territory. It's a full scale invasion. They are slaughtering people, the land is red with blood. Our army cannot cope with them.

Béla IV: *(to the nobles)* The Mongols have invaded us. What are you doing about it, eh? All that power you took away from the king? Will any king help you now?

Nobles: Please, your majesty, we give you full powers to deal with the enemy. Later we can revise the Golden Bull. We give you our word.

Béla IV: Good. (*To the messenger*) I shall lead the army myself. Send the Generals here to report.

(The nobles leave. King Béla gets down from the throne, goes down on his knees and prays to God.) God Almighty, save our nation from the Mongol hordes. Make my arms strong so I can wield your sword to drive the invaders out of our land for good. (Pause) I promise to dedicate my dearest daughter Margit in your service. Though only nine years old at present, she will serve you all her life until death. Accept my humble sacrifice, O merciful Lord, and help me to keep this land Christian. Amen.

Lights fade. Burst of battle sounds: horses neighing, people groaning on the battlefield. Suddenly, the bugles ring and sounds of jubilation. 'Mongols are gone', 'Mongols have fled'. Church music takes over. Amidst hymn singing, Margit enters holding on to her father's arm.

Margit: Where are we going, Papa?

Béla IV: We are seeing the Bishop, darling.

Margit: Why am I dressed up like a bride?

Béla IV: (*avoids her question*) From today on you will live in God's house.

Margit: What? Not with you and Mama? (*starts to cry*).

Béla IV: Listen, darling, there is no home for a woman better than a nunnery. (*Kisses her on her forehead.*) I will give you a whole island for it.

Margit: Oh, that would be fun, Papa. I can play hide and seek with my friends.

Béla IV: (*a sigh*) No, not for that, my precious. It would be to set up a nunnery in your name.

Margit: Ssh, here comes the Bishop.

Music. The Bishop enters from the opposite side. He is carrying a big cross. Béla IV hands Margit over to him. Wedding chants rise. Margit cries and grips her father's arm, whereupon he disentangles her hand and pushes her towards the Bishop. Margit's cries continue. Lights fade.

Lights go up again. Margit, now a young woman, is dressed as a nun. She is surrounded by lepers. They are all pushing and shoving to get close to her. A priest is shouting to stop them.

Priest: Hold it, don't push. You, you, line up. One at a time. Don't panic, she will see everyone. (*Goes to her*) Are you all right, my lady?

Margit: A bit tired, but I will try to see them all. (*Pause*) Is it true that my mere touch cures lepers?

Priest: Most certainly. They wouldn't be here otherwise, in their hundreds. You only have to listen to them talking about it. Because a large number of people here are still pagans. They trust the devil more than our Lord. Your touch will convert them to Christianity.

Margit: Oh, dear, I feel tired. Can we do it tomorrow?

Priest: (*harshly*) No, dear Lady, you'd better finish today.

Béla whimpers.

Curtain comes down. Lights fade.

Nagyanya comes out crying, she picks me up and sits down in the rocking chair. 'Such a young girl and made to live a life of loneliness.' I lick her face to tell her I understand why she feels like that. 'How terrible that a little girl is made to leave her parents to live among strangers.' Nagyanya rocks gently but doesn't speak for a while. We sit silently. I look around to see where all the lepers have gone. She understands my puzzlement and says, 'They were only puppets, drágám, just as we too are puppets of some superior power, but we don't know who.' She took a deep sigh. 'We should go to Margit sziget one day and look at the place where once poor Margit cured lepers.' (Alas, we never did make it to Óbuda). 'But even then Béla IV is my favourite king. He was a true royal.' I wondered in what way could I be like him. 'He was a good king and ruled his people justly. He kept his promise to God. He didn't change his mind, it takes courage to do that,' she said. How could she praise him, after crying over the fate of an innocent girl?

'It took Béla IV fifty years to make the land prosperous again. But guess what? Another horde of invaders loomed on the horizon. This time the threat came from the west. Isn't it funny, drágám, that this land should be invaded in turns, from east and west both. When eastern invasion finished, the western hordes would invade. I'm not joking, szívem. After the Mongols, the French arrived making claims over our land, followed by Luxembourg, followed by Poland and Romania. So many battles.' She looked at me. 'Is it getting too difficult for you, szívem?' She asked me as if my answer could change her mind, but surprisingly it did. 'Why don't we stop here today? Making puppet shows is some work.' What she said next surprised me. 'My heart is heavy, I can't stop thinking of poor Margit. I want to say a prayer for her soul,' and then added, 'for her father too.' Suddenly she got up and put me down. 'We'll stop now, no, no walk this morning. You go on the terrace, I'll see you at lunch.' She led me down the stairs and left me to choose how to spend the rest of the morning.

...

Next morning Nagyanya was her old self. 'Today's lesson is more tricky. The Ottomans were not just some invading horde, they were a rising military power in Europe.' I wagged my tail to say I had full faith in the puppets to make me understand the most difficult of discourses. She looked pleased with my positive response and kissed me on my nose. Then once again, she vanished behind the curtain. I settled down to digest the next phase of history.

Magyars & The Ottomans

A play in two Acts

:

The players:

Mátyás Corvinus IV, the King of the Magyars

Szilágyi Mihály, a nobleman

Hunyadi János, a Transylvanian warlord

Sultan Sulieman

Warlords

Nobles

Courtiers

Audience

Voice over: *In the next two centuries, many reforms were legislated. Again, the Golden Bull was brought back, which reduced the king's powers by much. A constitution was drawn up which forced the kings to consider the welfare of the people. A university was founded, and agriculture was developed, and many industries started. All this improved the living of the people. But within a century, decline set in. The Ottomans appeared on the horizon. For nineteen long years, Magyar kings fought them but with little success. In the end it took Hunyadi János, a Transylvanian warlord, to unite all the warlords under one banner and drive them out.*

MAGYARS & THE OTTOMANS

Music and battle sounds. Lights go up. Magyar soldiers enter from the right and Ottomans from the left. They clash with spears and swords.

Hunyadi: (*Enters stage right, riding on horseback*) Good soldiers, brave men, fight on, fight until the enemy is ousted. (*Rides out*)

         Sounds of victory.

Hunyadi: (*Enters riding, stage left*) Brave soldiers, you've driven them out of Transylvania. Now we have to push them out of Serbia. Fight them! (*Rides out*)

         Sounds of battle and then victory cheers go up.

Hunyadi: (*Enters riding, stage right*) Keep going, keep it up, follow them until they are out of Bulgaria. (*Rides out*).

         Sounds of battle.

Hunyadi   (*Enters riding, stage left*) My brave soldiers, we must stop the Turks. Keep up the fight, one last push and raise the siege of Belgrade. (*Rides out*).

         Sounds of Jubilation. Church bells ring. The Lords Prayer is sung in Latin. Warlords gather.

         Voice over: *With the Ottomans defeated, once again, the throne became blood-stained. The need for a king was urgent. Szilágyi Mihály, a nobleman, takes the matter into his own hands and calls a meeting of the warlords.*

Szilágyi: Hunyadi János died driving the Ottomans out of the country.

Warlord 1:   They may return. The king is dead. The throne is empty.

Warlord 2:   We should import a strong king from abroad.

Szilágyi:	Do you want a foreign king again?
Warlord 3:	(*looks at everyone*) What does everyone say? (*No one speaks*). Hunyadi became a regent to young László, as good as being a king. (*Pause*) That gives his son, Corvinus, a right to the throne.
Warlord 2:	It's not the same as a royal descendant.
Warlord 3:	Why not? Hunyadi united us against the Ottomans, and fought four fierce battles - not one, not two, not three but four – against them, drove them out of the land. Isn't that enough?
	Silence.
Warlord 4:	Why don't we try him then? If he doesn't prove his mettle, we can depose him and invite a foreign king.
Szilágyi :	Good thinking. Send a note to the Ecclesiastical Office right away to arrange a Coronation for Mátyás Corvinus.
	Music. Mátyás Corvinus enters, followed by warlords. The Bishop enters leading a Coronation procession of priests. Amidst hymn singing and litany, Mátyás is crowned with the title Mátyás Corvinus IV, the King of the Magyars.
Mátyás:	(*on the throne, looking through some papers*) Yes, it's a good design. I want the best material used both for the palace and the church. Commission the best artists to make frescoes on the walls and ceilings. Spare no cost, I want the castle to be the best in the world.
Noble:	It will be as you say, Your Majesty.
Mátyás:	Wait, here's another decree. Set up a printing press too. It's the latest development in Europe, we don't want to be left behind. Set up a library also. We'll need it for the printed books.
Noble 2:	We will do your bidding, Your Majesty. This land will be the shining star in all Europe. Magyarország will be known as the most advanced nation.

Mátyás:	(*astutely*) It's not enough to be a shining star, you need a standing army. Increase the number of mercenaries to 30,000, and call it the Black Army. We need to be vigilant against the Ottomans, and forever ready to go into action against them.
Noble 3:	Indeed, Your Majesty. We will make sure the Black Army becomes the supreme force in Europe.
Noble 4:	Your Majesty, it may be a good time to extend our borders to the West. The Austrian king is losing his grip on Vienna. We should put the Black Army to good use.
King Mátyás:	I see the point. (*Thinks*). Call a meeting of the army generals. We'll see them tomorrow, first thing in the morning. (*Gets down from the throne*) I will now take a tour of the Vár to see how the building is progressing. (*Exits*).

Lights fade. Music.

1490 A.D. Church bells ring mournfully. Announcement: Mátyás Corvinus IV is dead. Church bells continue to ring. 'The King is dead, long live the King'. Funeral service.

Warlord 1:	The King is dead. Fifty years of peace. Now who?
Warlord 2:	We are surrounded by strong kingdoms. Choose one. We need a strong monarch.
Warlord 3:	True. We cannot risk the Ottoman invasions again.
Warlord 4:	Hmm. What about the Hapsburgs?
Warlord 1:	No, the Anjou kings are stronger.
Warlord 2:	King Ludwik of Poland is a better choice.
Warlord 3:	No, the Anjou Kings from Naples.
Warlord 4:	No, no, no, the Romanian Kings are the best.
	They start shouting each other down. Swords flash and severe fighting ensues.

Battle sounds, fighting and killing, slaughter and devastation.
Jubilation by the Turks. Shouts of 'Allah O' Akbar'.
Mournful music.

Sultan Sulieman is on the throne. Enter: two courtiers.

Suleiman:	What news do you bring us?
Courtier 1:	The country is now divided into three parts: We are in the southern part, and the Hapsburgs in the northern.
Suleiman:	What about the eastern part?
Courtier 2:	Transylvania is declared as a separate principality, and will be ruled by a governor.
Sulieman:	Their governor, not ours?
Courtier 1:	Certainly not ours.
Courtier 2:	Unless we invade it.
Sulieman:	Now is not the right time. Let the dust settle a little. We must first win the trust of the people. What about the castle?
Courtier 1:	That is ours. They called it the Vár.
Sulieman:	Turn the church into a mosque.
Courtier 2:	Already done, Padshah.
Sulieman:	Make the Vár as my palace. Add a new section for the harem. Fly the Ottoman flag from both the palace and the mosque.
Courtier 1:	It will be done, Insh'allah.
Sulieman:	And yes, build more mosques, madrasas, music schools and art centres. We want the best houses to be built, to encourage Turks to migrate here. Every Kingdom needs people. Without them, a King is no more than a beggar.
Courtier 1:	Padshah, minarets are already higher than church steeples, the muezzin's call drowns out the Christian chants.

Sulieman:	Don't harass the Christians. We should show mercy to the infidels and win their goodwill. They are free to follow their religion, on payment of extra tax.
Courtiers:	Allah is merciful.

Islamic Music and dance. Lights go down.

Voice Over: *For another fifteen years, the push and shove of battles continued. But the Ottomans like the Romans stayed on. All through their two-centuries long stay, they were disliked so much that when eventually they were defeated in 1699 and driven out of the country, the Christian rulers made sure no sign of their rule was left, no trace of Islamic architecture, no palaces or mosques, only the Turkish baths were preserved.*

We'll stop here, today.' Nagyanya came out. I got up and rushed to her, wagging my tail. 'Good, I'm glad you enjoy the shows,' she patted me. 'Even then, drágám, I think I'll give them a little of rest now. It's hard going for me, what with making puppet costumes and finding out historical facts. So no puppet shows for a while, I'll have to think of some other method of teaching history.' I should have been glad not to have to sit there any more sifting through history day after day, but I felt sad at the loss of the show, especially of an excellent puppeteer, who could put on so many different voices to match so many different people! 'We won't go on the walk today,' she declared, 'I feel like resting a bit. You go and sit on the terrace.' I was taken aback, not expecting a sombre end to such lively and colourful shows.

That evening she remained in the same strange mood, still dwelling on the historical ups and downs. I was waiting for the story session, but she said there was going to be no animal story. 'You know, the history of kings is rather distressing. Kings lead to wars, wars lead to the devastation of land and the starvation of people. Do you think humans are peculiar that they can't live without destroying each other?' She then looked at me and said, 'Are animals the same? Do they have kings that bring about wars? Tell me?' What could I tell? What did I know about animals? Sitting on a sofa, doted upon by an old lady, given food and shelter, bathed and groomed, could I ever know what animal life was like?

'I'll sing you an English nursery rhyme tonight, about kings and wars, and hope you are not kept awake by the sabre-rattling and sword-swishing song.' She pulled the table over and started drumming on it, producing a loud marching beat of invading armies. I sat up and surprised myself by moving my paws to the tune. The thought flashed across my mind: is it the drumbeat that takes soldiers to war?

The Grand old Duke of York,
He had ten thousand men,
He marched them up to the top of the hill
And he marched them down again.

When they were up, they were up,
When they were down, they were down,
And when they were only half-way up,
They were neither up nor down.

She was right. I was so full of the drumbeat that it took me awhile to fall asleep, and even then my dreams were full of armies and battles, victories and defeats, loot and devastations, slaughter and bloodbaths.

†

MY FIRST HOLIDAY
‡

The history sessions started to peter out. I was sorry because it was rather fun to see human glory reduced to puppetry. Nagyanya complained that the work involved in making period puppets was enormous and she was too exhausted to continue. Oh, well, all good things come to an end, I thought, and hoped the closure of the theatre wouldn't bring back the dreaded history talks. When a few days passed without a sign of Nagyanya taking up the talking thread, I was much relieved.

The summer was getting hotter. The only cool time in the day was early morning or late evening, and people made the best of both times. I made sure I took a few rounds of the terrace in the morning, breathing the cool air soughing through the trees. The rest of the day I sweltered, my body heaving with sweat and my tongue salivating non-stop. Even retiring to the kennel was no relief. The enclosure became hot as hell. I began to understand what High Summer meant, and wished Sirius hadn't gone up to join the sun, doubling up on the heat already too much for comfort. I could hardly look up to confirm the story of the Dog Star, such was the blaze of the sun on the eye. Maybe, I thought, I shouldn't blame Sirius, he went up when the world was icy and the sun not strong enough to melt it on its own. But having gone up with the best of intentions, Sirius is now stuck there, still helping out the sun, although the ice is all gone and the planet well into global warming.

One morning the Old Lady asked my mistress, 'Zsuzsa, when do we go to Balaton, it's getting terribly hot, szívem?'

'Oh, yes, I forgot to tell you, Anya, Judit said the cottage is available from the beginning of next week,' my mistress said.

'Oh, just as well I asked,' the Old Lady sounded put out. 'Never mind, shall we then plan to go on Monday?'

'Yes, and with a little push, we can stay there till the end of the month, depending on when Judit's friend arrives from the US.'

'Why anyone would come to visit Hungary in the hot weather, I fail to understand.'

'Naomi – Medgyes Judit's friend – is doing research on Gypsies, and the summer is the best time for her to catch them at Balaton,' my mistress reeled off the information. 'I must go now, I'm already late, we'll finalise plans this evening, I'll check my leave dates also,' and giving me a ruffle, she was gone.

Nagyanya was all smiles. 'Did you hear that, szívem?' she turned to me excitedly, 'this woman is coming all the way from America to talk to our Cigányok. Well, well, well, things do change! She may want to interview you too! You never know, do you?' I wasn't the least interested. 'Just in case she does, let me tell you something about the history of the Cigányok, or Gypsies as everyone calls them, the little I know.' Oh, no, I thought, not the rambling talk again. I got up to wander away but no go; immediately came the reprimand. 'Where are you going, Béla, sit down and stay put, it's only a short lesson,' she commanded sternly. I stopped short mid-step, exactly like her puppets.

'Now, between the Gypsies and the Jews – the two have much in common - who do you think came to Hungary first?' I hadn't the foggiest, so I just gave a snort. 'Maybe we should leave it to Judit's mother to tell us about the Jews; you know, she was a Jew before she converted to the Catholic Church, and Judit's friend from America, you know the Indian woman, what's her name? Oh, never mind, she'll tell us about the Gypsies. That's excellent. Two wandering migrants down the centuries – brave and resistant to all pressures and persecutions.' I had no idea what she was saying. I was about to doze, when she gave me a push and said, 'No flutter, flutter of your eyes, unoka, we have to think of packing for the holiday. Come on then, up you get.' I jumped up, again like a puppet, and followed her to her room.

That evening my mistress confirmed that Monday morning was a better day to leave for Balaton. Sunday would not be so good; the traffic would be impossible as everyone from Budapest would be heading for Balaton. Nagyanya was delighted with the confirmation.

'Shall we take food supplies with us?' she asked.

'No, no, don't do that,' the mistress said. 'We'll get everything there.

Tihany isn't that expensive, not too many people go there to stay, most are day-tourists. No need to take too many clothes either, there's a new washing machine in the cottage.' Then she added, 'but don't forget to take Béla's utensils, they certainly won't have anything like that,' and planted a kiss on me. I welcomed her concern with a rapid flicking of my tail. The excitement was catching on.

'When is the Sun's eclipse? It happens in Balaton, doesn't it?' Nagyanya asked.

'No, Anya, not this year, definitely not this year. It's still a few years away. Don't worry, you'll know it when it is, there will be much hype about it. I must go now, have to prepare something for the meeting tomorrow.' The mistress knew there would be more questions if she stayed.

The weekend was one long activity of preparing for the departure. On Monday morning, we set out for Tihany. This was my first holiday with my two mistresses. In fact, I had no idea what a holiday was and how it was different from everyday living. I soon found out.

The first treat of the holiday was the journey itself. Nagyanya and Mistress sat in the front and I at the back, next to the window, my eyes fixed on the moving landscape outside, my ears remaining attentive to the conversation between the mother and daughter. I was still new to the family, so listening to anything enlarged my knowledge of the household. 'Keep your eyes peeled, Béla, you'll see lots of animals on the way. Remember the animal stories? Now you can see them, live and wild in the fields.'

'Hardly wild, Anya,' the mistress interjected. 'More like farm hands, put to work round the clock by farmers.'

'You are right, home pets are better off,' Nagyanya conceded.

'For that we'll have to ask Béla.'

'Oh well, in time, we may. Did you ring up Bori about the holiday?'

'No, actually, it was Judit who reminded me of our annual slot for the cottage,' the mistress said.

'I suppose we've been busy with Béla,' the Old Lady said and then turning back said to me, 'haven't we, drágám?' I squealed excitedly at the attention given to me.

'Anyway, we'll make up for our silence,' the mistress said. 'They may invite us for Tishah B'Av.'

'Oh, I forgot all about it. When is it?'

'July 24th , this year. We'll catch it just nicely.'

'We'll take Béla with us,' Nagyanya said with determination. 'I can't remember if the Jews accept dogs?'

'I don't know. We'll find out soon. Béla can stay out if they don't want him inside.'

'They can't be good Hungarians if they don't include a dog among them.' Nagyanya wasn't taking that.

'On the contrary, good Hungarians make their dogs live outside,' the mistress quipped.

'Oh, but not a small vulnerable puppy like our Béla,' the Old Lady said, stretching her arm back to give me a tickle. She saw that I was fixed on the landscape which was whirling around with great speed.

'Oh, look, Béla, horses, can you see those animals with long necks? Do you remember Nagyanya's puppet show, the first one which had Árpád fighting on his horse?' She looked back excitedly to see if I showed any sign of recognition. This was the first time I had seen a real horse. There were just four or five of them, brown, black and white. I liked their tall and stately look, particularly their tail, long and bushy and elegant, just like their sleek and graceful necks. 'The horse is a noble animal,' Nagyanya was saying. 'Have I told you the story of the Horse and the Dog? Hmm, I'm not sure. One day, I must take you to see Árpád on his horse, a big statue on a very high pedestal in Parliament Square.' She turned to the mistress, 'It is in Parliament Square, isn't it Zsuzsa?'

'Yes, yes, in Parliament Square.' The mistress was concentrating on driving, her eyes fixed on the road.

I too was keeping my eyes on the fields. The horses were now gone, some other animals were coming into view; smallish and in huge numbers, white fluffy bodies scattered all over the field, looking very still, like the horses. I was still wondering about them when I heard Nagyanya say, 'Those are sheep. They look cuddly and have woolly coats.' I didn't respond because I didn't know what 'cuddly' and 'woolly coats' were. She was saying, 'It's from sheep that we get wool for our coats and blankets for the winter.' While I was making sense of what Nagyanya was telling me, there was a sudden stirring in the animals, and they fell into a single line and started to walk away. I was amazed by the quick change in their behaviour. We had not yet left the field when they were almost out of sight.

We passed a few fields without any animals. 'Look over to the other side, quick, Béla, those are the goats.' I moved to the other window to see them, they were standing quite close to the road, looking at the passing cars from the other side of the fence. It was their horns and big bulging eyes that caught my attention most. Then all of a sudden they started running and calling out 'maa…maa'. I liked the sound, it was gentler than my own bark. Nagyanya was saying, 'Now, Béla, them you should recognise. Remember, the goat in the Chinese Zodiac?' Yes I did, especially the story of how the goat ran hard against the horse in the race to get to the palace. But in real life, they seemed nervous, running helter-skelter with maa…maa. 'Farmers use goats to keep the fields free of weeds. They will eat anything,' Nagyanya elaborated.

New fields were coming into view. I could see even bigger animals wandering leisurely. 'Those are the cows and bulls, but more cows than bulls. I'll tell you a story about them next time. Indians consider cows as sacred, even the bulls at times. There are lots of stories about them.' I was glad Nagyanya knew stories of so many animals.

We were now on the Highway. The roar of the whizzing traffic silenced us abruptly. The landscape started to revolve rapidly. It was a while before the mistress took a side road, leaving behind the sharp buzz of the highway.

'You can talk now,' Mistress said. 'I get quite tense on the highway. We should soon be in Tihany. Judit said she'll be at the cottage to see us in.' I sat up, all attention to see the place. We passed through the town centre, it was full of crowds of tourists. 'There's the Abbey, Béla, look up to the hill, can you see?' I followed Nagyanya's direction and saw a big church looking down at us. Will we go up there? was my first thought. 'That's the Benedictine Abbey. Remember, the history lesson? When was it?' She put the question to me, as if I could answer it. 'It was in 1055 that King Andrew I invited Christian monks to convert the Magyar pagans. Can you remember now?' Of course not, how could I?

'Oh, look at the lake, Zsuzsa,' Nagyanya exclaimed as the Lake came into view. 'Isn't it lovely! Why is water so soothing to the mind?' She never lost an opportunity to philosophise. I think I took my habit from her. She was right too. Looking at the vast lake was indeed a balm to the soul – whatever the soul is. 'I love the idyllic surroundings of the cottage; no tourists, no restaurants, no promenade stalls,' Nagyanya was saying, 'I feel I'm heading for a monastery.' I hope not, I thought, what would I do without her.

'For me, it's sailing and yachting. Each to her own, Anya,' the mistress chuckled. 'There's Judit!' she waved.

'And Bori too,' Nagyanya added, 'Oh, I can't wait to meet her.' The car stopped, the door opened and everyone was welcoming everyone. I waited to be let out. 'Oh, look, the dog!' someone exclaimed. Nagyanya rushed to let me out. I felt a bit sheepish and kept close to her, but soon they were fussing over me, which encouraged me to run around in excitement, and show off some of my puppy antics. It raised much laughter. I felt at home.

'Let's sit down, Ilona, I'm waiting to hear your news.' Bori Néni led Nagyanya to the chairs neatly laid out on the lawn.

'Nothing much, Bori. You know how life plods on. The only news is we have adopted a puppy. Zsuzsa found the little thing abandoned by the road, so brought him home.'

'Good for you, Ilona. A dog adds much to one's life. Now, Judit,' she called out, 'shall we have lunch out here? It's nice enough.'

'Good idea. Come, Zsuzsa, let's fetch it, everything's ready.' Judit led my mistress into the cottage. I followed them to see what it was like inside. All on the same level, it looked very comfortable with sofas and carpets. I made myself at home on the rug and listened to them talking. It seemed that Judit was my mistress's boss. I was pleased that I had made a good impression on her. She appreciated that I didn't jump all over the furniture.

'Zsuzsa, Béla's (my name raised much laughter!) dishes are handy in the boot, szívem. It's best to serve him in his dish.' Nagyanya never forgot me. I ate with relish and then stretched out and looked at the lake. It was so different from the trees and hills I had seen from our terrace or on walks, nothing like this, a sheer expanse of water. The afternoon passed in eating and chatting. I was so absorbed by the new surroundings that I hardly noticed time had passed and our hosts were leaving.

'Dinner at our place tonight, Ilona, (expostulations from my mistresses!) no, no, definitely tonight with us. From tomorrow you are on your own,' Bori Néni was adamant. 'So, see you at 6. You will also meet Bea and Attila, but alas Takács is away in the States,' Judit said.

'Ah, what about sailing, then?' My mistress showed concern. 'Well, what about it? It shouldn't stop us from sailing,' Judit announced, 'we'll go as usual, and leave the young and the old to fend for themselves.' Much waving and laughter as they finally left.

That was the beginning of an unforgettable holiday. 'Shall we all have a siesta?' Nagyanya yawned as the hosts drove away. 'Good idea, I feel exhausted,' the mistress said, clearing up the lunch table. I followed them in, with the full intention of taking a siesta myself.

The Kálmáns were only a few houses beyond ours. It seemed to us we wouldn't have to walk far, but surprisingly it still took us a good ten minutes, since the houses in between were set in spacious grounds. I was curious to know the link between the two families, so I made sure I gave a sharp ear to all that Nagyanya and the mistress were saying.

It surfaced that Bori and her husband András, now dead, were old friends of Ilona and Sándor's. Judit was Zsuzsa's colleague; Bea and Attila were Judit's and Takács' children. Phew! I got all that worked out and now was waiting to meet them to put faces to all the names I had heard in one afternoon. Their house was quite big and set on an upward slope. Nagyanya whispered, 'Who could own such a place these days? Just as well András was a party member in the heyday of communism.'

They were all waiting for us. Bea and Attila, Judit's teenage children, took to me immediately, which brought out an excited response from me. 'Now, Béla, behave yourself. Don't jump on them. Sit down.' I quickly backtracked and made sure I did not make Nagyanya ashamed of me. The rest of the evening I sat and watched the two families enjoy each other's company. The youngsters helped their mother to lay for dinner. The long table full of food was an impressive sight. I remember wondering whether animals also had food rituals. Or did I? A mere puppy at that time, could I have thought of such complex matters? Anyway, although I was served my dinner separately and on the floor, I still felt I was part of the community.

'Are you celebrating Tishah B'Av?' Nagyanya asked over dessert.
'We wouldn't have bothered but with Attila here, we can't pass up any Jewish festival.' Judit smiled indulgently, looking at her son.
'Quite, as Nova Jews, we'd better not,' Attila said drily.
'Lapsed Jews more like it. Ask Nagyanya, she'll tell you,' Bea retorted.
'I've heard it many times before.' I didn't like Attila's tone. For myself, I wanted to hear it, whatever it was.
'Go on, Nagyanya, tell that Jewish joke, it's so funny and says it all, I'm sure the Nénis will enjoy it.' Bea was already laughing. Nagyanya laughed

too. 'The joke is on Jewish grannies, but really it is more than a joke. It is said, that at the slightest rumour of pogroms, the grandmothers lined up the family and went through the history of Jewish persecution: from the first exodus led by Moses to all the others that came after.'

'Did you too, Nagyanya?' Attila said cheekily.

'Don't be too literal, Attila,' Judit said quickly. 'Yes, Anya, go on.'

'The point, Attila, is that these persecutions became so much part of the Jewish psyche that a fear of pogroms was the first reaction of grandmothers, and yes, I am very much part of it.' She paused to see his reaction, and then continued. 'So, for the Jews every festival becomes a revival of every exodus through history, sealed and stamped with memories of the deaths and slaughters of their ancestors. Now comes the Jewish joke. On Purim, Jews thank God for saving them from the Persian slaughter; on Chanukah, they remember how the Greeks butchered them; during Passover it's thanksgiving for deliverance from the Egyptians.' I found it quite funny but didn't know how to join in the laughter. 'The whole year is one long list of remembrance of Jewish misery and misfortune, slavery and serfdom and their exodus from every land – and that includes this country too. I'm not talking of the Middle Ages, but as recently as the last War.' Everyone had stopped laughing.

'All that is going to change, Nagyanya,' Attila robustly. 'Jews now have a different view of themselves, and so there will be no more pogroms or persecutions.'

'That's what they thought when Moses led them across the Red Sea,' the grandmother retorted.

'But no longer, take it from a Nova Jew. So, there's no point in telling the same stories, over and over again.' Attila said sharply.

'Never mind.' Bea overturned Attila's diktat. 'Even though you've heard my story, I'm still going to tell it to the Nénis. And you are staying put to hear it.' And I was surprised to see that her brother did.

'In that case, I'll have to tell mine,' Judit said laughing, 'I'm the important link, but, Bea, you go first.'

Bea started on her story. 'It was our eighteenth birthday – ha, ha, the joy of twins is to share birthdays, isn't it, Attila?' She stuck out her tongue at him. 'Anya and Apa were throwing a big party, we both had invited a huge number of friends. Our family tradition is to give the gifts, first thing in the morning of the day. Well, surprise, surprise, the gift was an announcement by our parents that we were Jews! That our family from both sides were Jewish! Can you imagine how we felt? We had grown up without any religious orientation. But in post-'89, as the socialist chains were coming apart in the Soviet countries, people discovered they were free to voice their thoughts or to make their choices. And here we were, Attila and I, something special, a religious anchor, a distinct link with Israel. Do you remember Attila?' I didn't understand too much, as my history lessons hadn't touched on the Jewish people.

'So, so, so,' Bea was saying, 'I was thrilled to be something different from others, and was determined to make a display of it too. I went straight into researching the cultural and religious history of the Jews. Both of us,' she looked at Attila, 'decided to follow Jewish practices, religious and cultural, to the word, didn't we?'

'Yes, we did indeed. But you changed, I haven't,' Attila said proudly.

'Hang on, I'll come to that in a minute,' Bea snapped. 'So, I started living like a Jew. I celebrated every festival, following the rules of the rituals most meticulously. I ate kosher meat and observed hygiene of the body to the letter – that is a woman's body, which - please note - is considered different from a man's. I did this round the year, enjoying every detail as if it were a special treat from the gods. Then looking for an exciting follow-up, I decided to travel to Israel. Rather than be a backpack tourist, I wanted to link my trip to Judaism. So I picked the most conservative of the Jewish sects and wrote to them, asking if I could become member of their sect. The idea was to return to the origins of Judaism.'

'That was the mistake you made,' Attila said pointedly. 'You should have gone for one of the reformed sects, as I did, and look, I'm still going strong, whereas you've collapsed.' I was following their argument, and must say he had a point there.

'True, but it would still have ended the same way, because it was me, not you. Congratulations, laddie, we disprove the theory that twins behave identically.' Bea wasn't letting her brother get away with anything.

'That's identical twins, you weren't those, Bea,' Judit reminded her.

'Anyway, this sect welcomed me with open arms. When I arrived, a young rabbi came to pick me up from the airport. I had also read up a lot on the conflict between Israel and Palestine, so I was watching everything with a hawk's eye. On the way from the airport, I saw signposts of "No entry, military area". When I asked the rabbi about them, he said they were refugee camps, supervised by the military. "Which refugees?" I asked. "Palestinians," was the short answer. "Aren't they Israelis?" I persisted. "Yes, Israeli Arabs," he said flatly. That was my first shock on arrival.'

'One would think you were anti-Semitic,' Attila said aggressively. 'Your sympathy for the Palestinians makes you blind towards the injustices Jews have borne throughout history.' I was afraid of a fight breaking out. But the others were listening to both youngsters with some amusement. So I relaxed and put my animal fear aside.

'It's not just their attitude to Palestinians, but their view of women that shocked me,' Bea said passionately.

'You won't find it better in other religions,' shot back Attila.

'Let her speak, Attila, she has a right to give her view,' the mother admonished him.

'I've heard it many times. So, if you would excuse me,' Attila got up, 'I have a concert rehearsal.'

'Oh, when is the concert?' my mistress asked.

'On this Sabbath. All the members are my age and Jewish. We play only Jewish folk music, and our performances take place only on the Sabbath.'

'That sounds very interesting,' my mistress said.

'I love the Jewish fiddle,' Nagyanya announced.

'I play that. If you want to come, I can reserve seats for you.'

'That would be wonderful.' Zsuzsa looked at Judit, 'Are we all going?'

'We can, although we have been to Attila's concerts plenty of times,' Judit said tactfully.

'Just let me know how many tickets,' Attila said to Zsuzsa and left.

Bea waited until he was gone, and then continued. 'He gets like that whenever I speak about my Israel experience. Anyway, so to carry on with my story, I was saying that when I argued with the rabbi about the woman issue, his defence was that it's only women's bodies which were a problem. It was just a matter of women observing a few rituals to cleanse their bodies after menstruation before they say prayers, or before coming in contact with the husband. Can you imagine one half of the human race is considered unclean and made untouchable?' She looked at everyone - all women now, with Attila gone - and let her statement sink in. 'Not only that, but there's much more,' she went on. 'A woman mustn't ever say no to her husband for the physical contact, and of course, no contraception either, and of course, women could not be in the open part of the Synagogue, they must hide upstairs behind the lattice! When I pointed this out to the rabbi, he said it is to keep women safe from men's eyes.' Bea had the whole Jewish anti-woman list pat to the last detail. 'I just laughed in his face and said, why don't men put blindfolds on their eyes and leave women in the open.'

'What did he say to that?' the mistress asked.

'Not much, as you would guess, but what broke the camel's back was the Jewish prayer - the biggest affront to women is the First Prayer of the morning. Every morning, the Jewish men thank God for not making them a woman.' This brought out sounds of general disbelief from my mistresses and even her mother. 'I never knew that', 'So openly, it's amazing', 'How can the Jewish women take it?' Bea was pleased at proving her point against Judaism. 'I was so angry that I wrote a poem about it. Shall I recite it?' 'Yes, yes', everyone said. Bea jumped up and gave a dramatised recitation of the poem.

A Jewish Woman's First Prayer of the Day
(after the Jewish First Prayer of the Day)

Thank you, O Lord, for not making me
a man, though he be in your own image.

Cast as the first human, you made him the ruler
of your creation, to protect the good and shun
the evil. But he wavered from your intent, and
set himself as the master over the weak: women,
children and animals.

O Lord, he stops at nothing.
Cruelty, torture and killings
are no barrier to his over-reaching self.

Nature itself he pillages, rapes and uses
all living beings for his own insatiable
greed, until stark desolation prevails.

O Lord, I thank you, at the start of every morning,
for your compassion and empathy for the weak,
and for instilling in me the same. I promise to stand
by all those who are in need of care and concern.

I thank thee in all humility, that my body is a mere
instrument of Your Will, to people the Earth.

I thank thee, O Maker of Life, for making me
a woman, and not a man in your own image.

Amen.

A burst of clapping and laughter from the audience. I did my bit by going over to her and wagging my tail. 'What did the rabbi say?' my mistress asked.

'That was the breaking point between us, he couldn't take it,' Bea said proudly. 'So, I returned home after three months, happier than when I went to Israel.' She looked in turn at her own mother, 'I think you were disappointed.'

'Not at all, drágám. Remember I grew up as a Catholic, didn't have a clue about Judaism.' Judit looked at her mother and said, 'I don't know about Anya, though. Were you disappointed, Anya?'

'Remember, it was me who converted to Catholism and christened you as a Catholic. It was a gesture only. Under the Communists, practicing religion wasn't permitted, but one could observe the basic rituals.'

'Nagyanya, tell them your story.' Bea was in the full swing of story-telling.

'Not today, enough of stories for our guests. They must be longing to get to bed.' She looked at me. 'Even the dog looks tired. Let's all go to sleep then.' She got up from the table. There was a lot of leave-taking with thanks for the food and stories.

'What are you people going to do while Zsuzsa and I go sailing?' Judit was holding up the departure. I suppose she wanted to plan the holiday for the old people.

'We'll go on walks, go up to the Abbey or take a bus to the centre, maybe visit the Hermit caves or just sit by the lake.' Bori had a long list. 'And go across to Siófok by boat,' my Nagyanya added.

'Good, so that settles it,' Judit said.

'Will you join us for Béla's constitutional walks?' All eyes turned to me. 'That's too early for me, Ilona. I'll come around a little after breakfast.'

So we said goodnight to them and set out for our cottage. As soon as we got inside the front door, we went straight to our beds, for rest and deep sleep.

Next morning, the mistresses were up early, unpacking and setting up the place. I sat waiting to be told where to go for my nature call. The mistress saw me sitting and looking at them. She understood and immediately got my lead and marched me off down the road. The sun was just getting up and the lake looked calm. It was a good spot, within close view of nature. That fixed the place for my routine for the rest of our time there. On our return, Nagyanya had set the table with breakfast, and my bowl ready for me to lap up. The mistress said she would run up in the car and fetch a few food supplies. While she was gone, I took a round of the front yard. Nagyanya warned me not to go too far, in case I fell into the lake. I took her seriously, only later did I realise she was making sure I didn't get lost.

The mistress was not yet back when Bori Néni arrived. I suppose she had come to fetch us for the walk. Nagyanya suggested they waited for my mistress to return. Over hot coffee, they caught up with each other's news. Not very long after, the mistress arrived. She was glad to see Néni. I think she wouldn't have been at ease going sailing without getting her mother involved in something.

'So where are you going today?' the mistress asked.

Nagyanya turned to Néni and said, 'What about the Hermit caves? I have to admit all the times I've come to Balaton, I've never visited the place.'

'Is that so?' Néni showed surprise. 'Well, that's where we'll go then. Ready for a brisk walk of one kilometre?' she said getting up. I was the first to get to the door.

'Shall we take it easy and saunter along the promenade?' Nagyanya bargained.

And so we set out for our first sight-seeing. We sauntered along the lake. The caves were a little way out, almost at the far end of the promenade. I followed them quietly. While they chatted I looked at the lake. It seemed to say something to me but I couldn't put it into words, I mean into barks. I remember I did produce a few sounds but they didn't quite say what I felt. All I could think of was that the lake was one vast sheet of water and yet something much more, calm and soothing. So we walked on slowly and steadily and arrived at the caves. We went in and nosed around the rocks and saw the space where the hermit had lived for years. I was hoping to hear something interesting about the hermit, after all, his way isn't so common. To my regret, the notice board didn't shed much light on the man. It was cold and dark inside.

After a while we came out. It was a relief to be in the sunshine again. There were no people around, apart from us.

I heard Nagyanya say to Néni, 'Last night, the grandchildren took over the evening. What about grandmama's story of the camps? I know, I know, you have told me before, but it was sometime ago. Shall we sit down on this bench? I want to look at the lake while listening to you.'

'Thanks for asking, Ilona. It's not often I am asked to talk about my life. I'm happy to look back on it,' Néni said and started on her story.

'I was born in 1925 in this very town. We were a big family, all three generations living under the same roof. I remember a happy childhood with siblings and friends in the street. Although I had a strong sense of being Jewish, I was not aware of any anti-Jewish feelings. It was only in my early teens when the 1938 laws came in restricting Jews from many jobs and even university entrance that I came to know about similar laws instituted by Horthy way back in 1921. Ironically, it was Horthy himself who had quietly let some of the laws lapse. So, by the time I was ten and going to school, the situation was much better. And now we were back to square one, with anti-Semitism rearing its ugly head again, and it was some head too. The anti-Jewish laws became even worse.' Néni's voice shook.

'The news of what was happening to the Jews in Germany struck terror into the Jewish community. "Will the same happen here?" they asked each other. When I returned from school, my parents and grandparents would ask me if anything nasty happened to me in school. "Did the teacher say something about your being Jewish? And your classmates, do they say things to you?" they would ask anxiously. A shadow hung over my family. I wasn't joking when yesterday I told the story of the grannies lining up the children and giving them a run-down on the history of Jewish pogroms.'

'Oh, no, I didn't doubt it at all,' Nagyanya assured her. I was seeing another side of the Old Lady. I had never seen her so attentive, shaking and nodding her head at Néni's words.

Néni went on. 'Once again, it was Horthy who came to the rescue of the Jews and tried to relax the anti-Semitic laws. But we never knew what was going to happen. It was like being on a swing, now up now down. That was the last thing the Jews needed. Then came another bombshell. In 1944, Horthy was called to Germany and put under arrest by Hitler, and the Nazis installed the Arrow Cross, a rabidly anti-Semitic Party. The terror had struck. Even though there was no television in those days, the news would spread among the Jewish communities, no matter what their nationalities were.'

'The Holocaust was just round the corner. I was 19. What is sad is that we could have escaped the horrors of Auschwitz. As Germany began to lose ground, the Nazis speeded up the destruction of the Jews. Here, in Budapest, the Arrow Cross thugs went into final action against the Jews. We were stripped of our possessions but not our families, since it was important to make sure each and every Jew was tracked down and centralised. A ghetto was created for the purpose, a place behind the big Synagogue. The Allies were closing in on Germany, time was running out. The "vermin" of Europe had to be exterminated before that. The biggest number of Jews killed were from Hungary, not counting the 10,000 who were shot on the banks of the Danube. The rest were put on cattle trucks and trained off to various concentration camps, to be gassed with millions of others.' Nagyanya sighed and put her hand on Néni's shoulder. I realised something sensitive was happening, so I went up to Néni and sat at her feet. She bent down and picked me up.

'One has to admire human resilience,' Néni continued, 'I remember it didn't seem too bad in the beginning, since our family was all together, even though we were treated like animals by the guards. But as soon as we got to Auschwitz, we were taken off and separated from each other. I was put in the young women's ward. I won't tell you what went on there. It is not for human ears, let alone animals.' She rubbed my back for what seemed like ages. 'The worst of all that time there, we didn't have a clue about what was happening to the other members of the family. It was only when I returned to Budapest and looked for my family that I was told none of them had come back.' Néni stopped and wiped her eyes. Sitting in her lap, I could show my compassion by licking the hands that were holding me. Nagyanya was crying too. Néni continued the terrible tale.

'Between the Americans and the Russians, Germany was at last brought to a halt in its destruction of Europe. The Holocaust of the Jews was a lesson for humanity never to follow extreme leadership.' She paused. 'The survivors – most young - were put on trains and escorted back to Budapest. I located a few relatives among the Jews who had returned – Kati Néni among them – but no sign of my parents or siblings. Was this the price I paid for being a Jew? The Communist State organised gatherings for Jews as therapy or just communal solace. They all asked the one question: was being a Jew worth it? Each survivor stood on the podium to tell his or her history. I made up my mind to put my Jewishness behind me, in fact I had left it behind in the camp. And like many others, I converted to Catholicism – not because of belief or conviction - and we decided never to look back, never to mention our past to others or even each other. It was safer not to do so. I made sure that I went to church every Sunday and was seen praying on my knees and crossing myself.

'There I met András, young and lost like me, who had also converted his Jewishness to Catholicism. Common to us was our suffering and our lone selves without families. We got married in the church and vowed to bring up our children without their ever finding out their Jewish background. We started a new life. Hungary was now a Communist State. It embraced a policy of equal treatment to all Hungarians of whatever ethnicity – it wasn't so easy to erase our Jewish background, lapsed though we were. We both joined the medical line, determined to put our shoulders to the new system. When a child was born to us, we were given a house to start our new life. We would have loved to have a larger family – I had five siblings, me the only survivor!' She took a deep sigh and tears rolled down her face again.

'The New Soviet Republic did not allow the Churches to practice their religion, but people could follow their beliefs quietly without much show. Christian Churches were allowed to christen children or marry young people, but nothing more than that. Churches were left to run down. Neither people or the State were concerned. Judit was a child of the new state. She joined the Young Pioneers and learnt ballet, singing and dancing, and often performed in the new socialist operas. She grew up without any knowledge of her Jewish forbears.' Nagyanya nodded her head, in approval of their decision.

'Jews were happy with the protection of the State. They were assured of a roof over their heads and food on their table. But humans are a strange species, they are never happy with what they have. A discontent was growing beneath the ten years of the rebuilding the state. When it exploded, the Russians moved in with tanks, and we finally had no choice but to give in.'

'I think it was the best that happened to us,' Nagyanya said.

'It was, especially for the persecuted people, Gypsies included. They received a more sympathetic treatment.'

'No matter what people say about the Communists, they cared for people. When all this euphoria of democracy settles down, people will realise that we couldn't have had better under another system.'

'That's right,' Néni agreed, 'it's the fashion now to condemn everything communist, but after the war, as victims of the Holocaust, both Jews and Gypsies needed an upliftment, emotional and economic, to get back on their feet.'

'But all that has passed away. We are back to free wheeling and dealing in all things now.'

'Not our world, Ilona. You heard Attila last night.' Néni got up. We started to walk back.

'Good luck to him, that's all I can say,' Nagyanya said more positively.

'I will certainly go to his concert.'

And so they talked about things past and present. 'Look, a sailing boat!' Nagyanya pointed to some white thing on the lake. 'That could be Zsuzsa and Judit, couldn't it?' I looked closely at the thing she described as a sailing boat. It looked so light and airy, just rocking gently. I was curious to know how it felt to be on it. I hoped the mistress would treat me to a ride. 'If you see a surfer, it will be Bea. I must say she's pretty good. Why wouldn't she be? She's on the lake all the time.'

'On a sunny day like that, who wouldn't be out on the water,' Nagyanya said.

'Except us,' was Néni's reply.

It was almost lunch time by the time we got back. Néni didn't want to stop for lunch, she said she didn't eat very much at noon. I was ready for my grub and wished Néni would move.

'Shall we go to the Abbey tomorrow? I can come round at the same time?' Nagyanya agreed heartily and said, 'Let's plan to explore something new every day.' I was all for doing that.

The mistress arrived in the afternoon. We were all ears to hear about her sailing.

'There was some trouble with the sails, but we worked it out, so we are pleased with ourselves. Anya – and you too, Béla,' she picked me up, 'should come for a trip one day. Yes, Béla,' she held me up and as if she was telling me a secret said softly, 'to be sailing on the lake is the only way to see it.' She seemed a different person to me.

After the meal we all slept, being truly tired out by our first day at Balaton.

...

The rest of the week passed, with everyone doing their own thing. As promised by Néni, we went to a new place every day – new at least to me. The visit to the Abbey I really liked. It was on top of the hill. Judit made sure we didn't walk up and asked Bea to drive us there. It was a treat to stand on the rock, and look down on the lake. Nagyanya and Néni planned to spend a lot of time in the church itself, but the question was where was I going to be left? Usually dogs are not allowed in churches, but Nagyanya never gave up hope of reversing the rules. She asked the Warden if they could bring me in, assuring him I was the best behaved being on earth. He looked at me and winked, to which I replied with a soft bark. That raised some laughter. I wouldn't have minded sitting outside and looking at the view below, but Nagyanya wouldn't have that.

I followed them around, as they wandered through every part of the church looking closely at plaques, paintings and frescoes. King Andrew's body in the crypt was the high point. I heard them say that it was him who had invited the Benedictine monks to set up the Abbey. Oh…h, yes, it did ring a bell all right for me. It must have been two hours at least before we emerged from the church. The lake was still there, and I must say I preferred it to the church artefacts.

'Look over there, Ilona,' Néni pointed out in the distance, 'can you see the Inner Lake?' I saw a smaller lake, its surface bathed in the sunshine. 'We should go there one day and then walk to the hot springs, only a couple of kilometres.' Néni was keen to make it sound an easy outing.

'I'm game,' Nagyanya said, 'and so I'm sure is Béla.' I gave a jump and raced ahead by way of consent. 'Gyere, Béla, gyere, come back , we are not going down yet,' she commanded me.

We walked in the Abbey precincts, in and out of various buildings, and then wandered leisurely through the gardens for another hour. It was coming to lunch time, and I heard Nagyanya inviting Néni to have lunch with us at the house. This was good news as I had started getting messages from my stomach.

We started our descent by the easy walk down to the lake. It was a treat for me to see it from different levels. There were lots of people on the waterfront, swimming or sunbathing, children racing each other, dogs outrunning them. It was a perfect holiday world. As my eye shifted back to the lake, I saw some boats, calm and floating on the water, it was a still day. I tried to look, even from that far, if I could see my mistress. Once at the waterfront, I lost the view to the parapet.

On Friday, we went to Attila's concert. Their band, Red Sea, was performing on the open stage. The square was packed with people. I looked around to see if there were any other of my species in the audience. I could see two or three but they were far away, I had no desire to race up to them, and anyway I had to be on my best behaviour. 'No running around and barking is totally out,' Nagyanya had instructed me. So I stayed put and listened to the music, and when not the music, to the conversation floating around me. It seemed that Attila's band played Klezmer music. Most of the audience were young men, and they were clearly enjoying the music. I wondered if they were all Nova Jews, like Atilla.

'Lots of the tunes are copied from some well-known bands,' Néni whispered to Nagyanya, who said. 'It doesn't matter, as long as they are good.' I agreed with her and thought they were good.

So ended our first week: ancient caves, Christian abbey, Jewish concert! What next? was my last thought as I hit my bed.

...

On Tuesday, Néni picked us after lunch to take the boat trip to Siófok. This was going to be a taster for going sailing with the mistress later in the week. She wanted to make sure how I reacted to being on the water. Well, I passed the test with flying colours. Not only did I show no nervousness – after all being on boat is not being in the water, like Nagyanya's bath tub - but I positively enjoyed the noisy surge of the boat as it proceeded across the lake to Siófok. I was looking forward to being in the town, but it turned out to be a busy town, full of shops and pubs, packed with tourists. I wondered why they wanted to go there. It must have been the boat trip more than the town itself, as we hardly got there before we turned back to catch the next boat home.

That evening when the mistress got home and asked how I had fared on the boat trip, Nagyanya reported that I had no problems with being on the water, and that I would certainly not have any with sailing. 'Good,' promised the mistress, 'I'll talk to Judit, and you will duly receive an invitation, probably for this weekend. Naomi is arriving next week, Judit will have her hands full then, we may even suspend sailing for a day or two.' I liked the evenings when the mistress and Nagyanya exchanged news of what each of us had done during the day.

Next morning, Bori telephoned to say that Kati, a relative, had arrived. 'The reason I'm ringing up, Ilona, is to say that she has come by car and could take us to the Inner Lake, it will save Bea having to drive us up. It will also be a change from hanging around the promenade.' The plan was that we would drive up to the lake, leave the car there, walk through the woodland, not more than two kilometres, and arrive at the Hot Springs, spend some time there and then catch a bus back, pick up the car and drive home. The prospect of going through vineyards, orchards and fields of lavender was too good an offer to turn down.

'Come, Béla drágám, let's pack some lunch and spend the day away. After the long walk, we will soak our tired feet in the hot springs.' I squealed at the mention of bathing, which didn't draw much sympathy from her. 'Come, come, don't be such a fusspot, hot springs do you good, improve your health if anything.' She wasn't giving way to my fear of a dip in the water, and got busy with putting a picnic together of sandwiches, fruit and drinks. We were picked up soon after. I took to Kati Néni immediately; she said if she wasn't driving she would have loved to sit with me at the back. That pleased Nagyanya, and me too.

I was captivated by the lake. The water was so calm that the sunlight seemed almost a part of it. What would the lake look like at night? I would have liked to know. The Nénis sat down on the bench. I ran about a little, but kept close to them. I heard them talking about the lake, how once it was a volcanic crater, and then got filled with water over the centuries. It was very peaceful, not many tourists about at that time of the morning.

Néni was saying, 'Remember, Ilona, I told you that when I returned from Auschwitz, I found only one relative among our family survivors.' She turned to Kati, 'That's her. It was just the two of us, the rest all gone, not even a sign left.'

'You have to accept that as the will of God, Bori,' Kati Néni said. 'It was so long ago, drágám, why think about it now?'

'No, just telling, Kati. Ilona was asking me the other day.'

Kati turned to Nagyanya, 'You see, Ilona, in some way Bori and me followed different paths. I did not bother to change my identity, no conversion and hence no surprises for the next generation. With the help of a communist state, my Jewishness gradually dissipated. And it hardly mattered.'

'You may not admit it, Kati,' Bori Néni said, 'but I think somewhere deep down, you still harbour the old beliefs. Otherwise, why come all the way to celebrate Tishah B'Av?'

'To meet the family, stupid.' Kati hugged Bori, 'I wouldn't miss the occasion for anything. Oh, no, that's my one-day-in-the-year-pilgrimage-to-my-ancient-roots.' Néni laughed heartily. 'Thanks to Attila for bringing back the prodigal aunt. Who knows we may all yet revert to becoming Jews, like our migrant ancestors.' She put her arm around Bori's shoulder. 'One thing is certain, you may take on another persona, but people don't let you. Once a Jew always a Jew. The other day I was shocked to hear a neighbour say, "Oh, the Lázárs, the people at no. 52? They are zsidók!" '

'That's it, Kati. Sometimes I wonder if Attila is right. Come, let's begin our walk then,' Bori Néni said getting up. 'There is too much beauty around to worry about religion.' The walk to the Hot Springs was something I will not forget. Not so much the vineyards or even the orchards but the fields of lavender captivated me. The purple of the flowers and the scent they exuded overwhelmed my senses. I saw the bees hovering over every stem, burrowing their heads way into the deep of the petals, their wings catching the sunshine as they stuck to the stamen, like glue.

The Hot Springs were teeming with people. Children were splashing in the bubbling waters. The Nénis were talking about the general belief that washing the body in the Spring water would rid it of illness. The bath houses were full of people come to cure themselves, but the Nénis didn't go in. 'Nothing wrong with us,' they said laughing. 'Let's sit on the terrace and sip coffee, and watch the ill and the ailing getting restored.' 'No miracles here, please, we are atheists!' Nagyanya laughed heartily. Oh, it was fun to be with them. I sat down, my eyes taking in the blue quietness of the lake, but my ears attentive to their conversation. I wouldn't have wanted to miss their talk for anything in the world.

...

Ironically, next morning Bea came with a message from Bori Néni that she had gone down with some bug and wouldn't be able to come. Bea thought she had overdone the trip to the Hot Springs and needed to rest for a day or two. What with Tishah B'av coming she didn't want to be ill then. Nagyanya looked downcast.

'Oh, yes,' Bea said remembering as she was leaving, 'she won't be able to come to the Gypsy concert, because Tishah B'Av goes on until Saturday. It's disappointing. I want to go to the concert too.'

'Well, that's it then.'

'No, wait, actually, come to think of it,' Bea said thoughtfully, 'Tishah B'Av starts at sundown on Friday and ends at the same time on Saturday, and the concert doesn't begin until later in the evening, and…and, let me think, oh yes, I can take time off surfing. So yes, we can all join you, not sure about Attila. I must go now, meeting a friend in ten minutes.'

'Remind her we are off on Sunday,' Nagyanya called out. 'I do want to see her before we leave. Who knows when we meet next.'

Nagyanya told the mistress about Bori Néni's illness and saw how disappointed her mother was at the cancellation of the boat trip to Keszthely and suggested we went sailing with her instead, since that was one of the things we were definitely going to do before leaving Balaton. The prospect of being on the lake in a sailing boat sent thrills into me. Nagyanya also brightened up. 'Will it be all right with Judit?' she asked.

'No reason why not. Let's make it tomorrow. I just need to tell her. We'll go by car. Our boat is anchored a little distance away, a spot for all boats, like a parking lot.'

'What do we need to take, apart from a hamper?' Nagyanya was already into preparations.

'Nothing. We just have to make sure we have enough life-jackets.'

'It's a pity Bori is down with a bug. I would have liked her to be sailing with us.'

In the morning, I heard Nagyanya getting up earlier than usual, even before the mistress. It must be the excitement of going sailing, I concluded. I too had kept on waking up, thinking of being on the lake, rather than looking at it. What a thrilling prospect! I could hardly keep still. I followed Nagyanya around while she prepared a hamper, as if I could help her with packing. By the time the mistress woke up, we were both sitting on the sofa, ready and waiting for her. When she saw us she was so touched by our earnest demeanour that she rushed over laughing and hugged us fondly.

The drive to the boat wasn't long, but I could sense an excited expectation in Nagyanya. I too had fixed my eyes on the road. Very soon a huge number of boats came into view. I squealed with joy. I was put on the lead as soon as we got out. Unfortunately, going to the boat involved walking on a plank. The moment I realised the precariousness of the walk, I started to show signs of fear. The mistress picked me up and carried me across. Once inside the boat, I sought out a corner and sat still to compose myself and watched Mistress and Judit organising the preparation for sailing.

Mistress was unwrapping what she called life jackets. 'Anya, you may not like this, but it is essential for both you and Béla to keep these jackets on the whole time. This will prevent you from drowning if by any chance you fall in the water.' A squeal escaped my throat. 'Now, Béla drágám, you mustn't be frightened,' Mistress said picking me up, 'Judit and I are here to make sure you and Anya are safe during sailing. You don't have to fear anything, just enjoy yourself. Okay?' I licked her face to say yes, okay. She gave me back to Nagyanya to put the life-jacket on me, she already had hers on. 'Now, Anya, we'll go through the technical drill to make sure you understand what is happening, you too, Béla, pay attention. Judit, go ahead.'

'Right, folks, this is a sailing boat, which means it runs in the old-fashioned way by sail, and not by engine power. It was in such boats that the Arabs sailed all the way to South-East Asia. Now then, Zsuzsa and I, between the two of us, sail this boat. How is it done? I'll tell you. You see that part sticking out of the back of the boat? That's the rudder. I'll keep control of that to steer the boat and you will have to work the sail, once we've rigged it. Sit on the side of the boat where I tell you. Sometimes I will ask you to change sides, when I want to change direction or when the wind changes. This means you have to undo the rope, and cross the boat to sit on the other side. As you cross the boat, the boom which holds the sail will be swinging across the boat, so be careful your heads. You'll also have to lean your body over the side of the boat to balance it if it's tipping at all. But be careful not to fall into the water. Everything's clear, Néni?' Nagyanya nodded her head vigorously and I gave a loud bark. 'Oh, yes, do you see that little door, it leads to a cabin below. If you feel sick or tense, you can go down there to rest until you feel well enough to come back up.' This cheered me up, there's nothing like having an alternative in a crisis.

'Now, all of you will be doing the crewing. Néni, you will get your instructions from Zsuzsa, and Béla will assist you.' She stopped to look at me, as if to see if I understood. I rolled my neck in imitation of the nod I saw Néni doing earlier. 'Good, now then,' she went on, 'the most crucial time for the crew is when the wind fills up the sails so much that the boat starts to tilt, sometimes even tips over. If it is not brought back to position, then, ho, ho, ho, we all fall into the water (I couldn't help squealing again), no, no, Béla, you won't drown because you have a life-jacket on. So no worries, drágám, you are safe.' Judit patted me, Nagyanya hugged me closer and the mistress came over to give me a kiss. 'When this happens, ' Judit went on with her tale of sailing, 'all of you will have to lie down flat on the boat's edge opposite to the sails that are bending over to kiss the waters, and hold on to the ropes with all your might, as hard as you can - and hey presto! the sails will go up again, shaking the wind out. It is the best moment, great fun to watch the way the wind resists leaving the sails, the sails wanting to shed the wind, and the waters playing cool.' Then she saw me listening attentively. 'Oh, yes, Béla, we need your doggie instincts at this stage. The moment you can sniff the wind getting up, give three consecutive barks to warn me that it's coming. Okay, ship-mate?'

Judit walked over and took up her position at the rudder. 'Oh, yes,' she shouted across, 'I forgot to mention that when I shout "Lee-ho", it means I am about to turn the boat, the boat may tilt, at that very moment you need to go into action. Okay, Néni?'

'Okay,' Nagyanya shouted back. I was amazed at the loudness of her voice. This encouraged me to give vent to mine. I jumped out of her lap and went to the mistress giving a salvo of happy barks. 'Can I sing a song about a sailor?' Nagyanya called out to Judit. 'Of course, Néni, sing it loud enough for me to hear,' she shouted, 'and make sure the sails and the wind hear you too. Watch, everyone, here we go out onto the lake.' 'Yippie' we all shouted. We were leaving the land behind, a smooth sensation of being afloat gripped me. I was still enjoying the sensation when I saw Nagyanya grabbing Mistress's hat and placing it on her head, shade her eyes from the sun with her hand. Then pretending to be a sailor, she started to sing. I rushed to join her, doing a jig to the tune.

> *A sailor went to sea, sea, sea,*
> *To see what he could see, see, see;*
> *But all that he could see, see, see,*
> *Was the bottom of the deep blue sea, sea, sea.*

If I ever felt thrilled in my life among humans, it was that morning. A wide expanse of water lay before us. A surface of calm and steadiness, even though the water splashing against the bow created some noise. I looked up to the mast, the sails had a beauty of their own, defiant in their triangular spread. I marvelled at the ingenuity of human invention. It was in these tiny vessels they sailed all round the world. I was so engrossed in these thoughts that I hardly knew when Nagyanya came over to me. We both sat looking at the lake. A few surfers appeared. One of them looked like Bea; Nagyanya waved to her. It was Bea. 'How is it going, Néni?' she shouted across. 'Good, very good,' Nagyanya responded vigorously, and I gave some very loud barks to the tune of 'A sailor went....' as if to say, yes, it was wonderful to be afloat on the water.

The sailing was so smooth we were surprised it was already lunch time. Nagyanya's hamper revealed many delicacies and wine to go with them. I was given my repast separately as usual. Having lapped up mine, I watched them eating together. It made me think again why animals eat alone by themselves. Is it something humans want them to do, or is it a natural habit with them? I got my answer only when I began my second life in the wilds.

Feeling the weight of food in my stomach, I wondered if the crew was allowed a short siesta in the cabin. Nagyanya saw my eyelids drooping and warned me against it in no uncertain terms, 'No, Béla, no siesta today. Surely, we can't trust the sails to the wind.' Mistress and Judit certainly weren't relaxing. As soon as they finished eating, they jumped up, this time swapping their positions. Mistress took over the rudder, and Judit became the crew. I was so overcome by food-ennui, that I made sure I sat out of sight to get a few winks.

Soon I was carried away to another world, borne by winged dreams. I was flying, wings of huge white sails were lifting me up and up and up, like Sirius I was heading for the sun. If only I could have stayed in that state, I would have been the happiest creature, but dreams are not for ever. Something was changing. My wings were pumping harder, colliding against something dark and threatening, like a solid wall forcing me downwards. My eyes opened, and I immediately felt a twitching in my nostrils. It was the wind. I jumped up and barking rushed to the crew at the back. The sails were blowing up, looking like bellows.

'Lee-ho, lee-ho,' the mistress was shouting. The wind had begun to push the sails down, tipping them into the waters. Judit was shouting the orders, 'Down, down, lie down flat, Néni, put your weight down, you, Béla, hold on to Néni, the sail must be pulled back. Keep going, it's getting up.' She was ducking to and fro, turning the rudder. With so many hands, the sails soon began to rear their head. We shouted victory, mistress echoed us from the front. We could hear the wind receding and saw the sails going back upright, and the lake regaining its composure. We sat watching the water rippling softly in the sunshine, the sails staying calm and sedate. 'Shall we turn back now, Judit?' Mistress shouted down the boat. She was given the okay sign. It seemed too early to me, but then I saw more boats were appearing on the lake. It was getting crowded and noisy. Maybe it was time to go home.

The rest of the week – our last in Tihany - raced on with one thing or another. First the long-awaited guest, Naomi Ezekiel, arrived. Nagyanya was surprised since she thought she wasn't arriving until the end of the week. The mistress said she had come earlier to be with the Kálmáns, for Tishah B'Av.

'Have we got an invitation?'

'No, Anya, Jewish festivals do not welcome gentiles, friends or foes.'

'But aren't some of the Kálmáns almost gentiles?' Nagyanya wasn't backing down.

'Not really. Judaism never gives up its claim on Jews who may have converted or lapsed. There's always hope of the prodigals returning. Then there is Attila, the Nova Jew, to see they do.'

'Oh, but Naomi, she's not Jewish?'

'Of course she is, she's an Indian Jew; again, she is what you would call a lapsed Jew but a Jew, nonetheless.'

'Goodness, I didn't know there were Indian Jews!' I had never seen Nagyanya so baffled.

'If you hadn't heard of them, that doesn't mean they don't exist. They haven't made news in history, because there have been no Indian persecutions of Jews – no pogroms or Holocausts.'

'I'm floored. I thought she was a Gypsy. Isn't she doing some work on cigányok?'

'But, Anya, that doesn't make her a Gypsy.'

I didn't like the mistress getting edgy with her mother.

'Are we going to meet her?'

'Yes, she wants to meet you. You can ask her as many questions about Indian Jews as you want. She won't mind. I've invited them for dinner.'

'Who else?'

'Rácz, her Roma friend, he's the one she's working with on the Gypsies. He's a Macedonian Gypsy.'

'There we are,' Nagyanya said triumphantly, as if somehow she had won the argument. 'Did you hear that, Béla, we have a Cig...er...a Gypsy guest this evening – and a Jewish guest too. We'd better getting cracking with preparations. Now, Zsuzsa, is Naomi kosher?' That was the wonderful thing about Nagyanya, she could change her perception of people in the flick of a second.

Naomi came earlier. I took to her immediately. She fussed over me. Nagyanya told her that I was a Gypsy breed – I have no idea whether that was true or not, sometimes I think Nagyanya exaggerated the words of the man who looked at me when I was brought to the house. Never mind, I said to myself, enjoy the attention, Gypsy pedigree or not.

'I tell you what, Néni,' Naomi said, 'we will get Rácz to confirm Béla's authenticity as a Gypsy migrant.' They laughed. I didn't like her tone. Was she poking fun at Nagyanya's insistence on my being Gypsy or the importance given to me as a dog? Anyway, I decided to ignore it. So did Nagyanya, since she was keen to know about Indian Jews.

Naomi said that there were many stories about the Jewish migration to India. Some said the earliest Jewish arrivals were around two thousand years ago, while others came in medieval times, and some as late as three hundred years ago. There were around four big migrations, all were by the sea route. Strangely enough, the Jews didn't make their way inland, they settled on the coast. 'I am from Kochi, my ancestors were the earliest Jews to arrive in India. In fact, it is said that they could have been one of the "ten lost tribes" which can't be accounted for. Some Jewish groups include that in their prayers.'

'Jews did very well in India,' Naomi went on. 'All professions were open to them. If anything, it was the Jews who were closed to Indians, but that's how it goes in India. All communities are exclusive. "No intermarriage and no inter-dining" is the slogan all round, and that suited the Jews.'

'Thanks, drágám, I'm sorry I am so ignorant,' Nagyanya showed much gratefulness.

'Not at all, Néni. It's not you, it's the European history. Everyone knows how up and down the Jewish migrations have been in this part of the world, even in this country. When workers were needed, the gates were opened to the Jews and they made the best of the opportunities, doing better than the natives who then turned against them. So the kings banished them, put them on the road for yet one more migration to somewhere else. This was not just back in the Middle Ages but even in the twentieth century. It's general knowledge.' She stopped to see if Nagyanya was still interested, then carried on. 'There has been so much anti-Semitism in Europe that Europeans remain unaware of those countries – mind you, very few - where nothing like that happened.'

'What about Israel now? Are the Indian Jews, like other Jews, returning to the homeland?' Mistress also asked.

'Yes, they are. It's inevitable, really. But quite a lot of Jews migrated to Australia, and of course to the US.'

'The other Israel!' Mistress laughed

'Indeed, that's where my family chose to go. It was as late as the '60s when they migrated. And I must say I've become very American, but not Zionist,' Naomi emphasised. 'Have I answered all your questions, Néni?' she said good-naturedly.

'Yes, drágám, thank you so much,' Nagyanya said gratefully.

'And this Gypsy research, Naomi,' Mistress asked, 'what got you into it?'

'I'm writing a book on the Holocaust. Often people don't bother about what happened to the Roma, which is a pity really. The Nazis saw both Jews and Gypsies as "vermin" who deserved to be gassed. But my interest is in their exodus from India. The funny thing is that the Gypsies left India because they were considered untouchables by the higher castes and made to live like animals; the Jews went to India and were welcomed by the natives.' She laughed, 'What a see-saw, really!'

'Is Rácz providing you with material?' Mistress wanted to know more about him.

'No, not really, Rácz has no time for the Roma.' Naomi laughed. 'He thinks they must get off their backsides and do something worthwhile. You'll hear him speak of the Roma in much stronger terms, I assure you.'

'Shall we have a drink?' Nagyanya seemed to have lost interest in the conversation, 'or wait for your friend?'

I was curious to meet Rácz. So I went over to the window. The evening was laying a shadow on the lake. I looked up to see if there was a moon out, but there was no sign of it. I would have liked to see the moon reflected in the water. I was still lost in these thoughts when I saw a man walking up. He saw me and waved to me. I leapt up and ran to the door. While everyone was welcoming him with words and smiles, I used the whole of my body to show my joy at seeing him. My tail wagged, my body turned and turned, my legs tapped, my ears went flat and eyes all soppy. Was my behaviour over the top? It was strange. There's no doubt that I felt a pull towards him. Was this symptomatic of a tribal link with him? Or was it because he was the first 'Gypsy' I was meeting, a name I had been hearing ever since my arrival in the house?

Having heard something about the plight of the Gypsies from Naomi, I thought Rácz would give the inside view of the atrocities against his community. But then I remembered she had said he had little sympathy with them. I wanted to know why, so I settled down to listen to him. Nagyanya poured him a drink.

'The Roma have problems with their view of the world,' Rácz said. I noticed he used the word Roma instead of Gypsies. 'They are still back in the Middle Ages. Music, fortune-telling, dole-outs, begging or thieving is all they want to do. This is the twentieth century, I tell them. What with Human Rights backing them, they can think of doing better than in the past. But they go on clinging to their old ways. Even the Holocaust hasn't changed them. 500,000 Gypsies were gassed at Auschwitz – agreed, not as many as the Jews, but at least the Jews learnt a lesson from it. Not the Roma. They go on as before, as if nothing has happened.' He spared no words to condemn the Roma.

'May be they need a support system to encourage them,' Nagyanya said softly.

'But they do have it, every sort of support is given to them.' Rácz was getting intense. 'The State is ready to back Roma initiatives with funds and other help, the Roma just have to ask. Already there is the National Roma Council and the Roma cultural paper. Believe me I couldn't run a radio station and bring out a Roma paper without the help of the government, no way at all.'

'Do you have a distinct plan?' Mistress put him to the test. Naomi decided to take a back seat in this discussion.

'Yes, I do. Education is the first step. All progress depends on educating the young. You look at the history of any class or community, education was the first step. Take it from me, without education, there will be no change in the Roma community, ever.' Rácz launched out on his views. 'Roma must send their children to school, instead of out to the streets to beg. With the prospect of Eastern Europe coming into the European Union in the next decade, the options open to the Roma are immense. Next step is work, maybe they can apply for funding to start small businesses rather than look for easy money off the street.'

'Do they like what you say?' Mistress asked. I was surprised at her tone.

'Do you expect them to?' Naomi laughed.

'I don't go around telling individual Roma. I bring out a Roma magazine and run a Roma programme on the radio. My crusade is to bring the Roma into the twentieth century, the end of it to be precise. The older generation will never accept what I say, but the younger people might come round to see what's at stake.' Nagyanya smiled at his statement. Was she thinking of Attila? 'You know, while listening to you, I was wondering if Macedonian Roma are different from the Hungarian Roma.'

'I don't think so,' Rácz laughed, 'it's half a dozen of one, six of the other. The basic mentality is the same. It's depressing.'

'Right, is that a hint, Rácz?' Naomi laughed. 'Maybe we should talk of something else.'

'I want to go to the Roma concert on Saturday,' Nagyanya said. I noticed she didn't say 'Gypsy'.

'That's definitely going to be the standard "Gypsy staple", that's what the tourists want,' Rácz announced.

'And are you going to relay it on the radio?'

'I will but with a twist. I shall interrupt it with my comments, pointing out how the Roma play to the "Gypsy" image. My aim is not to brag about the Roma in Hungary, but to say that we should break out of the typical Roma images, i.e., singers and entertainers.'

'What do you see the Roma doing?' Mistress asked.

'Whatever other Hungarians do.'

'The Roma aren't in the same position,' Mistress ventured further.

'You could say the same about the Jews,' Naomi said.

'With a difference. The Jews kept to themselves, but they had a notion of the work ethic, the Roma don't,' Rácz wasn't backing down from his stand. 'And when I make a stand on this, they attack me. I am boycotted socially.'

'That's what happened to Judit's mother too, and it's still happening,' Nagyanya took Rácz's side. 'Her grandson doesn't like it that she renounced Judaism in the past, and refuses to embrace it now.'

'The third slogan is: stop living in out-of-town ghettos. Can you believe they are still doing it?' Rácz was getting impassioned. 'They can't get out of the old Indian habit. They were forced to live outside the city, but that was eight hundred years ago, why continue to do it into the twentieth century? No, really, it's time they began the diaspora from the ghettos, that's what I tell them, and they don't like it.'

'The communists said the same, "No nomads in the new Soviet republic", and put the Gypsies, er, the Roma in apartment buildings. But it didn't do them any good, did it?' Naomi challenged Rácz. 'Except turn them into street-operators, gamblers and layabouts.'

'Come, food's on the table, it's time to calm our minds,' Nagyanya announced. That was just what was needed to change the course of the discussion. I was certainly exhausted by following the arguments to and fro.

The concert was a bit of disappointment. Somehow the music failed to touch me. Was I influenced by Rácz's opinion? It was difficult to tell. There were a lot of Roma families there. As promised, Naomi and the Kálmáns turned up for the latter half. Nagyanya and Mistress wished them a happy Tishah B'av, I did my best to convey my greetings by circling round them excitely, shaking my tail rapidly accompanied by barks.

By the time the concert finished, the sickle moon was beginning to show with more light. Everyone marvelled on its beauty, but I think the Kálmáns lingered over it longer. Could they be saying a prayer to the new moon? I wondered if the lunar movements had any importance for the Gypsies – I could not bring myself to call them Roma; somehow, the word did not have the same resonance. Each to themselves, I said. Nagyanya and Bori promised to keep in touch for the rest of the year, and not leave it to the meeting next summer in Balaton.

When we got back, I made a point of going to the window. I wanted to see the moon in the water, but the lake remained dark. I knew there was a moon in the sky, but it remained out of sight, perhaps it was over the other side of the roof. After waiting for sometime, I noticed the sky lighting up a little, although I couldn't see the moon itself. I decided to give it a little longer, even though my eyes were flickering with sleep and my limbs longing to stretch out. There it was! I sat up with a jolt. A luminous curve on the edge of a dark circle was resting on the lake. Could I have asked for more?

Before we knew it, it was time for us to leave for Budapest. The Kálmán family came to say goodbye to us, even Attila came, although he didn't stay for long. Bea didn't come, she was having a surfing lesson. Naomi was there too, she was moving into the cottage that afternoon. Amidst much waving and kissing, goodbyes were said, and eventually our car pulled out of the driveway. I turned to look through the back window, to have a glimpse of everyone standing there, wanting to store the image in my mind.

We drove in silence for a while. Nagyanya broke the silence, 'Pity we weren't asked to Tishah B'av. I would have liked to have been at the ceremony.' Mistress didn't say anything. Nagyanya went on, 'I can just see them sitting at the table, women's heads draped with lace head scarves and men in skullcaps, their faces lit by the nine candles of a Jewish candelabrum - reflecting the sunset outside - listening to the reading from the Torah.' She stopped as if she could hear the words, and then went on, 'And the New Moon, with the sun gone down, just beginning to show up, a tiny sickle barely perceptible unless you are looking for it.'

'Oh, Anya, you are being romantic. Every religious ceremony is the same in the end,' Mistress said realistically, and then in an attempt to change the topic, added, 'How did you like the Roma concert?'

'Yes, yes,' Nagyanya seemed non-committal, 'it was good.'

'Not an honest reply, Anya.'

'I have to admit, after listening to Rácz, it was impossible to respond to the Roma the same way as before.' She turned back and putting her hand out to stroke me said, 'But that doesn't include you, unoka.' I could hardly tell her that my response was no different from hers, even though I had come to accept Gypsy migrants as my ancestors. We were now on the highway. 'Another half hour and we'll be home,' Mistress announced.

That was my first holiday, and although many more followed, they were nothing like the one I had that summer.

†

8

THE NEIGHBOURHOOD

‡

Five years of my life have passed. That means I have covered half the mileage of my life expectancy. Generally, the mid-point in life is considered the best time to pause, look back and meditate on past experiences, especially if one wants to write about them. It seems to make sense. Why should I wait to talk about my life at the end when the senses withdraw inwards and lose their desire to engage with the outer world? Or, worse still, why wait until nostalgia and self-pity become the reason for telling my story? No, I have decided that now's the time to recreate myself while passion and desire are at their height.

One starts at the beginning always, though not all beginnings are the starting points. The memory of my life previous to the one that began in the Buda hills is a blank in my head. Someone once said that you create memories in the act of remembering. Why should I do that? They lie beyond the pale. What's not there was never there, why should I make much of it, and turn it into an obsession? It is the second year, the year of my second birth in a new home, that I will begin my story with. The first two years of my life, which I consider as my early history, was my golden age, my childhood, the point of all returns.

In those years I simply luxuriated in the warmth of love and care. It was like being in the sun, night and day. I had two mistresses to adore me as if I was a child born into the family. Life became secure inside the house. So when not too long after I was shifted from the Old Lady's bedroom to the front hall and then to the terrace I almost felt as if I was being sent to the dog-house. I felt wronged and resentful at being weaned so quickly - a mere two months! I didn't want to be on my own, but I suppose that's what growing up is about.

Gradually the concentric cycles of my world became wider. In easy stages I began to look at the outside world. From the inner sanctum to the terrace, then to the street, and eventually up to the woods from where I saw the river Duna hugging the two towns as a mother her two children. From Jánoshegy, the topmost hill that looks over the twinned Buda and Pest, almost the whole city lies open to a wide view. We went there whenever we had guests from abroad. 'It's a good way to start them on Budapest', my mistress maintained, 'after all, it is our capital city'. 'And we are proud of it', the Old Lady would pipe up, 'aren't we, drágám?' she would ask me. She always talked to me, and I loved it. If I have any pride in our city, the credit goes to the existence of Jánoshegy.

Whenever we went by car to Jánoshegy, the Old Lady came too since looking at the town from up there is a treat even for the locals. Walking up to it was even better. It took about one hour to go round and round the hill's lower girth as if performing some sort of penance. On arrival at the top, you are rewarded with a most wonderful view. Many a time I have stood there looking down at the panoramic view while listening to my mistress telling her foreign guests the history of this country, from the Romans to the Magyar kings, the Turks, the Hapsburg colonisers and the communist Russians. 'There's the castle, the closest to our view. It lies on the Buda side, that's where we are now', she loved giving the spiel, and I benefited from listening to it. 'The palace and the church both have been there - a very strategic position - since medieval times and have served as the stronghold of the rulers, in one way or another, of kings, invaders and liberators'. At times, she sounded like a tourist guide. But it was all grist to the mill for me, since I tend to forget a lot of what I hear. So the repetition is welcome.

'Old Buda – Óbuda, in Hungarian - over there to your left, just behind that hill, I'll take you there - is really run down these days', my mistress would be saying while thoughts of mortality occupied my mind. 'But at one time it was the proud home of the grand settlements of the Romans. The place is still full of the remnants of their life style: the mansions, the theatres, the baths and some grave-monuments.' At this point, the guest would raise the question of the Turks. 'Oh yes, the Turks were also in Óbuda but hardly any ruins of their culture have survived.' Ruins! A sadness would come over me. Ruins! that's how all power and glory ends. 'No archaeological diggings have unearthed mosques or houses?'

And invariably my mistress would stop at this point as if the echo of her statement bounced back on her. The guest would then follow up by saying, 'Strange, hardly three hundred years ago and yet nothing remains of them. What about the Turkish baths?' 'Oh, there are those, they were kept in use as the idea of baths took off with the Hungarians.' 'What about their tombs?' 'Oh, yes, I forgot Gulbaba's Tomb - you can't see it from here – much run down; the Turkish government wants to restore it but I'm not sure if the renovations would improve it.' I remembered the Old Lady and Vera Néni talking about it; a rundown monument, the mortal abode of a holy man to whom the truth of all things was that they ended in nothing. As if in continuation of my own thought, the guest said, 'It fits in with the Islamic notion of death and the memory of the dead.' 'What's that?' I wanted to know, too. The guest explained, 'Mohammed said that all signs of death should be obliterated from the face of the earth'. How true! A silence fell on us. Why should the memory be kept alive of that which is dead? 'Interesting,' my mistress broke the silence, 'but a difficult notion for Christians to understand.' 'I agree,' the guest said, 'still it is a wise thought, and much cleaner environmentally.'

To return to my own state, once thrown out of the nest, I had no choice but to look around and make the surroundings my own. There was the road right outside the gate that sloped upwards and downwards, telling me the world was much bigger than my own front yard. Yes, I saw the truth of it and tried to catch a glimpse of things and places out of sight. I could hear the noise of traffic, the constant rush of cars on the main road, going down from our gate, just round the corner. And the upward turn, as I discovered not long after, led to woods, a mere ten-minute walk from our house. These woods are very popular with the townspeople. On holidays and weekends many catch buses to them to get away from the pollution of the city, whatever the season.

Walks became a very important part of my routine. The Old Lady was absolutely set on this point. A dog must be taken out for walks, she used to say, and I was taken out twice if not three times a day. Three types of walks were arranged for me. In the morning every day, the Old Lady took me out around our own streets. Sometimes she would stop to buy something at the corner shop, sometimes we met people on the street and she had a little chat with them; at other times we just walked around two or three streets, passing the dogs behind their gates who invariably barked at me - barking and running along the whole length of their fences, as if resenting my being out when they were in. Sometimes I would let out a growl or two, but most of the time I just ignored them. It bothers me that for dogs barking is the only outlet for their emotions (well, okay, wagging of the tail too), too many responses are tied to it. Whatever the biological reason, barking must overtax the energy supply of our bodies.

Now, of course, apart from the regular exercise, the reason for dogs to be taken out for walks is to make them perform their job twice a day. Unfortunately, the dog-shit on pavements has become the proverbial curse of city life. But what can dogs do? People have tried to invent all sorts of methods to solve this stinking, fouling problem, but not much gets resolved. Walking on the pavements remains an act of bravery for most pedestrians. I often hear mothers saying to their children, 'Look out, there's dog poo', and then 'Oh, God, these dogs'. I have to say that I've become so sensitive to this indictment of us that I get as much into the hedge as I can manage; a little manure for the soil, that's the best I can do.

Whenever there is a city clean-up campaign, dog-shit raises its ugly head. Slogans like 'Dog-haters of the world, unite' are raised against dog-lovers. The other day my mistress read out from a local paper that our district was notorious for dog mess, and that the owners should train their dogs to use the house toilets. On the front page was the picture of a dog using a urinal. Interesting idea! I am in favour of it. After all, if humans could make the move from the wilds to privies, why not dogs? The Old Lady was really tickled by this and told the story of Ágnes Néni who claimed that her cat had been trained to use the toilet. Oh, yes, we know how clever cats are, they can do anything! I couldn't help thinking over the toilet proposition and came to the conclusion that dogs could adapt themselves to the squatting-type of toilets but the throne-type might pose certain problems of balance while performing. People will have to come up with a new type of toilet for dogs altogether. There's something for a clever mind to chew on!

My second walk of the day is in the evening with my mistress after she finishes her supper. We go up to the ridge and walk a little more extensively, I suppose for the benefit of both herself and me. Exercise makes both body and mind healthy. I breathe the air deeply, smelling the scent of the spring, or the heat of the summer, the melancholy of the autumn and even love the cold winds and the slipperiness of the snow in winter. Whatever is going is welcomed, as far as I am concerned. But the spring and early summer are the best times when the blossoms on the lindens and the wisteria are in profusion. To walk underneath the tall lindens and breathe in their scent is to be transported to a world of pure perfume. On the more mundane side, we meet a few regulars, with whom a short exchange of greetings is always on the cards, but nothing very lengthy as my mistress is rather tired at the end of the day, and I have nothing very much to say to other dogs, apart from sniffing them a few times, giving out a few growls and scuffing my back paws on the ground in some excitement. In fact, I prefer not to get into the dog-life too much at that time as I love the serenity of the late evening. I just want to savour it in silence, and look up at the millions of stars so brilliant against the dark sky, though a bit paler when the moon is out. Oh, the trees then take on a different colour, looking unreal, almost magical in the moonlight.

The third type of walk belongs to weekends, generally much longer and takes us out further into other hills. Going on this sort of walk often means that a guest is coming with us. On such occasions, the Old Lady did not always come with us as she found long walks too hard on her knees. The purpose of these walks is to explore the many woods and forests embedded in the surrounding hills. Not many cities could boast of such extensive wooded areas overlooking them. These walks are special outings and don't form part of my routine. It is the terrace which is my regular domain and from where I see the world go by and since so much does, it is fun for me. I learn a lot from just sitting and looking out.

Our terrace is spacious. A large chestnut tree towers over it on the road side, and opposite it at a right angle facing the side wall of the house two lilac bushes form a little grove where I spend most of my time from spring onwards. Besides the shade they provide in the hot months, the purple and white blossoms in early spring fill the air with subtle scent, transforming the terrace into a paradise. Robins and sparrows inhabit the bushes, chattering and fluttering in and out of them at all times, especially at sunrise and sunset. Listening to them, I wonder in what way their chirpings are different from dog barks. Well, of course, they are pleasant and mellifluous unlike the harsh barking of dogs. A visitor from England once remarked that dogs in his country don't bark. In defence, my mistress pointed out that the Hungarian dogs do not live indoors; their outdoor habitation makes them responsible for the protection of the house against burglars and intruders, and hence they must bark. I think she was a bit defensive against criticism of what is our inherent nature. After all, she said later, what's a dog if it doesn't bark? It's a poor bargain to lose one's instincts in return for domestic privileges. And I think she is right.

Once I saw a woodpecker knocking on the chestnut. It was quite frightening to hear the persistent sound of its pecking. It's a beautiful bird, I like its look, but when it gets going on knock, knock on the tree, I feel compassion for the wood. I find myself thinking of it and hoping it will take to the chestnut and come to it more often, so that I could listen to it more. Not that the squirrels may be too happy with it. They are the permanent inhabitants of the tree. It's their territory, really. The woodpecker's loud peck peck might upset them. They go up and down without making much noise. Sometimes I hear their chip chip, but more often than not they go about their nut-picking without causing any disruption in the atmosphere. The cat next door watches them too, but unlike me it has a design on them. The squirrels manage narrow escapes. Not once has the killer caught them, I am happy to say. I have taken to issuing warnings to them much ahead of time to ward off the evil pounce, by giving a volley of barks.

In the summer, the long afternoons prove rather uneventful, but for the song of the cuckoo that floats down from the woods. It is an amazing sound, eloquent and lofty. The lilt in the twin syllables – cuc-koo, cuc-koo - lifts the heavy summer air and hovers in the sky like a humming bird. To listen to its far-reaching mantra is to be transported to another level of existence. Alas, the bird never stays too long in one place. One hears it one day and the next day it's gone. The pigeons are just the opposite. They are always there, huddled high up, under the eaves of houses, cooing away night and day. Some people hate them for the mess they make. But to me they provide company with their deep, soul-searching cooing. In fact, the rhythm inspires me to meditate on many things. I stand by pigeons, even though I now know that doves are more eloquent at cooing. But you see, they are not so profuse, they don't sing that often, don't even come round that much.

When I first saw the doves on our terrace, I took them to be pigeons with a different look - the fawn skin and the beautiful black ring round their necks. Of course, I soon found out that they were not pigeons. My mistress called out to her mother, 'Anya, come and see, a dove in the garden.' The Old Lady leant out of the window, and said, 'Where's the other? It should be a pair.' 'Listen, it's going to sing', my mistress hushed. And it did, sedate and deep, a note of perfect fulfilment. This brought the other dove promptly (just as the Old Lady had predicted), cooing in response. It was a treat to hear their combined lilt. Unfortunately, they didn't go on for long. Ever since then, I have wished they would alight on our terrace more often. I like the idea of doves always in a pair, and that black ring on the smooth fawn body is something. I find myself thinking of it, almost feeling it on my own body. But, you see, the pigeons are always up there, under the eaves to keep me company.

Despite the luxury of a nice high terrace which gives me a good view of the road up and down, I am stuck behind closed gates. Even then you'll be surprised how much I find out about the world. For example, the other day, I could hear someone talking at the gate of the man who lives three houses up from us. I was glad both men spoke loudly because I could then catch everything they were saying. Apparently, it was a passer-by who had stopped at the gate, shocked and surprised that in this dog-infested, dog-barking district the man's dog didn't bark! The owner was explaining that the dog was of the husky breed which is found in Lapland and Greenland, those cold Northern regions towards the North Pole. 'A dog that doesn't bark! difficult to believe,' the man was hard to convince. 'But it's true isn't it, Husky? You don't bark, do you?', he said to the dog. 'He likes talking, try him', he challenged the man magnanimously. Both men laughed. 'He might even tell you stories of faraway places. See his eyes, unusual and mysterious, they hide secrets of those dark snow-tips of our planet.' The owner was being carried away, promising exotic and eerie entertainment to the passer-by. I ought to try it myself next time I see his dog on the street. I made a mental note to have a good look at his eyes. It is surprising how little you may know about your street and the people, though you may have been living there for years. That's modern life for you, I concluded.

The same passer-by was going past our gate now. I had seen him before and recognised him as the man who hated barking dogs. I have heard him blow his top when dogs suddenly leap up from behind fences and start barking. 'Oh, piss off', or louder still 'Fuck off', he barks back at them, making them go berserk even more. They start chasing him along the fence, sometimes quite a length. At such times, I am not sure who is more fierce, the dogs or him. And if he finds the owners standing by, he shouts at them even more ferociously, 'Why don't you bloody well keep your dogs under control?' They are so baffled by this direct address and by his uncommon manner that they just stand there, staring at him. At times I have feared they might let the dogs loose on him. He does look slightly crazy with his white goatee beard and white hair. I bet he gets maa-maa calls from young lads, they are bound to have a go at someone who looks like him, though I must say to me he looks young despite his overall white look. The puzzling thing is that even when he is fuming at the dogs, his eyes seem to be laughing behind his thick glasses, the sort of smile that spreads down from the eyes looking like crow's feet. No wonder he was so taken up with the dog who doesn't bark. For the same reason I myself am in his good books. 'Good dog', he always says to me as he goes by. Once I heard the old lady whisper to her daughter 'the crazy Englishman', but I know better.

Dogs! There is more to dogs than barking and fouling roads, I can tell you that. Now, one day I saw a bunch of dogs pass by our gate. I stood up at once to find out what was happening. From the gate I could see them heading up the road. I gave a quick half a dozen barks to attract their attention. They stopped and looked back. This time I gave out a howl to make sure they knew I meant it for them. Two of them turned back and came down to the gate. Surprisingly, they didn't bark at all. They sniffed me thoroughly, urinated at the gate while I made growling sounds to tell them I was interested in what they were up to, wandering about in the open. They gave me searching looks, as if putting me through an examination, sniffed me on the nose again, spurted more urine on the gate and then headed back to their mates who were waiting for them. They never looked back. I was mystified at their lack of response to me. I craned my neck to see what they would do next, and just managed to catch sight of them turning right on the ridge road. The woods! Could they be heading for the woods? A twitch of regret gripped me. They could have taken me with them. But the gates. No wonder they gave up on me. Now that I know where they go, the next pack of dogs I see I will join them, even if I have to jump over the gates.

There are other things that happen on the street which are not as intriguing or even interesting. The bulk of events relate to cars! Cars, those monstrous things I hate so much. And their alarms that go off at all times, day and night. I hate them, my reaction is so terrible. The moment the alarm goes, I jump up and start chasing my tail furiously. They are worse than ten thousand dogs barking in unison. At times I think of the white-haired Englishman when I am going crazy biting my own tail. What can be the equivalent of it in human beings? And the number of cars that go up and down this street! Often it's the same driver! What the hell is he - I say 'he' because it never is a woman - doing whizzing up and down? And the wretched techno music blaring out. That's it, that's all there is to life for these people - speed, speed of wheels, speed of music, speed of the senses. If I could put a curse on them like the Indian gods, I would reduce their cars to slowness, turn them into tortoises left to their own bodily resources, no gadgets, no machines.

One day I was sitting lazily on the terrace, quietly looking at the chestnut tree shedding its blossoms when I heard loud techno music cascading down our road. Oh God, I protested, there goes the peace of the morning! Five minutes later the same car came back, still blaring away. When I heard it the third time dashing down at even greater speed this time, I leapt up to give the driver a good lashing with my stored-up reserves. But the car was faster than me and raced past, disappearing out of sight. In the same instant I saw something white and small flung up in the air, like a furry ball tossed up at a sports-fair. I was at the gate by then and saw a man walk up to centre of the road, lift it, hold its dead body and say, 'Meghalt', dead, gone. 'Szia, jó élet macska, most meghalt'. He stood there bidding good-bye to a dead cat which had been alive a moment before. Then he saw me and smiled, a strange whimsical smile. A silent communion passed between us, sharing that split second that marks life from death.

He came back to the pavement, held the white limp form up to me, long enough for me to see it, and then dropped it in the gutter. "Szia, élet', he shook his head at the departed life, looked at me for a longish moment, and then went his way. In the minute he had held the dead cat to me, I caught sight of a frozen smile on its face, the smile cats have on their faces. It was still there, but looked more like a sad grin then.

All was still and normal on the road now, as if nothing had moved on it for a long time, The emptiness bothered me, I turned and dragged myself back to my spot to dwell on the passing illusions of living and dying. Poor cat. A remorse came over me as I remembered all the grievances I had had in the past about cats and their privileges over dogs. But they can die more easily too I found out that day.

9

DEATH IN THE FAMILY

‡

For two whole years I was in seventh heaven. What with the Old Lady doting on me and her daughter taking me out for walks, I didn't have a wish left in the world. The world couldn't have been a happier place. What with bedtime stories, history lessons and puppet shows, I was growing up into a knowledgeable dog. As I settled down into a routine life, I noticed that the Old Lady didn't keep too well. Every day when the young mistress got back from work, she asked her if she had taken her medicine. Another time I heard them talking about regular visits to hospital for treatment. The young mistress said she would arrange for the van service to take her there and bring her back too. After every visit the Old Lady would be exhausted and remain in bed until next day. I was greatly alarmed at her condition and insisted on being with her.

My mistress noticed it and assured me things were not too bad, but gave me strict instructions not to make noise or worry the Old Lady in any way, that her mother needed absolute quiet for resting. No more puppet shows. Did I understand that? I assured her I did. My kennel had been moved to the hall sometime back, but now it got shifted out on to the terrace. I was again told not to make a racket at the door or to get up to any mischief as that would wake up the Old Lady. Of course I complied with every word, but I wasn't too happy because I think my mistress didn't give enough thought to how I could be made to do my bit in a time of crisis. In fact, I knew I could be even more company for her mother in her illness than when she was well. I felt aggrieved, but it wasn't for me to argue. All I could do was wish her to get better soon so that we could be together again, and do all the things that made us both happy with each other.

Fortunately my mistress soon realised that putting a curfew on me took away something from the Old Lady too. I bet she must have said something to her daughter, because thereafter I was allowed to be with her on the strict condition that I would not make any demands on her. Of course, that's the last thing I would have done. We already had a good rapport with each other and had developed an understanding of each other's needs. We gave in to whosoever's need was greater. When she needed rest I made sure I remained in one place and did not create any racket by barking at cats or chasing squirrels up the trees or growling at the birds just because they hopped too close to me.

While I sat in my kennel outside I kept my ears open to the sounds from the house. When I heard her up and about to get some food or to potter around the house, doing one thing or another to exercise her body, I would ask to be let in and follow her about, making her talk to me, so that she would feel less lonely. But when she settled into her chair to read a book or talk to a friend on the phone, I would keep very still and sit down, putting my face flat on the table, listening to her. This amused her greatly and she would say, 'You funny thing, I don't know where you learnt to sit like that, with your face so flat out.' I didn't either but found the posture very restful. Whenever I became conscious that this dear lady was dying I would show signs of nervousness, she would spot it at once and take me into her lap and assure me that she was fine. I would then calm down. Sometimes when she looked quite bright and normal, I wondered if they had got it all wrong and that nothing much was the matter with her. I would have given anything to make that true. It was on such occasions that she would tell anecdotes from her life. Memories of the past were astir. Vague images began to materialise. Childhood in the countryside, teenage years with siblings and parents in Budapest. Once in such moments of recollection, she whispered to me, 'Don't be sad, drágám, when I am gone.' I whimpered and snuggled up to her. 'There's a saying, "Set the caged bird free,"' she waved her hand away. '"If it comes back it was yours, if it doesn't it was never yours." I feel like that, szívem, waiting to be set free.' She sighed deeply.

The fates were proving against us. The treatment was not having much effect. She started to stay in bed more and more. The house lost its vibrations, and life became wearisome for me. I would remain in my kennel for a good part of the day, wondering when she would be back on her feet again like old times. But reality was taking a different turn as I found out. I began to hear my young mistress tell the various relatives who came to see her that her mother was getting worse. She said the doctors had told her that the cancer had reached a terminal stage. Should she be in hospital then? they would ask. No, my mistress would not hear of it. She said her mother had lived in the house for forty years and she wanted to die in it. When I heard these words, I whimpered. My mistress saw me and called me to her and patted me. I felt grief in her touch and licked her hand many times to tell her that I was sad too.

The visits of the relatives were not a good idea. Many came and stayed for tea or supper, chatting and laughing with her. Initially they were good company for the Old Lady. But gradually it appeared that their goings-on about her past was not all that cheering for her. Memories of people, places and events were turned inside out, as if it was already her wake. They would sigh about the ways of fate and exchange meaningful glances with each other. Oh, people! people! Why do they jump the gun and rush to receive death? At such times my mistress would break down and cry, which gave the visitors a chance to console her. It is unbelievable how insensitive their behaviour was. I didn't like what was happening and showed my resentment by directing discreet barks at them. But much as I wished them dead and out of the house, their chatter did give me a glimpse of the Old Lady's past life.

She was a true Budapesten, born and bred in the Buda hills. Her parents lived further up in the hills. Ilona - that's what they called her - was bright but not academically minded. So, in the days of socialist streaming she found herself sitting for középiskola, the polytechnic equivalent of gimnázium, that trained young people for factory or clerical jobs. She soon realised those options were not of her choice and asked to be allowed to sit for the nursing exam and was selected. She did her training for the set period. It was the happiest day for her when she received her diploma and became a real nurse. I now understood why she was such a good carer of people in distress. I was thinking of myself. I know the healing touch of her hand.

Hospitals may be a dreary place for people who are ill, but for people who work there they are good meeting places, especially if they are young. This happened to Ilona too. She met her husband there - a heart surgeon. Doctors marry nurses - a very common phenomenon! Perhaps seeing to other people's illnesses, doctors long to be taken care of by someone else. And who could be better for it than a nurse? So, on and off duty,

Ilona and Sándor met, chatted and fell in love. The sterile hospital turned into the Garden of Eden and they announced their engagement. People congratulated them, saying what a good couple they would make. At the wedding there were flowers and gifts and endless toasts to their happiness. Soon they had a child - the only one born to them, my mistress - and they settled down in a normal matrimonial house. Home, child and companionship. It was to last forever.

Things went well for many years. Their daughter grew up into a young lady, with a promising career before her. What more could they desire? But the fates are fickle, and things started to go wrong for Sándor at work. His very success proved his undoing. He had acquired a great reputation as a heart specialist, but even that didn't save him from the unfortunate incident that brought him disgrace. To his misfortune, one of his patients was a politician of high rank. He was a member of the Party and had been a heart patient for many years; only regular medicine and caution had kept him going. But recent check-ups showed that he needed a heart bypass. Dr Sándor operated on him; everything went like clockwork, and rest and recovery were to follow. But the fates struck for the ill-starred family. Signs of failure began to show in the patient and he was rushed into intensive care. He took an unexpected turn, went into a coma and never came out of it.

Well, surgeons are not gods, and their scalpels by no means crosses. But if you are rich and influential you expect no mistakes in your treatment. The man's family was convinced that he did not need a heart bypass and that the surgeon's advice was wrong. In the socialist period law courts were a clearing house for weighty complaints and the person concerned was called upon to answer the charges without a defence. It became a public case and Sándor was duly charged with negligence. In the end it was his luck, 'szerencse' - Hungarians are prone to seeing everything good as pure luck - that he was cleared. But it broke the man and demoralised his family. A year later he died. My mistress was on a scholarship in the USA, and had to rush back. The mother and daughter clung to each other; my mistress wanted to stay and give up her studies, but the Old Lady insisted that she went back and finished her degree. When she returned after a year, they formed a new family unit - mother and daughter - and started another sort of life. It was 'szerencse' again that the state did not shift them to another dwelling. The mother ran the house and the daughter earned. This very household of cheerful well-being to which I was brought two years ago again lay in shadow.

At times when the Old Lady was alone in the house, she sat in her chair and just looked out of the window into the distance. I could read her thoughts. My heart went out to her, and she knew from the whimpering in my throat what I was feeling emotional. She would put her hand out and rub my neck, and her look would say, 'Don't. I am not sad. It's been good, and things don't go on for ever.' But I wished they did because she was my dear Nagyanya and I loved her. Thereafter her condition deteriorated fast and it seemed only a matter of time when it would end. We could only wait.

One evening I felt something was going to happen that night, the sort of inkling animals still retain through their instincts. Just as well because it makes us better prepared for the worst. They say that when dogs howl it's because they see death approaching, that they actually see it coming through the door to take the dying away with it. As I sat thinking of death and looking out of my kennel I thought the dark had never looked so dense and the night so forbidding. I decided not to sleep that night; every time my eyes closed I would jerk myself awake. The house had to be guarded that day. I was going to be tested for my ability to keep unwanted strangers out. My eyes were glued to the gate. I was so tense that every little sound startled me. I nearly jumped out of my skin when the door of the house opened and my mistress came out.

'Come, szívem', she said crying, 'she wants to see you'. She picked me up and carried me upstairs to her room. There she lay, the dear Old Lady, my Nagyanya, looking fatigued and played out, but still with the same benign smile on her face. She took me from her daughter and held me in her arms very gently.

'How's my unoka today?' she asked most tenderly. Knowing her state I could hardly suppress my sobs. 'No tears now, szívem,' she commanded as she ran her hand down the whole length of my body, from the head all the way down to the tip of my tail. She kissed me on my nose and then looking straight into my eyes, said, 'I know you love your Nagyanya, and that makes me happy.'

She took a deep sigh. I stayed still, waiting for her to say something more. She pulled me into her lap and said she would sing me an Indian lullaby. I shuddered and my vision blurred, making her image swim in my eyes. Her voice wafted on the air, falling softly like dew on my ears.

Sleep, young princess, sleep.
Sleep, because I love you,
Your beauty overwhelms me,
I will keep a watch over you.

Close your eyes, my princess,
Let your soul drift away to
A happy land of silent peace.
Look, the moon awaits you.

'Keep this song in your heart, Béla, together with your Nagyanya.' She kissed me again, what was her last kiss, and put me down. 'Now, show me where your kennel is,' she commanded. When I showed reluctance, she persisted, 'Come on, I want to see you go to it,' and gave me a slight push. I suppressed the terrible howl rising in my throat and hiding my sorrow, slunk away as fast as I could, obeying her as I had always done.

Those few minutes spent with her left me in the grip of a terrible trauma. I sat so still in my kennel that a passer-by might have thought I was a mock dog. I watched every shadow that crossed our terrace. The silence was frightening. Slowly a strange sound of stealthy motion and faint chip chip made inroads into that deathly quiet. It was coming from the chestnut tree. What now? I asked, arching my body. I dug my eyes into the tree and saw something crumpled up under it. I was about to move to it when I saw a whole group of squirrels coming down the tree's thick trunk. What were they doing at this time of the night? I was still asking questions when three or four squirrels were already around the crumpled mess on the ground. I lifted my paw but then stopped. They were now dragging the mass up the tree. Could they be ants instead, only giant-sized, because their labour seemed more like that of ants? I froze into absolute stillness. Next moment I saw that what they were dragging was a dead squirrel.

Inch by inch, they were pushing, pulling and propelling the dead body of one of their own. Why up the tree? Didn't animals just leave their dead where they died? Wasn't that one of the differences between animals and humans? It seemed not. It seemed death rites were essential to all living beings. The squirrels continued to move and were making progress bit by bit. They were up the tree now, where more squirrels were waiting to take over from them. Had they waited for the night to bring the dead home?

What last rites would they perform? Would they eat the body? A feast of the dead? Consumption as extinction? A sort of rebirth, a reinforcement of the living?

A rattle at the gate made me jump. It was as if someone had tried to come in. I quivered with apprehension. Who is it? I was terrified. Something was certainly astir. In that moment, something at last broke through me and I heard myself howl, a long painstaking howl, an unending howl at the long shadow that was stretching towards our door. I knew then that I was seeing Death come through the gate and go into the house to get the dearest person on earth. I had hardly recovered from my confrontation with the shadow that had fallen on our house when I heard the young mistress talking on the phone, crying hysterically, 'Please come, come now, she may be dying'. I scarcely knew what I was doing, squealing and going into long howls. Will Death come out the same way that it went in, only this time carrying my Nagyanya and heading for the other world? Could I stand up to the might of Death, and make a name for dogs as saviours? Could I snatch my Nagyanya out of its clutches and send it off empty-handed? The fever of grief was upon me, making me a victim of heroic delusions.

The Old Lady's death was a blow to her daughter. Now she was orphaned and alone. She had only herself to think of, and of course me, not a happy thought for a young woman. I too was left orphaned. I promised to myself I would try and live up to the expectations Nagyanya had of me. I thought of the long days when I would be alone in the house, with no one to talk to and be with.

How many good things could I say in praise of my old mistress? She never put herself first in anything, not even with me. Although she had never recovered from the death of her husband and the social disgrace that went with it, she never let that rule her life. She was very accommodating to her daughter, never made undue demands on her and even insisted that she took every opportunity to go abroad for holidays and conferences. She was a great influence on me in this. I follow her example in not restricting my mistress's life on account of me - well, at times I do, perhaps when I forget. But I try not to pull a long face or sulk when she has to go travelling, although it's not the same for me now without the fun and company of the

Old Lady. I am all the poorer without her.

The memory of the week between the Old Lady's death and her funeral when I was left to my own resources to face the terrible loss will stay with me forever.

†

10

THE NIGHTS

‡

The loss of the Old Lady was difficult to bear. It triggered off the old trauma in me. The distress brought back the old fears, and made me severely paranoiac. The world became a place to fear and take flight from. My mistress was in no condition to run around fixing appointments for me with the psychologist. But as this was not the first time, she knew how to handle it herself. She may also have spoken to the psychologist since as soon as Nagyanya's body was shifted out by the undertakers she took me indoors. I was in a terrible state when I saw the body being carried out. I admired my mistress's control. She remained calm and matter of fact, but I knew underneath that façade she was as distraught as me. As the car drove away carrying her mother's body, she shut the gate behind her and turned to deal with my problem. I was whimpering, tears flooding my eyes. She picked me up and walked into the house, now silent and empty.

She kept me indoors with her, until the funeral was over. This was what I needed, a reassurance that all was not finished, and that death does not stop life's normal course. We were both aware that we were trying to smooth over a terrible bump in our lives. But unlike me she had many things to organise: arrangements for the funeral, cars to take people to the graveyard and bring them back to the house, for the feast afterwards. She was on the go the whole time. Burial did not seem an easy task. I thought how strange that while the deceased was at peace, the living were caught in the throes of the last rites. It was difficult to see death as the final end with so much activity going on on account of it. I was grateful to be near her, whether in front of the TV as a distraction from the thought of her mother, or while she wrote letters to people, informing them about her death and the funeral service, or on the phone, receiving calls from people. It was enough for me to be in the vicinity and know what was happening. I licked her face, snuggled up to her, sat at her feet, and let her know I was there just as she was there for me. We needed each other. To be isolated in times of crisis is no way to get over it.

After the funeral, life had to resume its normal course. I was put back outdoors, in my kennel to do the rest for myself. It was right too. In the end you have to do that final bit for yourself, or go under. To become a liability to my mistress was the last thing I wanted when she had her own grief to cope with. The best then I could do was to put myself back on my feet and relieve my mistress of the extra burden of looking after me. I kept on saying to myself, I can't go on like this forever, I have to make a stupendous effort to find my way back into the world.

The passing of the day was not so bad, but the nights still proved difficult. As the shadows deepened, a fear would grip me, setting my nerves on edge, and ending all possibility of sleep. After that I would remain awake for hours, going over the death of Nagyanya, thinking back on all the incidents leading up to it and reliving my last meeting with her. When sleep would come, I would fall into those dozes that at best bring nightmares. What could I do? I had no more control over my mind than the planet had over its revolutions round the sun. I can understand why people take sleeping pills. God should pity those who cannot sleep, and send them dreams, which would make them sleep. Ah, dreams! If only one could ask for dreams and get them, like going to the chemist for medicine. I want a four-dream packet of DreamSleep, please. No, I don't want just sleeping pills, but a packet of dreams. No such thing available? How can that be, with all this technology and pharmaceutical advancement? Surely, someone has come up with a patent for DreamSleep? But no, one cannot buy dreams, and even sleep is difficult. Those pills don't always work, certainly not through the whole night. What can one do then to pass sleepless nights? Some say, get up and do something, which I did many times. I would spend many hours prowling around the terrace; but it never brought me sleep, only tired my body out. I would then have to lie down, without sleep and without dreams.

I noticed another change in me. I related to what was happening around me in a very strange way. It seemed whatever I saw didn't leave much impression on me; I didn't react to people and events although they were part of my everyday routine. For example, if I saw people I already knew well, I wouldn't recognise them or respond to them in the familiar way by barking happily or wagging my tail in excitement. It was as if I wasn't seeing them. Instead, I became aware of the more unphysical side of reality. I heard sounds so distinctly that I felt I could almost put flesh on them and see them moving about in the air. I realised that my grief was colouring the world for me. I feared the coming of the night, but at the same time felt assured by the shadows that stalked the dark. I felt I knew them.

The world seemed to be made up of sounds only. They came from everywhere, near and far. From the stillness of the night, from the silent trees, from the sleeping houses and even from within me. They came from a distance too; from the woods and from the valley at the edge of the woods; they rose like giants advancing to engulf me. I was becoming schizophrenic.

As I lay awake for hours, I would hear savage animal yells coming from the hills. I knew wild boars and foxes lived in the woods. I had heard them before, but now the sounds changed into vivid bodies. I could literally see wild animals coming out of their hideouts, prowling about in the thick forest, stalking the woods to claim back their territory from humans. Sometimes I thought the growls sounded more like dog barks. Could there be wild dogs up in the woods? Once I heard Vera Néni tell Nagyanya how her neighbour's dog, a big Alsatian, had gone missing one day. He never came back, couldn't be found. People claim that once dogs are on the loose, they head back for the Buda hills and become wild again. I remembered those four dogs I saw one day. They did seem to have a common bond, and the same aim. They certainly knew where they were going. Were they now wild inhabitants of the woods? I listened to the barks carefully next time and compared them with our own barks down here. Or was I imagining too much? Maybe the wild dogs bark, I argued, or maybe they don't. Once on their own ground, why would they need to bark? Not like the domesticated ones who do so out of frustration at their captive state, because they are forced to perform many tasks: guard the property, scare away intruders, attack thieves and burglars. There was no end to my mind running around in circles - another way of chasing my own tail - and proliferating thoughts. But they did pass many wakeful hours for me.

It wasn't just the sounds from the hills that scared me, but the trees around me too. They took on a threatening aura at night. They shook ominously, their tall trunks groaning with deep rumbles, and their shadows cast by street lights moaning at some unknown loss. The birds sheltering in the trees looked sinister as they clung to the branches, watching something intently I couldn't see. At night the trees would undergo a total change, from being a safe haven for the happy little day-birds to becoming the battle ground for the alien birds who sought shelter in them. Perhaps it was these birds of doom, the harbingers of ill-omens, who struck such terror into the little inhabitants of the tree and me below, a being already depressed.

On one moonlit night, the owl hooted. The suddenness of the hoot was startling. I was terrified by it, the way it suddenly rang out as if it were an oracle declaiming a message from the gods. It went on all through the night. The sound cut the air, sharp and eerie. It came from the next-door neighbour's tall straggly tree. The hoot shot like a bullet, shattering the peace of the night. The stillness that followed between the hoots was even worse. It hovered over me like a premonition of some doom waiting to fall on earth. What worse fate could befall us now? I asked trying to shake off the superstition from my mind. Some call the owl the bird of wisdom because it sees in the dark, but in that week of emotional despair it did not provide me with any way to overcome my grief.

On another night it was from the hills that my terror came. The night was very still when I heard terrible sounds of a chase and scuffle in the woods, quite close to the valley. The night silence was rent by savage growls. I crouched further back into my kennel, hoping they wouldn't spill over on to our side. Gates would prove no hindrance to such outbursts. There were thuds and growls as if the animals involved were tearing each other apart. The monstrous noise went on for so long that I got worse and worse. Fortunately, at some point I must have fallen off, probably out of the sheer terror of it never ending.

When I woke the sun was already up. I heard people talking about a fox as they went past our gate. Apparently that morning a policeman had found a dead fox on the road, and enquired from the residents if they had heard anything in the night. Did the dogs bark? Did they hear noises in the night? Everybody was cautioned against the wild animals coming down from the woods, and asked to make sure their dogs were safely inside the gates. Maybe extra barricading should be put up at the valley end of the woods, people deliberated. They were afraid of finding wolves and foxes in their gardens, or walking straight into them on the road, returning home late at night. I suppose people were thinking of the wild boars and the danger to children. Everyone talked about it for a few days. The local newspaper carried the news. Everyone had some story to tell about the wild animals in the woods. Some repeated stories of the dogs returning to the wilds. A Pandora's Box had opened. It seemed a bit over the top. I was too occupied with the death of Nagyanya to dwell on the savaging of a fox or the awakening of natural instincts in domestic dogs.

It was not just the woods that towered over me with their invasive wildness, but even our street erupted with uncontrolled emotions, adding to my trauma further. One night a scream rent the dark; a woman was screaming. Good heavens, I sat bolt upright. What now? Is someone else dying? Or being strangled? Or is the woman in the grip of a nightmare like me? The scream rang out again. I whimpered, making groaning sounds, stifled in my throat. It's the loss of someone. What does one do with it? How do you come to terms with the permanent absence of someone? The night was witness to the inability of people to overcome their afflicted state. Night revealed people, animals, birds and even trees as different from their day selves. Night and day, two aspects of the planet. Could it be that the planet itself is schizophrenic?

On the street itself, shadows hissed and flickered like fire in the night, harrowing me with their ever-changing shapes. They changed constantly like some mythical beast. I was convinced I was hallucinating. My fears were perpetuating new shapes. Sleep was so sporadic that it gave them no chance to play out their terror in dreams. When will things get better for me? I was getting tired of being miserable.

One night - I think it was past midnight - I saw a minibus stop outside our gate. Was it a shadow looking like a car, or was it a real car? Next moment, it became a rhinoceros breathing terror into me. What could I do against it? I crouched in the back corner of my kennel, leaving our safety in the hands of the fates. It took me a little more looking before the monstrous shape reverted to a minibus, which is how I saw it first. Even then I remained cautious. What was happening so late in the night? Someone to meet my mistress? Three people got out and looked up and down the road. Then they slipped across the road and were at the gate of our neighbour opposite. They took a bit of time before they opened the gate slowly and went in. I was puzzled by their measured moves. I came out, went to the gate and looked closer at the van. Someone was sitting at the wheel. What was up? There wasn't enough reason for me to set up an alarm, because nothing seemed wrong in people going into a house or sitting out in a van. An hour must have gone by. I decided to wait and see, and hung around at the gate. But the men didn't return. Ah, they must be asleep by then, I thought, forgetting about the minibus. The thought of sleep made me return to the kennel to try my hand at it myself.

I was jolted out of my doze by a loud flutter in the chestnut. The street was empty now, the street lights were off, and the minibus was gone. There was a glimmer in the sky, assuring me that the worst of the night was over. A peculiar silence hung over the hills. I thought of the animals in the woods; they must be calming down and retreating to their dugouts to sleep and recover from their night prowls. The sun must be slowly filtering through the thick forest growth. It must be nice to be up there, I couldn't help thinking. Returning to my own world down here, the trees were coming alive with bird noises, growing from indistinct murmurs to morning twitters. It soothed me to hear them. If only I were like them, I could be at peace with myself in the night.

By seven, I became aware of a commotion in the street. The occupants of the house opposite were at their gate, trying out the lock on it. I suddenly remembered the men at the gate and the minibus. I moved quickly to our own gate to find out if it was something connected with what I had seen last night. People walking down for the bus were stopping to ask what had happened. Soon I worked out that there had been a burglary in their building last night. There was much clicking of tongues and shaking of heads. I could have been the prime witness to the burglary, and thrown considerable light on what was otherwise proving mysterious to them. But who would think of a dog as a witness?

When my mistress came out they asked her if she had heard anything in the night. No, she hadn't. They warned her to be cautious. The keys, they went on about the keys. Apparently the burglars had used proper keys to open the gate, the door to the building and to the cellar. They were terribly indignant that the burglars had conducted the burglary so neatly. In the cellar, they found four stools drawn up in a circle and cigarette butts thrown around. So, while the burglars were having a chatty time, smoking and deciding what to burgle, the residents slept through the whole operation. Every household in the building had had huge boxes of big jars of preserved vegetables and fruit for the winter - all were gone!

As I was listening to their description, images of loaded donkeys and caves were flashing through my mind. The dream! What was it, the dream I had last night? It was coming back. I was in the woods when a line of donkeys came along; they were fully loaded and finding it difficult to move. From nowhere four wolves materialised. They started to chase the poor donkeys, who started to bray. I took fright and ran for home. While I was running I woke up. Now I knew that my dream was an instant translation of what was happening on the street - the burglars loading the van with the goods, and the minibus moving. It was the noise of the motor running that had woken me up. The whole thing was turned into a dream! So, was I sleeping, or was I awake? Or part sleeping, part waking, and dreaming at the same time? No wonder I woke up, feeling good, not in the usual wracked state. There was hope for me. The hallucinations had retreated into my other world, they were turning into dreams. A funny thought struck me. Do people become burglars because they can't sleep? Could I have formed a dog-burglary band? Rounded up all the sleepless dogs of the world and had fun invading all prohibited areas, instead of becoming miserable and alone in the kennel? Dog Burglary Private Ltd! How about that? My tail wagged like a reed swept by strong winds.

A clear image is a good omen. I felt I had already turned a corner. Through the night I had come to see the light. The emotional despair from grief and loss I had clung to so religiously had found an expression. Instead of fearing the coming of night, I promised myself, I would now trust its restorative quality.

†

11

THE BOY AT THE GATE

‡

The other day I was sunning myself in the front yard when I saw a young boy standing at the gate. There was something special about him, the way he stood looking at me. At first I didn't know what to make of him, but then something struck me about him - it was his smell. I could smell him. Driven by my instinct, I jumped up, but then stopped and very cautiously and slowly advanced towards him. I stopped midway as I noticed he was screwing up his nose and the whole nostril area was quivering with frenzied sniffing. I made another slow move and got to the gate. As I came close to him, though still on the other side of the gate, he switched himself sideways and started to rub his body against the metal. Good God! I exclaimed, he is going to lift his leg at any time! The imitative instinct passed into my own limbs and I started to move sideways too. He was now scraping the ground repeatedly with his feet, as if they were paws. But while his attempt to go into action was somehow failing, I, having taken my lead from him, could not wait any longer and performed freely myself. What an immense feeling it was, an utter relief which only bodily functions can bring. In peeing promptly, my main purpose was to help him to relieve himself in the manner of dogs, as that seemed to have been his intention. So, in another bid to encourage him, I went into a circulatory motion again and lifted my leg against the gate and spurted out more. He tried to copy me, but something was certainly hindering him. After all, he was a human and was used to doing it on two legs instead of on three like the canines.

I felt sorry for him, and thinking he needed some consolation, I licked his hand which was resting on the gate. I was taken aback when in quick return, he licked me back, and raised his head, and gave a bark by way of greeting my compassionate gesture. But, strangely enough, it wasn't a complete dog bark, it sounded more like a rattle than a bark. I was thoroughly confused by what was happening, and out of fear backed off quickly.

Before I knew it, I was barking furiously in self defence against the unknown phenomenon. The boy's face also changed from playfulness to fear, and he burst out crying. I am accustomed to children bursting into tears when I pursue them with my barking, but what I was not expecting was to see the sheer disappointment on the boy's face. A nervousness came over me, and my bark rose to a pitch, becoming more hostile.

My aggressive barking brought my mistress out, 'What's up with you, now? Mi a baj?' Then she saw the boy whose cry now became a wail at seeing someone appearing. He was almost having a fit. My mistress smacked me hard - I hate her doing that - and ordered me to return to my corner at once. When she does that to me I feel my tail curving in and my dog spirit deflating. I feel humiliated. As I slunk down in my corner, I heard her trying to quieten the boy.

'Come, come, stop crying. He's a good dog. He won't bite you.' As the boy's sobbing subsided, she asked him, 'Where do you live?' She repeated the question many times but the boy wouldn't say anything, except cry in a hoarse, barky way. I was watching carefully with my ears all pricked up for more information. By this time my mistress was catching on to what I had already sensed, i.e., there was something strange about the boy. That was the end of my interest in him. Let her sort it out, I thought, it serves her right for scolding me before a stranger. I put my face down, stretched out and watched them with droopy eyes. 'Where do you live?' she was still repeating for the umpteenth time. This time he made a gesture up the road. 'Come, I'll take you home, shall I?' To my surprise, he nodded vigorously and grinned, wiping his eyes and looking in my direction. My mistress unlocked the gate and took his hand, but he pointed to me and said in a funny way. 'Him too.'

'What, the dog?' She threw a stern look in my direction. 'I don't think so. He was naughty, he made you cry.' She again took his hand and was moving, but he shook his head and pulled her back, 'No, no, I want him to come,' he spoke quite clearly now, in a human way. My mistress gave in reluctantly. 'Okay, I'll get his lead.' And she went in. I immediately stood up and looked at the boy, my tail swishing fast and a rush of sounds vibrating in my throat at the prospect of a walk. To my great surprise, this time, he gave a clear, hearty bark. 'A dog! He's a dog!' The realisation swept over me like a revelation. I bounded up to him and gave a series of happy licks to his hand. He was inside the gate now as my mistress had left it open. He responded instantly and bending down to my level, gave out another volley of barks. I bounced up and caught his neck in my mouth as is the canine habit of playing with each other. A terrible scream issued from the door. It was my mistress, she looked petrified to see me at the boy's neck. Within seconds I felt a series of wallops raining on me. 'Stop it, at once. You'll stay here, if you don't behave.' Then she noticed that the boy was in great spirits and that I wasn't attacking him. I saw a shadow pass over her face, something closer to fear than shock, as she nervously started to put me on the leash.

She took the boy's hand and motioned him to walk. 'Now, to your place,' she said rather sharply, dragging him at a great pace. She was anxious to get rid of him. She hurried up the road, keeping a sharp eye on him all the time. He changed sides swiftly to walk beside me. I turned to him too, but kept my play instincts in tight check. I was afraid of upsetting my mistress further. But when the boy suddenly let his hand fall on me as if it were his front paw, all restraint went and I responded with a matching bounce. My mistress made no attempt to stop him or me. In retrospect, I think she decided to find out what was happening. All of a sudden, the boy started to move his hips sideways as if he was moving his tail and then suddenly gave a jump and put his hands, like front paws, on my back. I gave out a squeal, responding to his touch. He immediately went down on all fours. A chase of bounding, jumping and grabbing limbs started. My mistress stood aside, absolutely panic-stricken. She could hardly believe what was happening. I was beyond the usual reprimands. For once I couldn't care less for orders and obedience. I had found a human-dog and wasn't going to miss the extraordinary fun of mixed play. Vaguely I knew we had taken over the road, and that the occasional car passing by had to manoeuvre round us.

I have no idea how long it went on. Seconds? minutes? hours? The next thing I knew was the screech of a minibus, and a woman jumping out, calling 'István, István, gyere, gyere.' But there was no stopping István. He was firmly on his fours and beyond control. The woman rushed back to the minibus and got out a leash and a collar, all the time saying, 'Jó kutya, jó, jó, gyere, gyere'; and at some point, amidst this kutya-calling patter, she grabbed him while he was circling round me and threw the collar on him, holding the leash tightly at the same time. I could also hear my mistress screaming and yelling at me to stop. I was beyond all hearing as I hadn't had such free bouncing, pawing and biting since my puppy days. As soon as the woman was in full control of the boy, my mistress shook herself out of her hysterical state and grabbed my leash. She pulled me away most ruthlessly. Even in that excited state, I felt her grip speak of the fright she had taken.

She rushed me down the road at a speed I could hardly keep up with. She was almost running. It took me awhile to come out of my own euphoric excitement to realise what a terrible state she was in. She never spoke a word to me, not even to scold me. She banged the gate behind her, and pushing me to my kennel, left me to regret my behaviour. But my body was still in the throes of a peculiar experience. Why would a human behave like a dog? Was there a desire in the boy to be an animal? Could it be possible that the human form is just skin deep, and under it all we are the same - simply animals? These were difficult thoughts, and there was no way I could answer them in that exhausted state. I was played out physically and my little brain could not dwell on such matters. My eyes were closing every second and a haze of sleep was drawing over them.

†

12

THE EXTENDED FAMILY

‡

It was just after the New Year celebrations, Epiphany was not over yet. The traditional wheat was getting longer in the pot under the Christmas tree as a thermometer of family prosperity. All these days my mistress had been busy seeing friends. Visitors were still coming round to exchange Christmas and New Year greetings.

This particular morning I noticed my mistress was preparing open sandwiches with slices of cheese and ham. I at once knew a visitor was expected. There must have been a telephone call I missed hearing. Relatives always called beforehand to make sure you were going to be home. It made sense to save themselves a long journey across the city. And the receiving family also didn't want to be caught unawares. Hence, the making of the sandwich platter. The house too had been given a quick tidying up.

So I sat down at the window and waited to see who was coming. Of course I could have asked my mistress. A few barks when she was at the sandwiches, and she would have said, 'Oh, yes, Vera Néni is coming, silly.' And now here was Vera Néni, the bell was ringing. I jumped up and rushed to the front door. With me romping in excitement, my mistress had a job getting out. I followed her to the door and couldn't wait to give a few licks to Vera Néni She was my favourite visitor as she always talked about everyone and everything. She was a real storehouse of information.

Vera Néni was my mistress's aunt, her mother and my mistress's mother were first cousins. Her mother had died before Christmas, a few weeks previously. I didn't know anything about it. So, one day when I saw my mistress leaving the house in a total black outfit, I got worried. It brought back memories of the Old Lady's death. I hovered around her making whining sounds and sniffing her dress, she bent down and rubbing my neck, gently broke the news to me. 'It's all right, darling, it's Vera Néni's mother. She died last week, today is her funeral.' I was shocked. Many a time I had visited Néni's mother with my mistress. Thinking of those times and her affection for me, my eyes swam with tears and my whines took on volume. Seeing me in such a state of distress, my mistress made me sit down and look at her, and said, 'It's okay, calm down, darling, she was old and ill and better that she died than went on living.' That's what people had said to my mistress at the time of her mother's death. All deaths are a chain of associations. I remembered how grief-stricken she was then. I put my head in her lap and could not stop whining; she understood what was going on inside me, and stroked my neck gently and kissed me many times.

And now, here was poor Vera Néni. This was the first occasion I was seeing her since her mother's death. I wanted her to know how deeply I felt her loss. I licked her feet and put my front paws on her and tried to reach her face. My ears were flat down and my tail was going at full speed. My grief and joy at seeing her poured out of me. Vera Néni stroked me and kissed me and we all made our way to the house. My mistress stopped at the door, asked me if I wanted to stay out. Before she could finish her sentence I was already inside. I would not miss their conversation for anything in the world, not even for the brightest morning outdoors.

My mistress fussed over Néni, made her sit in front of the fire and got her a coffee immediately. Then pushing me a little aside as I had sprawled out at Néni's feet, she made place for herself on the sofa beside her. She took both her hands in hers and rubbed them most gently. 'I'm so glad you've come, Néni. It must be awful to be by yourself in times like these.' This was enough to break down Néni's restraint and she burst into tears, my mistress hugged her and patting her head consoled her, 'Now, now, you can't go on crying forever.' I jumped up and started to lick Néni's arm very rapidly. In an attempt to protect her from my over-excited affection, my mistress told me in no uncertain terms to behave myself. 'Stop that,' she said with a quick slap on my back, 'Néni doesn't want you to be all over her. Sit quietly or I'll have to put you out.' That sobered me up quickly. I didn't want to go out. So I went over to my window seat from where I knew I would get a good view of them.

Vera Néni was calming down a bit and my mistress was saying, 'One's parents don't go on living forever, Néni. Eighty-eight is quite an age. You must think of her. You wouldn't have wanted her to live in pain.' Néni blew her nose and wiped her eyes, and nodded her head at my mistress's wisdom. 'I can't forget her suffering. It was awful to watch her.' She fell silent. My mistress too remained quiet. 'I've hardly slept since her death. If only one could die without suffering.'

'But one doesn't,' said my mistress. 'Death means pain and suffering. We all have to go through that.'

'Hers was so much. It was too much, it didn't seem fair. And the doctors, they did nothing.' Néni's voice rose. My ears pricked up as I heard grief changing to anger. 'My mother was in such terrible pain that anybody would have taken pity on her, even a dog, but not the doctors.' I always have to fight a rush of resentment in me when the worse sort of human behaviour is attributed to dogs. Generally dogs are seen as loyalty incarnate, but in moments of personal grief, people reveal their prejudices against animals.

'They wouldn't even take her pain seriously.'

'Well, don't forget, Néni, the doctors are more concerned with the illness.'

'No, Zsuzsa, a doctor has to think of the person also. He is there to relieve the patient of pain. I am not even asking that he should have made her better, just done something about the terrible pain. He could have given her something, some pain-killer, that's all I was asking.' She paused and then blurted out. 'It's not true, I was asking for more. I wanted them to put her out of her misery; oh, istenem, how I wished her some peace, even if it meant death.' For a second she was calm, and then she burst into bitter tears again.

'You mustn't blame yourself, Néni. It's not allowed in this country, not yet. You can't just put people to death, as if they are dogs.' I started again. My mistress looked at me. I gave out a growl to let her know I was upset by such statements. She understood my feeling and called me to her, 'Not you, silly, you are not a dog.' She patted me. 'And anyway, it's just a saying. Sit here now.' Insult after injury, but I swallowed it and sat down at her feet, snuggling up to her.

'It wasn't just that, Zsuzsa,' Vera Néni continued, 'It was everything. The doctors didn't know their job.'

'It's the same with all of us. None of us know what is expected of us. The laws are changing so fast, we don't know where we are.'

'Even when someone is dying?'

'I know, I know, Néni.'

'The last days...' Her voice drowned in a cry.

'Tell me, Néni, tell me everything. It will be good to put everything behind you,' my mistress said softly and waited for Néni to speak.

'I haven't spoken about this to anyone. It's been so painful. And even if everything is changing around us, it should never be as bad as it was with her.' She stopped for a second as if deciding on something.

'I know, I know.' My mistress waited.

'You know when mother had her second stroke, she had to be rushed to hospital. Well, of course, I went with her. Just as well I did. You know what they did with her? They put her in a ward with twelve other people. I was shocked. This wasn't like the old Socialist times. Still, I thought, well, times have changed, we are into a different system. The nurses took charge of her, made her chart etcetera, and told me to go home. They didn't want me to stay. They said they would be doing tests on her, and I needn't be there. Mother was unconscious, of course. So, I took the details of the ward and went home to get some sleep. It wasn't easy to go back to the empty house, Zsuzsi,' her voice broke. My mistress stroked her hand.

Vera Néni wiped her tears and continued, 'The next day I set out quite early. When I got to the ward, I found it empty, stark empty, not a single bed in it, none of the twelve beds of the day before, and the people on them. I was so dumb-struck I could hardly move. Then I heard myself calling out in a loud voice, like a mad person, "Mother, mother," I was shouting like a lost child. "Where are you, Mother?" My voice was echoing in the empty room, and then, as if by miracle, I heard my mother's cry coming from far away. She is alive, was my first thought. I could recognise her cry, even though it was faint.' Néni couldn't go on.

I was moved by Vera Néni's words. Mother! Suddenly the word picked up a resonance. For the first time in all my years I became aware of its wholeness. Where is my mother? I could not suppress the whimper rising in my throat. What happened to her? I envied Vera Néni's feelings, sad as they were. Can one have a mother for the asking?

'Where was she?' I heard my mistress ask. She wanted Néni to go on. 'Why was the ward empty?'

'Don't ask me', Néni sounded remote. 'I stood there in the empty hall and wondered what had happened to my mother.'

'And where was she?' my mistress asked again. She was determined to help Néni ease her grief.

'Most of the patients had been sent home. They were waiting for me to discharge Mother.'

'What?' my mistress was incredulous. 'Why were they discharging people?'

'The whole wing had to close down; shortage of money.'

'Before even diagnosing the patients?'

'They said they had done all the tests, and found nothing wrong with Mother.'

'What?' My mistress expostulated again.

'Yes, they had already put her in the discharge room.'

'And this was from where you heard her answering you?'

'I don't know now. Was it her, or was I imagining it? You see, Zsuzsi, once I found myself standing in that empty room, I lost all my bearings.'

'Oh, how dreadful!' My mistress groaned.

'The worst was when they said there was nothing wrong with her. It was just blood pressure.'

'And the stroke?'

'The blood pressure was excessively high, and the blood flow got blocked, the brain went out of function.' She took a deep sigh.

'And the treatment?'

'She would need some therapy, and they'd arrange for it. But where was she to go? I asked them pointedly.'

'Yes, which hospital?' My mistress repeated.

'I could claim the free ambulance service for moving her to other places, if I needed it. Or keep her at home, they said.'

'Home?'

'Yes, they wanted me to take her home and look after her.'

'How could you?'

'That's what I said to them. I had a full-time job, I said. I'm away most of the day. Who is to look after her when I am away to work?'

'What did they say?'

'That I'd have to make arrangements with friends or hire carers. And that was it, they wouldn't say more. "The ambulance is ready to take her home", were their final words.' Néni stopped as if there was nothing more to relate.

The dog across the road started to bark. I could hear a vehicle chugging away outside. I got up to see what was up. A hospital van was standing there. The men had gone in to bring the patient out. Some old people were sitting inside, all looking very resigned. I had seen the van many times before, but today it looked different. The dog stopped barking.

'It's unbelievable what's happening to this country.' My mistress broke the silence.

'The old socialist security is gone, Zsuzsi. Now it's full-fledged capitalism. Everything is put out to privatisation.'

'It's frightening.'

'Taking mother home was like carting a dead carcass around. Mother knew what was happening. She looked at the nurses with pleading eyes. They hardly understood what she was asking them. She turned the empty stare on me. I knew what she was asking. All I could do was to communicate to her in unspoken words that I would if need be.'

'Oh, Néni,' were the only words my mistress could say.

Néni took a deep sigh, 'What else could I do, Zsuzsi? I accepted that it was the end, and got working on getting leave from work.' My mistress nodded. 'But then something else happened. One should be thankful for small mercies. In the end it was a private nursing home that came to my rescue.' While Néni was speaking I saw two men across the road, helping an old woman to the van. It didn't seem an easy job. The family members let them do it.

'Private nursing homes in this country?'

'Yes, Zsuzsi. It's known as "Changes and Choices".' There was bitterness in Néni's voice.

'How did you find out?'

'You know Kati, Illyés Kati in the department?'

'Yes, yes', my mistress nodded.

'Fortunately she heard about my leave and came to me. She said there was a nursing home in my district.'

'Oh, istenem!' The dog outside was barking again.

'Yes, right under my nose.'

'How did she know about it?'

'She was trying to get her ill father in somewhere.' People sitting in the van were greeting the old woman.

'What's happened to her father?'

'He's a terminal case now. She was running around, looking for a place for him. Someone told her of this home. But she couldn't get him in because she lives in another district.' The van was moving away now. The son of the ill woman closed the gates behind it.

'And you are in the same district,' my mistress had worked out.

'Yes, and would pay only minimum charges. I couldn't believe my luck.'

'Good for you, but don't fall for it. It's a come-on, Néni. Once we are used to privatisation, it will become as expensive as gold dust.'

'I know, I know. But it did seem a blessing at that time - only two weeks ago', Vera Néni's voice broke. The dog was still there, looking up and down the road. Then it saw me in the window, and gave a string of barks.

'Oh, Néni.'

'It was as if she went to hospital to die,' Néni sobbed. I couldn't bark back. The dog looked baffled.

'Poor Néni.'

'Still it was good,' Vera Néni wiped her eyes. 'They were very human.'

'What did you have to do?' I went back to the sofa, and sat down at Vera Néni's feet.

'I called the number; they said they would take her in, but not for another two days. I had no choice. But those two days were terrible. Mother just lay there, looking at me with a steady gaze, never saying a word. But I knew what she was asking. "I would, if I could, Mother".' I began to change my position.

'Would you have?' my mistress said softly.

'It would have been kinder. She was in great pain, Zsuzsi. Something needed to have been done.'

'It must have been terrible for you. In a way, it was better to have her in the nursing home.'

'Now I see,' Néni's voice hit a note of enlightenment, 'why in the end she became willing to be admitted.'

'Why?'

'It was easier for her to execute her plan there than at home. Yes, that was it. She didn't want to implicate me. Oh, Zsuzsi, that was just like her.'

'You haven't said what it was.'

'Once she was in the nursing home, she took her life in her own hands and stopped eating. Do you see?' My mistress didn't know what she was supposed to say. 'And I let her do it, which I couldn't have done at home.'

'I see.' My mistress waited to hear more.

'There they immediately put her on the drip, but her resistance to it was so great that it had no effect on her. All that time I kept mum. You are the only one I am telling, Zsuzsi. I have to tell someone, otherwise I'll go mad with guilt.'

'There's no guilt involved, Néni. You did what she wanted you to.'

'It was over in two days. She died peacefully, simply sank into oblivion.'

A silence fell. Even I didn't move. They had exhausted all words, and now there was nothing more for them to say. I felt my mistress's hand go over my back, ruffling my coat, and I quietly arched my back up to her, letting her know that I was grateful for her reassurance. Then the telephone rang and my mistress jumped up. While she was talking on the phone, I licked Néni's feet, and when she responded I stood up and put my head in her lap, making faint noises in my throat. I wanted her to know that I had heard everything and knew how she felt.

'Let's eat something, Néni. I have made cabbage soup. Something hot to warm up on.' She got up and Néni followed her. I waited for my little snack since I had had my main meal in the morning. We were all in need of some nourishment. Concern for old age, illness and death had exhausted our nerves. Grief had drained us of energy. After tucking into my snack, I stretched out to have a few winks.

I was woken up by Vera Néni's voice. It was dark outside, but her voice sounded even darker. I could sense fear in it. What could they be talking about now? I looked at their plates. They were having coffee and desert. At least an hour must have gone by.

'Did she ever call you, Zsuzsi?' Vera Néni's voice was searching for something. It was abrupt and afraid of the answer.

'Call? Who?'

'Mother. Did she call you in the last month, some time?'

'No', she said, thinking hard, 'No, I don't think so. Why?'

Vera Néni waited. Something was going to come out, I thought. I could feel my ears going up. 'Because, Zsuzsi, she called many relatives to complain about me.'

'What? What complaint?'

'She told her sister that I wasn't looking after her properly.' She was hovering over what she really wanted to say. I stood up.

'But it wasn't true, was it?'

'No, how could it be? Really, Zsuzsi, I am not praising myself, but no one could have looked after their mother as I did.'

'I don't doubt it, Néni. What is it that's worrying you?'

'So why did she say it to people?' I waited.

'It doesn't matter now, Néni, does it?'

'But people might think....'

'Forget the people, Néni. They don't matter.'

'Listen to me. Do you know what she said to people?' She was about to say it. I was tense. 'That I was trying to poison her.' There it was out. My mistress was stunned.

'See, it does matter.' Suddenly the agitation was gone out of Néni's voice. But she still wanted to know, 'Why did she say that, Zsuzsi?'

My mistress had recovered from the shock, and was once again trying to put Néni's mind at rest. 'She must have got confused. You told me that she wanted you to poison her. Didn't you say that?' The question left Néni speechless. She was aghast at my mistress's directness. My mistress went on, 'Poor woman wanted to die in a dignified way, instead of being carted around from hospital to hospital and put on drips, and seeing the whole system of care and medical assistance collapse in this country. She would have kissed the hand of the person who would have put a pinch of poison on her tongue.'

A shiver ran down my back. I was too familiar with that gesture. When I am ill, this is exactly how my mistress gives me medicine. She holds open my jaw and puts a tablet on my tongue, pushes it further down into my gullet, then closes my jaw, rubbing my neck at the same time to make sure the tablet goes down and is not thrown out. As she releases her grip on my jaw, I kiss her hand gratefully. Could she have been thinking of me when she said that? She looked at me; and sensing my fear, blew me a kiss to calm my troubled thoughts.

'Yes, but why confuse me with her own wish?'

'Perhaps, to provoke you into doing that.'

'It was terrible when people rang up to tell me that.'

'Why upset yourself for others' stupidity? They had no business to call you. Such callous people.' My mistress is rarely angry.

'No, Zsuzsi, they were trying to protect me. Suppose somebody had reported it to the police. They would have arrested me. Who would have looked after her then?'

'You would have. Because the police wouldn't have believed an old woman.'

'I wish I had spoken to you before,' Néni said quietly. 'I was in agony all those days when people kept on ringing up to tell me what mother had said to them. I would cry and think: this is what I get for wearing myself out and looking after her - social disgrace.'

'Be honest, Néni, you would have done it, if you could have brought yourself to it. If you love someone, you wouldn't hesitate to put them out of their misery, would you?'

I gave out a sharp bark, not happy with what she had said.

'You are thinking of pets, Zsuzsi,' Vera Néni said in a calm but sure tone. 'Doing it to human beings is not right. I know there is much in the air about euthanasia and all that, but I wouldn't play god with anyone. I did keep silent while my mother fasted herself to death, but I would not have poisoned her knowingly. No, that wouldn't have been right, Zsuzsi.'

By this time I too was ready to tell off my mistress how wrong and careless she was in her statement. I got up and moved about restlessly, knocking into my plate and spilling the water all over the place. My mistress scolded me and told me to return to my place, but she knew that it was a protest gesture from me. What she said next showed she understood me.

'You are right, Néni. I was speaking carelessly. Our control over animals misleads us to thinking we can do the same to human beings.' Good, I thought, at least she regrets her reckless comment. Vera Néni's belief and my protest made her retract. I could now return to my nap.

When I woke up, Vera Néni was gone, and the house was silent. My mistress was deep in a book.

†

13

OLD MAN WINTER

‡

It was now into the third week of January and everybody was getting fed up of the winter. The snowfall had been heavy this year. If everyone was complaining of still having to wear many layers of winter clothing, I was growling no less at having to spend most of my day in the small kennel. There was no way out of winter, I reasoned with myself, except time itself. One just had to make the best of whatever was there. Moreover, I reminded myself that the end of January means the beginning of Spring. So, when my mistress broke the news of our going to the farsang on Saturday, I cheered myself up to no end. The radio announced that there would be a carnival in the centre with a special winter chase on the Lánchíd. Oh, that wonderful bridge with its two grand arches - more like city gates - the pride of Budapestens.

They always talk about its clever technology, how it was built way back in the nineteenth century and how it linked the two separate towns of Buda and Pest; to my ears they seem to pun on 'lánc' and 'link'. I too admire this wonderful bridge and love to walk across it; it has a magic of its own. So I knew in order to get to Lánchíd, one had to go through the city - always my mistress took a longer route on such occasions – travelling by tram across the Duna over Margithíd. On one side, one saw the river divide into two to skirt round Margit sziget, and on the other side, one looked across to Lánchíd itself. The view always enthralled me; I made sure I stood by the door and did not miss anything by looking at both sides alternately.

So when my mistress broke the news to me that we were going to the Winter Carnival that Saturday, I felt cheered up. She tickled me in the ribs and said how lucky I was to be there to watch Old Man Winter being chased out by winter-weary people. Oh, happy, happy pagan minds who invented rituals that linked the living with Nature, and played chasing games with the seasons. To be on Lánchíd at any time with the Duna flowing below is a treat for me, but this was going to be the real thing, I concluded.

On the Saturday I was up early and waited outside my kennel for my mistress. She emerged from the house, in bright clothes, singing cheerful greetings, and we set out for the Lánchíd. Soon we saw lots of people going in the same direction. It seemed the whole city was heading for the bridge. Dressed in fancy costumes, and carrying animal masks, some with animals painted on their faces, they looked a happy crowd. I too had to have my mask, not to conceal my identity but to announce it. So I was all muzzled up and put on a leash as the law decrees for all dogs in Budapest. Although I hated to wear it, over the years I had got used to it, especially as without its clamp there would be no outings for me.

The journey to Lánchíd is long by public transport, at least three changes, but I didn't mind. The more the merrier, I thought. Yet most unreasonably when my mistress took the tram no. 6, I felt disappointed. I would have liked to go by the Metro, so I could see the old ladies who in this season sit in the entrance selling Spring flowers. They pick them in the morning, bending over the still damp earth and then tie them up in bunches and lay them out neatly in their baskets to sell them and make a few forints. I was looking forward to going past them and sniffing the scent of the early Spring from the woods. But now I wouldn't be able to see the first snowdrops all snuggled up in their green leaves and held out to rushing commuters. Well, I thought, dogs don't have a say in things. Maybe, I'll have another outing in late Spring and see bunches of bluebells instead, placed in the same baskets. To put myself in a happier frame of mind, I reminded myself of the journey over the Margithíd, and the fun of changing to tram no.2.

Lánchíd was crowded with people fully clad with winter wear, gloves and hats. Though the sun was shining - as it usually does in our city, bless it - they looked cold and chilled. People were trying to keep themselves warm. Many were moving from one foot to the other to keep their circulation moving, some were doing it by singing and others by blowing on their hands. And all were waiting for the fun to begin. Misrule is the pulse of carnivals. Masked and costumed, men lead a riotous protest against Old Man Winter who was refusing to go, even though he had outlived his time.

Everyone waited for the signal which would tell them to go into a collective attack on him with sticks and stones.

Suddenly a loud cheer went up; I pricked up my ears and craned my neck to see what was happening. The chase was to begin from the Buda end where the city woods are and where wild animals live. The crowd stirred with expectation and the piggy-backed children rocked excitedly on their dads' shoulders. I had my eyes fixed where the bridge began, determined not to miss anything. And there it was, a moving column of human bodies with animal faces. For a moment, anger hit me in my guts. How dare humans pretend they know what animals are! But the feeling passed and I reminded myself that I had as little to do with wild animals as did humans. I too did not know what it was like being a beast of the forest. A feeling of betrayal came over me, and made me brood over my sad state of being neither an animal nor human.

What a roar! It shook me out of my brooding. It soared higher than the chains that held the bridge. Animal calls rose into the sky. The brayings of the boars, hogs, deer and foxes filled the air. Excitement all round. I wanted to set up joyful barks but the muzzle prevented me from joining in the fun. The animals were charging down the whole span of the bridge at a great speed, making fearsome noises. I could see their faces clearly as they went past us. A sensation of recognition ran through me. And now they broke into a riot, in pursuit of something running ahead of them. A volley of human abuses and blood-thirsty animal calls were being hurled at this invisible enemy flying before them. People beat their feet to terrorise the fleeing enemy, bursting into a most gutsy song and clapping their hands as loudly as they could.

Old Man Winter, go away now,
We love snow, fires and glow,
but too long you stay, go away today.

Chorus:
Go away, go away, too long you stay.

Spring is here, buds and leaves.
White is pure but green the tree,
So, why don't you flee.

Chorus
Yes, why don't you flee, flee, flee away now.

Old Man Winter, go sleep in a cave.
Wake up next year, we'll see you again,
We'll wait for you but now go away.

Chorus
Oi, now, now, Old Man Winter, go away, go away.

The 'go away, go away' chant stabilised the mock aggression. Earlier, the chase was accompanied by abusive words and rude gestures. I was much happier with the song, which was chorused over and over. I too hummed it under my breath, moving my body, and swishing my tail rapidly, keeping the beat in the air. When it came to the end people shouted 'Once again', 'Once again'. So, the masked figures walked back to the starting-line and did another chase. The crowd was beside itself, and sang even louder; I too went faster with my movements. My mistress looked at me as she sang; she bent down and running her hand down my back, synchronised my body movements with the rhythm. She knew I too was telling Old Man Winter to go away, so that I could lie in the sun on the terrace and forget all the sad thoughts that sometimes come over me.

But all good things come to an end, and soon the atmosphere started to dampen down. The masks were removed and revealed ordinary human faces behind them, laughing and waving at the cheering crowd. They were now passing us, holding the animal masks in their hands. I had a closer look at the shapes and faces of animals on the masks, and felt a twitch in my throat. Was anyone of my kind in those heads? How was I ever to know if there are beings like me up in the hills? I must find out one day. It would be good to have a glimpse of the place my ancestors may have inhabited in some remote past. I had never felt this longing before, a distinct sensation ran through my body.

An announcement was being made now about the awards for the best costumes and masks, to be given out at a special ceremony later in Vörösmarty Tér. Everyone began to leave, chatting, humming and whistling the chant. I was still in the grip of the strange longing that had swept over me, when my mistress gave me a tug to come along, saying we were dropping in at Vera Néni's. 'Let's go and give her the news of the farsang', she said ruffling my ears. I tried to shake myself out of my thoughts. 'Poor Vera Néni, she's not well, we'll cheer her up, sing her the Old Man Winter song, shall we, drágám?' She whistled the tune and I managed to gather a rumble in my throat from behind the bars of the muzzle. Anyway, visiting Néni, I decided, would be exciting, even if the smell of old age and death hung there along with the real cobwebs.

So we trundled along to Vera Néni's who didn't live far off from the bridge. The Duna was at a low ebb. Even from above, it looked a bit chilled. It must also want the Spring, I thought. More sun, more water from the melting of the snow. Do rivers have memory? Would Spring-time bring back memories of old times when there were no dams to hinder, limit or divert its natural inclination? Do we ever remember what it was really like before? Thoughts were rushing on like the awaited thaw. Another tug at the leash and I knew I wasn't being fast enough.

†

⋮

14

SPRING CARNIVAL

‡

Well, much as poor Old Man Winter had got chased out of the woods, there was no sign of the winter ending, thick snow still sprawled everywhere. But common wisdom assures one that change is built into time, and that seasons follow one another. I also knew that the date of the Busójárás, the Spring Carnival, that year fell on March 1st. So I sat on the terrace waiting for the snow to start melting. Its solid look put it beyond doubt that it wasn't going to melt despite the folk festival that proclaimed the end of winter. Going to the farsang made me want to see the Busójárás, as in a natural cycle the ending of one season makes the beginning of another.

One day I heard my mistress talking on the phone. She was promising to take someone to see the Spring Carnival in the historic town of Mohács. Hearing the exciting news, I couldn't help letting a booming rumble escape my throat. It made her look my way, where I was sitting listening to her conversation, all very tensed up wanting to know if I was included in the trip. She indicated to me that I would be going along too. I was about to break out in a display of excitement when she put her finger to her mouth, signalling to me not to make a nuisance of myself and to go out at once. I sat on looking at her, wanting to know more. Then I heard her say we would be going by boat. This was too good a news to sit still on. So, I rushed out on to the terrace and bounced around to work off my excitement. 'All depending on the weather', were the last words I caught on the way out.

And would you believe it, the next day, the weather took a turn. More snow started to fall. My heart sank. First it was slow, but soon it worked itself into thick blinding sheets. A record fall for some decades, the weather forecast announced. It continued to fall for two full days, bringing everything to a halt. The radio blared at all times about the traffic jams and many cars and people stranded on the road. When my mistress didn't get back from work by her usual time, I got anxious. Was she stuck somewhere? Had her car failed? Would she get some help? I couldn't stop imagining the worst. As night fell I got nervous and jittery and feared I might have an attack. What would I do if something happened to her? I couldn't help thinking of myself. More hours went by, still no sign of her. It was quite late in the night when at last I saw her at the gate. I was beside myself with relief and jumped up on her to lick her face and tell her how relieved I was to see her. I made it difficult for her to get into the house. She rubbed my back and assured me she was fine and now home, safe and sound. At last I calmed down, left her to feed herself and went to my own kennel.

As I was falling asleep I kept on opening my eyes to see if the snow was abating. You see, my mind was on one thing only - the trip to Mohács to see the Spring Festival. There was still time, I calculated. The snow could be gone within a week, and we still had two weeks to March 1st.

I was ready for sleep after fretting for hours over my mistress's safety, but what with the howling wind and the snow flurries lashing around and the constant barking of the dog next door, I didn't think I was going to get much sleep. Between waking and dozing I was asking myself why do we dogs bark for everything - whether it's joy or anger or fear, it's always the same. It was early dawn when I finally gave up waiting for sleep and sat up looking out to see if the world had changed since last night. No, the snow was still there, still falling and gave no sign of letting up. Not good news, I admitted reluctantly. And as if in confirmation of my own prediction, I saw the snow-plough go up the road, flashing its light and heaving against the thick snow. It always started early before people set out for work. This was it then, I concluded. It meant more snow was coming. Well, so be it, I thought, and lay down. There was no point in fighting the elements. I settled down to the winter routine of waiting for the snow-plough to come past our gate. I knew the driver. He always whistled at me and I made sure I ran to the gate and gave him the seasonal welcome. I like to keep up contact with familiar faces. It lifts the greyness of life. I looked up and saw the house chimneys sending out thick gusts of smoke, an indication that waking and work do not stop, whatever the weather.

The sun rose and shone but couldn't budge the snow. It felt cold too. I worked out it must be not above -5 degrees centigrade, and it continued to be around that for the whole week. There was a constant activity of people clearing the pavements and their drives. Many went on ski trips. I saw cars loaded with ski equipment and also families with children pulling toboggans and heading for the hills. The house chimneys gushed out yet more smoke, and front windows along the road constantly reflected the flickering blue of television sets. Why not? I thought. People have to find their own way to survive the elements. I too was trying to come to accept the fact that most probably there wouldn't be a trip to Mohács.

Then on the eighth day, a thaw began. The temperature went up in the night and by the morning one heard occasional sounds of plopping as chunks of snow fell off telephone wires. As the wind blew, the trees shook and shed much of the snow resting on their branches. My ears went flip, flip the whole time. The air was full of the sounds of the thaw. I listened to every plop, every stir alive around me. That night, in my deep sleep, I heard a gurgle outside our gate. I woke up, and immediately knew the snow was turning into water. By the morning the sound got louder. It was like listening to a river leaving its source up in the mountains. In me too a whisper was growing distinct. Mohács! Mohács. Good, we can now go to Mohács. There was still a week to go, I counted, enough time for all this to clear. I was thankful that the temperature had not gone down so low as to leave the Duna frozen for long. To confirm my calculations, my mistress patted me that evening, and said she'd better start making arrangements for the trip as the weather was going to be good the following week.

Well, believe it or not, we were on the way to Mohács five days later! The snow was completely gone. I thought Old Man Winter must be in his cave now, if not yet sleeping. My mistress was ready with some snacks and wine for the journey. Our guest was to meet us on the Duna strand, where the hired boat was waiting for us. From home we set out very early by car. I sat in the back, my head right out of the window to feel the morning breeze and the early sun on my face, but also to show off to the passers-by that we were going on a special trip. The guest, a young man from Vienna, was already there, waiting for us. He befriended me right away. But I was wary of responding to people too quickly, especially the male acquaintances of my mistress. It was good to keep my distance until I was sure of what her feelings were towards anyone.

We boarded the boat immediately and it pulled out without losing any time. We were away. Here was the Duna, spread out before us. I was all eyes and nose. We stood out on the deck, although it was not warm by any means. My mistress and the guest were well wrapped up as it felt more cold on the water. Fortunately, my animal body remained free of any need for extra coverings. My mistress was telling her guest about the battle of Mohács, and how the Magyars were utterly routed by the Turks. The battle of Mohács, she said, was the watershed of Hungarian history. I waited to hear about the Busójárás, but the guest kept on asking questions about the Turks in Hungary. I gave up in the end and looked to the river where far more interesting things were happening. There were ships and boats and barges moving up and down from Budapest. I would have liked to know from where else they had come and to where they were going, but my mistress was saying nothing about them. So I turned to thinking about other things. I watched for the bend of the Duna, of which I had heard so much, but when it didn't come and we had sailed long enough, I concluded we were going in the other direction, down the river instead of up. Now I could see how straight and pointed the course of the river was, unbending and undiverted.

My eyes were quickly moving from one bank to another. The surroundings had changed many times: from industrial to fenland, to farmland and to high hills, quite dense at times. Twice I caught sight of deer in the fields, just standing and watching things, and once I saw two of them bounding away into the hills. Why is it, I wondered, they could go wherever they wanted and I had to be looked after for everything? Something wasn't right there. But I didn't get any answers, much as I dwell on these matters from time to time. Was I suffering from the national trait of Hungarians - *Kutya a baj*?

I was so engrossed in the wonders of the passing landscape that I was startled by my mistress's announcement that we had arrived at Mohács. Hours must have gone by, yet it seemed we had barely started from Budapest. I quickly took up my place at the railing, not wanting to miss anything coming into view. The Duna was quite wide here.

'Oh, look, the *busók!*' my mistress pointed, 'in the boat, can you see them rowing, that boat over there, coming from the other bank?' She was keen to make sure her guest did not miss seeing these Dionysiac figures. I pressed further against the railing to make sure I didn't lose my look-out place to him. What made it difficult to locate the boat was that the passengers hardly looked like people. Looking more closely, I saw that the figures were wearing big masks, which were supporting a complex set of horns. There were at least twenty busók, looking strange and grotesque in their masks, especially against the waters. There was something unreal about the boat, it looked as if it was coming from the unknown. Then I heard the clinking of bells, the sort you associate with farm-oxen returning from a hard day's labour. It was strange to hear the sound bouncing off the waters.

My mistress was explaining that this was the ritual entry of the busók as they are supposed to come from the Underworld. Our boat had stopped so as not to disturb the ritual. We could see the busók clearly now as the boat went past us heading for the shore.

A big noise went up. It came from the Mohács side. I looked and saw the bank full of people. They must be the people of Mohács, I thought, waiting for the busók to arrive, bringing with them all that Mohács needed for the Spring. There was so much excitement and expectation in the crowd. I noticed a lot of them were wearing masks and costumes and using rattlers to announce their welcome at the ritualistic arrival of the busók. They were also holding a long three-pronged pole, the sort Poseidon, the Greek ocean-god, carries. I remembered Nagyanya's stories of pagan gods. The boat was now almost there and preparing to moor itself. People broke out into a song as the busók disembarked. One would have thought gods themselves had descended amidst humans.

We had a very good view of their landing and the people going into a frenzy about it. I could also see the busók more clearly now. Mostly tall, they were wearing the traditional countryside dress of white broad-bottomed cotton trousers, trimmed with lace. I sympathised with them, knowing how vulnerable human limbs are in the elements, but soon I detected long-johns peeping through at the edges! At least the upper half of their bodies were covered in long tunics of goat fleece, which gave their masks quite an authentic look. Their horns were big and of different shapes: straight up, tightly curled, hugely twisted and spread out, and all in red and black. The illusion of so many goats maa-maa'ing brought out the herding bark in me, which made me wonder if I had a bit of the shepherd dog also in me, apart from the Gypsy food-gatherer. The people presented the long three-pronged pole to the busók, and immediately I understood what they were - spades to dig and turn the earth and make it fertile. Did Poseidon use his to dig the bottomless ocean?

And now amidst lots of bell-ringing and rattle-sounding and maa-maa'ing, a procession was being formed. The crowd now turned right round and proceeded to the city, with the busók in the lead. It was a marvellous sight for which I had waited since January. At last I was among the goats that are supposed to take over the cold wintry malaise and get you worked up into a frenzy of activity. It was like being in a dream, where all things happen. I was dying to join them.

My mistress got our own boat anchored and we disembarked to follow the crowd. Of course, I had to submit to the muzzle at once. But what did it matter if my mouth was bound, my mind and feelings were free and perceiving. I was in Mohács at a pagan ritual of ploughs and earth and horns and dangling bells, and the bleating of goats replacing human speech. It was an uplifting experience. I pulled at the lead to tell my mistress to keep up with the crowd moving fast ahead. We started to follow them, but she was still slow and we lost sight of the procession. She was looking at the programme to find out what events were taking place. A reception was being held in front of the Városháza, where the mayor and other city officials would be making the opening speeches. No point in going there, she declared, we don't want to listen to politicians. So, that's where everyone was going. I wasn't happy at the decision but I had no choice, although I sulked to let her know that. So now we proceeded at a slower pace and looked around at the street and the stalls. We were going past food and drink stalls where the owners were setting up the tables and mulling wine in big pots. 'Let's stop here; we need to warm up', she said suddenly. 'Let's have some food and hot wine, shall we?' she said to her companion, and then whistling to me, 'This way, drágám.' That was it, I gave up. The procession was disappearing from sight. Well, I thought, since I'm being deprived of the fun, I am not going to be compliant.

My mistress suggested they sit down at a table and order some wine. The smoke was rising from roasting and grilling, live with the smell of the fat being poured on the meat. A huge black pan was ready with grilled black sausages, sizzling fatty pork, chicken pieces and kebabs - ah, Turkish food! It was making me crazy with hunger. When the wine arrived in big plastic glasses for them and nothing for me, I decided to kick up a fuss. I jumped up and put my big paws on the table, almost knocking the drinks over, indicating that I needed a drink too. 'Get down, at once,' my mistress commanded. I did but then back I went again, persistently. This happened two or three times, until she realised I meant to have some wine and there was no point in trying to cow me down. The stall-keepers were greatly amused; I was certainly providing some entertainment. A bowl of steaming wine was laid out for me, my muzzle removed and everyone stood watching to see how I would drink it. The wine-drinking dog would be a story told by many. I went around the bowl a few times, estimating the temperature of the wine. It didn't take long for the steam to cool down; so I went for a first lap-up. The crowd clapped. My mistress was laughing and her guest was very amused at my eccentric ways. After that it was a matter of lap lap, and soon the wine was gone. Another round of clapping, and I sat down, proud of my feat, and aptly vindicated.

My mistress now turned to her guest and suggested they have some lunch while the crowds were still busy in the square. He admitted he was quite hungry. He chose a plate of mixed meats, and she black sausage and mustard. They ordered bread too. She then looked at me and brought out my food tin, smiling and cajoling me with the pictures on it. Oh, no, I thought to myself, I am not letting her get away with that. It's the animal day and less than real animal food will not be acceptable to me. So I gave her a very cool look, not responding to her baby-talk. Not taking notice of me, she dished out the food from the tin. I paid no attention to it. When their food came, up I jumped in protest and put my paws up, shaking the table with my weighty complaint.

'No, your food is there, now don't be naughty.' She was not going to give way this time.

We'll see, I murmured to myself. I kicked over the bowl and spilled the food and then back at the table, stood up on two legs, with the front two on the table itself. The sequence was repeated again. The stall-keepers laughed and waited to see if this was the day they would watch a dog eat black sausage and mustard. And it was. The battle between my mistress and I ended with a bowl of black sausage and mustard and fatty pieces of traditional pork being put before me. Everyone stood around, watching me start the demanded meal. As I tucked into the mustardy sausages and started to devour them with relish, there was a burst of loud applause from the watchers. The goats may be horned and vegetarian, but I am hornless and love meat.

After that treat I was ready to lie down and have a sleep, but there was no possibility of that. It seemed the reception in the centre was over; we could hear the rattlers approaching and young people dressed up as fairies and elves were wandering back. My mistress clamped the muzzle on my mouth and we set out to see the Carnival. The whole street was taken over by stalls of local curiosities, ceramics and traditional clothes. The busók were now mingling with the crowd in twos and threes. Their masks looked grotesque and lacked any visible outlets, and left me wondering how they saw their way around. The horns were the things that intrigued me most. Equipped only with ears, I was fascinated by the largeness and fierceness of the horns.

The crowd was growing now, more people were arriving; families, young lovers, and even older people were out and about. Ice creams and candy flosses mixed with the swinging of the rattles and outbursts of 'maa-maa' calls. Sometimes people looked at me, perhaps feeling sorry for my bound mouth, but I wasn't bothered. There was enough sound there without adding dog barks to it. It took us awhile to get to the town square where other activities were going on. The local dance group had just started as we got there. Skirts and aprons and embroidered blouses were twirling around while the boys hopped and kicked high in their long boots and riding trousers. The music was exciting. My mistress was telling her guest how folk culture got an uplift during the communist rule and was given an equal status alongside the classical.

The next dance my mistress told her guest was from the Croatian community. 'Croatians in Hungary?' he was surprised. 'Oh, yes', she enlightened him further, 'there are several ethnic communities in Hungary, with full political and cultural rights.' 'But not in Croatia!' he said ironically. 'Is the Hungarian government taking a stand against the Serbs?' 'Well, it all depends what they get out of it,' my mistress said. I wasn't interested in their discussion. But the man persisted and said, 'Do Gypsies also have full rights?' I waited to hear her reply. It brought back memories of my second day in the house when the veterinary man had declared me as the probable descendant of the original Gypsy dog. 'Oh, yes, but with the Gypsies there are problems of cultural beliefs.' Her remark brought back memories of the Old Lady who had very different views on the Gypsies, and her discussions with the American woman in Balaton who had come to do research on Gypsies.

An announcement was heard that in half an hour there would be a dance by the busók. As if in reply to it, horse carts started to arrive with busók walking along them. The drivers were local men and women dressed up in fancy clothes. The carts varied in their decor. Some had vineyard decor: the canopies of the carts were trimmed with plastic grapevines, over the wheels hung huge-sized wine bottles and troughs and drinking bowls; others displayed Dionysiac symbols with wine jars, horns and testicle-shapes hanging from the sides and knocking against the clinking bells next to them; then there were others which came loaded with agricultural tools, with three-pronged spades hooked on to the side of the cart. I was puzzled by the significance of the three-prongedness of the tool. What could it mean?

In looking around I spotted a huge bonfire in the middle which was to be lit in the evening for the torch-light dance by the busók. I don't like big fires; they make me anxious. So I hoped my mistress wouldn't decide to stay on into the evening. While I was dwelling on my reaction to ritual fires I saw some busók walk to the centre and set something up. Next moment there was a very big bang. It filled the place with smoke and smell which got everyone coughing. I got frightened by the noise and slunk back to my mistress, who assured me all was well and patted me a few times.

Suddenly a sound of stamping ran along the ground, as if the place was about to be invaded. Some thirty horned goats were gathering on the south side. The illusion of the busók being goats was quite real, although everyone knows goats don't walk on two feet. It was the way the busók walked, slow and swaying, and the way the painted eyes on their masks were so still and staring that the illusion of thinking of them as goats persisted. Maybe, under the thin veneer, humans are no different from animals.

People started to arrive from all directions. The word had gone round that the busók dance was starting shortly. I made a move to go to the front row to get a better view as being on my fours reduces my height by far against any human, even a child. Since I'm not one of those ferocious big dogs – thanks to the Old Lady's persistence in showing me the mirror -

people allowed me to go to the front, which meant that my mistress and her guest were also given way to follow me. It made me feel good to get them a privileged place.

A hushed silence fell on the crowd before another lot of fire-crackers were let off, making a big shattering noise and filling the square again with clouds of smoke. At the same time, through the haze was heard a steady clinking of bells, signalling that the dance was beginning. As the smoke cleared, a large column of busók came into view. Looking strangely grotesque with their large bodies swaying to the clinking bells, and the huge horns balancing on their heads, their faces hidden behind equally grotesque masks, they advanced in a slow and measured way. I couldn't take my eyes off them; they were not like real goats, light and nervous and vulnerable. These things were heavy and meant to do what they had come for. The illusion of their being goats which I had felt earlier had vanished, but the reality still remained illusory.

My thoughts were rung out by a louder clinking of bells. As I looked the bulky figures were twirling around and swaying their bodies so that the bells hanging from their leather belts were making a voluminous sound, announcing their arrival. But I soon realised that the belts looked more like penises, with mock testicles backing them. With the three-pronged forks lifted high in one hand and the other hand dropping on their fronts with aplomb, they shook the bells furiously, moving their limbs in a jerky fashion. A ready laughter from the crowd greeted their action. As the bells sounded louder, the busók bodies began to lift and move faster. I began to feel the same rhythm in my body. This went on for a while. People watched without moving. At last they gave a flourish to the forks – ah! penises in action! - and brought them down, staking them into the ground, pushing them in harder with repetitive movements. People broke out into loud clapping and laughed uproariously.

What happened next was more curious. The busók started to go round their staked tridents, as if they were some sort of totems, jumping and landing in a trance-like manner. I felt gripped by a hysterical sensation, as if a force was about to erupt out of me. My body had no will of its own. Inwardly it was imitating the dance. I became so oblivious of my surroundings that when a noise rose in the air I had difficulty in remembering where I was.

The carriages which had been parked on the side were waiting for this moment. It was the wheels that had made the sound as they got into action. The carriages were now entering the arena. Driven by beautiful young maidens, they added a new dimension to the ritual. The women were dressed in their traditional clothes and scarves, waving and smiling at the onlookers. The carriages circled the arena, before arriving in the centre where the busók were finishing up their totem dance. The maidens took out the wine casks and poured the wine into huge drinking mugs. Looking closer, I detected that the wine casks were shaped like testicles. Everyone noticed and roars of laughter followed. The maidens were now handing the mugs to the busók. How were they going to swig it, wearing such impenetrable masks? Were they going to take them off? I waited. Oh, how slow of me! Of course, the wine was not for drinking but a libation to be poured on the ploughed ground! The busók took the drinking mugs and with a gesture of upward movement, poured the wine over the tridents with an upright flourish. It was a magical sight. The crowd cheered their action with thunderous clapping, mixed with excited laughter. Ho, ho, ho! my jaw too relaxed - as much as it could when held by the muzzle - seeing human ingenuity at inventing what they think is Nature! Oh, clever, clever minds that can create such lovely illusions.

I looked around among the viewers to see how the women were reacting to this very Dionysiac rite. I caught many faces openly laughing, though with a touch of shy reserve. The maidens from the wagons took the mugs back from the busók and put them to their mouths. This was too much. The crowd were beside themselves with laughter and clapping. And now the busók climbed into the wagons, put their arms around the maidens and waving at the crowd, rode around the circle once, before exiting on the south side, from where they had entered an hour before.

I was still experiencing the strange sensations the ritual had excited in me when I saw the people dispersing. What a restless crowd, I thought irritably. Can't they be still for long enough to finish a good experience nicely? 'Come on, szívem, it's over', my mistress said, giving a pull at the leash. 'That was fantastic', the man said, 'I haven't seen anything like this before'. 'Oh, good, I'm glad it was worth your coming all the way', my mistress sounded pleased. 'What next'? the man was ready for another ritual. 'Nothing much, really', she replied, looking at the programme, 'more traditional dancing, some folk music and some story-telling and that's all, really.' 'It's a pity', he said regretfully. My mistress was quick to point out, 'It's coming to 4 now, and if by 5 we don't start back, I can't be certain what time we'd get to Budapest.' 'Hmm. Well, it can't be helped then', he said, relinquishing his desire to see more. 'How about just having a quick look at the place where the Battle of Mohács actually took place?' I was wrong, he didn't mean to give up so easily. 'Just a quick glimpse of it?' he asked, persisting. 'Sorry, not possible. The site is outside the city. I'm not even sure if it's the original place.' Even though I too would have liked to visit the battleground and put a face on my history lessons, I was still glad that my mistress wasn't going to chase history, not after the wonders we had just watched.

So, greatly relieved at the prospect of not trooping around to catch the dust raised by the Turkish and Magyar horses four hundred years before, I was ready to head for the boat. Tracking back the same way, strangely enough, I found nothing to interest me. Not even the food stalls, nor the startling rattlers, not even the fun-making youngsters. My imagination was still in the grip of the astonishing ritual of horns, forks and bells. The event was over, but I was sure my mind would weave it into dreams. So, on the journey back, I planned to head straight down for the lower deck and sleep. Not even the sights of the Duna would keep my eyes open.

†

15

SPRING MATING

‡

There were clear signs of Spring everywhere. All the snow was gone, pavements no longer slippery, the air much fresher, and the light on the increase with each day of the calendar. The days too were becoming longer. The trees were beginning to break into bud. Soon the leaves would be opening out, I mused, shimmering and shining as the breeze ruffled them. Once again, the world would change beyond recognition. It was time it did, I thought, as I moved out onto the terrace. Who would want to stay indoors, or even in the kennel, cosy as it might be, when such loveliness pervaded the world outside? And the warmth of the sun was just what I needed.

One morning - I think it was the day after the radio had announced the first day of the Spring - my mistress, as she was leaving for work, bent down and stroked me affectionately and said, 'Now, you be good, drágám; don't let the Spring season run away with your good sense.' This was not her normal parting shot. So, what was on? I wagged my tail and licked her hand, although I didn't get the drift of her remark. I got up and followed her to the gate, making the usual noises at her leaving. I always do that, every morning. I never like to have her out of my sight. The thought 'She is going now, will I ever see her again?' always bothered me. She shut the gate behind her. I stuck my nose through the bars of the gate and watched her drive away. The road was empty now. I returned to my chosen spot against the wall and sprawled out in the sun. It was wonderful to feel the warmth seep into my body after months of cold weather.

I was half dozing when I heard a commotion up the street. Nothing new, I thought, the dogs must be barking at someone passing their gates. Not worth getting excited about. I told myself to stay put. But soon I became aware of something unusual. Instead of the usual barking bouts from various dog quarters, the sound of a collective squealing was in the air. Ah, here we go! I smiled, understanding my mistress's remark at last. Spring and mating arrive together, I should have remembered. Trees may remain quiet as they burst and sprout in the new season, but not dogs. They must squeal and whimper as the sweet agony of sex takes hold of them. The squealing now was growing every minute, but overlapping with it came a woman's voice. This was unusual. The voice was rising above the dog-squeals. Curiosity got the better of me. My tail wagged and I felt a yearning inside me as I leapt up to the gate. Pressing myself against the bars, I craned my neck to see as far up the road as I could.

And there it was - five dogs and a woman were bunched up in the middle of the street. They looked in a real tangle. The dogs were all round the woman and preventing her from walking. What a way to behave! I gave out an angry bark. Why involve a woman in your copulation chase? I was ashamed of my species. Now they were getting closer and I could see that one of the dogs was a bitch - needless to say she must be on heat - and the other four were dogs trying to get near her. All of them were rolling down willy-nilly and coming closer by the second. I could see them more clearly now. The woman was speaking in a foreign tongue as she was desperately trying to shoo them off in a half-frightened, half-commanding tone. But the dogs weren't listening. All their faculties were concentrating on the behind of the bitch who, in turn as it were, was seeking asylum with the woman, now coming in front of her, now rubbing against her legs and stopping her from moving. An Alsatian was ahead of the other three dogs in getting closer to the bitch. Once he almost got on her back, half mounting her. His squeals were becoming more acute with every fresh attempt.

'Go home, doggy, get away from me', the woman was putting a commanding tone into her voice. But since the doggies were showing no sign of leaving her, she thought she could get rid of them by moving across the street. But no, they too moved with her. In fact, the dogs were not following her, they were not even aware of her, their instincts were fixed on the bitch. They went where she went. The woman looked harassed. She began to move about to every part of the street to shake off the amorous pack, but the bitch immediately followed her wherever she went - onto the pavement, back on the road, across the road, to the left of it, to the right of it. It was as if she had signed a protection contract with the woman, and had become her ward.

It looked like a zig-zag game. The Alsatian was still in the lead. The next-in-line was a mixed-breed, keeping up with the leader. The other two dogs, one looking rather shaggy with hair falling helter-skelter over his body, even on his eyes and face, wasn't showing much drive in his movements; the other with a close-shaved skin and long ears was equally ineffective. He seemed more interested in mimicking the others rather than in acquiring the booty for himself. I could do better than him, I thought, scraping my paws on the gate, if only I were on the other side of the fence. Though ahead of all others, the Alsatian wasn't getting anywhere, either. In the meantime the rubbing, pushing and squealing went on as they all continued to roll down the road, like a ball of gathering moss. The cavalcade was now passing my gate. I could see the woman more clearly. I recognised her as the Indian woman living up the other end of the road. I knew about her from a remark by Margit Néni, who was always curious to know about anyone new in our street.

Despite all odds against getting the better of a pack of dogs, the woman hadn't given up trying to make the dogs understand that she wasn't part of their mating-chase. 'Oh, go away, go somewhere else,' was the continual mantra she kept up while making her way down to the main road. I could hear the panic in her tone. Clearly she was shaken at the prospect of the dogs not leaving her at all. They were still waylaying her at every step, trapping her movements and stopping her from reaching the bus-stop. The bitch was determined not to leave her side while at the same time turning and twisting her back to thwart the Alsatian's every attempt to mount her. He'd get her in the end, I could tell. Even I began to feel some excitement generating in me. But it was nothing in comparison with what was happening the other side of the fence. I was more of an on-looker really, I murmured in self-justification of my own little instinctual response.

Now they were outside my gate. I felt a surge of domesticated morality run through me, I heard myself giving out a bark or two in quick succession at my peers to stop them from misbehaving with the woman. But my compassionate defence of her didn't even get noticed. I was embarrassed at not being able to get much attention by my thick, turgid bark. I tried a higher note but still without any effect. The squeals continued and the woman's strange utterances continued to fall on deaf ears. They went past me, moving down towards the main road. I quickly turned my head to follow the action, making sure I got a good angle on the scene. I wanted to know what would happen next. From my position I could see the road and the bus-stop on the corner. By now they had reached the corner, and still nothing had changed.

The woman was looking up the road to see if the bus was coming. Obviously, I thought, the arrival of the bus would be the key to her escape. The cars were whizzing by and the dogs continued to circle round her, the bitch snuggling up to her and now beginning to snarl at the Alsatian. The other dogs were showing signs of frustrated desire. Their movements were becoming more aggressive as they started to compete with the leader. Still no sign of a bus. Then something changed. The woman started to look up and down the road in quick succession. What did she have in mind? Before I could think of something she shot across the road. She has decided to go down to the tram stop, I made a quick guess. Good thinking, I cheered from my post. Like her, I was sure this would trick the pack; they wouldn't follow her across the road. But would you believe it, as she rushed across, so did the rest! And still in the same orbiting, squealing fashion; the bitch hugging the woman's legs, the Alsatian grabbing her back, and the others close behind. I heard myself bark out a volley of abuse at my compatriots. The woman stopped in the middle of the road, stamping and gesticulating furiously at them to return to their side of the road while the cars were whizzing by, honking at her to get the dogs and herself off the road. There was such a din. The woman got to the other side eventually, but so did the rest. The bitch was determined not to leave the protection of the woman, and the others not to leave her.

What I saw next increased my admiration for the way the human mind works. I salute its cunning. The dogs hardly got to the other side when the woman turned round and shot back across the road again as speedily as she could. But the bitch saw her and ran after her at top speed. I held my breath as a car screeched to a halt, within centimetres of the hairy dog, another honked furiously as it jammed hard on the brakes to avoid running over the bitch. Both drivers shouted out to the woman something about the pedestrian crossing. I didn't like their insolent tone. Did they think it was her doing? They must have been blind not to see that the woman was having trouble herself. And the dogs, they remained impervious to the chaos they were causing. Oh, I was furious at everyone.

Now back on this side again, the woman was trying to work out what to do next. The bitch was still clinging to her leg, determined not to leave her. I was nervous she might trip the woman, or even bite her. But then I remembered that sexual instincts override all other impulses. The woman was now looking up the road. What would she do? My heart went out to her. No bus was in sight, and the dogs had begun to compete with the Alsatian for the bitch. Then I saw the woman raise her hand to stop the whizzing cars. A good move, I swished my tail. She should have thought of it earlier, I growled with hindsight. But no cars were stopping. Many passed and not a single one took notice of her. That's the modern world for you, I groaned. No one cares if you are in trouble. Anyone could tell she was desperate, but not a single vehicle stopped.

I waited with apprehension. The bitch was now getting snappy and the Alsatian more aggressive in his leaps, and the others more competitive with him. How is the woman going to get away from this lot? I despaired. What was happening to the bus today? Why wasn't it coming? I was angry. I could hardly see a way out for her. Then I saw a car stop. The woman rushed to it and spoke to the driver, who was saying something to her. What was he questioning her about? Wasn't it clear that the woman was in some straits? She was shaking her head and turning to the dogs, shooing them away vigorously. Silly man, did he think she was asking for a lift for the five dogs? But although the woman was denying ownership of the dogs, the dogs were refusing to leave her side. I was on edge. Oh, God, don't let the man drive away, I prayed. What will she do then? In that split second she did something very clever. She walked away from the car to make sure the bitch would follow her and all the dogs the bitch, and then quick as lightning she turned around and shot back. The driver was holding the door open for her, she got in banging the door behind her like a thunderclap. And the car sped away. Whoosh! I jumped with joy. She's got away, now you lot can do whatever you like, I gloated, and didn't even stay to see what happened to them. I had had enough of them. It was time to recover my nerves with a snooze in the sun.

†

⋮

16

SHOPPING IN TOWN

‡

Spring was now in full swing. Trees were filling out with blossoms. All that twiggery and brownishness was giving way to fresh delicate flowers. A transformation was afoot wherever one looked. I watched the hills and waited for them to change from their solitary look to a communal white and pink. It was wonderful, one could almost hear the spirit of Spring at work. But the weather remained whimsical. I could hardly keep up with its moods. The winds cut the air with loud sheet-sounds, and the storms hovered over the horizon. People restrained their pruning impulse in case the frosts returned. Wait another two weeks, they said to each other, and winter would be gone. And so it was. Soon the earlier fluctuations between rain and sun began to even out, and one could tell what sort of day it would be like by just looking up at the sky in the morning.

So when, on a Saturday in April, my mistress got my muzzle and the lead out I knew we were going shopping. Hurray! went my tail wag wag and my feet tap tap with excitement. We were going to the city! Even the horrid muzzle was not enough to dampen my spirit. I know its raison d'être is to act like a shield for people against the canines, except that it's us, the dogs, who have to hold the shield against ourselves. A funny reversal of purpose! Anyway, I look on the brighter side and treat it as a necessary bit of gear for an outing. To be in the city centre is always exciting for me. I would accept any restriction for it. While my mistress was getting it ready I couldn't stay still. My feet danced and my barks drowned out all sounds until the muzzle was clamped on my jaw. The restraint on the one end only made the freedom of the other all the more frenzied. My tail was going crazy.

Soon we were in the midst of shimmering roads. The sun was filtering down through the tall chestnut trees, collecting little shadows from the sprouting leaves and the tight little buds. In the parks, the lilac bushes were loaded with purple and white flowers, filling the air with a profusion of scent. Daffodils and tulips were still around, claiming the last of their glory.

My mistress announced we were going to the District VII shopping centre. It wasn't a very swanky plaza, like the ones which had started to mushroom all over Budapest since the '90's. This one was opened in the early '80's when signs of change were first appearing. It's a middling sort of shopping place, but one which I like for a particular reason. There are other areas like District VIII, where I hear lots of Gypsies live, and which is considered a risk area by foreign businesses. So no new centres brighten up the run-down buildings there. Shops are still small and locally run, not much to shop at, whereas District VII has quite a few new department stores. The one where my mistress was going to shop has four levels, and they are packed with shops selling modern gadgets. My mistress was looking for a new hi-fi player, and for that it was still good, the prices much lower than at the new swanky plazas. You don't pay for the latest style and for the new-style building. As dog entry is not allowed in department stores I have to be tied to one of the rings outside. Hurray! I say, I'll sit and watch the world go by, out of hearing of the nasty techno music that goes on inside.

Another plus point to this store is that its frontage faces the impressive building of Keleti Railway station. Built in 1891, it stands grandly looking out towards the river Duna. All this I know from overhearing my mistress when she gives a potted history of the country to her foreign friends. It makes my outings more challenging to me. Tied to the black iron rings outside shopping centres, I can play twenty questions with whatever view of the city I have.

Going to Pest involved some travelling. Starting with catching a bus round the corner from our house, then a tram and then the Metro. In the bus going down to Moszkva Tér, I said to myself at least this time I'd meet my metro-ladies. They would be there for sure, selling late Spring blooms; not so exciting as the early snowdrops but still fresh with scents from the woods. I will slow down when going past them to get a whiff of the wilds. I don't know why but somehow, I feel an affinity with the old sellers.

Escalators! The pride of the underground system. But I couldn't use them. My mistress tried various ways of helping me to get over my phobia of them but I wouldn't budge. I could not adapt myself to their congested steps, their sudden stopping at times and people rushing past as if a fire had broken out somewhere. The worst was getting on and off them. You had to attune yourself to their constant appearance and disappearance, and manoeuvre hopping on and off, risking breaking your limbs trying to do it. My mistress understood my trauma, and eventually came up with the solution that we should use the unmoving escalators instead. It is tough on her to forego the easy ride on the escalators, especially going up, but I rationalise it by saying that it's a good exercise and would keep her fit. For me it's fun. I can go up or down in easy bounds.

The trains are not a problem for me. I like waiting for them on the platform and see them come shooting out from the tunnel. The automatic doors are even more exciting with everyone squeezing in within seconds. When we get in, my mistress signals to me to take up a place against the closed door in the main section. I suppose it's best to keep out of the way of people. Some people aren't very tolerant of pets travelling in trains. I don't mind going into corners where baby prams are also positioned - on brakes of course. To my delight, it means that I can have a glimpse of the baby sleeping inside, or see it playing with its own hands, or making cooey-cooey sounds to no one in particular. Sometimes when they catch me looking in, they stop and stare at me, not afraid of my strange looks, but just struck by seeing something new. At such times, people smile and pat me on my back and wave at the baby. Pets and babies bring out a good response in people.

The ride to Keleti is longish, which is good. One can settle down for a bit and enjoy looking around. There are always new things to watch, new people to see, especially backpackers from all over Europe. Trains from western Europe arrive at Keleti station. So the Metro here is very crowded, and the escalators jam-packed with travellers heading for trains, or coming off them. Some you can see hurrying in case they miss their train. That's why I don't like the Metro ticket inspection conducted there. At times I think the inspectors go for the tourists because in nine cases out of ten ticketless people are bound to be foreigners. The inspectors never listen to any explanations, such as, 'We didn't know where to buy tickets,' or 'We couldn't see the punching machines,' or 'The machines weren't working.' They don't waste any time listening to the excuses, but immediately start writing out the receipts for fines, saying nothing whatsoever. I think cities ought to make some concessions for tourists' ignorance of the place. After all, these people bring bags of money to spend. Come to think of it, I've never seen my mistress punch a ticket for me. Am I a ticketed or ticketless traveller? Does she get a monthly pass for me? It wouldn't be worth it if I'm not using the transport every day. Sometimes an incident gets my mind going.

If the ticket inspectors were the only predators on tourists, it wouldn't be too bad. The pickpockets are much worse. This city is famous for their exploits. They swipe everything off people. And again the tourists are targeted. I was witness to a hair-raising experience of their operations. It was at Keleti Metro, on its long escalator going up. Being on the unmoving escalator I had a clear view of their method: how they target a person, how the victim is approached, distracted and then pick-pocketed in broad daylight of all their possessions.

It was a Friday, the Metro train had just deposited a huge mass of people - we among them - on to the platform. The mass surged towards the escalator - one escalator! at a major railway station - and lo and behold! an army of ticket inspectors stood blocking the exit like a barbed wire across it. Despite that, many users – invariably the locals - still slipped by since the inspectors couldn't stop everyone. My mistress and I weren't stopped, so we headed straight for our own escalator, absolutely free and uncongested. As we were climbing up steadily I noticed a group of five men and women, very blasé with an out-for-trouble manner. Even as I was looking at them, I saw something pass between them and suddenly they all scuttled up, aiming for an Asian woman higher up who had a backpack and a biggish handbag on her arm. I felt my tail harden and my ears pricked up. Then I saw one of the two women walk up and stand on the step above the tourist. While one held out a map before her, the other started asking in pidgin English, 'Please, where Centrum?' Two of the men had come alongside the tourist, standing on the same side as her handbag, and one of them held his coat on his arm in a way that it covered her bag also. The other man formed a back wall so that people behind couldn't see what was going on. The escalator was moving all this time. I could see what was going to happen next. I had heard about the famous pickpockets of Budapest but had never witnessed their craft before. I was ready to give out a loud bark as a warning to the woman but my mouth was tied up. I stopped and made sounds with my feet to attract the attention of people but the escalator was moving and I was losing sight of the culprits. My mistress gave a tug at the leash to make me carry on. As I looked again, the woman with the map was standing with her eyes fixed on the tourist while the other was keeping the patter going about the Centrum. Then the Asian woman turned round and asked someone three or four steps down, 'Which bus to the centre, John?' In reply, the man shouted back, 'Watch those people.' At that point the woman looked down at her bag, saw the coat over it, flung it off instinctively and screamed when she saw a hand moving towards the inner pocket which was bulging, probably with passports and holiday money. At that point the man called John rushed up, and pushing past the others and shouting something, tried to catch the man, who along with the others instantly made himself scarce, forfeiting his coat into the bargain. By this time the escalator had reached the top. I heard the man say to the woman, 'Check the bag, check if everything is there.' The woman was quite shaken and said, 'Yes, yes, everything is here; the zip is still closed; God, they nearly took everything.' I felt like saying to the man, 'What the hell were you doing down there when you could see your wife - or whoever - being pickpocketed?' and almost added, 'You deserve to lose everything for your laissez-faire attitude; staying put, watching the pickpockets clear out all your possessions.' No one stopped to ask the pair if they could help or call the police. No, everyone went their own way. I wanted to stop but my mistress didn't want to get involved either. As we came up to the top I saw another man come up the escalator and stretch out his hand to the couple for the coat, abandoned by the fleeing pickpockets. The tourists flung the coat at him. I looked back one last time to see where the man with the coat was going, and saw him disappear into the café on the right. So that's their den. I made a mental note of it in case I had to give witness. Well, that was a memorable experience, especially as the gang was foiled in their aim.

Once out in the open we passed chess players on stone seats, deliberating over their moves most abstractedly. I wanted to stop and watch at least a few moves, but a tightening of the leash was a clear signal that there was no time to do that. So we hurried up to the road where the shopping mall 'Arzenál' is. What a name! I cringe every time I hear it. Yet I looked forward to sitting outside it and looking across to the big Railway Station. After my mistress secured me in the iron ring and disappeared through the doors, I settled down to quiet musings. But soon I became aware that a whole row of shops was blocking my favourite view. Even buses were stopping there. I couldn't believe it. All this change since my last visit to this place? How long ago was that? Or is it that the world is changing faster these days?

I was still moping over the loss of an open view to Keleti when my eyes caught sight of a dog who seemed to be in perpetual motion. It was going up and down a mound over and over. When I dug my eyes deeper into the scene, I detected that what looked like a mound was in fact a drunk, fast asleep. The dog was tied to the leg of a stall table under which the man lay bundled up like a sack. It looked as if the sack had been there for many hours, if not days. Was the man dead? I raised my nose and moved it about vigorously to sniff out the smell, but it was too far away, and my basic animal instincts, alas, much reduced.

Soon I realised I wasn't the only one intrigued by the view. All the people at the new bus-stop had turned round and were watching the dog caught in this compulsive upward and downward motion. Amused murmurs were astir in the crowd as they saw the irony in the pairing of an obsessive canine with an oblivious human. Oh, istenem, I sighed, all this romanticism of drunks and dogs and beggarly city pavements. The table under which the man was sprawled out, perhaps dead by now, looked like a newspaper stall. It was empty at the moment. The man's body was blocking the entrance to the Játszék Szalon, just behind it. People inside were standing with their noses pressed against the glass door to see what it was that was amusing others on the street so much. Since their own exit was barred, the most they could do was to wait until someone moved the man. Although the dog was firmly tied, it still managed to extend the rope every time it made its way up the man's body to the top of the table. I looked carefully and could slowly make out the object which was inspiring this compulsive action in the dog. On the table lay a half-open bundle, with food spilling out. Aha, I knew at once - it took a fellow-canine to detect the method in the dog's madness. With constant cycles of motion the dog was stretching and pulling his leash to loosen it so that it gave enough leeway to reach the spilled-out food. I soon became aware that I wasn't the only one on edge about the dog's success. The watching crowd too looked tense, like at football grounds before an expected goal is scored. I shot up on all fours, my tail so straight that it was hurting me. Now, it's coming, there it goes, and now almost there, there it goes again, almost through, the bundle moves, shakes, opens and now almost, almost, it's done, and now at last the food is in the dog's mouth! A burst of loud clapping greets the scorer. Well done, my tail eased, and started to fan rapidly, but alas no salutes could issue out of my mouth as my muzzle kept strict control over my instincts. I felt proud of belonging to a species which could not be outdone at surviving.

The dog was so busy digging into the heap that the cheering watchers received no more than a cursory glance from him. There was nothing more now to hold people's interest and they soon started to catch their buses. The dog was still at his feast when the police van arrived. The people in the Játszék Szalon must have called the police as they were losing business by a blocked entrance. As two of the policemen picked up the drunk, the dog gave a yelp. No muzzle on this one, I noticed. The police paid no attention to him and carried the man to their vehicle. The dog started to bark at them. The door of the Játszék Szalon could open now. The proprietor came out and told the police that the dog belonged to the drunk and had better be taken with him. After a consultation with each other, one of the policemen untied the dog - by now quite nervous and erratic - and threw him into the vehicle after the drunk. I saw him falling on the man, at once starting to lick his face most lovingly. A shiver ran through me. What will happen to him, if the man is dead? I had heard some terrible stories of what happens to stray dogs in cities. Good acts go the same way as bad ones. A dog's loyalty comes cheap when the master himself is homeless.

My sad thoughts were interrupted by the arrival of my mistress. As she was untying me I licked her hand profusely. She was taken aback by my wanting to snuggle up to her. 'Mi a baj?' she asked in surprise, 'What's the problem?' I would have replied, 'Kutya a baj', if I could have made her understand the problems us poor dogs suffer at human hands.

†

⋮

17

PASSING OF TIME

‡

Two years on from the time I started giving an account of my early days, I now want to go over the last part my life in the Buda hills, the place I once loved so much. Of course, I am not dead, nor a ghost speaking from the other world. I'll come to that later. But here I want to relate the years when the tide was already ebbing, the sun on its homeward journey and the moon waning. Sadness grips me when I think back, but then I myself chose to go the way I did.

Well, the two years after the death of the Old Lady went by without any events worth recording. But a life-story shouldn't just record exciting happenings. Even though general routine was all there was, and nothing much notable happened in this period, it was perhaps a significant phase of my life. Without talking about it, I cannot possibly tell you what followed. I strongly believe that there is a continuum in life, that every event is linked to another. The tenor of this period was very mundane, but still I treasured every minute of it. Although it was quite predictable and lacked excitement, it was never boring.

Waking up in the mornings after a good sleep always proved satisfying to me. There was never a time when I opened my eyes and didn't feel good about being alive, especially when the sun shone bright, and my mistress came towards my kennel, greeting me with a ruffle and a pat and twirling the lead in her hand. I responded eagerly, leaping out to greet her, my tail swishing at the prospect of going on the morning walk, even though it was nothing more than a quick round of the block to answer the call of nature. We would meet other mistresses and masters and their dogs also on the same errand. Greetings were exchanged between owners and sniffs between the pets. Having achieved the main aim of the outing, we would then turn back home. My mistress would fetch me a drink before dashing back in to get ready for her work. Like me she did not partake of any breakfast, a Magyar habit of reserving the best of the appetite for the midday meal. So, I settled down on the terrace to watch the morning scene: people hurrying to work, or rushing to the corner shop for a last minute buy for lunch or dinner. In contrast, I stayed still watching the world spinning at a fast pace. I must say I didn't feel the lack of not going to work, didn't feel envious of humans for their belief in the work ethic. I liked the stillness of my terrace life.

My mistress was the epitome of rush and haste. Her departure for work was at nothing less than lightning speed. She tore out of the house showering kisses and advising me to be good for the rest of the day, threw open the gate, dashed into her car, drove through, and finally leapt out again to close the gate behind! But despite all the break-neck speed, all the years I was with her, she never forgot even once to take leave of me. She would then drive down the hill at a speed that left me worrying over her safety for the rest of the day.

As I trundled back to my morning spot for a quiet meditation, I vaguely thought of the three hours ahead before Erzsi Néni would arrive to dish out my lunch. Time never weighed on me. I never felt lonely. There were always people waving to me, no matter how many times they went by. I had a good reputation up and down our street. I never startled passers-by with abrupt barking or racing along the fence of our house making them nervous by my persistence. They even said, 'Hello, doggy, how's life?' as they went past the gate or threw a hurried salutation in my direction, 'Good dog, lovely morning'. Children were the best. They lingered at the gate, wanting me to go up to them for a chat, as Zsófi used to, before her family moved away. The child would invariably complain, 'Oh, Mummy, why can't we have a dog?' 'Because, darling, then we won't be able to visit Granny at Balaton. You know she doesn't like dogs,' Mummy would reply tactfully, looking directly at me, before dragging the child away.

I would hang around at the gate waiting for the postman, he came around mid-morning. I liked our postman. He always greeted me as if I was an old friend, ruffling my coat through the bars. Every day he would crack some new joke, which I hardly understood, let alone laughed at. 'How are you today, mister? Have you finished up all the flies bothering you?'

What was the drift of that remark? My wagging tail would bring out some clarification but not enough, 'Be like our leaders, comrade, swat the hell out of anyone who has something to say, finish them up, okay?' A quick pat and, thrusting the day's mail in my mouth, he would roll down the slope with his bag swinging behind him. He was a jolly man, I liked his light-hearted manner.

Time for forty winks, I would decide, taking the letters to the box at the front door to keep them out of rain or snow. Lunchtime would arrive with the clanking of the gate as Erzsi Néni undid the lock and came in, making a set of sweet noises at me. She was very fond of dogs. I tried to match her enthusiasm by responding to her warmly, but I could never bring myself to showing any feelings for her. She was very serious and proper. My mistress knew how I felt about her, but there was not much choice. Momentarily, an urge to escape her would rise in me, as she would never lock the gate behind her when she came in. But where would I go? And the thought of causing anger and anxiety in my mistress, stopped me from playing truant. Erszi Néni was the only neighbour, near or far, who offered to serve out my lunch every day. That being over, the afternoons went by quickly with legitimate snoozing. The road would also go quiet, not too many people passing and disturbing me in my siesta.

Waiting for my mistress' return in the evening was the heaviest part of the day. It weighed on me. The hills lost the sun earlier than the plains. The dark set in quickly. People plodding back from work seemed different from their bright enthusiastic selves of the morning. They walked by listlessly, hardly saying a word to me or even looking my way; it made me wonder if they were the same beings who passed me in the morning. Anyway, the one thing good about time is that it does pass. When the street lights came on, I knew it wouldn't be very long before my mistress arrived. Instinctively I knew when her car was about to pull up at the gate. Even before she got out of the car, I was there and beside myself. I could hardly keep still and pranced about like a maddened bee at seeing her after what seemed like ages. She too responded to my joy, talking to me all the time while picking up the mail and opening the front door. Even before the door opened, I hopped onto the sofa in my reserved space, and waited for her while she made herself a drink first, before sitting down next to me and opening her mail. I moved close up to her, putting my paws in her lap. It was heavenly but it didn't last long as she would soon be up again to get herself supper, and put mine out for me, telling me to hurry up with it. Time for the last routine – no, there was still one more after this – another quick round of the block to answer the evening call of nature. I hardly finished eating when she would be out with the lead, looking relaxed in a red track-suit – the fashion of the day.

My mistress always set a fast pace when we went on our evening walk. I am never sure if it was because she wanted to get back home quickly, or I needed some boisterous exercise before the long inactivity of the night sleep. Though we met more or less the same owners and pets, the atmosphere lacked the oomph of the morning stroll. Everyone looked a bit sombre and preoccupied. The pets too related less to each other. Perhaps like me they were also thinking of the television time. And sure enough we sat down before the television as soon as we got back. I am lucky – maybe, all dogs are – that I am allowed to be a viewer.

The habit of watching television over long winter evenings is not always a wasted time. At times the most trivial things become a source of knowledge. Television became my window on the world. My mistress watched the news every day without fail. I remember her mother calling out to her, 'Drágám, the news is on.' And my mistress would come running, no matter what she was doing. I too got into the habit of finding a space for myself in front of the box, and tried to understand the ways of the world. In my early days it was these evenings together with my two mistresses that gave me assurance of a good home.

After the death of the Old Lady, my mistress continued with the old habit, and I kept company with her. Watching television in the evenings diversified my routine, but most of all it gave me time to be with my mistress, as she was away at her job for the whole day. My mistress was keen on the news, and listened most attentively to what was reported. I, on the other hand, waited for the programme that followed it. She knew it, and even though she preferred to go to bed, she stayed on.

This particular serial was about the life of wild animals in forests and jungles. I liked to see how they lived all by themselves, something I didn't have any experience of. It was amazing to see how many different animals there were out there. I had seen only cats, birds, squirrels on the terrace, and...er...maybe a horse, cow and sheep on the way to Balaton, but I am not sure. On the screen there were so many animals, and all so very different from each other. My mistress sometimes told me their names, like I have seen grown-ups telling young children. 'That's a monkey, a monkey, and that's a giraffe, can you say gi-ra-ff'. Well, of course I couldn't. But inside my head I stored their names, and later could identify lots of them in pictures or on screen by their human names – thanks to my mistress. The list was getting longer: lions, tigers, elephants, hyenas, wolves, apes, bears, snakes, rhinoceroses and many others.

The best thing about this programme was that I could watch my kind of species without exposing myself to an arduous life in the wilds. I mean, when I looked at them, I couldn't stop feeling how much better off I was. Just look at them, I said to myself, they are all on their own; okay, okay, perhaps they did start off with a family, but not for long, they wouldn't have things made ready for them, not like me with perfect supervision of my every need, from morning to evening. No, they had to fend for themselves, and my God, how exposed they were to dangers – not only from some alien elements, but for goodness sake, from each other too! Now, this predatory behaviour is missing in human society, I am sure of that. People on our street don't tear each other apart, just because the shop is sold out of whatever they went to buy. No, this sort of feasting on each other – from the big and powerful to the small and helpless, didn't fit in with my view of existence. I was sure I was better off where I was. But I did like to watch from a distance what it was to be a free animal. After all, I thought, when all is said and done, I do belong to the animal species, and must have some sort of awareness of what they are about.

While I was watching the doings of animal species I found my mistress had given in to sleep. I was about to nudge her – as the Old Lady used to, saying, 'Come, drágám, wake up, the bed will be more comfortable' – when suddenly the screen went crowded with dogs. Here was my own tribe. Now people say that recognition needs cognition, and dogs don't have much of it. But they are wrong. How do babies recognize other babies? As soon as they see another of their kind, they show excitement, feel a pull towards them. I felt the same and was determined to watch the screen, leaving my mistress to sleep on. I got so engrossed in the pictures that I didn't even mind the full-scale snoring coming from her.

It must have been a bit of time before the film finished. I could have gone on with other things, but felt obliged to wake up my mistress. I pulled at her a few times, gave a few soft barks and waited. She got up with a start, switched off the TV, put me out, locking the door behind me. All very quickly. It was as if she literally threw me out of the house. I felt discarded. Was I being too touchy? As a consolation, I reminded myself that my kennel was not a hole, and the terrace not a wilderness.

†

10

HARSH WINDS

‡

On the one hand, time passed slowly in everyday routine; on the other, it moved at break-neck speed. I had remained unaware of the harsh winds blowing our way, until I sensed a tension in the air. A sudden rush of visits from friends and neighbours indicated that something unforeseen was happening. They would come in at all times and start talking to my mistress in hushed tones. They would ask her to come out to the gate, and panic-stricken look up and down the road, pointing to certain houses, informing her about the incidents that took place that morning. This was becoming an everyday happening. Even in the evenings, my mistress would hardly get back from work when people would start knocking at the door. I felt a bit aggrieved because I missed our evenings together. So I decided to get to the bottom of this agitated reporting. Whenever someone came and took my mistress out, I would follow them and edging up to them listen carefully. They were all saying the same thing: that strangers were walking up and down the streets in our area, pointing out houses to each other, checking the numbers on the gates, comparing the buildings with the pictures in their hands, and then stepping back and viewing the house in question at some length.

When one resident, after seeing them from his balcony, stomped out and challenged them for their intrusive behaviour, these strangers apologized most politely and said that they were returning to the country of their parents - or even grandparents - who were no longer alive. So? the resident would say aggressively. These people would then relate that in the estate of their deceased parents, they had come across photos and the address of the house their parents had owned when they had lived in this country, several decades ago. Now that the country was no longer Communist and had begun to open up to the outside world, they thought they would visit the old country and identify the area and the house their parents had called their own. At this point, the resident would firmly inform them that he had bought the place thirty years ago, and that now the property legally belonged to his family. Whereupon the strangers would hastily assure the owner that they had no intention of trying to reclaim the house, but that they were merely retracing their steps into the past to look for their roots.

It turned out that these returning émigrés - Vera Néni's word for them - did not mean what they had said, and did file claims with the City Council, pressing for repossession of the property of their forebears. The residents were shocked that their Government was encouraging property reclamation by the descendants of people who had left the country of their own free will. What about those who didn't flee? They were sorely indignant. People like them stayed back to build a new equal society from scratch. Now what was going to happen to them? Was the government going to protect their rights? If not, where would they go when strangers threw them out of their own houses? My mistress tried to calm their anxieties, saying it might not come to that. 'What about your house? Has anyone been around?' they enquired earnestly.

It was fortunate that nobody had turned up at our gate. If anyone had laid claim to my mistress's house, I would have fought them tooth and nail. My anxiety ended when I heard Vera Néni shed some light on the history of the house. 'Don't worry, Zsuzsi, no one is going to claim your house, because there can't be any descendants of the family – can't think of their name – who could own it,' Vera Néni said. 'Well, try to remember, Néni, it's important,' my mistress pressed her, 'what makes you say there can't be any descendants. How can you be sure?' 'Because they were Jews,' Néni replied, as if it was the last piece in the jigsaw. 'So?' My mistress was puzzled. 'Because in 1944, they were all sent to Auschwitz. ' A Pandora's Box was opening up. Néni told the story.

'I think they were called Medgyes, but can't be sure, I'm going back half a century, Zsuzsi,' she laughed. 'There were four children, parents and grandparents, eight in all. I knew them through Erzsi. We were both teaching in a primary school. Erzsi was greatly in awe of the family who came to live opposite them. She said they were very rich. The man was a banker and his wife was an artist and very beautiful. They lived rather well and in style. What you read in books about the war history of our country, we saw it all. By 1944 our resistance to the Fascists broke down, and the Hungarian Jews were rounded up and sent to Auschwitz. We could do nothing. When the war ended, and some Jews came back, we hoped to see our family too, I mean the Zollmans. But there was no sign of them, all eight of them, grandparents, parents and four children.' 'How old?' my mistress could hardly speak. 'Between 10-16. None of them came back.' She fell silent, as if honouring the dead. 'Erzsi said the house remained empty for a year, all locked up. But it's no good leaving a house unoccupied. So, after a year, the government started to allot them to officials, the houses were rather nice.'

'When did we go in?' I could hardly hear my mistress. 'When your parents got married. Sándor was already a surgeon by then. Medical doctors often had to have a surgery at home for local people. It was a way of reducing pressure on hospitals.' She got up to leave. 'Anyway, Zsuzsi, there is no fear of anyone turning up to claim your house.' After Néni left, my mistress remained sombre. It took her a few days to come out of it. I left her alone. I myself was shaken by the story. Is it all a matter of luck whether one is alive or dead? Is 'szerencse', the word most commonly used, crucial to our existence?

It was one thing to be endangered from the émigrés, another to be under threat from amongst themselves, their own comrades. The gap between the rich and the poor was widening. The rich were becoming richer and the poor even poorer. Shouldn't they blame the Government for it? Wasn't it awful that residents were being pushed out by those with whom they had lived as neighbours for some decades? The old system is crumbling, people lamented. They reminded each other of how they had put up with the new laws way back when the Communists had taken over and divided big houses into smaller apartments, so that every one could have a dwelling. It wasn't easy for the owners, it took them time to get used to the new policy but they did, and all credit to their commitment to making a just society. But now the political stand was changing again, back to where it once was.

Feri Bácsi, who lived four houses down from us, said Gábor was an example of how poorer people were being dispossessed by the new moneyed class. Gábor was popularly known as the resident drunkard. People joked about his drunkenness, but accepted him as part of the street life. But now, look what was happening to him. For years he had lived in the annex of the big house at no. 30 János út. Agreed it was more like a shack than a proper tenement, but a roof over Gábor's head nonetheless. Way back in the '50's, when all property was nationalized, the original owners were allotted only one section of the house for their use by the City Council, and the rest of the space was divided into smaller flats and given to families in need of housing. But now, with the collapse of the Communist regime, the original owners were wanting to get their house back. They started working on poor Gábor – not popular with the rest of the residents - and offered him cash (the going market rate) to buy his shack off him, which in its heyday was a stylish annex to the big house. Of course the poor fool was overjoyed to see so much cash. He boasted that he was on the way to becoming rich. With so much cash in hand, he saw a better life ahead, much better than what the Communists did for him. He went back to the country with plans to buy a cheaper place there and live off the rest of the money. Well, you can guess what happened to him. Sure enough, he was back in the area, having spent all his money but no sign of a house anywhere. His drinking became worse, and then he disappeared altogether, not to be seen again. They shook their heads at his fate.

Feri Bácsi had hardly finished the saga of Gábor, when Laci Bácsi said, What about Ádám? Hadn't he too fallen foul of the change-over to a market economy? he said. Ádám was a technician engineer, who had been allotted accommodation in the big house, again years ago. I liked Ádám, he was much more friendly with me than Gábor, who behaved rather drunkenly, frightening me with his loud and unseemly manner. Whenever we ran into Ádám on our walks, he always stopped and chatted with my mistress, but unmistakably it was to give me a pat and a ruffle and tell me what a good dog I was. It was a sad moment when I learnt that he was no longer going to be living in the area. People heard his story in shocked disbelief.

Ádám lived at no.16, up from Gábor's place. It was a small apartment building, housing some ten families. His was a one-room flat. He became a victim of the same sort of dealings as Gábor. Next door to him lived the Kovács family. The husband was a bank clerk but now he had plans to set up a real estate agency. The wife was a translator-interpreter and, people said, made good money. They had two growing daughters. With economic prospects in the near future, they looked for a better life-style, and wanted to expand on their living space. So they offered to buy off Ádám's apartment with ready cash. He too was thrilled to see so much money, as he also had plans to open up a small business of home electrical repairs. But like Gábor, Laci Bácsi emphasised, he was tricked into what he thought was a good bargain, and ended up living in congested accommodation with four others, who also probably suffered from the same illusion of being better off with money in hand.

It terrified the residents to think they could be the next victim of greed and ambition. Every day people were reporting such dealings where property expansion was being carried out by the nouveaux riches minority at the cost of the subsidised worker. And it had been only a few days ago that I had been confident predatory practices did not exist in human society!

That wasn't all. People were also complaining that our hill was under great pressure from developers. Some even coined a phrase to describe the phenomenon. "The Buda hills are shaking," they groaned as they heard the sound of machines felling the trees on the slopes, clearing patches of land to start building houses for foreign buyers, perhaps again the second or third generation of expatriate Magyars, who wanted to settle down in our historic city, in stylish newly-built houses, for a price next to nothing. I was saddened to see the residents up and down our hill so anxious about their future, when at one time they thought their comforts would last out at least their own lives.

†

⋮

19

CYCLONES OF WAR

‡

My cosy routine-oriented life was getting shock after shock from the outer world. If the changes at home were leaving people feeling insecure, the news of the terrible happenings in the countries south of us, left them stunned. A war of vengeance was raging in the Balkans. The TV and newspapers were full of it. More violence than heroism, they said, it was nothing less than savagery. It sent shock waves among the people in our area. They stood at street corners comparing notes in disbelief. How was it that not so long ago in the same country, different communities – religious and ethnic – had lived together as one people? Why is human society so unpredictable? I made sure I caught every word of what they were saying, the only way I could understand what was at stake for them. But at least, I thought, it wasn't happening outside their own front gate.

As days went by, more soldiers could be seen on TV with guns marching here and there, or sitting atop tanks and shooting into the distance, supposedly at the enemy. It was very unfamiliar to me. I had not seen anything like that before. In the end, it was pictures which made me understand more about what was happening. At that time I didn't know too much, but three years on, I have found out a lot more about the ways of the world. Since then nothing else seems to happen in our world but wars, wars, wars.

People huddled around the television all times of the day to get live reports from Yugoslavia, a country once a model of multi-ethnic population. Now it was breaking up into smaller republics, from being one nation to becoming many. Someone said, 'What else did you expect when an empire breaks up? Of course, wars follow hot on its heels,' and gave examples from history to prove his point. The reports of Serb aggression, first against the

Croats, then the Montenegrins and now against the Bosniaks, left little doubt in people's minds who were the instigators of the bloodshed. The Serbs declared themselves as the defenders of the old Yugoslavia, and vowed to keep it as one nation. The minorities must submit to them, the Serbian majority. The Balkans was once the country of their ancestors, the others were immigrants, who arrived from somewhere else. The Bosniaks, the Macedonians, the Croats, the Slovenes, the Albanians and the Roma, all of them, they shouted, had no reason to be there. People couldn't bear the cold rigid faces of these perpetrators of war who styled themselves as the supreme power over all other communities in Yugoslavia. Even I began to feel hatred for these thugs, such was the effect on me of everyone's indignation towards them. I could recognize them by their hateful faces when they appeared on TV

Looking back I now remember that the blood-letting had begun even before the Old Lady died. She used to get quite upset at the news, as she had some relatives living in Croatia. Oh, istenem, what will happen to them? she would mumble. She used to get on the phone to Vera Néni, and ask her to come over. Together they would ring up relatives in Croatia to find out if they were all right. Later the two would talk for hours about the old days and how these families came to emigrate there. She had warned them against going. She didn't like either the Croats or the Serbs. She said they both had racist genes, not like the Magyars who were tolerant of so many minorities, she even counted the Roma among them.

Even at that time, neighbours who like us had relatives there, came to make emergency calls to find out what was happening to them. Not everyone had phones in their houses in those days, and not all public phone booths were fitted for calls abroad. Medical doctors were given telephones as an exception to the rule, on account of emergencies. Seeing me agitated by a flow of visitors at all times, the Old Lady would say, 'People don't always need you, drágám. Remember that. Never miss a chance of helping others.' She was a compassionate soul. It pained her to hear panic in people's voices as they shouted into the phones, 'Are you okay? What's happening? Are the children okay? Leave in time. Don't hang on to the property. If you live, you will have it again. What did you say? Yes, yes, come here, your old country. We'll take care of you. The Council is opening up shelters for refugees. Don't delay. Don't leave it until too late....' Then the line would get cut off. Oh, dear, it's true that things don't get better with time. But what could a dog do? I was a helpless witness to the tragic events.

The news that the situation was getting worse, not better, left people dismayed over the safety of their relatives. Bombs, fires and smoke dominated the TV screens. Refugees were running and fleeing in all directions. Soldiers strapped with guns   barricaded all exits and entries, pushing and pulling everyone through a narrow opening, as if they were animals; trucks and tanks drove at high speed past refugees, leaving little room for them even to walk. People gasped in disbelief as they watched scenes of atrocities. They were thankful that their country did not go through the same sort of bloodshed at the time when it too declared its independence. But who could say, they shuddered at the thought of it, that the same won't happen here? Did anyone ever think Yugoslavia would become a battleground?

Sleep did not come easily to me after watching the news. I lay awake for long hours, unable to wipe the horrific images of pain and suffering from my mind. I whimpered as I put myself in the place of these ill-starred wretches, flushed out of the safety of their homes and set on the road to nowhere. The thought alone terrified me.

People's fear of war began to overshadow their lives. As the saying goes, if you really dread something, it will happen to you. Soon, pictures of the fleeing minorities on the screen became a reality on our streets. The refugees were arriving at our front gates. They came from different villages and cities but were driven out of their houses by the same criminals.

Then suddenly, like the desert sands, the war shifted to Bosnia. This time the Serbs took after the Bosniaks, committing atrocities on them, bombing them, and setting their houses on fire. What I saw on the screen was blood-curdling. My mistress tried to stop me from watching, but I didn't budge. I wanted to see everything, everything that human beings were capable of doing. The same scenes were repeated day after day, but now the Bosniaks were called Muslims. This brought out greater hatred in the enemy. I knew that the Magyars too had no love for Muslims, but they didn't agree with what the Serbs were doing to them. The reports of rampant ethnic cleansing and brutality continued.

The family two doors away came to ask if they could ring their relatives in Bosnia. My mistress was surprised. Did they have Muslim connections? She never thought of them as different from anyone else. They had lived next door for many years. Now it turned out that a cousin of theirs had married into a Muslim family. My mistress like her mother believed that one should always help others, no matter who they were. She asked them in, as she would have anyone in the area. But as their luck would have it, the lines were dead, no links working. My mistress tried to console them, but they knew the worst must have happened to their relatives.

Further up the road, another family told my mistress about their Croatian relatives in Omarska. They had been settled there for two generations, yet the Serbs would have them go to Croatia, now that it had become a separate country. But it wasn't that simple, because they had never lived there. And the Croats in the new Croatia didn't want them either. So they had nowhere to go. Cruel, how cruel humans could be I had never known.

Well, not a week had passed before we began to see groups of bedraggled people on our streets. It was very scary to see humans in such a condition. The sight of some of them lurking outside our gates, made me leap up and rush to the gate, barking at them most viciously. When I saw them cringe with fright, I felt ashamed of my behaviour. Fortunately, it was the weekend and my mistress was home. She came out and ordered me to stop growling at them. She then tried to find out what they wanted. It turned out that they were looking for the family next door. My mistress personally showed them to the house. I begged to go with her, promising to behave myself, but she wouldn't budge. I watched from the terrace. There was much crying and weeping when they were welcomed by the family. It made me feel even more remorseful at having added to their grief by my reaction to them earlier.

More refugees began to arrive. This time they were not looking for relatives, as they had none in our area, they were simply begging for food and shelter. My mistress again proved compassionate and served them hot bread and coffee on the terrace. Their hunger was evident from the way they wolfed down the food. They told terrible stories of torture, killings and inhumanity in Bosnia. They had somehow managed to escape the camp at Omarska where all Muslims, and some Croats too, were being kept as prisoners until slaughtered. One Bosnian woman named Nusreta, a former judge in her country, related incidents of utter brutality, beyond all belief, how the guards regularly took women into their halls and raped them, even girls hardly past puberty and feeding mothers. Some never returned, they wept thinking back to the time when they had to face living in conditions unimaginable to anyone who had not experienced them.

My mistress wept for them. So much suffering caused by humans on humans! I was brought up to believe in the nobility of humans and the savagery of animals, unless they were domesticated. But the truth seemed different. My mistress's compassion made each of them want to tell her their story.

Esmuda, a school teacher, from another camp at Trnopolje, spoke of how the women were ordered to clean the blood-splashed walls of the Red House the day after their men had been executed there in the night. They had to wash the blood still warm from fresh killing, and not show any emotion. If they cried, the guards brought down a whip on them. This was repeated the next day and the one after and all days that followed. They wept bitterly when they thought of what their husbands and sons must have gone through before their throats were slashed by the butchers. The accounts of the daily slaughter was hair-raising. Esmuda related how one day the women saw the guards jumping on a body, a whole bunch of them. Suddenly a woman amongst them screamed as she recognized the body. The bundle was her wretched husband. 'What are you doing to my husband?' she yelled out. It was lucky they didn't hear her, drunk as they were on sadism. Later that night, they took the wife of the man to their barracks, and while the same guards gang-raped her, she was told she needn't worry about her husband finding it out. He had died that morning.

Another spoke. This time it was a man from the village of Kozarac. Shahabudin broke down as he related how one morning they woke up to the town - 25,000 Muslims - almost reduced to ashes. The night before the houses had been marked in paint for incineration. The surviving few - they couldn't understand why some were left out - were herded in droves to the top of the mountain at gun-point. As they were stood in rows and shot at close range, he pretended to have been hit, and fell down. After the bodies were left to rot in the open, he made his escape. He could hardly believe he was alive to tell the story. On the one hand, listening to them made me hate human beings, but on the other, I could not help feeling an admiration for human resilience at survival.

This brave man, Shahabudin, was determined to lead all the Bosniaks – the term they used for themselves, rather than 'Muslims' as the rest of the world did – back to each of the places in which they had been stripped of their property, religion and humanity. He was determined to organise a survivors' association. 'We the survivors are appealing to the European Union to bring the butchers to justice, to get our homeland back for us. And God willing, we will rebuild our houses, open up shops and cafés and raise new minarets, higher than before, sticking it to the Serbs.' The high note of Shahabudin's last word was drowned in rousing applause from his co-survivors. Not being able to join in applauding him, I got up, walked up to him, rubbed my nose in the ground and sat down at his feet.

Humans, humans, humans! I was no sooner ready to sink into the pit of man's savagery, when I rose buoyed up by the resolution of the victims to overcome it.

†

20

MISTRESS'S NEW JOB

‡

Compared with animals, human beings are a pretty versatile bunch. Whereas we are single-minded in our approach to things, they handle a number of experiences on different fronts without much difficulty. Although people were quite disturbed by the rapidly changing face of the Balkans war, they continued to live their lives without letting the horrible events impinge on their day-to-day affairs. This instinct in humans sets them apart from other beings.

My mistress too put the horror of the ravages in the Balkans on the back burner, and continued with her life. One day she broke the news to me that she was going to change jobs. 'How would you like your mistress to work in a sales company, eh, drágám?' I couldn't grasp the full implication of the change but, nonetheless, gave a bark in agreement, a sort of happy sneeze. What did I know about differences in jobs? I worked on the principle that whatever made my mistress happy had my total approval. I waited to know more about it.

Well, I got my first shock when she told me that she was going to come home even later than before. This was bad news for me, as it meant that she would be even more tired and maybe our television viewing would have to be trimmed down or scrapped altogether. Yet the walk after supper could not be dispensed with, as it was an essential part of my dogginess to defecate out on the road rather than in our own garden. I particularly enjoyed the walk in the evening. I wondered if it was part of my animal nature to respond to the coming of darkness.

But that wasn't all. Next came the bombshell. She said that the new job involved some travelling. This grieved me more as I had never been separated from her from the day she found me in a ditch by the busy highway. So what was I going to do? How was I going to live by myself when she was away? How would I go on walks? Would a few spins round the garden replace the twice-daily call-of-nature outings? My head throbbed while I grappled with many questions, all to do with my own concerns. I moped around the house, especially during TV, watching to make sure my mistress would notice it, which she unfailingly did. Sensing my anxiety, she hugged me and tried to calm my fretting heart, told me that I must look at it from her point of view also. This was the first opportunity for her to travel abroad. She said she had never travelled before and had always wanted to. There were so many restrictions that only the most resourceful people could clinch it. While her mother was alive, she turned down jobs that involved going away from home. But now she would like to. She said that she always wanted to see more of Eastern Europe, and this would be the chance of a lifetime for her, especially as it would cost her nothing. I knew I was not the same to her as her mother, but still I felt unhappy at her admission.

Like the Old Lady, I was concerned with my mistress's safety in the countries which were going through political upheavals. She sensed my concern and said, 'You worry too much. I'll be fine. I am not going there alone. We are going to be a team of technicians and sales supervisors. So, you have no reason to worry. Okay?' She gave me a tickle and a kiss to make me feel better.

The question was how was I going to survive in her absence? Who was going to take me on walks, look after me at nights, feed me in the evenings, and what about the weekends? I wasn't making it easy for her. But neither was she for me. She told me that the answer to all my questions was: Erzsi Néni. No, not her! She would be the last person to make up for my mistress' absence. I took a tumble and clamped my teeth into the cushion. This shocked my mistress. She gave me a smack and told me sternly to behave myself. It brought me back to the realization that after all I was only a dog, not that it put an end to my protest. I slunk under the window table and whined, refusing to come out when my mistress tried to make up with me. I wasn't having Erzsi Néni all day and every day, I made it very clear to her.

Well, seeing my determination, my mistress changed her attitude, and tried to appease me. She put out a dish of crisps for me, which was always a treat for me. But, no, I wasn't giving in. 'Look, drágám, you are being very unreasonable. After all, if you use your stubborn head, you will realize that every day you are without me for many hours, and only for a few hours with me. Isn't that right?' No, it wasn't. I gave a sharp bark. 'All right, all right, I haven't forgotten the TV time, but don't you forget all the night hours you are outside the house. So, if you count, you are with me only – let's do the count,' she said, literally doing it, 'One hour when I get back home, one hour on the evening walks, and another two after we get back and watch TV. So, no more than four hours in the whole day, okay, let's say five at most. So, really, it's not a big crisis if I am away. Now, be reasonable, come out and stop making a big hoo-ha about it.' She paused to see my reaction. I kept aloof. I felt intensely resentful. Why doesn't she have a companion? I wouldn't be ownerless then. The two could take turns to stay at home to look after me. Was I being selfish? Or did I really want her to have someone living with her? Was I becoming a romantic in my old age? My silence continued.

'All right, put it this way. Let's try Erzsi Néni once, and if you don't like it, I will make other arrangements,' my mistress said craftily. Hardly a compromise, I thought. 'After all, I am only going to be away for two days. I'll be back by the weekend.' She paused to see if this produced some reaction in me. I remained unresponsive. 'Look, I said next time I will make other arrangements, maybe someone has started running kennels, then you too can go on holiday, and have a good time with your own comrades, yes? I promise.' Well, what could I say? She couldn't go on sitting on the floor, coaxing me to come out. That was the end of my standing up to her – the first time in all the years.

†

21

CARERS & KENNELS

‡

The following week my mistress left for Russia, on her first assignment to promote colour televisions for her company, Television World. The winding down of State control meant a boom in private businesses. Anyone with entrepreneurial push was taking to the capitalist road. My mistress's trip was to last three nights, including the day of departure and the day of arrival back. As I stood at the gate bidding her bon voyage I put on a brave face, but it was difficult to hide my low spirits. She herself was not altogether happy at leaving me alone, but at least after all these years, she was putting her own interest before consideration for others. And I was only a dog, I reminded myself. I must adjust myself to her new life-style. 'Call no man happy until he is dead,' the refugees had quoted some old sage as a way of coming to terms with their fates. Had I ever thought I would be alone in the house without my mistress?

I too decided to accept my fate and make the best of it. As usual I made use of my terrace time in observation of things and people. But constantly I found myself counting how many times I would be seeing Erzsi Néni every day, and on top of that, the time on the walks. The thought alone made me cringe. The arrangement was: she would come in to take me out for the morning walk, lay out lunch for me (as usual), come in the evening to give me my supper and soon after take me out on the scheduled walk; and finally would put me out of the house, before going home herself. One thing more, my mistress informed me tactfully that she had told Néni she could watch our TV; this would be a special treat for her, she explained, as hers is only a small black and white. It would also mean, she rubbed this one in, that I too would be able to have my daily staple of television viewing. 'After all,' she shot this one straight into my heel, 'drágám, you wouldn't be able to operate the machine all by yourself, would you?'

By the time lunch hour arrived, I had gone over again and again the number of times I would be in the company of Erzsi Néni. Thoughtful as my mistress was in making the minute arrangements for me, I decided to forgo the intimate television viewing with Erzsi Néni. Food and walk were essential and could not be avoided. Having made up my mind, I decided to stick by it. The hours went by after this self-inflicted decision. It didn't seem long before I heard the clinking of the gate. Erzi Néni came in. She was more cheerful than usual and asked me how I was, saying that I mustn't mope about my mistress's absence as she also loved me. I tried not to show too much aversion to her, but gently turned my face away so as to discourage her in her artificial talk. It was the high pitch in her voice which was most difficult for me to endure. Since I didn't bounce up and down, she soon went away.

After eating my lunch, I settled down for my usual nap. As sleep was overtaking me, it passed through my dozing mind that I would no longer be calculating how many more times I would be seeing Erzsi Néni for the rest of the day. A few hours must have gone by when I was woken up by the usual clinking of the gate and in came Erzsi Néni. She went into the house, brought my tinned food out, and in her hand she carried the lead. Oh no, I had forgotten the after-supper walk. I lost my appetite immediately. She coaxed me into eating half of what she had put out, and then she marched me off for the walk.

I had never walked so reluctantly in all my years. I tried to cheer myself up with the thought of meeting the other regulars, but unfortunately everyone asked her the one question I did not want to hear, 'Where is Zsuzsa?', to which Erzsi Néni would reply with full details of my mistress's new job and the travels involved, plus the saga of her looking after me, including an aside that I was not too happy at Zsuzsa's being away. Even meeting my mates did not produce the usual feeling of animal fraternity in me.

When we returned, I went straight into my kennel. Erzsi Néni unlocked the door and told me she was going to watch the television for a while, did I want to join her? I did not come out, thereby declining her invitation. But it was too early to turn in. An hour later I saw her leave. She bid me a cheerful goodnight, asking me not to worry about anything, that she was just across the road, and if I barked loud enough, she would come across immediately. She called back from the gate that I must remember intruders were afraid of dogs, and not dogs of intruders – unless they happened to be ghosts. That did it for me.

I had a sleepless night. I had no idea what ghosts were, but the way Erzsi Néni said it sounded as they were some invisible demons who could materialize out of thin air. Every time sleep came over me, I thought I could hear someone lurking outside my kennel. I set up a bark, knowing most people are afraid of a dog bark. But ghosts are not people. Thinking it was good to put up a strong defence against unseen powers, I got out of the kennel while continuing to bark my loudest. I leapt up to the gate to make it as the front line of defence and raising my face gave a continuous howl, something I didn't know I could do. Looking up and down the road I ran along the fence on both sides, barking non-stop. People were still up, many lights still on, including Erzsi Néni's. Her curtain parted. The sight of it stopped me short in mid-barking, I didn't want her to come out to me. I quickly brought my full-throated barks to a few grunts, and walked back to my kennel.

Two or three hours must have passed. I woke up with a start. I thought I heard a scream in the house. I jumped out and raced to the door, barking loudly. I thumped at the door and stretching to my full height ran my paws down it most viciously. It was a warning to whoever was indoors that if any harm came to my mistress they would have to reckon with me first. Suddenly reality dawned on me, the realization that my mistress was away, and the house was empty. I slumped down with exhaustion. My eyes filled with tears in self-pity. What a wretch I was! Even when awake, I was fighting nightmares. I looked up at Erzsi Néni's window. No light had come on. Luckier than me, she must be deep in sleep.

Back in my kennel, I decided to put my mind into a more positive frame – perhaps a better defence against ghosts and bad dreams than baring my teeth and barking at shadows. I needed some sleep badly. So, I turned my mind to my mistress, visualising her somewhere enjoying herself. There was no point in making myself miserable. The thought made me think more positively about my walks with Erzsi Néni. After all, she was more than a lunch lady. She might have some interesting side to her temperament. That did the trick, the rest of the night went uninterrupted.

I woke up at the clinking of the gate. Remembering my last night's resolution, I got up and let Erzsi Néni put the lead on me. I had got my head round to not expecting too much from the walks, so tried to put some enthusiasm in my tread. Erzsi Néni stopped to chat with a few people. I stood by obediently, vaguely listening to their chat, but there was nothing very interesting. I did a little sniffing and rubbing with other dogs, but all very low-key. On the way back, Néni stopped at the store for shopping, and I waited outside. The rest of the day passed as usual. With the onset of the evening, I began to get nervous about a repeat of the night before. I thought if I stopped resisting the new arrangement, I might have a less traumatic night. So, when we returned from the evening walk, and Erzsi Néni unlocked the front door, I followed her in. She was mighty pleased and patted me for being good. But I didn't hop onto the sofa to sit beside her, no way, I said to myself. I sat on the floor and watched the television, with not much interest though. Most of the time I had my eyes closed. Nothing was the same without my mistress. And I wanted to keep it that way.

The third day and night passed the same way. It didn't get better, but fortunately, didn't get worse either. My mistress was arriving on the fourth morning. I never knew how terrible waiting for someone could be. I was going to the gate so often that in the end I thought I might as well sit there until she arrived. She had said it would be sometime mid-morning. Since it was the weekend, Erzsi Néni wasn't coming to do lunch for me. She did take me out for my morning do, which according to my plan was going to be the last. I was not having the same arrangement again, and my mistress would have to accept that.

And then I had a glimpse of my mistress in the taxi heading up our street. I stood up. She came through the gate. The joy of seeing her played havoc with my throat and tail. She was back at last, after what seemed like ages! I went into spasms of joy, jumping out of my skin, leaping, prancing, pouncing, catching my tail, circling the terrace at top speed, so overwhelmed was I with excitement at seeing her. After a while I calmed down and showed a quieter affection for her. We sat on the sofa together, my head in her lap listening to her description of what she did in Russia, and how exciting it was to see all the sights she had heard of but had never actually seen. While she was talking of her experiences, I was thinking whether she would be going to another place, and what would happen to me again. 'Now, tell me how was it with you? Are you kinder to Erzsi Néni now?' I squealed. 'Oh, dear, you are difficult, aren't you? What am I going to do with you, you fussy kutya, eh?' I responded with an even stronger squeal this time. I didn't care how difficult it would make things for her, but I wasn't going to go through that night's experience again. Making myself very clear, I settled back into our weekend routine, and looked forward to walks in the woods and then, of course later, television watching.

It was on our walk that I heard her tell someone that she would be going to Bulgaria next, in a month's time, and that from then on, it would be a regular schedule once a month, probably lasting five days each time. That did the rest of the walk for me.

'What about the dog?' the next person she was talking to asked.

'I don't know really. He is a fussy little thing, and I hate to think he is unhappy when I am enjoying myself.'

'It is a problem, isn't it? That's the reason I don't travel. Erzsi Néni doesn't have a dog, and so is happy to look after him, am I right?' A yelp from me warned my mistress, and brought the neighbour's dog to give me a compassionate lick.

'Did you hear that? That was what I faced when I got back this time,' my mistress looked for sympathy. The mistress and Aladár, the man, stood looking at me, as if I was a delinquent.

'You could think of putting him in the kennels,' I heard the man saying.

'I thought kennels were not allowed in our country?'

'Well, everything is these days,' he laughed.

'Where do I look for them?' My mistress saw a way out of the impasse, and since I did not know what kennels were, I could not react.

'You know the next hill down from the main road, well in the valley, a family has set up kennels. Apparently, it's big business.'

'Why not? Now that we can travel to other countries, we will need carers for our pets. Good entrepreneurship!' My mistress supported business ventures.

She meticulously took down the particulars from Mr Aladár and cut short the walk to make a call when she got home. I decided to listen to the conversation. It seemed she was happy with the response she got, and took down all the details of the rules and prices. As soon as she put down the phone, she picked me up and kissed me, giving me the good news.

'Now you can be in the company of your own kind, right? Let's see how you make out with them.' I responded with giving her a lick on her face.

'Good, you like it too. Now I can relax. So, the date is – let me check,' she fetched the calendar, '- it will be the week of December 1st, almost a month away. So, what do you say, eh, fusspot?' I put my paw on her shoulder. 'Excellent, so that settles it. Now let's celebrate.' She got up to get the bottle of Tokaj out, and pouring some in the best glassware for herself, and into the special glass dish for me, she toasted to my victory. So, all was well now that ended well. I slept soundly on the best Hungarian ambrosia.

...

It was a full moon on my first night in the kennels, which were located in the valley down from us. It was exactly a month after my mistress came to know about them. She brought me there after our morning walk, before leaving for Bulgaria. It took her a bit of work before everything got settled. There was a choice of individual or communal boarding. My mistress took the middle-line and arranged for a separate living space but communal free time. When she asked me, I gave my approval by hanging my tongue out and taking a leap. I really was excited at the thought of living with other dogs, something I had not experienced in all my years. My mistress handed me to the owner of the kennels, along with some papers on me, and while she bent down to say goodbye I was already looking around at the other dogs who were watching my arrival and giving soft barks to welcome me, a newcomer. Later I was appalled that I did not know when my mistress had slipped away.

Gradually I noticed the location of the kennels. Set in a valley, they were overlooked by the hills in the north. It was a change to look at the hills, rather than be in them. My kennel was made of wood and surrounded by a wire fence, which I didn't much care for. A security against my running away, I mused. Where would I run to? I would have liked to ask them. I settled in and took stock of my surroundings. Lunch time arrived. A young man brought some food, and put it in my dish, alongside which lay a bowl for my drink, which he filled with water. So far so good, I said, and headed for my dish. Well, I wouldn't say it was anything special. No taste to it. Since I am an animal, I thought, I shouldn't always give so much importance to food. 'Thou shalt not live by bread alone,' I had heard people say. Anyway, I decided to wash down the peppy taste with water. A surprise, I didn't like the water either. It seemed not so fresh. Was I being fussy? I found myself comparing the meal with Erzsi Néni's lunches! Well, well!

Nevertheless, I was resolved to make the best of this arrangement, and not jump at the first opportunity to be unhappy. So, I settled down for a siesta. My kennel faced the hills; I was still looking at them when my eyelids drooped. The sharp ringing of a bell woke me up. What was that about? I puzzled. Not a fire somewhere. No, it was the same young man coming back, but this time with a lead to take me out. I saw lots of dogs gathered together in an enclosure. They were all running around, bouncing, jumping, rolling over, grabbing each other by the throat, all this accompanied by a whole range of barks. I couldn't wait to get in. I had never played so freely with other dogs, always conversed with them while kept on the lead. To begin with I found it difficult to let myself go. So far, I had lived with one person, and did not know how to relate to so many, and of so very different sizes and types. As I stood overwhelmed by the panorama of canine variety, and was attempting to find a way out of my own constraints, a whole lot of them came running towards me. I responded to their welcome.

It was just the thing I needed. The memory of the dog-boy reminded me that I too could behave like a dog. And I did. It was such a relief to get out of my skin. I chased other dogs, jumped on them, growling while catching hold of them by their necks, rolling over, getting up again, rushing up to another, across to the other end, barking, sniffing. Being a bit short on dog behaviour in my upbringing, it wasn't all that easy for me at first, but after a quick observation of others, I successfully imitated them, having a load of fun into the bargain. It was exhilarating. The attendants made sure we played out our energies to the full.

Time up, we were led back to our enclosures, some dogs living in more communal ones. There was much noise and barking there. It was one thing to have a free range in the playground with a whole lot of dogs, another to live cheek by jowl with them. I am afraid I wasn't used to it, and was happy to be back in my own space. The hills looked a bit sombre by now, with an early sunset. I lay down to rest, truly I felt a bit exhausted. I think I must have had forty winks, because when next I opened my eyes, the full moon was looking down at me. The attendant came with my supper and went through the same routine as at lunchtime. I should have been hungry but didn't rush for the food. The memory of the morning repast proved discouraging. I thought I'd wait until I felt hungry.

As the night darkened, and the moon shone brighter, the dogs – I think there must have been fifteen of them – started to bark. They got louder as they picked up the pitch from each other. Soon it became one long howl. I came down to the gate and looked out to see why the terrible noise. I could see the enclosure on my right. It housed four dogs. They were all out, standing there and looking up to the moon and setting up a howl, and other dogs in the neighbouring enclosures were picking it up wholesale. I remembered Erzsi Néni once saying that dogs do that when they see ghosts approaching to take someone to the other world. But the moon is not a ghost, I argued. I gave them a 'shut-up, you ignorant fools' bark but it had no effect on them. In the end, I gave up and sat down outside, looking up at the beautiful moon, apologizing to it for the disgraceful behaviour of my species.

The noise, the barking, the howling went on all night. I could hardly sleep. Somehow the dark passed and the light dawned in the valley. But the day did not bring any enthusiasm with it. Having not eaten in the night, I went over to my bowl and found it was full of other creatures who must have been more thankful to have it than me. Soon I was feeling famished, and waited for the attendant to bring lunch. But alas, it seemed there was still some time to go yet. I began to get irritated, and by the time the food came, it tasted terrible. I could not eat it. The water too had scum floating on it. The bowls were not rinsed out, the old food and drink not thrown away before the new lot were put in. Oh, dear, I wished I wasn't so spoiled.

The exercise time too didn't prove as exciting and novel as it had done the day before. The dogs' irrational howls at the moon had made me rather contemptuous of them. Was the honeymoon over? I wondered. I think they sensed my snootiness and, unlike previously, they didn't jolly me into playing with them. It was left to me to join them or not. I had such little food in me that even though I wanted to be playful I couldn't. So, I sat down in one corner and watched everyone, not feeling enthusiastic about their pranks. Play time over, we were again taken back to our places. The dogs of the adjacent enclosure were ahead of me, they stopped and wanted to paw me around. Their gesture seemed playful, but I think there was a touch of viciousness there, maybe they were settling scores from last night. I didn't pay much attention, ignoring their lack of understanding of my intention.

I was really looking forward to food, as by now I was suffering from pangs of hunger. But the fates were really trying me out, as the supper was no better that day either. I hankered after some hot soup, here there was only mass-produced packaged food from big tins. What was I going to do? I closed all my smelling powers and got down to lapping up whatever was there in the bowl. I couldn't see much in the dark. The moon was late in rising, I thanked heavens for that, and prepared for the night. Suddenly, I felt as if things were crawling all over me. I used my paw to see if something had fallen on me, but couldn't see anything. Thinking something may have fallen from the tree, I took shelter inside and lay on my bed. Soon intense itching started. I got up and gave myself a thorough scratch to get rid of whatever had got into my coat, but to no effect. The moon was up now but I had no time to look at it or get irritated with the next-door dogs for howling at it.

The night passed between bedding down and getting up to give a horrendous scratch and then getting back once again to bed. By the fifth time I did that, I decided to sleep out, forgoing the comfort of a made bed. It was a sensible move as I did get some sleep in the end.

It was the third day. And not too much hope, except that the attendant noticed that I had slept out and was attacking my body. He returned with some powder which he sprinkled into my coat. It produced instant relief. I showed my gratitude by licking his foot. He had also brought new clean bowls for food and drink and took the old ones away. The food was still not so good, but I thought it was best to put something inside me. No sooner did I go back to my bed than the same cycle was repeated. It seemed the source of scratching and irritation was in my bed. How could I tell this to the attendant? Well, I was so desperate that I decided to play havoc with the bedding. I dragged the basket out, pulled out the bed clothes one by one and left them lying at sixes and sevens. When the attendant returned to fetch me for the walk I refused to go. He saw the rampage I had gone on, gave me a hard scolding, but went away and returned with replacements, sprinkling them with powder and leaving me alone with my wish to be by myself.

I lay down in my new bed and caught up with sleep. I was not sorry to miss the play time. Well, two days more of this, I said to myself, and then never again. The mistress will have to decide what to do with me. I am not going to put up with this again. This was the first time I had thought of her. Initially the euphoria of being with my own community and then the collapse of my health had kept home-sickness at bay. The food on the fourth and fifth days went back to the first and second days. Apparently, the owners gave a clean-up to things every third day, and if something didn't work out in between, it was your tough luck. The result was I longed to be back in my own home.

On Saturday morning, my mistress came to fetch me. By this time I was feeling so weak from malnutrition and bodily ailments that I had no enthusiasm to greet her. She was quite shocked to see me so dispirited. I heard her ask all sorts of questions from the attendant, and got him to call the owners, to whom she spoke quite sharply. She did not look at all pleased by their answers.

What a relief it was to get home. She sprinkled more powder on my coat, coaxed me to eat some hot bone soup with some vegetables, and put some warm milk in my bowl. There was no leaping and hopping for television, only a longing for a bed to lie on. The last thing I heard before I was overcome by sleep was a sigh from my mistress, 'Oh, drágám'.

†

22

THE ENGLISH COUPLE

‡

Fortunately, my mistress was not going somewhere again for another month. It seemed the company was looking into its sales policy which so far had been limited to the eastern sector. They were thinking of producing a new product which could be marketed in the West. This piece of news I picked up from her phone conversation with Vera Néni. It meant that she wouldn't be going away in the near future at least. I was quite glad of this reprieve. Both times my mistress was away had proved disastrous. On the one hand, I was ashamed of my inability to adapt myself to a new situation; on the other, what could I do? I was brought up as more human than canine.

The new job meant more socialization for my mistress. She went out a lot more in the evenings, and more people visited us. It meant that in both cases, we missed our television session. This left me feeling unhappy. Not again! I thought. I can't go on being unhappy with her every time she does something different from our routine ways. It was time, I reprimanded myself, I looked at the changes in our lives in a positive way. Reasoning with myself worked. It opened up a whole vista of fresh perceptions.

I started to know new things about my mistress and the visitors too. A lot were from other countries. As I was allowed to be in the room at such times, for the first time I heard my mistress speak English. I liked the sound of it. Her life had taken an unexpected turn. Maybe, maybe, at last she will meet someone. One evening she told me that an English couple were coming to dinner, who, surprise, surprise, lived up on Széhér út, the ridge road as everyone called it, the highest point of our hill. I must have seen them go by many times, but couldn't put a face to them. Strange how one can see people vaguely, but not know them. But then the world is a large place, even the road one lives on remains a mystery. One can never know everyone. 'You'll like this couple, drágám,' my mistress confided in me on the walk, showing me their apartment. 'They are young and very different from us, but like us, they love dogs. The English are known to be dog lovers. I've invited them for this Saturday. They want to taste Hungarian dishes. You can come in and listen to them, but don't be too critical of my English. Okay?' I rubbed against her leg, almost tripping her, and looked up at the balcony to see if I could catch a glimpse of the couple but there was no one there. Oh well, I would be seeing them soon, Saturday was literally round the corner.

I was on the terrace when they arrived at the gate. They came in without hesitation. My mistress came out and greeted them heartily. 'Hello, there,' the man said to me, shaking me by my paw, 'How are we today?' I responded by letting my paw rest in his hand. 'Oh, he's lovely,' the woman said, ruffling my neck, 'I'd love a dog like him.' I gave her a lick for praising me. 'Well, you can borrow him, whenever you like, Susan,' my mistress offered me on loan. I didn't like her saying that, as if I was an object to be passed around. Anyway, Bill and Susan Smith as they were called, went in and I followed them.

'The funny thing is, we knew your dog before we came to know you,' Susan said laughingly.

'It sounds more like, "If you know my dog, you know me,"' my mistress laughed.

'Well, we can know him more if you let us have him some time,' Susan repeated her earlier remark. What was going on? My ears pricked up.

'Look what we have here,' Susan took a video out of her bag. 'It's all about dogs in the U.K., a testimony to the English love of dogs. Would you like to see it?'

'I bet your dog would!' Bill interjected, 'Jokes apart, we thought if you are going to Britain, you might as well know a little about the dogs there.'

'I'd love to. Let's put it on.' My mistress welcomed the offer, and so did I. 'Come, drágám, come over here. See how it is in their country for dogs.' I jumped up onto the sofa and snuggled up to her. 'Jó kutya,' she patted me. 'He is Béla, my mother named him after a Hungarian king. Dogs are wonderful I think,' my mistress said proudly.

'True, but even then domestic dogs can have a bad deal as pets,' Bill said.

'Really?' My mistress was incredulous.

'You won't believe it but it's true,' Susan said. 'They get adopted for different reasons. Sometimes as toys for children to play with, and when they grow up and lose interest in the dog, they get abandoned, just taken to the countryside and left.'

'People just stop in the lay-by on the motorway, open the door and bingo, put out the puppy or puppies and drive away,' Bill added.

'That's how I found our Béla, didn't I?' my mistress hugged me closer.

Bill added, 'And if the litter is big, too many puppies born, the solution is to hold them down in boiling water.'

'Dog lovers like you are gotten at in another way,' Susan reported. 'Yes, dogs get abducted – especially those of old ladies, who then receive letters demanding a ransom to release their pets.'

'No, I can't believe that. It would never happen here,' my mistress said with national pride.

'Really, I'm surprised with so many Gypsies in Hungary,' Susan refused to give in.

'Watch out, darling,' Bill warned, 'you are airing racism.'

'But you know, it happens in the U.K. all the time,' Susan said excitedly. 'The abductors are either Travellers or druggies who make easy money from people's love for animals. You can read notices of a reward for finding dogs.'

Bill laughed. 'There we go, if not Gypsies, then drug addicts, or both.'

'Well, it seems we in Hungary haven't all gone savage yet,' my mistress said proudly.

Bill quipped, 'It will come, now you have become part of the EU community.'

My mistress put me down and got up, 'On that note, shall we have a drink? Tokay! Our gift to civilisation. Have you tried it?'

'Of course. You can't be in Hungary without tasting the best drink on offer,' Bill said politely.

'We have gone as far as three stars. Are you going further?' Susan was more challenging.

'Five.' My mistress was holding up the pride of Hungary. There were cheerful sounds of expectation from the guests. She poured the drinks, handed them round. With glasses in their hands, everyone settled down to watch the best show on earth. Me too.

The video was rolling. The screen was filled with dogs and masters. In turn, the guests were explaining what was going on, as everything was in English. It started with a single dog's life, showing how the pet should be looked after and cared for. The dog on the screen lived with a family:

parents and two children, one young, the other a teenager. Both were shown playing with the dog, racing it, doing mock fighting and rolling over on the grass, all looking very happy. For a moment I wished there were children I could play with. Maybe when my mistress met someone. Now we were seeing a doctor examining the dog and explaining something to the owners. I was familiar with this. Recently when I got back from the kennels my mistress had taken me to the vet. Then abruptly the scene changed to a room full of funny machines. Susan said it was a science laboratory.

A man and a woman in white coats were holding a dog on the table and giving it an injection. The scene shifted to the outside, where a large group of angry people were hurling shouts at the people inside. It seemed they were not happy at what was happening in the lab.

'These people are against science experiments on dogs,' Bill said. 'Do you have any such organization here?'

'Not heard of any,' my mistress said, a bit surprised by the angry crowd. 'What do they want?'

'They don't want any experiments done on dogs. But the scientists say if people want research on life-destroying diseases, they have to do experiments on animals to develop drugs that can save human life.'

'Isn't that reasonable?' my mistress asked.

'Not really,' Susan came back quickly, 'it's just an excuse for scientists to do what they want to. There's no surety their research would come up with a solution.'

'I don't think one should trust scientists,' Bill said, joining in. 'They are pretty blinkered. The latest thing with them is cloning. Already they have begun to clone dogs, because soon they want to get on to humans.'

'I thought it was a sheep. Wasn't it called Dolly?' My mistress tried to keep up with the discussion.

'Oh, that's an old story,' Bill said.

I was concentrating on the screen. It had changed to the countryside, a beautiful landscape with a crowd of smartly dressed horse riders: black hats, red jackets, rearing up on their horses, and a crowd of small dogs waiting below, yapping and squealing to start the run.

'This is a typical hunting scene in Britain.'

'What sort of hunt?'

'Hunting the fox. It's a very old sport and mostly old-style landed gentry indulge in it.' From his tone, Bill didn't sound much in favour of it.

'Many people are against it, because it is considered a cruel sport. You see the pack of dogs there?' Susan pointed to the dogs. 'They have been kept hungry on purpose to make them vicious for the kill. They will be raced by the riders to where they know foxes live.'

'Oh, that's terrible,' my mistress said compassionately, voicing my own reaction.

'Exactly,' Bill said with full force. 'You see, there are hardly any foxes left in Britain. Any sign of wild life is vanishing.'

'Our countryside has no creatures left,' Susan backed up Bill's statement.

'And the Dog Rights Group is demanding a stop to this cruel sport.'

'Will they be successful?' My mistress sounded doubtful.

'Not much hope. In a democracy, any issue is divided: some are in favour, some against. So nothing gets done.' Susan didn't seem hopeful.

A horn trumpeted the start of the hunt. All the horses set out at a canter but were soon at full gallop. The dogs were let loose to compete with the riders. I was gobsmacked by their stamina. They were jumping over hedges and ditches, keeping ahead of the riders, pitching for the fox holes. Then we saw a fox nearby in the open, looking alarmed by the terrible noise of horns, human yelling and dog yapping, instinctively knowing what that meant. Like lightning, it turned to the safety of its hole under the mound. When the riders reached the spot and reined in the horses, the dogs were already there. The noise of squealing, yapping, barking reached a crescendo. Shoving and pushing each other incessantly, they burrowed deeper and deeper into the fox hole to get at their kill. And they got it. They were now dragging it out into the open. A mauled bleeding piece of flesh, torn to pieces, hardly recognizable as a fox, was the booty of the day. Their mouths were dripping with blood. It was terrible to see what dogs could do.

'Oh, istenem,' my mistress was greatly distressed by the spectacle, her hand reached out for me.

'You see, there is no justification for it, as nobody eats fox meat,' Bill deplored the practice.

'It's just for fun. Now in Greenland, a country near the Arctic,' said Susan giving a counter-example of dogs' use for hunting, 'hunting animals is the only way the Inuit can survive in that harsh climate. So there is some sense in it, but in Britain it's all a game.' All this was getting confusing for me.

'That's why people are so much against it,' Bill added. 'Let me show you how the Anti-Hunt groups work,' he said, fast-forwarding the video. 'At the last hunt they kidnapped forty six-dogs from the kennels, on the grounds that they were rescuing them from a cruel sport. I couldn't agree more. I would readily support such rescue operations.'

'Isn't there an organization called something like RS...something in England, which protects home pets against any bad treatment by the owners?' My mistress wanted to confirm snatches of her knowledge about dogs in England.

'Oh, yes, there are some very strict laws about domestic pets.'

'Like what?'

'You are forbidden to use domestic pets for any sport,' Susan started to list them. Turning to Bill, she said, 'Do you remember last year they arrested three men who secretly ran dog-fights?'

'Oh yes, I do. It was in the local paper, wasn't it? I had never thought such things went on in English cities.' He shook his head in disbelief.

'There's nothing like that here,' my mistress said proudly.

'And if the RSPCA finds out,' Susan continued, 'that you leave your dog at home for long periods and go away on holidays - neighbours can tell on you - they will turn up at your door and take your dog away, giving it to a home that promises to treat it better.'

That went home to my mistress in no small measure. I stretched my head in her lap.

'Oh, istenem,' exclaimed my mistress, 'that's not fair! After all, the owners wouldn't have a dog if they didn't love it. Don't you think?' she asked pointedly. The discussion was hotting up, so Bill turned off the video.

'Yes and no,' Bill said. 'If you look at it from the point of view of the owner, okay, they can make some arrangement with a neighbour or someone, to come in and put the food out for the dog – you see, cats are not a problem – but what about the dog? Is he happy about it?' He paused for the question to sink in. I pushed my head deeper into my mistress' lap.

'Are you a member of this organisation?' my mistress asked.

'Not members, but in spirit we believe the same. There is so much abuse of animals. Take, for example, the kennels. Now people run them as a business. They take a lot of money from the owners, but don't give enough attention and comfort to the animal.'

Oh, dear, I thought, my poor mistress is coming under attack today.

'But what are people to do if they have to go abroad, not for pleasure but for work? Most countries have quarantine laws, don't they? What do they expect people to do? Bring their pets and dump them in quarantine kennels? That's cruel too. They can't have it both ways.' My mistress rose to her defence.

'The good news is that dogs can now be granted passports in the U.K., like other visitors. So hurray! No quarantine for dogs, at last!' Susan clapped her hands.

'You'll be able to take your dog with you,' Bill put the brighter side to view. 'Doggie can have his own passport.' He laughed and patted me on the head, 'Oh, I must tell you about a cartoon. It's absolutely hilarious, I saw it in the paper: a lady and a dog are sitting together in the plane, the dog by the window, and its owner is speaking to the air hostess, "Could you open the window? My dog would love to put her head out." Don't you think it's funny?'

Susan was cracking up, 'It was indeed, I remember that one, very good.'

My mistress barely smiled. She was still thinking back to Bill's earlier remark.

'Taking a dog on a business trip isn't practical, even if there's no quarantine. To keep it locked up in strange hotel rooms, while you yourself are out all day long, isn't any more humane than leaving it in kennels back home. Don't you think?' My mistress was rather snappy in her counter argument.

Nobody spoke for a minute.

'Hmm. It's Catch-22, I can see,' Bill admitted.

'Anyway, look,' Susan said, 'we'll gladly keep your dog, if you like. He is such a sweetie,' she reached out to pat me.

'Oh, thank you, I may take you up on your offer. My next trip will definitely be to Britain,' my mistress said quite categorically. It sounded as if she already knew about it. Was she hiding the news from me?

'Well, shall we watch the more interesting part of the video?' Susan suggested. 'You'll find it very interesting. Bill, could you fast forward, please? It's called "The Best Friend of Man". It shows how dogs can be trained to serve human interests without being treated cruelly.'

This sounded more cheerful. We waited while Bill was finding the right place.

'Did you know that dogs have been domesticated for 10,000 years?' Susan said.

'Yes, but cats have been longer,' Bill always won points over Susan. I looked at her to see whether she felt the same. I saw a cloud pass over her face. 'All right, here we are,' Bill stopped. I sat up.

The screen was lit up with a beautiful home, set in the countryside. Wow! What a place! The commentary ran over the pictures, giving details of the life of the dog. He regularly received medical checkups from a vet, was manicured by a specialist, taken on holidays and entered in fashion shows. You say it, he had it. I should have felt envious of his life-style, but I wasn't. I thought this wasn't being a dog.

'Would you like to live like that, dog? Would you, eh?' Susan asked me. I snorted and I think she got the message.

Next they showed a guide dog for blind people, very docile and obedient. He helped his master to cross the roads on a green light, went with him shopping and on walks. Bill and Susan clapped, but I felt sorry for the dog. He had to be on a lead all the time, and go at the same pace as his master, slow and watchful. At no point did he run or bounce or bark. Could he be a dog?

'Isn't it wonderful to see how a dog can be a guide for the blind?' Susan said with great conviction.

'Indeed, the man would not be able to go out at all without the dog,' Bill seconded her. 'It pays off to train dogs, I think. Watch the next one, it's even better.'

We now saw Alsatians - a breed that always sends shivers down my spine – being trained as drug sniffers. The experts were making them sniff drugs many times a day, and then tested their ability by hiding drugs somewhere and getting them to locate them, which some did quite accurately. In another part of the yard, the trainers were giving a provocative sort of training to other Alsatians. They were made to behave ferociously, although always kept on a lead. It wasn't their choice, was it? Next they showed dogs in different places; in prisons when prisoners were being interrogated; at airports and even at political demonstrations. These dogs could hardly protest against what they were being made to do. But nobody else was feeling like me, even my mistress seemed in favour of the police using dogs to catch criminals and drug dealers.

Next on the screen appeared landmine dogs. These were shown clearing landmines, the dangerous mess armies left behind after wars. I suppose here my fellow-canines were doing something worthwhile for humans. The video reinforced the worth of training dogs by showing many civilians without limbs in the war-torn countries. How can human beings be so cruel to each other? Here I willingly joined the company in lauding the nobility of dogs.

The next section showed a conference of doctors in favour of training dogs to detect cancer. I was puzzled. To train animals in their sense of smell was one thing, but to make them diagnose illnesses like doctors was another.

'Does cancer have smells? How can dogs be made to detect something internal?' Susan was puzzled, so was I.

'And how are the dogs going to indicate where the cancerous growth is?' My mistress added to the mystery.

'Well, we shall have to wait and see,' Bill said.

After all I had seen earlier on the video, I felt positively against all experimentation. Humans are a cunning breed, I concluded, they find out how to tap the best in animals for their own benefit. I don't have a very sharp sense of smell, but I think if they wanted to take me on, they could turn me into a cancer-finding dog, or a drug-sniffing or a mine-defusing or a violence-favouring canine. Could training dogs for human purposes leave enough of the natural animal in dogs?

While I was still juggling with riddles, the film turned to celebrity dogs. Now that was certainly disgusting. Human celebrities were bad enough, I always snoozed off whenever they came on the screen, but to see their diamond-studded and fur-draped dogs was more degrading. But to my surprise the present company clapped with enthusiasm, even my mistress! The film ended there, and just as well, as I thought I had had enough of human dogs for one evening.

'So when exactly are you going to Britain?' Susan asked. I sat up and looked straight at my mistress. My feeling was right, something had been going on behind my back.

'Some time next month. I will confirm,' she sounded a bit sheepish.

'Make sure we know a week in advance; we want to make sure we are around.'

'I will, I will,' she quickly covered up the fact that I had not been told.

'Now what about dinner, shall we proceed to the table?'

There was much oohing and aahing about it. 'Are we going to have palacsintas?' the guests chorused.

'Indeed. They are ready and waiting to stand the test,' was the elegant reply.

Candles were glowing, the dish was steaming, and it was time for me to part from human company. I would have liked to stay on and find out more about my mistress's plan for Britain. Perhaps they would talk about it while eating, but then I thought I would wait for her to tell me. Why hasten anxiety? Let sleeping dogs lie, as humans say. I quietly slipped out to do the same.

I must have dozed off, because the next I heard the guests was when they were leaving. It must have been fairly late, as the street was very silent. I stood up and followed them to the gate, wagging my tail.

'Goodnight, jó kutya,' Susan used the Hungarian dog speech, to make me feel at ease. I rewarded her effort with a special lick on her hand.

'See you soon, old chap. We'll sing dog-man songs when you come to stay with us, plenty of them in English, okay?' I sniffed in reply.

More goodbyes and goodnights at the gate. I went into my kennel to avoid meeting my mistress. But she stopped by, and kneeling took hold of my paw, saying most gently, 'You are not angry with me, drágám, are you? After the disaster of Erzsi Néni and the kennels, I had been looking around for a third alternative for your stay. Don't you trust me?' Tears filled my eyes and a lump obstructed my throat. I licked her face many times and could only make gurgling sounds, so overwhelmed was I by her kindness

†

23

BEING A GUEST

‡

The day arrived when my mistress had to leave for the U.K. A week before, she started to prepare for her departure, sorting out her papers, packing her things and making arrangements for the house to be looked after in her absence. The telephone rang constantly, people giving her last-minute information, or suggesting places to see and people to meet, or her boss giving her more instructions. It went on the whole time, it was nerve-racking for me. She realised that and apologised for the hectic atmosphere in the house, saying, 'You must understand, this is not like any other time. It's a journey westwards, drágám, very important,' she emphasised. If she made good contacts, she explained, and got some orders, her company would give her promotion.

This time I did not flap as usual at the thought of her going away, because I liked Susan – well, Bill too, but not as much - and was almost looking forward to being with her. This was the first time I was going to experience a stay with a family – I mean man and woman. I almost wished they had a child, and then like in the video, I could play games with him or her, I didn't mind whichever, boy or girl. Sometime back, I had learnt not to be partial in my gender preferences.

The day of departure arrived. My mistress said it was better if she took me to Bill and Susan's. She had to leave around lunch time for the airport, and she would have enough time to give the final touches to her packing after dropping me off at their apartment. So we walked up together. On the way my mistress gave me a little talk about how I should keep heart and not despair, since she was going to be away only for a week. 'Remember, this couple has given you a special invitation,' she emphasized, and urged me to enjoy the attention about to be showered on me, rather than keep missing her. We soon reached Széher út and she rang the bell on the gate. Susan appeared on the balcony and shouted that they would be down soon.

Being on the top floor, they took a few minutes to come down. Soon both were at the gate. They invited my mistress in, but she declined, saying she ought to be going on with her last minute preparations. She kissed me and handed me over to them, thanking them profusely for offering to look after me. We stood watching her turn the corner, and then I followed my hosts up to the third level. It was a bit of a heave up for me as I was not used to so many stairs.

'Welcome to our apartment,' they chorused with deep bows at the door. I played the game and went in with measured grace, and stood waiting for the next move from my hosts.

'Please sit, Your Majesty. What can we get you? Bill, fetch some milk for the honoured guest,' Susan said to Bill, who rushed with mock alacrity to serve me. I thought they were very funny. I would have liked to laugh if I could, instead I did a roll or two on the floor and gave happy barks. I lapped up the milk Bill put before me. I noticed a dog basket in the corner, apparently my bed. Of course, there was no terrace, and the balcony would get too cold.

'Come on, then, clever dog, show me where your bed is.' In reply to this test, I moved to the basket, and saw all sorts of imitation bones and other dog accessories there. I was very amused as I wasn't used to such things.

Soon I was served my meal. Well, that was the most privileged meal I ever had. People waiting on me hand and foot, making small conversation while I nibbled at my food slowly. The attention I had from my mistress was good, but nothing like this. Where would my mistress be if she did this to me three times a day? She would have to give up work and be in attendance on me all day long. This was my holiday, and Susan and Bill were doing their best to make everything special. It was time to sit back and enjoy being a guest.

The rest of the day I snoozed or took short walks in the house. I was given free rein to survey the premises, which consisted of just two rooms. The best part was the balcony. It overlooked the main road, where the buses rattled down at some speed. It was fun being on high and to look down on houses, cars, people, children and pets taken on their walks. Sometimes I would give a bark to make people look up. They would wave at me and say, 'Hello doggie, it must be good being up there, is it?' Yes, it was. I could also look at the hill opposite, across the valley, which I couldn't see clearly from the ridge where we took our daily walk. I knew it was there, because we passed the deep steps every day, but never took them. The Old Lady had found the up and down of the valley too much, and my mistress often discouraged me from lingering there, saying, 'Yes, drágám, I know you want to go there. It's all right to go down to the valley, we can do it sometime but we won't go up the hill from there. I have heard all sorts of things about it. So, don't fuss. Come, move on, quick.' Nor was the Old Lady keen on it. She called it the dark hill. She said Vera Néni once told her that sometimes domestic dogs ran away, took to the road, joined up with stray dogs and headed for the wilds to be with wolves and other animals for a free life. She would go to the extent of claiming that animals' natural place was in the wilds, and it was not fair that humans domesticated them for their own self-interest. She said some people claimed they had actually seen dogs with wolves prowling in the valley. Listening to this sort of talk always left me with much to think about, and I felt a persistent curiosity to see the 'dark' wood. Maybe my hosts thought differently about it. I started to think of a strategy.

For my evening repast, I was served a light meal, quite different from what I got at home. Nothing out of a tin, but bits of fresh meat in rice broth. I enjoyed it thoroughly. After watching me eat my meal with relish, Susan and Bill sat down to theirs. A nicely laid table, candles and napkins, wine glasses and shiny cutlery. I compared it with my mistress's plate in front of the TV. Was there something more to two people supping together than one by herself? I listened to their conversation, and could hardly help thinking of my mistress who had only me to talk to. It couldn't be much fun for her, I sighed. Why didn't she find a partner? It would be good for her, and I vowed I would support her decision, and adjust myself to suit her new life.

While I was busy planning the future of my mistress, Susan and Bill finished their supper, cleared the table and were standing with my lead ready to take me out for my constitutional walk. I jumped up with expectation. Where were we going to go? Maybe we'd go to the 'dark hill'. I wagged my tail. 'Good dog, don't get excited, we are not going far, just down the road for your jobbies,' Susan thought best to declare her hand. 'Tomorrow, you'll go on a special trip.' Bill nodded wholeheartedly.

So down we went and trundled along the ridge, straight up and down on the road. This was my usual evening route, I knew it well. What was new was that I was meeting different people. Many stopped to ask Susan and Bill if they had adopted a dog. There was much laughter when they were told that I was a 'guest' visiting them. They all made pleasant sounds at me and said how well-behaved I was. I, in the meantime, was looking at every man going by, wondering which one would be a good partner for my mistress. I was confident given the responsibility I could choose a suitable match for her from among the men passing, but how would I tell her who it was? I had no clue as to their names and where they lived. My imagination was fired by seeing two people living together happily. It made me ambitious for my mistress. I think somewhere at the back of my mind I was concerned with what would happen to her when I was gone – the Old Lady too must have felt the same.

On returning from the walk, I was ready to go to bed in my special corner, when Susan and Bill settled down to watch TV. I watched a bit but didn't find the programme interesting, so I decided to go to sleep. Once or twice I woke up in the night, thought I heard strange noises. The balcony door was left open, in case I needed to go out for a call of nature. I didn't need to but felt curious to see how the outside looked in the night. The moon was up, very bright but not yet full. I am an avid watcher of the moon, that's the only way I can keep pace with Time. As I stood looking at it I counted the days my mistress had been away – hardly one so far! Then I heard some strange animal calls. They seemed to come from the hill across. The dogs in the valley set up a howl in reaction, or was it in response? I too had an urge to bark, but out of courtesy to my hosts I kept control on myself. I looked at the hill, and thought I saw trees sway, not from wind but from something moving underneath. What could it be? I again hoped my hosts would take me there.

Still thinking of the hill I fell into deep sleep.

...

TRIP TO ÓBUDA

'Wakey, wakey, ' Susan's voice brought me back to where I was. She was carrying my breakfast. Bill clapped his hands, 'English breakfast for Your Highness.' He put down a bowl of milk-soaked chunks of bread.

'Did you have a good sleep, doggie?' Susan enquired. 'Hope you are not missing your mistress?' I got up and tucked into my exotic repast, too ashamed to admit I wasn't.

After lapping up my breakfast, I sat back and watched my hosts having theirs. What next? I wondered. Susan cleared the table and Bill came over with my lead. I jumped up wagging my tail and hoping we would go to the 'dark hill'.

'Bill, I think we should go to Óbuda today,' Susan said, 'It's better to stay closer to home on the first day, just in case any problem arises.'

'Very sensible. We do keep postponing the trip to Óbuda. Today then, mister, is the day for all of us to find out what the Romans did for Hungarians.'

Susan added, 'Don't forget the Turks, quite a few monuments in Óbuda to tell their story, the Tourist Guide says.'

Bill said, 'So, to the Turks, and also let's not forget the early Christians too – we'll do the whole lot today.' The names rang a bell. I remembered the bedtime stories by the Old Lady, about invaders and settlers.

Bill saw me listening attentively and said, 'What do you say, old friend? Have you been there?' I extended my paw to say no I hadn't, and would very much like to go with them. I had heard my mistress talking about it to her guests. Bill shook my paw and said, 'Good, you are happy at that. I think it's going to be a grand tour.'

'So, what's the batting order, Susan?' Bill asked. Susan had it all planned. 'First we go to the Trinitarian monastery, then walk down to Gulbaba, then go to the Roman ruins, and if we discover any other sites, we stop at them also.' 'Do we take a picnic?' Bill asked. 'No, we won't,' Susan said, 'I know a good café, a real Hungarian café, where we can have gulyás,' then turning to me, added 'and you can also have the same, doggie.'

I was happy that they were making me part of their family. I had already forgotten that this was my temporary home, and that I was there on loan. My thoughts turned to the nature of my existence. But this wasn't the time to dwell over it. I prepared myself to enjoy my time with these friends of my mistress's. Besides, I had not yet been taken there by her. I began to think my mistress followed rather set habits, and avoided going to less popular places. I was alarmed at thinking about her in a grudging way.

I went out on the balcony. It was already hot. The sun seemed to have taken over the whole sky, with hardly a cloud in sight. I was already feeling the heat and my tongue was hanging out. Could it be the High Summer, the month of July? Yes, it must be. All those bedtime stories came rushing to my mind. I remembered the Old Lady telling me about Sirius, the Dog Star, and the sun and why the hot summer was called the Dog Days. How long ago was that? I looked up to work out how close the two stars were in the sky, but the glare of the sun was so much, I could hardly see anything.

'Come, old scout, you and I to the wide world,' Bill was putting the collar on me, 'first to your morning call and then we take the bus.' I began to like Bill. He had a jolly style of talking to me. My thoughts once again turned to my mistress, wondering why she hadn't had a partner so far. Bill shouted out to Susan who was in the bathroom that we would meet her at the bus stop. 'Off we go, friend. I'll race you down.' And before I knew it he shot off, leaving me to run after him. It was hard for me to keep up with him. I had to be careful going down fast on the stairs, not being used to them. 'Here's the bus stop, mister; but first we take a walk down the road, for your doings, quick, quick.' I couldn't have been quicker, and then we raced back to the bus stop where Susan was already waiting for us. We could see the bus rattling downhill, one of those I had been hearing every ten minutes since the early morning. Bill put the muzzle on me, which to my discomfort prevented me from letting my tongue out on a hot day like this. But I was determined to enjoy my very first outing with my hosts. I still didn't miss my mistress.

Fortunately, the bus was not very crowded and I could sit by the window. Bill was explaining to Susan, 'The bus will cut out the centre and take us directly to Old Buda. As the crow flies, it's a straight line from West to East across the three Buda hills.' I was glad not to be pumping my lungs, but letting the bus wheels do the climbing and descending for me.

The bus was going up the last hill now. 'Can you see the monastery, Bill?' Susan pointed out through the window. 'Looks like a huge bird sitting atop the hill, doesn't it?' I craned my head to see how high up it was. 'Come over here,' Susan said pulling me on to her lap, 'you'll have a better view from here.' The bus was now almost at the top and was going along a huge wall on the left. On the right, way down, Óbuda was coming into view. 'The first stop is ours – the only stop, the bus then turns round and heads down.' Susan rang the bell and we got off.

'Oh, look at the view!' Bill exclaimed. 'The whole damn lot, Buda, Pest and the Duna snaking out to Szentendre and beyond.'

We stood at the parapet, silenced by the vast panorama.

'It's so lovely, why don't we sit down for a minute?' Susan said sitting down on the low parapet, and signalled to me to sit beside her.

'Just look at it,' Bill said, with a sweep of his arm.

'I dread returning to Britain,' Susan said in a dead tone.

'What? But that's home,' Bill said shocked. 'Why do you say that?'

'I like Budapest, it's a nice city, not like Manchester. I like living in the Buda hills. It's not crowded and so peaceful, unlike the sprawling industrial city where we live.'

'Nothing's stopping us from moving to the countryside. There are lots of villages around Manchester, and quite nice ones too,' Bill said reassuringly.

'What, live in a village?' Susan said in disbelief. 'Can you see me living in a village?'

'You never know, you may love it.'

'No I won't,' Susan was very emphatic. 'English villages are so parochial. I can't see myself living between the church, the pub and the village hall. No thank you.'

'I didn't mean "live there" in that way. We can continue to work and do things in Manchester as we do now, but live in the country.'

'It won't be the same,' Susan replied, and then added dreamily, 'I could live here forever.'

I felt with her. The prospect of staying with them every time my mistress went abroad appealed to me. I liked Susan, and Bill too.

'It wouldn't be wise to do that. Things are still not too stable in this country. I don't trust the politics here. The Communists are already back in power,' Bill said getting up.

'Anyway, we'll talk about it later. Let's go in now. The old church building is supposed to be magnificent, on a very large scale, but not in service, of course.' Bill took Susan's hand.

We went through the main gate which opened out into a very large garden, rectangular and full of flowers and bushes. 'The yellow building in front is the monastery,' Susan read out of the tourist book, 'it was completed around 1758 but within twenty years the Monastery was dissolved and the building was confiscated and turned first into a military camp, and then a hospital. Now it's a museum which houses a 19th century pharmacy....' She stopped and said to Bill, 'We don't want to see the museum, do we?'

'Not really, it's the Trinitarian Templom we are looking for.'

'The huge wall you see on the left, that's the wall of the old monastery chapel, now a mere shell,' she pointed out.

'You think they'll let us take Béla in?' Susan whispered.

'I'll ask the monk. Hungarians are supposed to be dog lovers, we'll find out soon.' Bill walked up to the desk. Susan and I waited at the door. He returned with a big smile, saying that the monk gave one look at Béla and okayed his entry. I did a little jig to let them know how happy I was to remain with them, even though I had to keep my muzzle on.

We went in. 'Oh, my God, this is magnificent, I have never seen anything like this before!' Susan exclaimed.

'Indeed, trust the monks to go the whole hog.' Bill was equally awestruck. If I could speak I would have said the same. The hall was vast and high-vaulted. The emptiness gave it a sacred aura. The architecture was embellished by decorations in vivid colours and patterns. Susan was reading out of the book. 'In 1738, some three hundred years ago, a Christian sect called Trinitarians arrived in Óbuda and built themselves a monastery on Kiscelli hill...' Listening to Susan, I was trying to remember if among my history lessons, there was a mention of this monastery. The Old Lady did mention a statue of the Virgin Mary of Máriazell which was supposed to have a miracle-making quality, but I couldn't remember whether it was here or somewhere else. I looked around but saw no sign of it in the chapel.

We must have been there for over an hour. In the end I wondered if we were ever going to leave the place. I was glad when at last we came out, the muzzle was getting too much for me. To my great relief, Bill saw my discomfort and took it off.

'Where to next?' Bill asked.

'Well, the two Roman places I have marked are closer from here, and we can get there now if we dart straight down, which we can't,' she traced them on the map. 'One is called Hercules Villa, a noble's mansion with mosaic floors, worth seeing; the other is the site of the military camp straight ahead, ruins of baths with some good columns still standing. There are other sites, like Aquincum, an aquaduct and another amphitheatre a few kilometres further away, but we won't go there today. I'm already feeling the heat.' I was grateful for that remark.

'So what do you suggest?' Bill wanted to get going. So did I.

'First we should go to Gulbaba's Tomb; it's a good walk, an avenue of trees all along which will provide us shade from the sun, no traffic and the place is set in a garden,' Susan said closing the book. 'Yes?'

'Yes, sounds good,' Bill said with a sweeping gesture, 'lead the way.'

So, we set out on the promised road, walking down along the walls of the monastery, which towered over us, so massive were they. Bill said that after the hugeness of the monastery he looked forward to the smallness of the tomb, a mausoleum is always a modest building. Susan thought it was built before the Kiscelli Monastery, when the Turks were here as rulers and at the height of their power in Hungary. I hadn't reckoned on visiting Ottoman sites, only the Roman ones. They'll be next, Susan had said. I must be patient, I reminded myself.

I liked the walk, it was thrilling to simply roll down the hill. The avenue of trees blocked the intense heat of the High Summer and made it cool to go at a leisurely pace. No fun in rushing to escape the burning sunlight.

Half way down, Bill and Susan stopped to look at the view. 'See all the bridges on the right,' Susan said, 'before they were built, the Duna had kept Pest separated from Buda. Since they were linked, together they make a marvellous city.' Bill mused over Óbuda. 'And the once flourishing centre, Óbuda, is now lost in a jungle of high-rise apartment blocks, courtesy of the Soviet period.' The irony was not lost on me. 'Look at the neat way the Duna steps aside, parting at the touch of Margit Sziget. Neat, very neat,' Bill mused poetically. It was strange looking down on an island. I hadn't seen an island before, let alone Margit's island. Susan was telling Bill the story of Princess Margit. It again brought back memories of history lessons on Hungarian kings and the Mongols, and why the island was named after Princess Margit. I remembered how the Old Lady had cried thinking of a nine-year-old being banished to a convent on this very island. Susan was saying, 'Margit proved to be so saintly that she wouldn't even wash herself above the ankles. How gruesome!' she said with a deep sigh. Bill added laughing, 'Still she was vindicated when the Turks turned it into a harem!' Since I didn't know what was a harem, I couldn't share the joke.

'Are we going there too?' Bill asked.

'No, it's a whole day trip, really. The convent ruins are worth a visit, the book says, so we can't do it today.' I was disappointed. It would have been good to have felt the presence of the little Princess in the ruins.

'So, what was that about wanting to live in Budapest? You don't mean it, do you?' Bill asked as we continued the walk.

'Of course, I do. I like it here, very much.'

'But this is not our country, Susan. We don't even speak the language, it's okay as a working holiday, but I can't think of shifting to Hungary for good.' Bill's tone was serious.

'Why worry about "for good"; who knows where we will be in ten years' time.'

'I know, we'll be where my job is...'

'You can look for a job here, plenty of jobs for Brits in Budapest itself,' Susan interjected.

'You know my contract is up next year.'

'Your degree in political science will easily get you a job at the Central European University here. They are crying out for people to teach International Relations.'

'Well, it seems you have given the matter a great deal of thought.' Bill was incredulous. I could understand his feeling. It seemed he had no inkling of it.

'Sure, I have,' Susan said, 'shall we talk over lunch? Now I want to concentrate on getting to the Tomb, unless we want to lose our way.' Was there a warning in Susan's voice?

As we took another turn downwards on the road, the tomb of Gulbaba came into view. Bill and Susan stopped to admire the beautiful structure of the dome. Its gold spike glinted in the sun. They were comparing it with the Christian churches, which didn't interest me so much. What appealed to me most was that the mausoleum sat in the middle of the garden, giving peace to the saint resting within. Another five minutes, and we found ourselves at the gates. Fortunately no one was there, so I went in without any problem. It was so different from the monastery, which was on a grand scale. This place in contrast was down to earth. There were rows of roses, different colours and types, the air was infused with their scent. We sat down on a bench and Susan read out from the book. Gulbaba was a Sufi saint who came perhaps from Persia, but nobody knows for sure. Although he was a Muslim, the book said, he was renowned by all for his devoutness. Even Christians came to make a wish at his tomb. I had heard the Old Lady talking about this place with Vera Néni, but to be here was balm to the senses.

'Shall we take a round of the place, and then move on to the Roman ruins?' Bill said getting up. I followed them as they wandered leisurely round the garden, going full circle to the mausoleum. We peered at the grave through the barred door. A simple stone slab draped with silk cloth. Gulbaba's body lay under there. This was my first time looking at a grave. My thoughts went to the Old Lady. She must also lie in a grave somewhere; was it in a rose garden? Does my mistress go to see her? My mind was beset by many questions. What happens to animals when they die? Do they bury their dead in graves too? Or do their bodies simply disintegrate and disappear into the earth?

'There are Turkish Baths just below here,' Susan was saying, 'Can you see that building over there, with little chimneys sticking out?' Susan tried to direct Bill's eye. 'Those are the baths, the only mark left of the Turkish presence in Hungary for almost two hundred years,' Susan said with a touch of melancholy.

'At least the Hungarians recognise one thing about them, even if it is the tradition of hot baths and robed bodies,' Bill said ironically, looking at the picture in the book.

'There is definitely an evasiveness in Hungarians when you mention the Turks,' Susan agreed. I knew that too well and could testify to it. My mistress would never say much when asked about the Turks.

'If you bend a little and look straight from the baths to the hill above,' Susan directed Bill's eye, 'you'll just catch the Fisherman's Bastion, a sort of promenade now. Behind it – you can't see from here – is the Mátyás Church. It was converted from the mosque and the Islamic structure completely eliminated.' I tried to follow her directions but couldn't see much.

'Ah, but it wasn't the Turks who built it,' Bill said, 'I know my Hungarian history.'

'Yes, that's right. It says here,' Susan said reading from the book, "the Vár was constructed in the fifteenth century by Mátyás Corvinus" – and hence the name of the church. So, yes, when the Turks defeated the Hungarians in 1526, they converted it to a mosque….' Bill interjected, 'And when the Turks were vanquished, the Christians converted it back to a church - the tourist site of today. Right? Call it the ping-pong of history.'

The puppet box rose in my mind, with memories of lessons on the Magyar kings and the invading Mongols. I could see the Old Lady's chin resting over the puppeteer's curtain and saying to me, 'Never mind the church-mosque to and fro, szívem, but take note the construction of the Vár was first started by Béla III – that's your namesake – before, alas, he had to abandon it.' She never missed an opportunity to highlight the grand connections of my name.

Having finished with Gulbaba's Tomb, Bill and Susan were deciding on the next move. Susan suggested we walk down to the road and take a bus to the Roman site, the one further away. The main drag was full of traffic, she said, nothing as idyllic as the one we had walked so far.

'And what about the restaurant?' Bill looked at his watch. 'I could do with lunch soon.'

'Me too, and I'm sure the doggie also,'- she didn't forget me - 'the restaurant is close to the Hercules Villa site, popular with local Hungarians. After lunch, we can walk back on the same road to Florian Tér - only a ten minute walk,' Susan said measuring the distance on the map. 'There was a military camp there once, and now there are some columns and sculptures scattered round. Quite interesting,' and then added, 'and if after that we feel like stopping at the big amphitheatre, we can do that.' 'Or go home for a siesta!' Bill said realistically, voicing my own preference.

'Agreed. Let's go then,' Susan said setting a fast pace, but not faster than me, something I have over humans.

We had hardly got to the bus stop when the bus arrived, which saved us waiting time. Susan was right, the traffic was awful, and the bus hot. Anyway, we got off at the underpass and crossed over to the ruins and remains right in the centre, with every sort of vehicle circling round them inch by inch.

More weeds than seats, the former camp turned out not to be so impressive. I think the main reason was the noise from the traffic. It had also become part of the Metro station; people went about their business, totally ignoring the remnants of grandeur the area must once have had. Like me, Susan and Bill were disappointed. It was nothing like what they had expected. The tourist book had given it too much of a high profile. I would have liked to sit and wait for my hosts in one place, but they couldn't let me out of their sight. After all, they said, I was loaned to them and they were responsible for me. What if I went astray? How would they face my mistress? Once again, my thoughts turned to her, and what it would be like to see her again. Only a day had passed since she left, but it already seemed like ages since I last saw her. I would be sorry to leave these people, whose wider perspective on things was revealing many truths to me. They were the first outsiders in my life who took me in and were making me part of their life, volatile as it turned out to be. Will they remain in my memory?

They instructed me strongly that I was to keep close to them, while they moved slowly, looking at all the bits and pieces lying around. Susan read out from the book on and off, and Bill tried to decipher Latin inscriptions on fallen stones and plaques. They had to shout to hear each other, with the constant noise from the traffic above and around. Anyway, within the hour they were through and ready to head for the restaurant. Bill was making noises about food. Fortunately, the restaurant was not far, and what's more, the owner allowed me in, provided, he said, I did not create any disturbance. He even let Bill take my muzzle off. How else could I eat my food?

Susan ordered the food in Hungarian. This was the first time I had heard any foreigner speak in our language. And I could tell she spoke it with a good accent. For the meal, she ordered gulyás and palacsintas and chocolate ice-cream for desert. While waiting for food to arrive, I looked at the other people there, and immediately placed them socially. I'm afraid living in a genteel house had made me class conscious. I heard Bill ask the waiter to make it quick. Like him, I could hardly wait to eat. Soon, a piping-hot gulyás was brought in a tureen, and warm crusty bread in a basket. Mine came separately. We all tucked in. It was delicious, the meat well cooked. Having cleaned up my plate in no time, and not wanting desert, I stretched out to rest my limbs. As I floated into my post-lunch siesta, I heard Bill saying that the choice of the restaurant was good, they should come there again.

I must have slept for half-an hour when I was startled by Susan's voice. 'I don't want to open a nursery in a village, thank you very much. What gave you that idea?'

'Isn't it logical to say that, instead of teaching in a nursery in Manchester – which now you say you don't like,' Bill spoke in an even tone, 'it stands to reason to say that you could open one in the village we choose to live in?'

Susan's voice rose in a pitch. 'I have told you I don't want to live in a village.'

'All right. So what will you do here?'

'I want to start a theatre in Budapest. There is a great desire in the English-speaking ex-pat community to have an English theatre here.'

'I never thought you were interested in theatre that much,' Bill said surprised by the revelation. 'When exactly did you decide on it?'

'It's been growing gradually. Teaching women's studies at the university - a point in favour of the communists, they gave jobs to the wives of foreign professors - ...'

Bill interjected. 'A policy to keep the wives out of mischief! You must never underestimate their astuteness!'

Susan laughed. I was relieved. I had sensed a tension in their conversation since this morning. I thought, wouldn't it be good to end our trip on this positive note. But it was not up to me to decide, I could only wait.

'Anyway, we can consider moving to Budapest, provided we both get something out of it.' I was glad to hear Bill coming round to Susan's idea. I would have been disappointed if he hadn't. I was still puzzled why my mistress didn't have a partner.

They looked at me and saw that I was ready to go back. They paid the bill and we set out on the journey home. Which home? It worried me to be so quick in changing my view of the world. Only a day, and I had already lost my bearings. Will I remember them? Do I have a memory? Do animals have memory? These questions continued to haunt me.

...

CHINESE PAGODA

I woke up to the sound of birds. Susan was standing by the balcony, looking out. 'Did you sleep well, doggie?' she enquired in a gentle tone. 'Come to the kitchen for breakfast.' I followed her hoping it would be the English breakfast again. It was and I gobbled up the bread in milk pretty fast. 'Today, we'll take the forest train and show you the whole of this hill, then we'll go up to see the Pagoda - it's the Chinese for a tower - and have a picnic lunch there. How's that? Happy?' I was still licking the milk off my whiskers but gave a wide flick of my tail to show that I was.

'Bill isn't up yet. As soon as he's ready, we'll be off. We'll take a picnic this morning. You want to sit and watch me?' She sang while she made sandwiches. I loved the sound of her songs, and wished my mistress sang more. My thoughts went to her and I wondered what she would be doing at that moment. Bill came in still in his night clothes. He was surprised to see Susan well into preparations for the outing. 'Isn't it too early to leave?' He didn't seem very enthusiastic.

'Start in good time, and return in good time, that's my motto,' Susan replied. 'We had agreed to leaving by ten, and that's when we will leave.'

'I wish you weren't so organised. It would be nice to relax some time.' I didn't like his tone.

'Well, do you want to go or not?' Susan challenged. I began to worry about our trip. I so much wanted to go. I made a throaty sound, in a pleading manner. They both turned to me to check if something was wrong. I licked Bill's hand.

'See, he wants to go,' Susan found an accomplice.

'I'll have a quick coffee and get ready.' It worked.

Within the hour we set out for the local wood, just a climb away. This walk was familiar to me, I had done it many times before. The hill train too I had been on a few times with my mistress, but not that often; so I was looking forward to it. I set the pace for my hosts by running ahead and then waiting for them, and when they caught up with me, I would run on further. It wasn't very long before we got to the station where the train stopped to pick up passengers. At this point Susan put the muzzle on me. I never liked having this contraption on but the alternative was not to go anywhere.

We got on the train and it set off chug-a-chug, a leisurely holiday speed. Susan let me sit by the window. I looked around to see if there were other dogs in the carriage. There was one, rather a big one. He too had a muzzle on. Looking at him had a mirror effect on me. I could imagine what I looked like. Still, dogs have no choice. It's not like being a child who would protest at not being given a choice. I had to remind myself that dogs are house animals whose lives are one long list of rules and commands. It was a depressing thought. I turned my mind to the scene outside. The view was not familiar to me. It looked down on the other side of the Buda Hills. A whole stretch of valleys, woods and hills were rolling by.

We got off at the last station and started the promised walk up to the Pagoda. I had not been to this one before. How is it that my mistress did not know about this place? Was she nervous going to places off the main paths? Another reason for being two, I reasoned. Susan removed my muzzle and took me off the leash. From sheer delight at being free, I ran backwards and forwards, almost in a frenzy. Susan and Bill seemed very quiet. 'Look, doggie, the Pagoda, can you see it?' Susan held me by the collar and turned my face upwards. 'We are going to go right up to the top. Up there, you'll be able to see all around, in all directions. Shall we then?'

The muzzle was clipped back. I looked up and saw a few people deeply immersed in taking in the view. I bounded up the stairs, for which I was scolded by Susan for rushing ahead. I must stay with them. Children might get scared by a romping dog, she explained. So, I had to remain between them. We started to go round slowly, stopping to take in the breathtaking view of the valleys at every turn. When we got to the top, Susan remarked that I was standing at the highest point of the city. We stood looking at the panoramic view. 'Hello there. Fancy seeing you here, Susan, Bill,' someone called out. 'Oh, hello, there. What a surprise, Peter.' My hosts greeted a tall handsome man.

'Looking very parental,' Peter said nodding towards me.

'Why, does he look like a child?' Susan patted me.

'Don't know about him,' Peter said, 'but you both look keen parents.'

'What about you? Married now?' Bill turned the remark back on him.

My ears pricked up. I rather liked the man. He had a smiling face and a happy manner. Why couldn't my mistress meet him? I would be thrilled to walk between them and have people ask if I was their child.

'No fear, not yet.' Everyone laughed. 'Anyway, you are still around, obviously. Why don't we meet some time?' He sounded sociable.

'Yes, come for a meal one day.' Susan extended the invitation immediately.

A ray of hope. Maybe Susan could invite my mistress too. That's how things start, I concluded. I promised to myself that I wouldn't be jealous.

'In the meantime, why don't you have a sandwich with us?' Susan patted the bag on Bill's shoulder. 'Down there, on the grass, yes?' Peter was happy at the idea. We descended. A table cloth marked our grass patch. Bill took out sandwiches and drinks. We were ready to eat and relax. While they talked, I kept turning and looking at every bit of the surroundings. The growth was impenetrable.

I looked up at the Pagoda, it was getting crowded. My thoughts went to my mistress again; I wondered what she was doing at that moment. Was she having a picnic too, maybe with someone she met? Wandering thoughts bring sleepiness with them. I was startled out of my doze by Susan's voice, 'Could I finish what I am telling Peter – if you don't mind?' She looked pretty upset. Peter was quick in saying, 'Yes, go on, I am waiting to hear more.' He eased the situation. He seemed the jokey type. I liked him. How old was he? But then, I didn't know how old was my mistress. Numbers! Numbers were what I had no grasp of.

Eventually everyone got up. Peter said he must leave, as he had set himself a longer walk before the day finished. He gave me a very friendly handshake and ruffled my neck. I licked his hand to show I accepted him as a friend.

We took the downward road, but we had hardly started down the path when Susan had an outburst. 'Can you not interrupt when I am talking to people.'

'Did I?'

'Yes, you did. And you do it all the time,' Susan persisted indignantly.

'That's how conversations go between people.'

'Don't tell me how conversations go. You cut me off when we are with people, as if I'm not there. And if I speak, you jump in, take up what I am saying and then ignore me. Why can't you wait until I have finished.' Susan's voice was rising. What was going on?

'Come, now, Sue. You are too touchy,' Bill was trying his best. He took her hand, but Susan shook it off. Bill shrugged his shoulders. They walked in silence. Somehow the surroundings no longer seemed exciting. Something had changed.

The train was crowded. Everyone was returning home. I got a seat by the window again, and became immersed in the view, this time coming at it from the opposite side. The city looked different in the setting sun. When we got home I was ready to turn in. I lay down on my bed and waited to see if Susan would be in a better mood. They seemed all right. She made tea and they talked about Peter. I was so relieved that things were fine with them that I fell into a snooze immediately, until I was woken up for dinner, followed by the customary walk. I was exhausted from the morning outing, so didn't really take in much on the road.

...

IN THE FOREST

Next morning, the first sound that tapped on my sleeping head was Bill's singing:

Open all the windows, open all the doors,
And let the merry sunshine in.

'Wake up, lazy bones,' Bill clapped his hands, 'time for breakfast, mister, mister.' I sat up quickly in obedience. Hardly awake, my first thought was, where to today? I was getting into luxurious habits. I wondered if anything special was laid out for me. Was I getting spoiled? Where would it leave me with my mistress if I expected new things every day? Soon I heard Susan talking to Bill about the day's plan. There we are, I gloated. I was right. This time we were going to go further than our own woods. They were planning to drive to the northern hills which were said to be inhabited by boars, wolves and even bears. Susan said, 'Doggie, doggie, we are going to show you the natural habitat of animals – animals of the wild.' Would I be lucky enough to actually see real wild animals - face to face?

Bill said he'd make a packed lunch this time. I was going to follow him when Susan said, 'No, doggie, the chef does not like anyone in the kitchen, not even me. Come away, we'll check the car.' So I raced down with her. Susan gave a running commentary on every part of the car and how one drives it. If I had been given the chance of driving that day, I would have done a good job, maybe even won a race. Susan said she was looking forward to driving on the highway, and I, going to the country.

When we set out, I got the window seat at the back. Immediately I sat up and stuck my head out, my eyes taking in every bit of the passing landscape, feeling the cool breeze on my face. Susan drove and Bill sat next to her. They chatted about their jobs and their future plans. I wasn't much interested in their talk, but wanted to sense if all was peaceful between them. As we left the city behind, the countryside was opening up. I was surprised how flat it was. I could see nothing but the horizon, a mere line dividing the blue sky from the green earth. Anyway, I wasn't going to be fussy, and after the initial disappointment settled back to enjoy whatever was rolling into view.

'Hey, mister, watch out for the deer.' Bill stretched out his arm and tickled me. 'Poor things, chased out of the forests, they now inhabit open fields, like cattle.'

'What can they do,' Susan said, 'when woods are cleared, they have no option but to wander down for a day's outing – just like you, doggie.' I wasn't sure what the deer looked like, but I kept an eye out for any moving bodies in the fields, stretching away as far as the eye could see. The circular motion was mesmerising.

'Look, doggie, there's the famous forest,' Susan was saying.

'No, not on the side, you dumbster, straight ahead,' Bill said in his typical way. A dense forest stood across the motorway, almost as if barring our way. Could animals live in such dark places? Something surged in me.

Soon, we came abreast of it. The forest now loomed over us, a massive stretch changed to a towering height. It sloped away to the left, bringing the valley beyond into view. Susan parked the car on the main road at a place where there were a few shops. We all got out. I was put on a lead and tied to a ring outside while they went into the shop to get a few eats and local information on climbing the hills.

I sat down to have a good look at the forest. It was so high that it dwarfed everything on the road. I tried to spot the wild animals through the impenetrable growth. When the trees moved I thought it was because of the animals' movements. If only I could have a glimpse of one. The hill rose straight up, sheer height. How were we going to get up there? Having walked up and down the city roads, I hadn't the slightest clue how we could scale a hill.

'Right, we are off,' Bill untied me. 'Are you ready to do the climbing?'

'It's not him, it's us,' Susan wisely pointed out. 'All the scary stories about the bears and wolves on the board in the shop. "Beware, beware" was the message. Didn't you read it?' Was there caution in her voice?

As soon as we hit the beginning of the path up, Bill untied me, saying, 'No muzzle this time.' I sprinted ahead. They called out that I mustn't go too far, in case the wolves waylaid me. The climb began to get steeper at every winding upwards. Susan was beginning to find it hard. She was stopping many times. Bill was offering to pull her along, but she refused, saying she wanted to do it on her own. We continued to climb with no end in sight, so high was the hill. The path kept on zigzagging more and more. All we could see were thick trees, no sunlight filtered through them. Susan was getting breathless; Bill was trying to take her mind off the effort by relating lots of stories. I wished I could have done something for her. I was also huffing and puffing, but salivating was proving an advantage.

'Look, Susan,' Bill exclaimed, 'the sky!' We stood and watched the bit of blue peeping through the trees. 'Come on then, just the last bit now. We should be there in a jiffy.' Bill didn't want to lose the momentum. We were only a few windings down from the top. Keeping the widening scrap of blue above in view, we soon emerged into a patch of land, the highest point of the forest.

'At last!' Susan heaved with relief. 'How long did that take us?' 'Almost two hours, not bad,' Bill confirmed.

It was enclosed by forest on all sides. It looked like a piazza, like I had seen on TV, where people came out in the evenings and sat in cafés, drinking and eating on hot summer days. Maybe the wild animals do the same, I thought. Do they socialise with each other by gathering on the common, and then withdraw into their reserves from where they hunt their kill in the undergrowth?

'There's no one here, just us and the doggie. We could be in a paradise of our own.' Susan was feeling romantic.

'It looks like it, doesn't it? Come, let's sit down under the trees, with sandwiches and a flask of ale, who cares if we never go down!' Bill lay down on the grass full stretch. Susan laughed, 'Not quite what the great poet says.' 'Here, mister,' Bill tackled me next. 'Sit and wait for your food, since dogs can't romanticise.' Bill's remark went to my heart. Am I really that brutish, and good at only eating and barking? But I did as instructed and waited impatiently. I was ravenous. Bill was right.

After that grandiose statement of love and ale, Bill and Susan lay down for a little siesta. I remained up, thinking at least I could guard my hosts against any danger from the wild animals. Another hour passed. I was alert to every stir from the surrounding denseness. What if we were being watched by animals? I bored my eyes into the thick growth, attempting to make out any shapes lurking in the trees ready to spring on us. I looked at my hosts lying stretched out, without any fear of bears or wolves creeping up on them. I am an animal and yet I was uneasy with those surroundings. What made them so confident about their safety?

A movement stirred in the trees. I shot up and gave loud barks aimed at any animal thinking it could get away with an attack on us. My action was a lot of bravado as I was feeling quite nervous and wished to turn my back on the wild animals inhabiting the forest. But my hosts were in no haste and continued to doze. I decided to prod them to be up. So I pretended I saw some animal in the bushes, and set up a lot of chasing and scraping the ground. In the end, I succeeded. Susan looked at her watch and decided it was time to make our move. Bill wanted to stay longer but Susan pointed out that we would be losing the sun earlier, and that it was wiser to start the journey. I was relieved.

While deliberating which exit to take, they remembered the warnings they had seen in the shop below: "Not all paths bring you down to the road. Make sure you come down by the one you took going up." On inspection, they soon discovered that there were many paths leading out of the clearing. There were at least four that looked like the one we had taken on the way up. Bill and Susan tried hard to identify the path we had taken, but weren't getting anywhere. The only way they could decide was by trial and error.

Suddenly Susan said, 'Hey, our doggie should be able to sniff our smells on the path. Why didn't we think of it before? Let him loose, Bill.' 'Now, mister,' Bill wagged his finger at me. 'Don't you take off on your own. Okay?' I was happy to be of some help, even if it was a test for me. I was sent down one path they thought we might have come up on. I sniffed the slope, stones and all but smelled nothing. 'We're waiting for the signal, doggie. Squeal, squeal.' Apparently, dogs squeal as a signal that they can smell familiar scents. Alas! I could not smell anything, and just looked emptily at my hosts.

We returned to the clearing, and I was sent down the next path. This formed a pattern for the all the exits they thought might yield the authentic one. But each time I tried hard to come up with positive results, alas, again I was not able to pick up any scent of ourselves on any of the paths. It became quite clear that relying on my smell was a waste of time. Time was ticking away. I could see the panic on Susan's face. She blurted out, 'Oh, doggie, doggie, you are hopeless. Why can't you help?' Bill too reprimanded me.

'One path must have our smells, mister, which one is it?' What could I do? If I no longer had my canine senses, was I to blame for it? I did not take kindly to their harsh words.

'What are we going to do now?' Susan was almost crying. 'Look at the light, we can't lose more time.' Bill tried to keep calm, 'I suggest we take the path we think most likely to be the right one – even if it isn't – and keep going. Let's move now.' He put the lead back on me.

To begin with, it looked as if the path was a good choice, but after a while it abruptly ended in a thicket. 'There's no way we can go back to the top,' Bill said. 'We can look around here for another opening.' We all got rummaging through the undergrowth to find some vestige of a path. One thicket showed some signs of trodden earth, we took it. We had hardly gone a few steps ahead when we heard some heavy movements and scrambling behind the line of trees on the right of us. I broke out into loud barking to make sure the animal there knew it was dealing with another animal and not some helpless humans. Time was against us. The sunlight was beginning to lose its brightness. There was no proper path to be seen, but Bill and Susan kept bashing down the undergrowth and fighting for just a little path that allowed us to get out of the forest. I kept close to them, whether out of nervousness or a sense of shame, I don't know. We had hardly covered much ground when we heard thudding and heavy scrambling again. This time the noise moved with us. Susan was out of her wits. I issued some very threatening barks and pulled at my lead to go after whoever was in the thickets, but Bill kept a strong hold on me. 'Keep your mouth shut and put your stamina into walking.' Susan hung on to Bill. Linked together, we three concentrated on making our way down.

Very soon we were barred by even denser growth. We looked around for another opening and found a path that also had signs of use. No sooner had we taken it that we ran into yet another cul-de-sac. As we were back-tracking to find another opening, we saw a very clear path. We could hardly believe our eyes and took it immediately. We had taken so many turns that Bill had no idea which direction we were facing now and whether we were heading for our final destination. He said as long as we kept moving, we'd get there in the end. He urged Susan not to give way to fear; as long as we didn't disrupt the animals' habitat, they wouldn't go for us. He had hardly finished speaking when there was a huge clatter and commotion in the trees as if a whole herd of animals was advancing. Susan started to run, Bill followed with me. 'Don't stop, keep going, I can see an opening ahead,' Susan shouted back to us.

Within seconds we were out into an open patch. We had hardly caught our breath when we saw a whole lot of people emerging from bushes, a little further down from us. Susan and Bill burst out laughing. It looked like a school party. 'Ah, fellow explorers!' they hailed them. 'You scared us out of our wits.' They explained how their noise had struck terror in us. Their teacher told us they too couldn't find the right path, and had been bumbling around for hours, fearing they'd never find a way out. He pointed to me and said that Susan and Bill at least had me to scare the animals away if some did appear, but they had none. I appreciated his compliment to my animal instincts but I knew that confronted with wild animals, I could in no way have defended my hosts.

Next, the three got working on how to make their way down. The leader had a compass and confirmed that we were facing in the right direction. Their aim was to reach their bus parked below. We slowly went round the clearing carefully looking for a path going down, but there was no sign of any. A shout from the students announced that something had been discovered. We hurried to them. Behind a thin line of trees, they had found a steep slope, with a bit of the road at the end. There were cheers and loud applause from everyone.

The teacher looked down the slope. It was so steep that a ball thrown would go down at lightning speed. 'Well,' he said 'that's it, lads. This is the way home.'

'How are we going to get down?' many asked.

'It will mean hurtling down,' he said making a diving gesture, 'rather than walking down, but there is no other option.'

'Can we run down?' The lads were getting adventurous.

'No, you'll break your legs, and I'm answerable to the school.' The teacher then issued precise instructions about how the descent was to be managed. 'Now everyone, listen carefully. I don't want you to be foolish and playful. As you go down, you'll gain more speed than you can manage. You'll find yourself running down, but you must control it, and the method is this. One, make sure you do it in small measures; two, aim your run to a tree, a branch or a bush or something. Take a rest, and then take another shot. In other words relay with yourself. Once you have reached the road, wait at the bus. Anyone not clear about what I have said?' he asked in a loud voice.

'Could we not run but go sliding down – I mean on our bums?' a girl braved the question. Immediately many voices joined her, some were even from boys. 'I want to do the same,' I heard Susan say. 'All right, let me say, whatever people feel easy with, go ahead. The aim is to get down there in one piece, without breaking your limbs, and before it gets dark. I will be in the rear to make sure no one is left behind in the forest. So, everyone, let's start.'

Laughing and chattering, a crowd of thirty-odd people started the steep descent. It was quite a sight: the daring running down, the cautious sliding on their bottoms and others interlocking arms to control an unnerving speed. I of course came down on my fours without any fuss, and realised that I had a natural advantage over humans in having four legs to manage a slippery slope. What was awkward for them, came naturally to me.

Everyone reached the bottom without any mishaps. Without delay and amidst much waving and victory signs, the school party drove away in their bus to be with their families, and we set off in our car. For me the day's events meant self-analysis. Sitting in the back seat, looking at the passing world, I was not taking in the view, but looking within to evaluate my role in the crisis that morning. I felt ashamed that as an animal I had proved no help in finding the way out of the wood. I did try to use my ability to identify the way but failed miserably. I was shocked to realise that my natural animal instinct was limited to smelling people and things around me.

Susan was still shaking from the experience, thinking back to the impasses that could have left us stranded. What if we hadn't met the school party, and had to stay in the woods for the night? We could still be there rushing around looking for a path out of the forest. She then fell silent and drove without speaking. But the tension was still there, I could sense it. At one time, she switched to the fast lane. Bill said, 'Watch out, it's a tricky motorway, lots of lorries...' That was enough to make her flare up. 'Excuse me, I'm the driver. So don't tell me how to drive.'

'Bloody hell, drive how you like. Let us all be killed then.' Bill was outraged by her response. They both seemed on edge.

The rest of the way passed in silence. It was night by the time we got back. We had hardly entered the apartment when a storm broke out. Susan threw down the keys on the floor, shouting, 'Take them, I'm finished with driving. I can't be pushed around any more, always, always you criticise my driving.'

'You're crazy, absolutely mad.' Bill shook his head.

'It's you who makes me mad, because you won't treat me like a human being. You interrupt me when I'm talking to people.'

'Bloody hell, making a big issue out of nothing. I'm fed up of these scenes, fed up, fed up....' Bill was kicking the door repeatedly. The house shook.

'Go on, abuse me,' Susan shouted. 'That's the only thing you can do, abuse, abuse, abuse. You correct me in everything, if I speak to people, if I do something, if I drive. You put me down in front of others the whole time. I can't take it any more. Can you hear me?' she screamed.

'No, I can't, and I don't frigging want to either, because you talk rubbish. The more I go along with you the worse you get.' He banged the table many times.

I started to bark furiously to stop Bill. Susan turned on me, 'And you stop it, go back to your place. I have enough here to deal with. Go, go now.' She looked so fierce, I slunk away to my mat. The shouting continued to and fro. I couldn't help letting out some barks to stop them somehow. Susan burst into tears. Bill continued to have an outburst. 'Christ, niggling me all the time. I get nothing else from you other than condemnation. I'm wrong in this, I'm wrong in that, wrong in everything I do.' He pulled down the books from the bookshelf. Fear gripped me. Was he going to hit her? I jumped up and was about to grab his trousers when he rounded on me, 'You shut your gob, frigging barking idiot. Go back to your place.' I backed off under the threat but did not stop barking. I didn't want to leave Susan without protection.

But Susan wasn't taking it either. She shot up and matching Bill's shouts, yelled at him, 'It's not you, it's me who's put up with your ways for years. You treat me worse than a dog,' her voice touched the highest pitch, 'and you are arrogant enough to say it's me.' She burst into a flood of tears.

Dog! I didn't realise dogs were the bottom line when it came to treatment.

'You are crazy, mad, mad. All this frigging feminism is driving me up the wall,' he stomped off to the bedroom, banging the door behind him with such force that the whole apartment shook. I stood up and taking the risk of facing an angry man, rushed to the door, barking full force, just to let him know that he and Susan had a well-wisher. I was expecting Bill to open the door and threaten me, but instead I felt a resounding slap on my back. 'Shut up, shut up, you beast, just shut up,' Susan pulled me back with such harshness that I could have wept at being treated like that when my only crime was to show compassion for the abused. She forced me down into the basket, glaring at me as if she was going to kill me. I was terrified. At the same time, I heard the bedroom door open, and Bill dashed out shouting, 'This frigging house is not worth a piss. I'm going.' I stood up, perhaps to stop him from leaving, when he shot out at me. 'Get out of my way, bloody nuisance.' I slunk away to my corner, 'And you, don't expect me back,' he thrust his face into Susan's and slamming the front door behind him, thudded down the stairs. Susan burst into screaming tears, 'Don't, don't come back,' and flopped down on the sofa.

Deathly silence ruled the apartment for what seemed like a long time. Hours must have passed. Susan lay there like a dead body. There was no sign of food. I was too frightened and sad to raise a demand for it. Instead I gave much thought to what had happened and why, but found it beyond my ability to analyse it. Susan got up once or twice to go to the toilet, but she never looked at me. I was careful not to upset her more than she already was. So I used these moments to slip out to the balcony to assess how late it was. There were fewer people on the street, so I reckoned it must be getting late in the night. There was no sign of Bill. Susan lay still with her hand covering her eyes. I wanted to approach her but was afraid to. With no purpose in remaining awake, I decided to give in to sleep.

I don't know what time it was when I heard the door open and someone come in. It must be Bill, I thought, and waited to see if he would come in to see Susan. But he didn't. I heard him go straight to the bedroom. Within minutes I heard him getting into bed. So, that was that. I wondered what tomorrow was going to be like. The rest of the night remained patchy.

...

THE REPRIEVE

I woke up to a silent house. Nothing stirred. Susan was still on the sofa. She looked very still, with no intention of getting up. There was nothing I could do but wait. Then I heard Bill go to the kitchen and put the kettle on. He came in and sat down on the sofa, making a little place for himself.

'Tea is ready,' he said. No response. 'Shall I bring it here?' he asked again. I was on tenterhooks. I wished with all my might that she would reply.

She nodded her head. He jumped up and returned with the tray, poured the tea and took it to her. She sat up. It was a relief to see her drinking tea. I could hardly control my excitement. He sat down next to her. It was good to see them together, though not speaking yet. They looked so forlorn. It was sad. I had seen them as an ideal couple when they visited my mistress. How little one knows about people. Susan had gone all limp, just overnight. She looked at me, and quite plainly I could see the thought dawning on her that I had gone without food since yesterday.

'Can you give him something to eat? He must be hungry.' That was enough. My tail started to go, and I slowly edged towards her.

'I'll get some milk and bread.'

By this time I was licking her feet, and conveying all the compassion I felt for her. She stroked me. Bill came back with my breakfast, he could hardly put it down so hungry I was to take it. I was so busy lapping up my milk and the soaked bread that I scarcely noticed Susan get up with some effort and go for a shower.

Bill came back with a mug of coffee and sat down on the sofa, watching me as he supped it slowly. When I finished I sat up licking my whiskers and waited for him to say something, not sure if I could approach him.

'Good?' he asked. I gave a happy yelp. 'I'm sorry it was a rotten day for you, for all of us, no fun going without food, was it?' He tapped on the sofa, indicating me to go over to him. This was a welcome move for me. He rubbed my neck gently. 'I'm sorry for yesterday. I know what you must think of me. But I assure you I am not solely to blame. I can't bear it when she is like that with me. Then I blow up. But trust me we are not always like this. It's unfortunate that you caught us like it. You must think I'm a bad guy. I shouted and abused Susan. Yes, I am ashamed of my behaviour. But you know, she can be very difficult at times.' He paused and looked out. 'Oh, dear,' he sighed deeply, 'What comes over one? What goes wrong? We are happy, and think it will last forever, but something small happens, and bang, it's gone.' He then turned to me and said, 'You won't think badly of me, will you, eh?' I was greatly moved by his words, and wished I could tell him I wasn't judging him. I had no business to do that. He became very thoughtful, 'I think animals are better than us. You are happy by yourselves, no partner, no conflict. What do you say?'

Was I happy? I had never thought of it. I must have looked bewildered. 'Oh, not to worry, I'm just rambling on,' he said affectionately, running his hand down my back. 'Anyway, it's fine now, but unfortunately, I have to go to the university for a meeting. Don't want to leave her alone, but I can't miss it. You look after her for me, please, and make sure she takes you out. I'll check if she's ready.' I wanted to follow him, but thought best not to push my luck. Instead I decided to go to the balcony to have some fresh air.

I was still sitting on the balcony meditating on Bill's remark about animals being better off than humans – "no partner, no conflict" - when I saw him at the gate leaving for his meeting. Then I heard Susan come in to the room, and rushed in to welcome her. She looked fresh after the bath. I was extremely happy to see her looking well, and made it very clear to her, wagging my tail, turning and twisting my body in joy and making throaty sounds. I could sense she was still sad. She patted me and let me put my head in her lap. 'I'm sorry I hit you yesterday.' She looked at me apologetically. 'I wasn't myself, and he was horrible.' We remained like that for what seemed like long time, with no indication that she would get up to do things in the house. I began to worry about lunch.

After a while, she put on the TV and lay down. I sprawled on the floor, hoping TV would provide some diversion with something entertaining to put her in a more cheerful mood. Well, would you believe it, the first programme that flashed on the screen had a lot of dogs in it. It was sheer luck we had bumped into it. I thought it would be good entertainment for Susan. There were a lot of dogs, I didn't know so many of my kind existed. People in uniforms were herding them to make them go up a plank into the back of a truck, which set out for the road. Soon a whole row of them were moving down the highway. Where were they going? It didn't seem like an outing. 'Oh, my God,' Susan said nervously. 'How horrible, why doesn't someone stop these people?' I sensed that something bad was happening.

The trucks were halted, and all the dogs were made to come down, and then led to a big hanger. We weren't shown what was happening there, but soon we heard a lot of barking and yelping and howling. 'Oh, no, oh, no,' Susan was crying. Then it became silent, and the men came out carrying huge bags. There was blood on their uniforms; the bags were thrown into the trucks, which set off for the road again. I was horror-struck and realised what had happened. 'See, doggie,' Susan said between her cries, 'See what happens when men finish using animals for their own purposes? These dogs were trained to hunt, but now they are too old, and cannot do what they did at one time. So they are being culled. Just like that.'

As she was speaking, the scene shifted to another place, streets upon streets where hundreds of dogs were being clubbed to death. People were shouting and clubbing dogs until they went lifeless. I was aghast to witness such cruelty, such blind fury in humans. I started to squeal. 'Oh, my God, don't, doggie, don't, you mustn't see,' she tried to cover my eyes. But it was too late. I had already seen it. 'Do you know why they are doing it? Because three humans have died from a canine infection, which they call rabies – that's the death of three humans, for which all dogs must be killed. That's what the Chinese government has ordered people to do. Oh, my God!' she could hardly speak from shock and horror.

'You and I have something in common, doggie. You can be killed, and I simply oppressed. That's what I see in Bill, the same killer spirit when he goes into spasms of fury.' We sat together silently as co-sufferers for a while, before Susan spoke again. 'I have no right to speak for myself. I have my use if I go along with him, but not if I want to be different.' She broke down again. I too was thinking about the rights of animals, but seeing her cry, I forgot my own helplessness and licked her face to tell her how much I felt for her. After all, she was human and should not feel cast out like an animal. I couldn't bear to see her so distressed.

'Do you know the story of the Horse and Dog?' she said wiping her tears. 'It will tell you how man - and I mean man, not woman – enslaved beings who were once free spirits, just to serve him.' It sounded nothing like the stories of Nagyanya, but still I sat up indicating that I was all attention.

'You remember the video we showed to your mistress about the British sport of fox hunting?' I was still trying to remember when she went on, 'It is a most cruel sport, but turned into a festival: horns blowing, scarlet-jacketed riders impatient to start, well-groomed horses waiting to be spurred on, dogs heaving with savagery and the country people ready to cheer the race – all this to kill one lone fox, who is perhaps interrupted in suckling her young, in an underground hole.' I couldn't recollect the scene, and anyway, it was the story of the Horse and Dog that I was waiting to hear.

'Once upon a time,' Susan started, 'a horse and a dog found themselves running alongside each other. This was at an annual hunting festival. The horse was carrying his rider and galloping at his fastest, keeping up with the yapping squealing dog who was sprinting ahead to get to the foxhole.' She grimaced, 'Man's victory over one small animal!' She paused. Snatches of the hunting were coming back to me.

'The dog noticed for the first time that the horse was much bigger and stronger than the rider.'

'Hey,' the dog hailed the horse, 'why do you have that man sitting on you? And why is he digging his spiky boots into your flesh?'

'Because he is my master and he has the right to spur me to go faster.'

'It must be painful, but you still do as he commands you. Do you ever disobey him?'

'Oh, no, I never disobey him. I did once but that was long ago when he stole me from my home in the forest, and put me under hard training.'

'You mean to say you didn't always live with him?' It was becoming a mystery to the dog.

'No, I didn't. I lived in the wilds, however I liked. I was my own master. But one day this man trapped me, took me home, started to ride me, whereupon I threw him off, not used to being ridden by anyone, but he would get up and do it again and again, until I gave up my free will and accepted my servitude. Now I do as he commands me.'

'Nevertheless, I admire your gallop. Did he teach you to run so fast?'

'You saw him digging his spiky boots into me. When he does that I feel such pain that I run as fast as I can. For this he calls me his best friend.'

'So it's not for love or loyalty that you do as he says.' The dog tried to get to the bottom of the horse's statement. 'He couldn't be your friend if he causes you pain,' he concluded. After a pause, he asked, 'Just now I saw something shining on your feet, what's that?'

'That's called my shoes – horse-shoes. They're made of iron. I have to have them nailed into my hoofs.'

'I don't have such things on my paws, and yet I can run as fast as you, if not faster.'

'Ah, but your training is different from mine. I wouldn't swap places with you. You see, you are deprived of eating meat. You are given the fox-meat to smell but not to eat. This excites you with the prospect of hunting down a fox. So, on the hunt day, you run faster than me because you know when you reach the foxhole, you'll be able to drag the fox out into the open and tear it to pieces.'

'How do you know so much about me?' The dog was amazed.

'Because, stupid, I see you do it on every hunt. Remember we both assist the hunter in killing an animal. But whereas I understand man's cunning, you don't.'

'How can you say that?' the dog challenged him.

'Because I am more intelligent than you. I see through the greed and craft of man.' The dog didn't like the snigger in his voice.

'What makes you think I don't?' the dog asked the horse to explain.

'Because even before my rider kills the poor fox, I see her blood all over your face, and her flesh in your mouth.'

At this very moment, the hunter's call 'Tally-ho' went up. The dog saw the rider's spurs going into the horse's flesh, whereupon the horse broke into a gallop. The dog leapt into a sprint to keep ahead of him.

'See, doggie,' Susan said finishing the story, 'that's you and me, the horse who knows he is enslaved, and the dog who does not.' I was so stunned by her remark that I could hardly find words to question her pronouncement on me as a dumb animal.

'But I'm not going to give up,' she said with determination, 'neither am I going to run away from it. I don't want to leave him or divorce him. I want to be together, and I think he does too. I want him to see that I have the same humanity as him. He must learn to give me space to express myself. I don't want him to interrupt when I'm speaking, or snatch my sentence and start saying what I was saying. Do you think that's unreasonable?' Was she expecting me to give an opinion? 'Oh, dear, it sounds very childish, but you know we give confidence to children by letting them express themselves, but not to us, not to wives. If I protest, he ssh-ssh's me, as if I am a dog.' I barked at the insult, a mere reflex reaction. 'No, I don't mean that. But you know, and I know that we can ssh a dog or a child, but shouldn't ssh a grown-up human being. But Bill does not ever want to hear that he is wrong, or that he needs to learn to accommodate me on an equal basis. When I do face him with it, he creates scenes, shouts abuses and lashes out at me. You think it's fair?'

She asked as if I could answer human questions and find the solution to human failings. As an animal, I suppose I should be grateful that I am spared the conflict that must arise from interdependence between two people.

Time was passing, yet Susan showed no sign of getting up. I began to wonder if there was going to be any lunch. So I went and sat by my dish. 'Ah, you want some food, do you?' she said with a pale smile. I gave a little bark. So she went to the kitchen. I followed her to make it certain that I was hungry. It wasn't long before I had my bowl of meat. I was ravenous and polished the food off in no time. Susan made herself a sandwich and sat on the sofa and ate it. She was still not herself, but there were no further emotional breakdowns. So far, so good, I said and passed the day between my corner and the balcony.

Bill came in late. He went straight to Susan, kissed her and said he was sorry at his outburst, but he could not help it. I heard Bill admit everything Susan told me about him earlier. Despite his apology, she remained self-contained. I supposed he might be apologising too many times, and not doing enough. Bill reprimanded me for not making Susan go on a walk. Anyway, it was decided that we would go out after dinner for my customary walk. For me, going in the open was so much better than going into a tray on the balcony.

Nothing special happened on the walk. When we walked past the lower valley steps, Susan pointed to the hill and suggested they go there the next morning. Bill agreed. 'People are quite negative about it. But why should we accept the verdict of others?' That's exactly what Susan says of herself in relation to you, was my answer to him as I walked behind them. We walked up and down the ridge road twice, and then returned home. I was glad to see Susan and Bill go to their bedroom.

Before I settled down for the night, I took a quick trip out. The moon was full and very bright. I stood looking at it for a while. I thought I heard Susan crying in the bedroom, and then Bill's soft voice talking to her. It had been a very emotional day. I was exhausted by it, and hoped to fall asleep quickly. But my mind was wide awake with images of the dog slaughtering on the TV and Susan's cries still in the air. In the end I must have fallen asleep.

'Szabó, Szabó', a woman's scream shot through the night. I was shaken awake. For a moment I thought it was Susan screaming, but when I looked at the sofa, she was not there. I waited to hear more. 'Szabó, Szabó', the cry shot out again. I jumped up and rushed to the balcony, the cry had come from the road. A big round moon was watching me. I looked down to see if someone was lost and crying for help. But there was no one. Then I saw an animal on the pavement. It was looking up at me. Its two eyes shone like diamonds. What was it? I looked closely. It looked like a dog, but bigger and a tail so bushy I had not seen it on any canine. Then it raised its neck to the moon, and howled very loud. A wolf. It was a wolf's howl at a full moon, an unrestrained howl. The next moment, it shot into the bushes but emerged immediately sniffing and searching. I stood without moving, watching its movements. It soon forgot the moon, and it seemed it was about to go when it looked up at me. The stare frightened me. I backed to the wall, as if to hide from the two searchlights. I saw it shoot down the steps into the valley. I was relieved to see it go. I stood there stunned. My thoughts turned to the woman. There was no sign of a woman. I waited a bit longer. No cry came again. A memory stirred. It was after the death of the Old Lady, one night I heard this very cry. Why tonight? There was no answer. I went indoors, and lay down to get some sleep. It was difficult to keep the wolf out of my mind. I imagined it making its way up to the woods opposite. I then remembered that Bill and Susan were planning to go up that hill. Maybe I'll see the moon-struck wolf. With that thought in my head, I quickly gave in to sleep.

THE DARK HILL

Bill's voice reciting poetry brought me back from the deepest sleep. Susan and Bill were sitting on the sofa having their coffee. There was no sign of any tension between them. At least something good had come out of the terrible events of yesterday. I quickly lapped up the milk in my bowl, and then waddled up to them.

'Your mistress called this morning,' Susan said, rubbing my back. 'She is coming back a day earlier.' 'That's tomorrow,' Bill added, 'so you'll have to leave us.' There was a note of sadness in Susan's voice. I licked her hand, just to say I would be sad too. I was beginning to feel I had two mistresses once again. 'Never mind,' Susan said, 'we'll come and see you, or we can talk through the locked gate. Two prisoners, remember?'

'What was that?' Bill asked.

'Nothing, a joke between doggie and me.'

'Come, then, let's go for our walk. Are we going before lunch or after?' Susan looked at me. I barked and pranced around.

'Maybe we should go towards the evening. That's the time the animals come out, we may even catch the wolf that everyone talks about.'

'So we go after tea,' Bill said, and then to me, 'Is that okay with Your Highness?'

The rest of the morning went as planned, a leisurely lunch, lazy afternoon, and then came tea-time. After tea, I sat looking at Susan, to indicate I was ready for the trip to the valley woods, as I came to call them. 'Okay, okay,' she said, and called out for Bill to take the lead. I was surprised, because I was never put on a leash when going for walks in the woods.

'We don't want you to run away with the wolf, mister,' Bill expostulated, 'your mistress will never speak to us again. She may even accuse us of murdering you. Ho! Ho! Yes.' Bill seemed in a good mood. I was happy for them.

I bounced ahead and waited for them at the top of the steps, which so far had remained a no-go area for me. I leapt down at the first indication of a go-ahead sign from my hosts. Wolf, wolf, here I come, I sang. Susan called out, 'Not so fast, wait for us.' But I couldn't. It was quite a drop. I left them to pick their way carefully down the fifty-odd steps. At the bottom, I looked up and down the road. There were some very big houses, with huge gardens. I imagined how the guard dogs in these spacious houses would set up a collective howl when they saw a wolf prowling outside their gates. I tried to think of myself in their place, but really I had been frightened by the Old Lady's accounts of the wolf. My best hope on this rare walk – I was sure my mistress would never come this way – was a glimpse of a real wolf.

Susan and Bill were down now. I apologised for my haste by wagging my tail a few times, and to win their favour, walked alongside them. I didn't know the way, so had no choice. Apparently there were a number of paths one could take. After some deliberation, they diverted to one which they thought would take us closer to the beginning of the wood. I was surprised that the hill wasn't very high or even unapproachable. Why would my mistress demonise it with heights and wolves? Was it to discourage me from seeing a real forest? Why? The thought persisted with me.

The path began to narrow, becoming dense with trees. There was no way the evening sun would get through the thickness. Something surged in me as we came up against thick undergrowth, and had to look for a path to put our next foot on. There was a drop on both sides, so one had to be careful not to roll down. I looked at my hosts every time to make sure which way we were going. They were deep in some sort of talk about the Buddha. I remembered the bedtime stories in which Buddha figured sometimes. The TV programme on animal killings also highlighted his non-violent philosophy, how even 2000 years ago he had protested against the killing of animals as sacrificial food for the gods.

Bill was saying, 'It's amazing how the Buddhists believe that the Buddha in his previous births was born as many animals, including a dog. You wouldn't find many religions accepting their prophet as a dog in some past birth.' My ears pricked up. I liked the idea of a human experiencing what it's like being an animal.

'I know some of the Jataka tales, but not the one about the dog. How does it go?' Susan seemed keen on knowing the story. We were passing a clearing.

'Shall I sit down on this tree trunk, and pretend I am a Buddha, telling the story of my birth as a dog?' Susan laughed, but thought it was a good idea. I wasn't sure what that meant. The next moment, Bill took up a funny position on the tree trunk and Susan found a log to sit on. I sat down by her.

'And so it happened that this time I was born as a dog, in the kingdom of Anuradhapura ruled by King Dharmeshwara, who was a Hindu. He had a large number of dogs as his hunting team, and they lived in the luxury of his palace. He did not allow any of his nobles to breed dogs, but let masterless dogs exist in the city, as and when they were born. Hindu priests sacrificed animals in the temples to please their gods. Now dogs were not considered as sacrificial, because they were seen as the lowest of the low, yet the Hindus did not believe in killing animals without reason. Consequently, these free-range dogs lived on the leavings of people's food and sheltered in the cremation grounds.'

'Ugh,' Susan made a noise. 'Poor dogs, I draw a line there, wouldn't you, doggie?' I certainly would, I agreed, issuing a few barks as an absolute rejection of such a habitation, boddhisatva or no boddhisatva.

'Don't forget, to become a boddhisatva you had to be in the lowest position. Besides, cremation grounds were an advantageous location, as people brought food to give to the dogs, in the name of the dead,' Bill reminded us. In his role as a Buddha, he remained unmoved and continued with his narrative.

'My birth had added yet one more body to this community. I was named Chitaranga, which meant, one attuned to cremation. I knew that I had a purpose in being born as the most despised animal, and had to prove that even a dog can attain wisdom and compassion and teach others to do the same. If I achieved this I would become a boddhisatva, and would be remembered as Amida Nyorai.'

'Are you listening, doggie?' Susan said, 'you too can be a boddhisatva and have a title for posterity. Isn't that great?'

'Now,' Bill continued, 'it so happened that one day when the king returned from his hunt, he couldn't find his favourite hunting thong. He was not happy at losing it. So his servants conducted a search to find it. After looking everywhere, they found it inside the palace gate, but it was all chewed up and torn to pieces, apparently by his dogs. Now, who was to incur the king's wrath by informing him that his much valued thong was destroyed by them? But they had no option. When the king heard it, he refused to believe his dogs were responsible, and ordered an immediate slaughter of the city dogs, certain that it was they who had done it. The Royal Death Squad arrived in the cremation grounds, with clubs to kill all the dogs living there. My community had no protection against being clubbed to death. They yelped and ran to save themselves against the brutal attack, but it is difficult to escape the cruelty of humans. The cremation ground was turned into a slaughter-house. Dead dogs lay in their blood, their limbs broken and severed from their bodies. It was a gruesome sight. It was time I did something. I heard myself shout out, "Stop. Stop this brutality. We did not chew the king's thong. Take me to the king. I will speak to him, I seek an audience with him." The Death Squad was stunned by a dog's demand to see the king, but they had to take me to the appeal court. The king had a ruling that anyone in his kingdom could ask for an audience and he would be granted one. They did not expect a dog to demand it, but they could not refuse it.'

Susan interjected, 'Isn't that awful, doggie? We are all the same beings, yet some have more rights than others.'

Bill continued. 'I stood before the king in the luxurious audience hall. All the nobles waited to see how the king would react to a lowborn animal demanding an audience with him. To make a case for the canine community was a real test for me.'

'O King, I am Chitaranga, a free dog in your kingdom. I come before you to make an appeal on behalf of my community, who live in dire conditions, looked down on by all, scavenging on the city-leavings and living in the city cremation grounds. We keep out of everyone's way and do not savage any belongings of the rich, let alone anything belonging to the king.'

'Who else could do it then?' the king asked in anger.

'It will require setting up a test to catch the culprits.'

'What test?' the king demanded.

'Please ask your ministers to bring your dogs here and have them served their favourite food in big quantity, so that out of greed they overeat and throw up,' I said humbly.

'How dare you malign my pets?' the king said in great anger.

'Your Majesty, you accord justice to all citizens in your kingdom, and though I am the lowest of the low, I am still your citizen.'

'Bring my dogs here at once,' the king ordered. 'And have them served their favourite dish in big quantity.'

Around twenty of the king's dogs were brought in. I had never expected to see dogs like that. They had nothing in common with us, the free canines. They were clothed and bejewelled and manicured beyond my wildest imagination, since they were not on a hunt at the moment. The dish served was rich with meat, followed by rice pudding with nuts and raisins. Yet they fell on their food in a common way, no different from ours. I thought, well, an animal is an animal, no matter how much it is humanised. Their greed was astonishing, they continued to eat without stopping. Everyone watched, waiting to see what was going to happen. The bowls were hardly licked clean when terrible noises ensued from the dogs, on account of overeating. The next moment they were getting sick everywhere. What came out with the food were big chunks of the king's thong! 'Your Majesty, your thong!' came the exclamations from the nobles. The king walked down from his throne to see for himself. His pets were still vomiting out chewed up pieces of his leather thong. King Dharameshvara was beside himself with anger. 'Take them away and have them whipped.'

'No, Your Majesty, you must not punish them. It is not their fault.'

I stood up for these canines, after all, we shared the same animal nature. 'These dogs are trained to help you to hunt animals. They are domesticated to serve man's needs. If animals are not allowed to live by their nature, they will lose discretion of what they should eat and what not. Greed and not need becomes their habit.'

The king looked at me in amazement. I knew it was time for me to tell him the Way of Compassion for all beings. 'Your Majesty, in your kingdom, animal sacrifices are made every day to please the gods. Do the gods drink their blood and eat their flesh, and only then bless humans with happiness? What sort of gods could they be who divide the natural world? We animals share the same Being with humans, who were also animals once.' The king was much moved by my words.

'Your words are full of wisdom, O Dog.' He turned to his ministers and said, 'Tell the priests that from today on, no animal sacrifice will be made for the gods. Disband the palace dogs. They must live a natural life and be free.' He then bowed to me and said, 'I salute you for teaching me the Way of Compassion for all beings.' With these words he left the Audience Hall.

'Thus in my rebirth as a dog, I became a boddhisatva, known as Amida Nyorai by some.' Bill fell silent. He looked very peaceful.

Susan broke the silence. 'A very moving story, isn't it, doggie?' I was watching Bill, whose eyes seemed to be fixed on something beyond us.

'My God, Susan, turn round slowly, a wolf is looking at me,' he whispered.

We turned to look but only caught sight of a very bushy tail disappearing into the trees. I made to go after it, but Susan held me by the collar. 'Stop, doggie. We'd better move, Bill; where's the lead, quickly.' Susan clipped it on me instantly, urging Bill to get up at once and follow her.

'By Jove, that was a handsome wolf, if there ever was one. Beautiful coat and bushy, bushy tail. What we see in books does not compare at all with reality.' Bill was taking his time. He was so overwhelmed by the sight of a wolf.

'Stop talking, Bill, hurry. We don't want anything to happen to the doggie.' I was resisting being dragged and tried to pull myself towards the slope, my one chance to look at a wolf. 'Doggie, behave now. We are going. Bill, take the lead, I can't do it. Hang on to him.' Susan could hardly speak for panic.

I tried to resist being dragged, but my lead was stretched to the full, the collar digging into my neck was enough to strangle me. No, there was no chance of my stopping Susan. She was rushing like a maniac through the dense growth at top speed. Within minutes, we came out into another clearing. 'Gosh, that was a close shave.' She stopped to take a breath.

'What a grand wolf, so majestic. The way it stood and looked at me.' Like me, Bill was still dwelling on the moment.

'Grand or not, I have to hand over my charge in one piece, not many.'

'There was nothing to panic about. It wouldn't have attacked us. It was only a wolf, not a tiger. Our guest might have been glad of saying hello to the species he is descended from, wouldn't you, mister?'

Yes, I would. How could I tell Susan she had made me miss the chance of a lifetime. Not only was my mistress afraid to let me come to a wolf-infested forest, but having come here and being in such close proximity to a wolf, my custodian also would not let me have even a glimpse of my ancestor.

'I don't see much logic in your statement. It's like saying our looking at chimpanzees somehow would give us a sense of our origins. What do we say to a chimpanzee, "Fancy meeting you, dear ancestor. Scientists tell me that way back in time I was like you, but now, we are very different. And why is that, eh?"' She then turned to Bill and said, 'What do you think the chimpanzee would say to me?'

'Would you like to hear a story about what he might say?' Bill offered to check Susan's manic speed. I was still feeling cheated out of meeting my ancestral species, but welcomed the diversion.

'Last time your story went on for so long that it brought a real wolf to the door. This time you can tell a story as long as you keep walking. It's getting dark, and I don't wish a whole pack of wolves to be waylaying us in this godforsaken forest.' Susan continued to move at a frantic pace.

'Now,' Bill started the story, 'it so happened that one night when a wolf came down from the forest in search of a meal, he was hailed by a dog behind the locked gate of a big house. The dog vaguely recognised his species, but could not work out why this one was wandering around in the middle of the night.'

'Have you lost your way?' the dog hailed the wolf as he passed him.

The wolf laughed and said, 'I live in the forest up there, I know my way only too well. I have come down to hunt a creature I could take back with me for dinner.'

The dog felt sorry for him and said, 'You wouldn't have to find your meals if you lived like me. I get good meals three times a day, and I don't have to hunt for them.'

'Well, maybe,' the wolf conceded. He surveyed the dog's surroundings, the nice big house, the garden and then rested his eyes on the dog. 'Your neck is rather disfigured. You have a nasty wound there.'

'I know, it's where I have to wear a collar.'

'What's a collar for?' The wolf was leading the dog up the garden path.

'It has the address of my owner. I must wear it, because if I get lost, people can take me back to the house. See?'

'Yes, I do, but it means you are never free to go where you like. And let me tell you, we of the canine race do not forget our way. We can go for miles into unknown territory and yet can find our path back, because we are guided by our ability to sense things, not like stupid human beings who have to carry maps and compasses to know where they are. Ha, ha, ha. So dear, dear enslaved canine, know this, that I would rather search for my meal than be given it.'

'But why? Why not sit back and have it given to you?' the dog still persisted.

'Because then I would not be a free animal. I would rather die than have my neck put in a collar such as the one on you, like a slave owned by a master – or mistress.' With these words, the wolf wandered on, in search for his meal.

The dog called after him. 'I see your point. If ever I get rid of this collar, will you be my guide?'

'I may or may not. When you look for freedom you shouldn't look for anyone's help. Go alone, you may or may not find others.' Having said this, the wolf turned his back on the collared dog and sauntered up the hill.

Susan said, 'It is true. You have to go alone, it's a matter of luck if you find someone else on the same path.' I was thinking too. It was the collar bit which was most telling on me. I began to feel the pull of the lead on my neck.

Although Bill's story relaxed her, Susan kept up the fast pace, until we came out onto the regular path that went up to the more commonly visited wood. From there, we turned down to the ridge road. Bill started to sing a song about an old man and his dog.

> *This old man, he played one,*
> *He played knick-knack on my thumb,*
> *With a knick-knack paddy whack*
> *Give a dog a bone,*
> *This old man went rolling home.*
>
> *This old man, he played two ....*

It had a jolly beat, all that rolling home, and Bill made it more funny by acting out the old man, but I didn't like the words. The singing relaxed Susan a little. But I was still dwelling on the story of the dog and the wolf. It helped me to walk the rest of the way. Getting home was now a matter of minutes. Once inside the apartment, she looked as if she had escaped a great crisis. It was different with me. There was a lot to think about. I lay down on my mat. Bill got my food and they sat down to a meal themselves. I was hungry, so tucked in fast while listening to their talk.

'Why did you get so het up about the wolf?' Bill said. 'After all, we humans don't have to fear wolves – tigers yes, but not wolves. They are only bigger dogs.'

'Because they are wild animals. They may take domestic dogs to be their enemies.'

'On the contrary, I would think they might despise them.'

What could that mean?

Having polished off my dish, I felt my eyes closing. The last thought that passed through my head was that I was going to sleep like a log. But that was not to be. I kept on waking up on and off, and in between having strange dreams. In one of them, I saw myself sitting in front of a mirror, and steadily looking at every part of my body, bit by bit. It was very disturbing to see myself obsessed with my body. This dream kept on coming in snatches. There was another in which I saw myself talking to the wolf through the gate of our house, and it kept on pointing to my neck and laughing raucously. This one made sense because of the story Bill told, but looking into the mirror, I couldn't make head or tail of it. I must have fallen asleep towards the morning. I was still struggling to get some sleep when

Susan came into the room.

One look at her and the strain from my own sleeplessness went out of the window. Sitting on the sofa she looked a complete wreck. Had she been crying? I got up and went to her. Automatically, her hand stroked my neck, but the next moment she burst into tears. I nuzzled up to her, and licked her face to ask her not to be so sad.

'See, doggie, you and I have the same problem. We both have collars of behaviour; if we don't act as we are told we are given a tough lesson. That's how it is for those who are not allowed to stand on their own feet.' Tears were rolling down her face. I couldn't understand why she was likening herself to me. What did we have in common? This human being and me, a mere animal dependent on human patronage.

The door opened and Bill rushed in. 'What's the matter, darling?' He hugged her, 'Why are you crying? What's happened? I thought you were asleep.' I moved over to make place for him. After all, what he could do or say to Susan, I couldn't. 'Now tell me, what's bothering you?' Susan shook her head. 'You are still not thinking of the wolf, are you? Wolves can't do anything to humans. Surely, you know that?' Bill waited, but Susan still wouldn't say anything. 'Not harking back to the other day?' Susan nodded. 'Now I did apologise, didn't I? I said I was sorry for losing my temper.' He paused to see if Susan would say something. 'Now, come on, you can't hold it against me forever if I speak harshly. You know I can't bear you going silent on me.'

'But you can't bear it if I say something too,' at last Susan spoke. It will be better now, I thought. They'll talk it out. 'So, what am I to do?' She looked at Bill questioningly. 'I can't take my collar off, can I?'

'What are you talking about?'

'The dog knows. We both have collars, don't we?' She sought me out as her accomplice.

'That's not fair, Susan. If you have a collar, then I have one too. We are both collared dogs, not free wolves.' Bill took Susan's hand and kissed her. She didn't resist. It was time for me to leave them alone. I walked out to the balcony.

...

HOMEWARDS

The sun was already up and shining. A bus went rattling down. Women were rushing along for milk and morning bread. Nothing could be wrong with the world. I saw the gate and remembered how I had waited there not so long ago with my mistress. It looked different from above. How many times had I passed through it in these last few days and would do the same this evening when my mistress came back to fetch me. It would be the end of my being a guest in this house.

†

⋮

24

BACK AT HOME

‡

I was home. Contrary to my foreboding, I was delighted to be back in the house with my mistress. My body continued to curl and twist with excitement, and my tail spoke volumes about my feelings at being with her. I couldn't be still, and she couldn't stop calling me endearing names. I was the homecoming for my mistress. She settled down on the sofa to tell me about her time away.

'I had a great time, drágám. I met so many English people - of course, who else would you meet in England but the English! But wait, no, not true entirely. There are so many different people in London, from so many countries. You can hear people speaking in languages one hardly knows of, let alone understand. You know, it's not the same here, nothing like it. Until recently, we were kept so confined, we hardly knew a different world existed outside our country. Anyway, how was it with you, eh? Tell me, did you miss me?'

I flicked my tail furiously to say that it wasn't so good, that I would have preferred to be with her. How could I be so barefaced in telling her a lie? How could I tell her I'd had a great time with her friends and thought of her only on rare occasions, and that I was sad to leave them? And how could I tell her what had happened between Bill and Susan? She probably wouldn't believe it. She was convinced that they were very happily married. And how could I tell her that I was a new dog, that I had gone through experiences which had changed me, that I had come to perceive the world differently, myself differently, and my relationship with her differently? Had I been able to tell her all this, it would have broken her heart.

Anyway, she lit the home fires and cooked a meal for herself and me. After we finished eating, she took me out for my night walk. When we returned I was looking forward to settling down to a bit of TV when she told me there was going to be none that evening. She must go to bed early and get up early to write reports on her trip. She had to give details of the conferences she'd attended, the business contacts she'd made to interest companies in their projects and hundreds of other things. She was afraid it was going to be early turning in for me too. For a moment I was surprised that I was going to be put out, unlike sleeping in the house as I did at Bill and Susan's place. But I had no choice.

She had cleaned my kennel and had made my bed with fresh coverings. I lay down to sleep. But there was no sign of it. I took a stroll or two on the terrace to settle my mind, but my eyes would not close. It was Bill's story of the wolf and the dog I couldn't get out of my head. I kept on scratching my neck with my paw and pulling at the collar. For the first time in all these years, I began to feel the weight of being a house pet. Why should I have the collar? Does my mistress think I would run away if I didn't have her name and address around my neck? I decided to find out. The best method would be to test her. What sort of test? I put myself to the task of devising ways and means to test how my beloved mistress regarded me. Another hour passed, but nothing definite was taking shape. I tried to calm my mind and closed my eyes. Tomorrow is another day, I thought, as my head began to drop.

I was woken up by my mistress reprimanding me for not being up. 'Come on, lazy bones, up you get, you can't sleep in like that!' Why shouldn't I? was my reaction. Don't I have the freedom to laze around if I want to? I did not move. I had found my first test.

'What's the matter with you?' She knocked hard on the roof of the kennel.

I continued to remain curled up. 'All right, stay then. I'm off to work. See you when I get back.' She went. Didn't she realise that I might want to have a lie-in, like humans? Did she pass the first test about my right to freedom? I took time to get up, making up for the lost sleep in the night. I was bent on exercising my rights.

At midday, Erzsi Néni came with my lunch. Although I did not much care for her, I usually welcomed her in a measured way, but today I made a point of not doing it. She tried to jolly me along but I did not respond. She wondered if I was feeling ill, and left me alone. After she was gone I lapped up the food.

That evening I decided to put my mistress to the second test regarding freedom of animals. As a habit when she came back I went into the house with her, and snooped around while she got the meals ready. This time I sat down and started to scratch my neck and made frustrating sounds at not getting a good scratch on account of the collar. She enquired a few times but when I wouldn't stop she removed the collar. 'All right now? Now scratch as much as you want.' That's good. No collar for dinner. Now, let's see about the walk.

After we had supped, and were setting out for our stroll, she said holding out the collar, 'Come, let me put it on you.'

I immediately set up a terrible whine and rushed to the gate, showing my keenness to go without the collar. 'Oh, no, you are not going without the collar, okay? No collar, no walk. Do you understand that? Come, now.' But I wouldn't budge and whined more. 'All right, then stay in the kennel, no TV either, if you disobey.' So that was it. I walked back, straight past her and went into my kennel. She had failed the test. No collar, no walk, no freedom.

That night, I had the mirror dream. I was looking into the mirror and examining my neck which was covered with sores. Had I scratched it so much? I was still looking at it when blood started to pour out. It was so gruesome that I started to yelp with all my might. I was yelping for help but no one came. I was still yelping when I woke up. It was dark. I felt miserable, and came out of the kennel to calm myself. A big round moon was looking down at me. I wondered if it was the moon that had made me dream so horribly. I had heard that women and animals behave funnily when the moon is full. I looked closer and saw that it had one more night to go to become full. I went back to the kennel to snatch a bit of sleep.

I was still dozing when my mistress turned up with my breakfast – a new habit she took to in England. 'What was happening in the night? You were making such a racket.' There was no sympathy in her voice. How could

I tell her that all through the night I had been beset by terrible nightmares. It was clear I was fretting to be a free animal. The days of domestic security were over for me. There was no doubt I was feeling uprooted from my collared life. I just had to accept it and plan how and when to depart from this house. I needed step-by-step plans.

That day, after my mistress left for work, not feeling happy with my behaviour, I began to plan my escape. The first step was to set the day. Do I leave now or tomorrow or the day after, or some time in the future? No, I thought I mustn't procrastinate, it was now or never. So, which day? I confronted myself. Today? No, I haven't said goodbye to my mistress. Tomorrow? Yes, why not? It was best not to delay it further.

Having set the day, the next question was what time? Should I depart when she was there; in the morning before she left for work? Or in the evening when she returned? Suddenly, it hit me that working out a plan meant I would never see my mistress again, my dearest mistress, who was the only person I knew closely in the world. Tears welled up. My vision lost clarity. The next moment I reminded myself that I was not human and that there was nothing in common between me and her, apart from her ownership of me. Humans have little compassion for other beings. It was clear I had steeled myself against her. And although nothing was going to cause me to swerve from my aim, the least I could do was to give her as little distress as possible. So I concluded I would leave when she was not there.

The collar! I had to have the collar off, else I would be brought back by anyone who could grab me. They might even ask her for money in return for finding me. I had to have the collar off when I made my escape. That seemed to be the most difficult operation. It required some thinking to plan the strategy.

And the last step - when should I say goodbye to her? The night before leaving, or the morning of the departure? I decided to leave it until the morning. That way any emotional upset would not have time to alter the course of my action.

Having worked out all the steps, I sat back and waited for her return in the evening. I planned to be at the gate to welcome her, a special gesture of reconciliation for my bad behaviour in the morning. It worked beautifully. My mistress was good-natured. She never stored things against anyone, least of all me. It went according to plan. She was delighted to see me waiting for her and wagging my tail. The rest of the evening went as usual, food and then the walk. I did not resist the collar for the post-dinner walk since I needed to do a last-minute survey of the escape route the following morning. The steps to the valley were still there. I carefully took note of the distance from home, especially going uphill. The departure must run smoothly. A slight slip and I would be back in the kennel.

After returning from the walk, my mistress sat down to watch TV and asked me to sit with her. I was waiting for this moment to execute the last step of the plan. My collar. The collar had to be taken off. I had to get my mistress to do it. Without that I could not risk leaving. We had hardly settled down when I set to scratching my neck. Within a minute I increased my scratching and started doing it furiously, making painful squeals at the same time.

'Is it the collar, drágám?' she asked very kindly. I looked at her with watery eyes and squealed even louder. 'Here, come, I'll take it off, you don't need it in the house.' She took the collar off. What a feeling! I could have been racing with the wind, it was so wonderful. 'But for going out, you must wear it. I don't want my soul-mate to be stolen by some lout, do I, drágám?' She kissed me fondly. And this was the person I was plotting against!

When it came to the time of being put in the kennel I set up the scratching again. 'What is it, szívem?' She rubbed my neck gently. 'I'll get some cream tomorrow. Why don't we leave the collar off until then, okay, is that better?' I licked her hand. 'You are not going to run away, are you?' O treachery, treachery! Most vicious betrayal in the name of freedom.

†

⋮

25

THE DAY OF DEPARTURE

‡

I woke up with a clear head. It was my last night to sleep like humans. I have heard that wild animals sleep during the day and are up in the night. Would I adapt myself to a different way? It might take time but I was sure to fall into my natural way. I wasn't worried. It was all in the future.

I saw my mistress come out with my bowl of milk, but I pretended not to be well, and turned it down. 'What's the matter? Is it the neck, drágám? Let me see.' She sat down to examine it. I squealed at the touch. 'Look, we'll go to the vet this evening, okay?' This would be the last time I would ever hear a human voice with genuine concern for me. My legs went weak. Something surged within me. Immediately, I steeled myself against having second thoughts on leaving. It was too late now. 'Look, drágám. I'll cancel the morning walk, we can't go without putting on the collar.' She was extremely sympathetic.

This was the time to say goodbye to her. I moved closer to her and put my head in her lap. She rubbed my back. Tears rushed to my eyes. I had to look at her. 'What's the matter, drágám? Why the tears, eh? It's only a bit of soreness. It will get right with the cream.' She held me close and kissed my eyes. If only I could tell her that my leaving had nothing to do with her. That if I had to have an owner, there could be no one in the whole world I would like better than her. But alas! Speech is what divides animals from humans. I saw her get into her car and drive away.

So, that was that.

All set to depart now, I waited for lunch time. As a routine Erzsi Néni never shut the gate behind her when she brought my meal. She would simply put the bowl down in front of me – all this time the gate would remain open – then she would turn around and go back. This was the moment I planned to make my escape. I waited. I heard the gate open. I watched her approaching. When she was half way, I jumped up, rushed towards her, knocked down the bowl and made straight for the gate.

'Oh, no, you naughty dog, what did you do that for? Right, you go without food.' While she was threatening me with punitive measures, I was out of the gate, and just for a brief moment I turned back and barked at her. It was simply to say, 'Do what you like, I won't be here to be punished, I'll be somewhere else, where neither you nor she nor anyone can reach me.' Having delivered my last words to the dog-owning humans, I sped towards the ridge.

I heard her screaming, 'Wait, wait, come back, come back at once, Béla.' For a split second, I stopped. The sound of that name rang strange. A series of snapshots rushed through my mind, taking me back to the beginning of my life. 'Béla', yes I was named 'Béla'. I remembered the first time I was called by that name. The vet had declared me a mixed breed, even perhaps related to a nomadic breed that had arrived in the Carpathians with the Gypsies. The Old Lady lost no time in naming me as Béla, saying it was a Gypsy name, and should be given to the descendant of a dog that came with them. When the young mistress reminded her that it might not be too appropriate to make a dog share its name with King Béla of Hungary, she poo-pooed the caution, and said why not? and that was that. She kept to her word and addressed me as Béla, but my young mistress rarely did. Even as I was leaving her for good, I wondered why she did not take to it, not that it mattered any more.

'Béla, come back,' Erzsi Néni's shouts continued. She had come out on the road, gesticulating helplessly, hoping someone further up would stop me. Fortunately, no one else came out. I started to run hard and made it to the ridge in no time. Memories of being on that road were flashing through my mind. I thought of Susan as I was running past her building. Would she too find her freedom? But now wasn't the time to think of her. I was leaving everything behind. I goaded myself to keep going.

I ran down the valley steps with a speed I did not think I was capable of. As I was running past the big houses, all the dogs rushed up to the gates, dumbstruck at a canine all on its own. They stepped back as I went past them. Were they scared of me, did they think I was a wolf come down from the forest? Suddenly there was a burst of howls. Their anguish hardly mattered to me. I did not stop. I had nothing to say to them. It was up to each of us to go our own way. I kept up the momentum, until I took the path up the hill, well on my way into the forest.

There was nothing to fear any more.

‡

⋮

ABOUT THE AUTHOR

RANI DREW is a poet, playwright and short story writer. She has written for stage and radio, and has produced plays in the U.K., China, Hungary, Romania, Spain and Macedonia. Her work has been published in North American, English and Indian poetry and fiction magazines.

Drew has travelled widely, teaching in Universities in Singapore, China and Hungary. During 1999-2000 she lectured at the University of Pécs in Hungary, where she taught theatre workshops, English literature, psychoanalysis and gender studies.

Her plays *Shakespeare & Me* and *The III-Act Hamlet* were performed for Shakespearean Festivals in Romania where they were awarded literary prizes. The Hungarian translation of the former also won a prize. Her play *Caliban*, a sequel to Shakespeare's *The Tempest,* was given a reading-performance by the Blue Elephant Theatre in London, and *Bradford's Burning* was rehearsed-read at the Attic Theatre, Wimbledon. *Eggs for Education*, a short play about top-up fees, was staged in Cambridge. In the past year, *Cleopatra* was staged in Punjabi by Rangtoli in Amritsar, India, and *1859-Darwin and the Victorians*, a Darwin-FitzGerald centenary play, in Cambridge.

Drew has published articles on Freud, women's writings and post-colonial literature. She is married and lives in England.

 | Published

Whyte Tracks print & design
Tuborg Havnevej 19
Hellerup
2900 Cpenhagen
Denmark

http://www.whytetracks.eu.com

Lightning Source UK Ltd.
Milton Keynes UK
UKOW042044161212

203730UK00001B/83/P